About t

Michelle Smart is a *Publishers Weekly* bestselling author with a slight-to-severe coffee addiction. A bookworm since birth, Michelle can usually be found hiding behind a paperback, or if it's an author she really loves, a hardback. Michelle lives in rural Northamptonshire in England with her husband and two young Smarties. When not reading or pretending to do the housework she loves nothing more than creating worlds of her own. Preferably with lots of coffee on tap. Find her at michellesmart.co.uk

Jackie Ashenden writes dark, emotional stories with alpha heroes who've just got the world to their liking only to have it blown wide apart by their kick-ass heroines. She lives in Auckland, New Zealand, with her husband the inimitable Dr Jax and two kids. When she's not torturing alpha males, she can be found drinking chocolate martinis, reading anything she can lay her hands on, wasting time on social media, or being forced to go mountain biking with her husband.

Award-winning author **Jennifer Hayward** emerged on the publishing scene as the winner of Mills & Boon's So You Think You Can Write global writing competition. The recipient of *Romantic Times Magazine's* Reviewer's Choice Award for Best Mills & Boon Modern of 2014, Jennifer's careers in journalism and PR, including years of working alongside powerful, charismatic CEOs and travelling the world, have provided perfect fodder for the fast-paced, sexy stories she likes to write.

A Dark Romance Series

June 2025
Veil of Deception

July 2025
Thorns of Revenge

August 2025
Surrendered to Him

September 2025
Bound by Vows

BOUND BY VOWS:
A Dark Romance Series

MICHELLE SMART

JACKIE ASHENDEN

JENNIFER HAYWARD

MILLS & BOON

All rights reserved including the right of reproduction in whole or in part in any form. This edition is published by arrangement with Harlequin Enterprises ULC.

This is a work of fiction. Names, characters, places, locations and incidents are purely fictional and bear no relationship to any real life individuals, living or dead, or to any actual places, business establishments, locations, events or incidents. Any resemblance is entirely coincidental.

Without limiting the author's and publisher's exclusive rights, any unauthorised use of this publication to train generative artificial intelligence (AI) technologies is expressly prohibited. HarperCollins also exercise their rights under Article 4(3) of the Digital Single Market Directive 2019/790 and expressly reserve this publication from the text and data mining exception.

® and ™ are trademarks owned and used by the trademark owner and/or its licensee. Trademarks marked with ® are registered with the United Kingdom Patent Office and/or the Office for Harmonisation in the Internal Market and in other countries.

First Published in Great Britain 2025
by Mills & Boon, an imprint of HarperCollins*Publishers* Ltd
1 London Bridge Street, London, SE1 9GF

www.harpercollins.co.uk

HarperCollins*Publishers*
Macken House, 39/40 Mayor Street Upper,
Dublin 1, D01 C9W8, Ireland

Bound by Vows: A Dark Romance Series © 2025 Harlequin Enterprises ULC.

Taming the Notorious Sicilian © 2014 Michelle Smart
King's Ransom © 2019 Jackie Ashenden
Married for His One-Night Heir © 2018 Jennifer Drogell

ISBN: 978-0-263-41861-3

This book contains FSC™ certified paper and other controlled sources to ensure responsible forest management.

For more information visit: www.harpercollins.co.uk/green

Printed and Bound in the UK using 100% Renewable Electricity
at CPI Group (UK) Ltd, Croydon, CR0 4YY

TAMING THE NOTORIOUS SICILIAN

MICHELLE SMART

This book is dedicated to all the staff and volunteers at the John Radcliffe Children's Hospital, with special thanks to the team on Kamran's Ward. Without their care, compassion and sheer dedication, my beautiful nephew Luke would not be here.

This book is also dedicated to the memory of Henry, Lily and Callum. May you all be playing together with the angels.

CHAPTER ONE

Francesco Calvetti brought his MV Agusta F4 CC to a stop and placed his left foot on the road as he was foiled by yet another set of red lights. Barely 7:00 a.m. and the roads were already filling up.

What he wouldn't give to be riding with nothing but the open road before him and green fields surrounding him.

He thought of Sicily with longing. His island had none of the grey dreariness he was fast associating with London. This was supposed to be *spring*? He'd enjoyed better winters in his homeland.

He yawned widely, raising his hand to his visor out of pure habit. After all, no one could see his face with his helmet on.

He should have gotten Mario to bring him home after such a long night, but being driven by anyone irritated him, especially in a car. Francesco was a man for whom *drive* had multiple definitions.

The light changed to green. Before twisting on the throttle and accelerating smoothly, he swiped away the moisture clinging to his visor.

What a country. At the moment it was like driving through a saturated cloud.

As he approached yet another set of lights, a cyclist on a pushbike just ahead caught his attention—or, rather, the fluorescent yellow helmet she wore caught it. She reached the lights at the moment they turned amber. If that had been him, Francesco mused, he would have gone for it. She'd had plenty of time.

But no, this was clearly a law-abiding woman with a healthy dose of self-preservation. She stopped right at the line. The car in front of Francesco, a large four-wheel drive, drew level on her right side.

She had the thickest hair he'd ever seen—a shaggy mass of varying shades of blonde reaching halfway down her back.

The light turned green and off she set, sticking her left arm out and turning down the street in that direction. The car that had been beside her also turned left, forced to hang a little behind her, with Francesco joining the convoy.

The road ahead was clear. The cyclist picked up speed....

It happened so quickly that for a moment Francesco was convinced he had imagined it.

Without any indication, the four-wheel drive in front of him pulled out to overtake the cyclist, accelerating quickly, but with the spatial awareness of a cauliflower, because it clipped the cyclist's wheel, causing her to flip forward off the saddle and land head-first on the kerb.

Francesco brought his bike to an immediate stop and jumped off, clicking the stand down through muscle memory rather than conscious thought.

To his disgust, the driver of the offending car didn't stop, but carried on up the road, took a right and disappeared out of sight.

A passer-by made a tentative approach towards the victim.

'Do not move her,' Francesco barked as he pulled off

his helmet. 'She might have a broken neck. If you want to help, call for an ambulance.'

The passer-by took a step back and dug into his pocket, allowing Francesco to stand over the victim.

The woman lay on her back, half on the pavement and half on the road, her thick hair fanning in all directions. Her helmet, which had shifted forward and covered her forehead, had a crack running through it. Her bike was a crumpled heap of metal.

Dropping to his haunches, Francesco yanked off his leather gloves and placed two fingers on the fallen cyclist's neck.

Her pulse beat faint beneath his touch.

While the passer-by spoke to the emergency services, Francesco deftly removed his leather jacket and placed it over the unconscious woman. She wore smart grey trousers and an untucked black blouse covered with a waterproof khaki jacket. On one of her bare feet was a white ballet shoe. The other was missing.

His chest constricted at the thought of the missing shoe.

He wished he could tuck his jacket under her to create a barrier between her and the cold, damp concrete, but he knew it was imperative to keep her still until the paramedics arrived.

The important thing was she was breathing.

'Give me your coat,' he barked at another spectator, who was hovering like a spare part. A small crowd had gathered around them. Vultures, Francesco thought scornfully. Not one of them had stepped forward to help.

It never occurred to him that his presence was so forbidding, even first thing in the morning, that none of the crowd *dared* offer their assistance.

The spectator he'd addressed, a middle-aged man in

a long lambswool trench coat, shrugged off his coat and passed it to Francesco, who snatched it from his hands. Francesco wrapped it across the woman's legs, making sure to cover her feet.

'Five minutes,' the original passer-by said when he disconnected his call.

Francesco nodded. For the first time he felt the chill of the wind. He palmed the woman's cheek. It felt icy.

Still on his haunches, he studied her face carefully, ostensibly looking for a clue to any unseen injuries. No blood ran from her nose or mouth, which he assumed was a good thing. Her mass of blonde hair covered her ears, so he carefully lifted a section to look. No blood.

As he searched, he noticed what a pretty face she had. Not beautiful. Pretty. Her nose was straight but just a touch longer than the women of his acquaintance would put up with before resorting to surgery. She had quite rounded cheeks, too, something else that would be fixed in the endless quest for perfection. But yes, pretty.

He remembered she'd had something slung around her neck before he'd covered her chest with his jacket. Carefully, he tugged it free.

It was an identity card for one of the hospitals in the capital. Peering closer, he read her name. *Dr H Chapman. Specialist Registrar.*

This woman was a doctor? To his eyes she looked about eighteen. He'd guessed her as a student...

Her eyes opened and fixed on him.

His thoughts disappeared.

Shock rang out from her eyes—and what eyes they were, a moreish hazel ringed with black—before she closed them. When they reopened a few beats later, the shock faded to be replaced by a look of such contentment and serenity that Francesco's heart flipped over.

Her mouth opened. He leaned closer to hear what she had to say.

Her words came out as a whisper. 'So there really is a heaven.'

Hannah Chapman leaned her new bike against the stone building and gazed up at the sparkling silver awning that held one word: *Calvetti's*.

She admired the explicitness of it. This belonged to Francesco Calvetti and no one else.

Even though it was 6:00 p.m. and the club wasn't due to open for another four hours, two hefty-sized men dressed all in black stood beneath the awning, protecting the door. She took this as a good sign—the past three times she'd cycled over, the door hadn't been manned. The club had been empty.

'Excuse me,' she said, standing before them. 'Is Francesco Calvetti in?'

'He's not available.'

'But is he in?'

'He's in but he's not to be disturbed.'

Success! At last she'd managed to track him down. Francesco Calvetti travelled *a lot*. Still, tracking him down was one thing. Getting in to see him was a different matter entirely.

She tried her most winning smile.

Alas, her fake smile wasn't up to par. All it resulted in was the pair of them crossing their arms over their chests. One of them alone would have covered the door. The pair of them standing there was like having a two-man mountain as a barrier.

'I know you don't want to disturb him, but can you please tell him that Hannah Chapman is here to see him?

He'll know who I am. If he says no, then I'll leave, I promise.'

'We can't do that. We have our orders.'

She could be talking to a pair of highly trained SAS soldiers, such was the conviction with which the slightly less stocky of the duo spoke.

Hannah sighed. Oh, well, if it wasn't meant to be, then... so be it.

All the same, she was disappointed. She'd wanted to thank the man personally.

She thrust forward the enormous bunch of flowers and thank-you card. She'd cycled the best part of two miles through London traffic with them precariously balanced in her front basket. 'In that case, could you give these to him, please?'

Neither made a move to take them from her. If anything, their faces became even more suspicious.

'Please? This is the third bunch I've brought for him and I'd hate for them to go to waste. I was in an accident six weeks ago and he came to my rescue and...'

'Wait.' The one on the left cocked his head. 'What kind of accident?'

'I was knocked off my bike by a hit-and-run driver.'

They exchanged glances, then drew back to confer in a language that sounded, to her untrained ear, as if it was Italian. Or she could have imagined it, knowing Francesco Calvetti was Sicilian.

Since she'd discovered the identity of her benefactor, she knew a lot more than she should about Francesco Calvetti. internet searches were wonderful creations. For instance, she knew he was thirty-six, unmarried but with a string of glamorous girlfriends to his name, and that he owned six nightclubs and four casinos across Europe. She also knew his family name was synonymous with the Mafia in Sicily and that his father, Salvatore, had gone by the nickname Sal il Santo—Sal the Saint—a moniker allegedly given due to his penchant for making the sign of the cross over his dead victims.

She wouldn't have cared if his father had been Lucifer himself. It made no difference to what Francesco was—a good man.

The man who'd brought her back to life.

The stockier one looked back to her. 'What did you say your name was?'

'Hannah Chapman.'

'One minute. I will tell him you are here.' He shrugged his hefty shoulders. 'I cannot say if he will speak to you.'

'That's fine. If he's too busy, I'll leave.' She wasn't going to make a scene. She was here to say thank you and nothing else.

He disappeared through the double doors, letting them swing shut behind him.

She hugged the flowers to her chest. She hoped Francesco wouldn't think them pathetic but she hadn't a clue what else she could give him to express her gratitude. Francesco Calvetti had gone above and beyond the call of duty, and he'd done it for a complete stranger.

In less than a minute, the door swung back open, but instead of the bouncer, she was greeted by a man who was— and Lord knew how this was even possible—taller than the guards he employed.

She'd no idea he was so tall.

But then, her only memory of the man was opening her eyes and seeing his beautiful face before her. How clearly she remembered the fleeting certainty that she was dead and her guardian angel had come to take her to heaven, where Beth was waiting for her. She hadn't even been sad about it—after all, who would be upset about being escorted to paradise with the most gorgeous man on either heaven or earth?

The next time she'd opened her eyes she had been in a hospital bed. This time, the fleeting feeling was disappointment she hadn't gone off to paradise with Adonis.

Fleeting feeling? No. It had been more than that. Adonis had come to take her to Beth. To learn she was still alive had been on the verge of devastating. But then, of course, sanity poked through.

As she'd come back to the here and now, and memories of her Adonis kept peppering her thoughts, so, too, came the revelation that she truly was alive.

Alive.

Something she hadn't felt in fifteen years.

Limbo. That was where she'd been. She, hardworking, practical Hannah Chapman, for whom bedtime reading consisted of catching up on medical journals, had been living in limbo.

In the weeks since her accident, she'd convinced herself that her memory of that brief moment was all wrong. No one, surely, could look like he did in her memory and be a mortal? She'd had severe concussion after all. Even the pictures she'd found on the internet didn't do justice to her memory of him.

Turned out her brain hadn't been playing tricks on her.

Francesco Calvetti truly was beautiful…

But in a wholly masculine way.

His tall, lean frame was clothed in tailored dark grey trousers and a white shirt unbuttoned to halfway down his chest, the sleeves rolled up to his elbows. In the exposed V—which she was eye height with—he wore a simple gold cross on a chain, which rested on a dark whorl of hair.

A rush of…*something* coursed through her blood, as if a cloud of heat had been blown through her veins.

Unsettled, Hannah blinked and looked back up at his unsmiling face. Not even the forbidding expression resonating from his deep-set eyes—and what a beautiful colour they were, making her think of hot chocolate-fudge cake—could dent the huge grin that broke out on her face. She extended the flowers and card to him, saying, 'I'm Hannah Chapman and these are for you.'

Francesco looked from the flowers back to her. He made no effort to take them.

'They're a thank you,' she explained, slightly breathless for some reason. 'I know they're a drop in the ocean compared to what you've done for me, but I wanted to get you something to show how grateful I am—I am truly in your debt.'

One of his thick black brows raised and curved. 'My debt?'

A shiver ran up her spine at his deep, accented voice. 'You have done so much for me,' she enthused. 'Even if I had all the money in the world I could never repay you for your kindness, so yes, I am in your debt.'

His eyes narrowed as he studied her a little longer before inclining his head at the door. 'Come in for a minute.'

'That would be great,' she said, not caring in the least that his directive was an order rather than a request.

The two-man mountain that had flanked Francesco up to this point, guarding him as well as they would if she were carrying an Uzi nine-millimetre, parted. She darted between them, following Francesco inside.

After walking through a large reception area, they stepped into the club proper.

Hannah's eyes widened. 'Amazing,' she whispered, turning her head in all directions.

Calvetti's oozed glamour. All deep reds and silver, it was like stepping into old Hollywood. The only club she'd been to was at the age of eighteen when her entire class had descended on The Dell, their sleepy seaside town's only nightclub, to celebrate finishing their A levels. It had been one of the most boring evenings of her life.

Compared to this place, The Dell had been grey and dingy beyond imagination.

And, in fact, compared to Francesco, with his olive skin, short black curly hair and strong jawline, all the men she had ever met in her life were grey and dingy beyond imagination, too.

'You like it?'

Her skin heating under the weight of his scrutiny, she nodded. 'It's beautiful.'

'You should come here one evening.'

'Me? Oh, no, I'm not into clubbing.' Then, fearing she had inadvertently insulted him, quickly added, 'But my sister Melanie would love it here—it's her hen night on Friday so I'll suggest she drops in.'

'You do that.'

It didn't surprise Francesco to learn Hannah Chapman wasn't into clubbing. The women who frequented his clubs were a definite type—partygoers and women looking to hook up with a rich or famous man, preferably both.

Hannah Chapman was a doctor, not a wannabe WAG. He allowed himself to take in her appearance more fully, and noticed that she was dressed professionally, in another variation of the trouser suit she'd been wearing on the day she was knocked off her bike. The lighting in the club had the effect of making her white blouse see-through, illuminating her bra, which, to his trained eye, looked practical rather than sexy. Her thick blonde hair looked as if it hadn't seen a hairbrush in weeks, and he could not detect the slightest trace of make-up on her face.

He'd assumed when he'd seen her at the door that she

had come with an agenda. In his experience, everyone had an agenda.

He slipped behind the bar, watching as she set the flowers and card to one side. He had never been presented with flowers before. The gesture intrigued him. 'What can I get you to drink?'

'I could murder a coffee.'

'Nothing stronger?'

'I don't drink alcohol, thank you. In any case, I've been working since seven and if I don't get an enormous shot of caffeine I might just pass out.' He liked the droll way she spoke, the air of amusement that laced her voice. It made a change from the usual petulant tones he was used to hearing from her sex.

'You're back at work already?'

'I was back within a fortnight, as soon as I'd recovered from the concussion.'

'Any other injuries?'

'A broken clavicle—collarbone—which is fusing back together nicely. Oh, and a broken middle finger, but that seems to be healed now.'

'You don't know if your own finger's healed?'

She shrugged and hopped onto a stool, facing him. 'It doesn't hurt anymore so I assume it's healed.'

'Is that a professional diagnosis?'

She grinned. 'Absolutely.'

'Remind me not to come and see you if I need medical attention,' he commented drily, stepping over to the coffee machine.

'You're about twenty years too old for me.'

He raised a brow.

Her grin widened. 'Sorry, I mean you're twenty years too old for me to treat in a medical capacity, unless you want to be treated on a ward full of babies, toddlers, and kids. I'm specialising in paediatrics.'

It was on the tip of his tongue to ask why she had chosen to specialise in children but he kept his question to himself. He wanted to know why she had sought him out.

He placed a cup in the machine and pressed a button. 'Do you take milk and sugar?'

'No milk but two sugars, please. I might as well overdose on that as well as caffeine.'

His thoughts exactly. He added two heaped spoons to both cups and passed one to her.

His initial assessment of her had been correct. She really was very pretty. Of average height and slender, her practical trousers showcased the most fabulous curvy bottom. It was a shame she was now sitting on it. The more he looked at her, the more he liked what he saw.

And he could tell that she liked what she saw, too.

Yes, this unexpected visit from Dr Chapman could take a nice twist.

A *very* nice twist.

He took a sip of his strong, sweet coffee before placing his cup next to hers, folding his arms across his chest and leaning on the bar before her.

'Why are you here?'

Her eyes never left his face. 'Because I needed to let you know how grateful I am. You kept me warm until the ambulance arrived, then travelled in the ambulance with me, stayed at the hospital for hours until I'd regained consciousness, *and* you tracked down the driver who hit me and forced him to hand himself in to the police. No one has *ever* done anything like that for me before, and you've done it for a complete stranger.'

Her face was so animated, her cheeks so heightened

with colour, that for a moment his fingers itched to reach out and touch her.

How did she know all this? He'd left the hospital as soon as he'd been given word that she'd regained consciousness. He hadn't seen her since.

'How about you let me buy you dinner one night, so I can thank you properly?' Colour tinged her cheeks.

'You want to buy me dinner?' He didn't even attempt to keep the surprise from his voice. Women didn't ask him out on dates. It just didn't happen. For certain, they thought nothing of cajoling him into taking *them* out to expensive restaurants and lavishing them with expensive clothes and jewellery—something he was happy to oblige them in, enjoying having beautiful women on his arm. But taking the initiative and offering *him* a night out…?

In Francesco's world, man was king. Women were very much pretty trinkets adorning the arm and keeping the bed warm. Men did the running, initially at least, following the traps set by the women so the outcome was assured.

She nodded, cradling her coffee. 'It's the least I can do.'

He studied her a touch longer, gazing into soft hazel eyes that didn't waver from his stare.

Was there an agenda to her surprising offer of dinner?

No. He did not believe so. But Francesco was an expert on female body language and there was no doubt in his mind that she was interested in him.

He was tempted. *Very* tempted.

He'd thought about her numerous times since her accident. There had even been occasions when he'd found his hand on the phone ready to call the hospital to see how she was. Each time he had dismissed the notion. The woman was a stranger. All the same, he'd been enraged to learn the police had failed to track down the man who'd so callously knocked her down. The driver had gone into hiding. Unfortunately for the driver, Francesco had a photographic memory.

It had taken Francesco's vast network precisely two hours to track the driver down. It had taken Francesco less than five minutes to convince the man to hand himself in. By the time he'd finished his 'little chat' with him, the man had been begging to be taken to the police station. Francesco had been happy to oblige.

And now she had come to him.

And he was tempted to take her up on her offer of a meal—not that he would let her pay. It went against everything he believed in. Men took care of their women. The end.

If it was any other woman he wouldn't think twice. But this one was different. For a start, she was a doctor. She was a force for good in a world that was cruel and ugly.

Despite her age and profession, Hannah had an air of innocence about her. Or it could just be that she was totally without artifice. Either way, she had no business getting involved with the likes of him.

If he was a lesser man he would take advantage of her obvious interest, just like his father would have done if he'd been alive.

But he would not be that man. This woman was too... *pure* was the word that came to mind. If she were the usual kind of woman who frequented his world, he would have no hesitation in spelling out how she could repay her so-called debt to him. Naked. And horizontal.

'You owe me nothing,' he stated flatly.

'I do...'

'No.' He cut her off. 'What you consider to be your debt is not redeemable. I did what I did without any thought of payback—consider the fact you are alive and healthy and able to do the job you love to be my payment.'

The animation on her face dimmed a little. 'So you won't let me buy you dinner?'

'Look around you. You don't belong in this seedy world, Dr Chapman. I thank you for taking the time to visit me, but now I have business to attend to.'

'That sounds like a dismissal.'

'I am a busy man.'

Those hazel eyes held his for the longest time before she cast him the most beautiful smile he'd ever been the recipient of, lighting her face into something dazzling.

Then, to his utter shock, Hannah levered herself so her torso was on the bar and pressed her lips to his.

They were the softest of lips, a gentle touch that sent tiny darts fizzing through his blood.

He caught a faint whiff of coffee before she pulled away.

'Thank you. For everything,' she said, slipping back down onto her stool then getting to her feet. Her cheeks glowing, she finished her coffee and reached for her bag, her eyes never leaving his. 'I will never forget what you've done for me, Francesco. You have my undying gratitude.'

As she turned to leave, he called out after her, 'Your sister—she has the same family name as you?'

She nodded.

'I'll leave word that Melanie Chapman's hen party is to be given priority at the door on Friday.'

A groove appeared in her forehead. 'Okay,' she said slowly, clearly not having the faintest idea what he was talking about.

'Your sister will know what it means.' A half smile stole over his face. 'Tell her she'll be on the list.'

'Ah—on the list!' The groove disappeared. Somehow the sparkle in her eyes glittered even stronger. 'I know what *that* means. That's incredibly lovely of you.'

'I wouldn't go that far,' he dismissed, already regretting

his impulsive offer, which had come from where he knew not, but which unsettled him almost as much as her kiss.

Francesco never acted on impulse.

That same serene smile that had curved her cheeks when she'd lain on the road spread on her face. 'I would.'

He watched her walk away, his finger absently tracing the mark on his lips where she'd kissed him.

For the first time in his life he'd done an unselfish act. He didn't know if it made him feel good or bad.

CHAPTER TWO

Hannah stared at the queue snaking all the way round the corner from the door of Calvetti's and sighed. Maybe the queue was an omen to stay away.

No. It couldn't be. Even if it was, she would ignore it. Just being this close to his sanctum was enough to send her pulse careering.

Meeting Francesco in the flesh had done something to her...

'Come on, Han,' her sister said, tugging at her wrist and breaking Hannah's reverie. 'We're on the list.'

'But this is the queue,' Hannah pointed out.

'Yes, but we're *on the list*.' Melanie rolled her eyes. 'If you're on the list you don't have to queue.'

'Really? How fabulous.' She'd thought it meant getting in for free—she had no idea it also encompassed queue jumping.

Giggling, the party of twelve women dressed in black leotards over black leggings, bright pink tutus and matching bunny ears hurried past the queue.

Three men in long black trench coats guarded the door.

Melanie went up to them. 'We're on the list,' she said with as much pride as anyone with a pink veil and bunny ears on her head and the words *Mucky Mel* ironed onto the back of her leotard could muster.

Hannah had guessed Calvetti's was popular but, judging by Melanie's reaction, she could have said she'd got VIP backstage passes to Glastonbury. Her sister had squealed with excitement and promptly set about rearranging the entire evening. Apparently Calvetti's was 'the hottest club in the country', with twice as many people being turned away at the door than being admitted.

Luckily, Melanie had been so excited about it all that she'd totally failed to pump Hannah for information on the man himself. The last thing Hannah wanted was for her sister to think she had a crush on him. It was bad enough knowing her entire family thought she was a closet lesbian without giving them proof of her heterosexuality—one sniff and they'd start trying to marry her off to any man with a pulse.

The bouncer scanned his clipboard before taking a step to one side and unclipping the red cordon acting as a barrier.

'Enjoy your evening, ladies,' he said as they filed past, actually smiling at them.

Another doorman led them straight through to the club, which heaved with bodies and pulsated with loud music, leading them up a cordoned-off set of sparkling stairs.

Her heart lifted to see one of the man mountains who'd been guarding the club the other afternoon standing to attention by a door marked 'Private'.

Surely that meant Francesco was here?

A young hunk dressed in black approached them and led them to a large round corner table. Six iced buckets of champagne were already placed on it.

'Oh, wow,' said Melanie. 'Is this for us?'

'It is,' he confirmed, opening the first bottle. 'With the compliments of the management. If you need anything, holler—your night is on the house.'

'Can I have a glass of lemonade, please?' Hannah asked,

her request immediately drowned out by the hens all badgering her to have one glass of champagne.

About to refuse, she remembered the promise she'd made to herself that it was time to start living.

She, more than anyone, knew how precarious life could be, but it had taken an accident on her bike for her to realise that all she had been doing since the age of twelve was existing. Meeting Francesco in the flesh had only made those feelings stronger.

If heaven was real, what stories would she have to tell Beth other than medical anecdotes? She would have nothing of real *life* to share.

That was something she'd felt in Francesco, that sense of vitality and spontaneity, of a life being *lived*.

Settling down at the table, she took a glass of champagne, her eyes widening as the bubbles played on her tongue. All the same, she stopped after a few sips.

To her immense surprise, Hannah soon found she was enjoying herself. Although she didn't know any of them well, Melanie's friends were a nice bunch. Overjoyed to be given the VIP treatment, they made sure to include her in everything, including what they called Talent Spotting.

Alas, no matter how discreetly she craned her neck, Hannah couldn't see Francesco anywhere. She did, however, spot a couple of minor members of the royal family and was reliably informed that a number of Premier League football players and a world-championship boxer were on the table next to theirs, and that the glamorous women and men with shiny white teeth who sat around another table were all Hollywood stars and their beaus.

'Thank you so much for getting knocked off your bike,' Melanie said whilst on a quick champagne break from the dance floor, flinging her arms around Hannah. 'And thank you for coming out with us tonight and for coming here—I was convinced you were going to go home after the meal.'

Hannah hugged her in return, holding back her confession that she *had* originally planned on slipping away after their Chinese, but that the lure of seeing Francesco again had been too great. It had almost made up for the fact Beth wasn't there to share Melanie's hen night. She wouldn't be there to share the wedding, either.

The wedding. An event Hannah dreaded.

She felt a huge rush of affection for her little sister along with an accompanying pang of guilt. Poor Melanie. She deserved better than Hannah. Since Beth's death, Hannah had tried so hard to be the best big sister they both wished she could be, but she simply wasn't up to the job. It was impossible. How could she be anything to anyone when such a huge part of herself was missing? All she had been able to do was throw herself into her studies, something over which she had always had total control.

But now her drive and focus had been compromised.

Never had she experienced anything like this.

Hannah was a woman of practicality, not a woman to be taken in with flights of fancy. Medicine was her life. From the age of twelve she'd known exactly what she wanted to be and had been single-minded in her pursuit of it. She would dedicate her life to medicine and saving children, doing her utmost to keep them alive so she could spare as many families from the gaping hole that lived in her own heart as she could.

At least, she had been single-minded until a car knocked her off her bike and the most beautiful man in the universe had stepped in to save her.

Now the hole in her heart didn't feel so hollow.

Since that fateful cold morning, her mind had not just been full of medicine. It had been full of *him*, her knight in shining armour, and meeting him in the flesh had only compounded this. She wasn't stupid. She knew she would never fit into his world. His reputation preceded him. Francesco Calvetti was a dangerous man to know and an *exceptionally* dangerous man to get on the wrong side of. But knowing this had done nothing to eradicate him from her mind.

That moment when she'd been lying on the cold concrete and opened her eyes, she had looked at him and felt such warmth.... Someone who could evoke that in her couldn't be all bad. He just couldn't.

'Come on, Han,' said Melanie, tugging at her hand. 'Come and dance with me.'

'I can't dance.' What she really wanted to do was search every nook and cranny of Calvetti's until she found him. Because he was there. She just knew it.

Melanie pointed at the dance floor, where a group of twenty-something men with more money than taste were strutting their stuff. 'Nor can they.'

Francesco watched the images from the security cameras on a range of monitors on his office wall. Through them, he could see everything taking place in his club. The same feeds were piped into the office where his security guys sat holed up, watching the same live images—but the only eyes Francesco trusted were his own. Tomorrow he would head back to Palermo to spot-check his nightclub and casino there, and then he would fly on to Madrid for the same.

A couple of men he suspected of being drug dealers had been invited by a group of city money men into the VIP area. He watched them closely, debating whether to have them dealt with now or wait until he had actual proof of their nefarious dealings.

A sweep of thick blonde hair with pink bunny ears

caught his attention in one of the central feeds. He watched Hannah get dragged onto the dance floor by another pink-tutued blonde he assumed was the hen of said hen party, Melanie.

Not for the first time, he asked himself what the hell Hannah was doing there.

She looked more than a little awkward. His lips curved upwards as he watched her try valiantly to move her body in time to the beat of the music. He'd seen more rhythm from the stray cats that congregated round the vast veranda of his Sicilian villa.

The half smile faded and compressed into a tight line when he read the slogan on her back: Horny Hannah.

That all the hen party had similar personalised slogans did nothing to break the compression of his lips.

It bothered him. Hannah was too...*classy* to have something so cheap written about her, even if it was in jest.

He downed his coffee and absently wiped away the residue on the corner of his lips with his thumb.

What was she doing here? And why did she keep craning her neck as if she was on the lookout for someone?

Since he'd dismissed her three days ago, he'd been unnerved to find her taking residence in his mind. Now was not the time for distractions of any sort, not when the casino in Mayfair was on the agenda. This particular casino was reputed to be one of the oldest—if not *the* oldest—in the whole of Europe. It had everything Francesco desired in a casino. Old-school glamour. Wealth. And credibility. This was a casino built by gentlemen for gentlemen, and while the old 'no women' rule had been relaxed in modern times, it retained its old-fashioned gentility. More than anything else, though, it was the one business his father had wanted and failed to get. This failure had been a thorn in

Salvatore's side until his dying day, when a life of overindulgence had finally caught up with him.

After almost forty years under the sole ownership of Sir Godfrey Renfrew, a member of the British aristocracy, the casino had been put up for sale.

Francesco wanted it. He coveted it, had spent two months charming Godfrey Renfrew into agreeing the sale of it to him. Such was Godfrey's hatred of Francesco's dead father, it had taken a month to even persuade him to meet.

What was more, if Francesco's spies were correct, Luca Mastrangelo was sniffing around the casino, too.

This news meant he absolutely could not afford to lose focus on the deal, yet still he'd found himself, an hour before opening for the night, giving orders to his hospitality manager to reserve the best table in the club—for a hen party of all things. He'd only ever intended to have Melanie Chapman's party on the guest list.

Under ordinary circumstances, free tables were given to the most VIP of all VIPs and only then because of the publicity it generated.

He hadn't expected Hannah to be in attendance, but now she was here he couldn't seem to stop his eyes from flickering to whichever monitor happened to be fixed on her.

Hannah tried heroically to get her feet moving in time with the music, aware her dancing was easily the least rhythmic of the whole club. Not that this seemed to put any of the men off. To her chagrin, a few seemed to be suffering from what her sister termed Wandering Hand Syndrome. One in particular kept 'accidentally' rubbing against her. When his hand brushed over her bottom the first time she'd been prepared to give him the benefit of the doubt, and had stepped away from him. The second time, when he'd been bolder and tried to cup her buttocks, she'd flashed him a smile and said in her politest voice, 'Please don't do that,' he'd removed his hand. Which had worked for all of ten seconds. The third time he groped her, she'd 'accidentally' trod on his foot. And now the sleaze had 'accidentally' palmed her breast and was grinding into her back as if she were some kind of plaything.

Did people actually *like* this kind of behaviour? Did women really find it *attractive*?

Just as she was wishing she had worn a pair of stilettoes like all the other women there so she could bruise him properly, a figure emerged on the dance floor.

Such was Francesco's presence that the crowd parted like the Red Sea to admit him.

Her sister stopped dancing and gazed up at him with a dropped jaw. The other hens also stared, agog, their feet seeming to move in a manner completely detached from their bodies.

And no wonder. A head taller than anyone else on the dance floor, he would have commanded attention even if he'd looked like the back end of a bus. Wearing an immaculately pressed open-necked black shirt and charcoal trousers, his gorgeous face set in a grim mask, he oozed menace.

Even if Hannah had wanted to hide her delight, she would have been unable to, her face breaking into an enormous grin at the sight of him, an outward display of the fizzing that had erupted in her veins.

She'd hoped with a hope bordering on desperation that he would spot her and seek her out, had prepared herself for the worst, but hoped for the best. She'd also promised herself that if he failed to materialise that evening then she would do everything in her power to forget about him. But if he were to appear…

To her disquiet, other than nodding at her without making proper eye contact, his attention was very much focused on the man who'd been harassing her who, despite trying to retain a nonchalant stance, had beads of sweat popping out on his forehead.

Francesco leaned into his face, his nostrils flaring. 'If you touch this woman again, you will answer to me personally. *Capisce?*'

Not waiting for a response, he turned back into the crowd.

Hannah watched his retreating figure, her heart in her mouth.

Melanie shouted over the music to her, her face animated, yet Hannah didn't hear a single syllable.

It was now or never.

Unlike the regularity of her life, where the only minor change to her schedule came in the form of the monthly weekend-night shift, Francesco's life was full of movement and change, hopping from country to country, always seeing different sunsets. Her life was exactly where she had planned it to be and she didn't want to change the fundamentals of it, but there was something so intoxicating about both Francesco and the freedom of his life. The freedom to wake up in the morning and just *go*.

He could go anywhere *right now.*

Hurrying to catch him, she followed in his wake, weaving through the sweaty bodies and then past the VIP tables.

'Francesco,' she called, panic fluttering in her chest as he placed his hand on the handle of the door marked Private.

He stilled.

She hurried to close the gap.

He turned his head, his features unreadable.

The music was so loud she had to incline right into

him. He was close enough for her to see the individual hairs in the V of his shirt and smell his gorgeous scent, all oaky manliness, everything converging to send her pulse racing.

'Why did you just do that?' she asked.

His eyes narrowed, the pupils ringing with intent, before he turned the handle and held the door open for her.

Hannah stepped into a dimly lit passageway. Francesco closed the door, blocking off the thumping noise of the music.

She shook her head a little to try to clear her ringing ears.

He leaned back against the door, his eyes fixed on her.

'Why did you do that?' she repeated, filling the silence with a question she knew he'd heard perfectly well the first time she'd asked it.

'What? Warn that man off?'

'Threaten him,' she corrected softly.

'I don't deal in threats, Dr Chapman,' he said, his voice like ice. 'Only promises.'

'But why?'

'Because he wouldn't take no for an answer. I will not allow abuse of any form to take place on my premises.'

'So you make a point of personally dealing with all unwanted attention in your clubs, do you?'

His eyes bored into hers, his lips a tight line.

Far from his forbidding expression making her turn and run away, as it would be likely to make any other sane person do, it emboldened her. 'And did I really hear you say *capisce*?'

'It's a word that the man will understand.'

'Very Danny DeVito. And, judging by his reaction to it, very effective.'

Something that could almost pass for amusement curled on his lips. 'Danny DeVito? Do you mean Al Pacino?'

'Probably.' She tried to smile, tried hard to think of a witty remark that would hold his attention for just a little longer, but it was hard to think sensibly when you were caught in a gaze like hot chocolate-fudge cake, especially when it was attached to a man as divine as Francesco Calvetti. If she had to choose, she would say the man was a slightly higher rank on the yummy stakes than the cake. And she liked hot chocolate-fudge cake *a lot*, as her bottom would testify.

'Thank you for rescuing me. Again.'

'You're welcome.' He made to turn the door handle. 'Now, if you'll excuse me...'

'Dismissing me again?'

'I'm a very...'

'Busy man,' she finished for him. God, but her heart was thundering beneath her ribs, her hands all clammy. 'Please. I came along tonight because I wanted to see you again. Five minutes of your time. That's all I ask. If at the end of it you tell me to leave then I will and I promise never to seek you out again.'

She held her breath as she awaited his response.

He eyed her coolly, his features not giving anything away, until, just as she feared she was about to run out of oxygen, he inclined his head and turned the handle of another door, also marked Private.

Hannah followed him into a large room that was perhaps the most orderly office she had ever been in. Along one wall were two dozen monitors, which she gravitated towards. It didn't take long to spot her sister and fellow hens, all back at their table, talking animatedly.

It occurred to her that she had simply walked away without telling Melanie where she was going.

'So, Dr Chapman, you wanted five minutes of my time...'

She turned her head to find Francesco staring pointedly at his chunky, expensive-looking watch.

He might look all forbidding but she could sense his curiosity.

How she regretted allowing Melanie to talk her into wearing the 'hen uniform', but it would have been churlish to refuse. She had denied her sister too much through the years. Dressing in a ridiculous outfit was the least she could do. Still, it made her self-conscious, and right then she needed every ounce of courage to say what she needed to say.

She swallowed but held his gaze, a look that was cold yet made her feel all warm inside. Seriously, how could a man with chocolate-fudge-cake eyes be all bad?

'When I was knocked off my bike I thought I'd died,' she said, clasping her hands together. God, but this was so much harder than she had imagined it would be and she had known it would be hard. 'I honestly thought that was it for me. Since then, everything has changed—*I've* changed. My accident made me realise I've been letting life pass me by.'

'How does this relate to me?'

Her heart hammered so hard her chest hurt. 'Because I can't stop thinking about you.'

His eyes narrowed with suspicion and he folded his arms across his chest.

Hannah's nerves almost failed her. Her tongue rooted to the roof of her mouth.

'What is it you want from me?'

Out of the corner of her eye she spotted the thank-you card she'd given him. Seeing it there, displayed on his desk, settled the nerves in her stomach.

Francesco had kept her card.

He'd sought her out and rescued her *again*.

She wasn't imagining the connection between them.

She sucked her lips in and bit them before blurting out, 'I want you to take my virginity.'

CHAPTER THREE

FRANCESCO SHOOK HIS HEAD. For the first time in his thirty-six years he was at a loss for words.

'God, that came out all wrong.' Hannah covered her face, clearly cringing. When she dropped her hands her face had paled but, to give her credit, she met his gaze with barely a flinch. 'I didn't mean it to come out quite so crudely. Please, say something.'

He shook his head again, trying to clear it. 'Is this some kind of joke?'

'No.'

'You're a virgin?'

'Yes.'

For a moment he seriously considered that he was in some kind of dream.

Had he fallen asleep at his desk?

Since the discovery of his mother's diaries ten months ago, he'd been consumed with rage. This rage fuelled him. Indeed, for the past ten months, his drive had been working at full throttle. Only a month ago his doctor had told him to slow down, that he was at risk of burnout. Naturally, he'd ignored that advice. Francesco would not slow down until he had eradicated every last trace of Salvatore Calvetti's empire.

And to think he'd almost missed those diaries. Had he

not given the family home one last sweep before emptying it for sale, he would never have found them, hidden away in boxes in the cubbyhole of his mother's dressing room. He hadn't even intended to go into his mother's rooms but the compulsion to feel close to her one last time had made him enter them for the first time in two decades.

Reading the diaries had been as close to torture as a man could experience. The respect he'd felt for his father, the respect that had made him a dutiful son while his father was alive, had died a brutal death.

His only regret was that he hadn't learned the truth while his father was alive, would never have the pleasure of punishing him for every hour of misery he'd put his mother through. Duty would have gone to hell. He might just have helped his father into an early grave.

He hoped with every fibre of his being that his father *was* in hell. He deserved nothing less.

Because now he knew the truth. And he would not be satisfied until he'd destroyed everything Salvatore Calvetti had built, crushed his empire and his reputation. Left it for dust.

The truth consumed him. His hate fuelled him.

It was perfectly feasible he had fallen asleep.

Except he'd never had a dream that made his heart beat as if it would hammer through his ribcage.

He rubbed the back of his neck and stared at the woman who had made such a confounding offer.

She looked ridiculous in her hen outfit, with the pink tutu, black leotard and leggings, and black ballet slippers. At least the other hens had made an effort, adorning their outfits with the sky-high heels women usually wore in his clubs. It didn't even look as if Hannah had brushed her hair, never mind put any make-up on. What woman went clubbing without wearing make-up?

Indeed, he could not remember the last time he'd met a woman who *didn't* wear make-up, full stop.

And she still had those ridiculous bunny ears on her head.

Yet there was something incredibly alluring about Hannah's fresh-faced looks. Something different.

He'd thought *she* was different. He'd resisted her offer of a date a few short days ago because of it; because he'd thought she was *too* different, that she didn't belong in his world.

Could he really have judged her so wrong?

What kind of woman offered her so-called virginity to a stranger?

And what the hell had compelled him to warn her groper off and not send one of his men in to resolve the situation? If he'd followed his usual procedures he wouldn't be standing here now on the receiving end of one of the most bizarre offers he'd ever heard.

It had been watching that man paw her—and her dignity when rebuffing his advances—that had made something inside him snap.

The rules were the same in all his establishments, his staff trained to spot customers overstepping the mark in the familiarity stakes. The usual procedure was for one of his doormen to have a polite 'word' with the perpetrator. That polite word was usually enough to get them behaving.

Francesco might have little respect for the type of women who usually littered his clubs but that did not mean he would tolerate them being abused in any form.

In the shadows of his memory rested his mother, a woman who had tolerated far too much abuse. And he, her son, had been oblivious to it.

A rush of blood to his head had seen him off his seat,

out of his office and onto the dance floor before his brain had time to compute what his feet were doing.

'I have no idea what you're playing at,' he said slowly, 'but I will not be a party to such a ridiculous game. I have given you your five minutes. It's time for you to leave.'

This *had* to be a game. Hannah Chapman had discovered his wealth and, like so many others of her gender, decided she would like to access it.

It unnerved him how disappointed he felt.

'This isn't a game.' She took a visibly deep breath. 'Please. Francesco, I am a twenty-seven-year-old woman who has never had sex. I haven't even kissed a man. It's become a noose around my neck. I don't want to stay a virgin all my life. All I want is one night to know what it feels like to be a real woman and you're the only man I can ask.'

'But why me?' he asked, incredulous.

Her beautiful hazel eyes held his. 'Because I trust that you won't hurt me.'

'How can you trust such a thing? I am a stranger to you.'

'The only men I meet are fellow doctors and patients. The patients are a big no-no, and the few single doctors I know…we work too closely together. You might be a stranger but I *know* you'll treat me with respect. I know you would never laugh at me or make fun about me being a twenty-seven-year-old virgin behind my back.'

'That's an awful lot of supposition you're making about me.'

'Maybe.' She raised her shoulders in a helpless gesture. 'I thought I was dead. When I opened my eyes and saw your face I thought you'd come to take me to heaven. All I can think now is *what if…* What if I *had* died? I've done *nothing* with my life.'

'Hardly,' he said harshly. 'You're a doctor. That takes dedication.'

'For me, it's taken everything. I'm not naturally bright—I had to work hard to get my grades, to learn and to keep learning. In the process I've been so focused on my career that I've allowed my personal life to go to ruin.' The same groove he remembered from the other evening reappeared on her forehead. 'I don't want to die a virgin.'

Francesco rubbed his neck.

*It seemed s*he was serious.

Of course, she *could* be lying. Having discovered who he was, this could be a clever, convoluted game to access his life and wealth.

Yet her explanation made a mad kind of sense.

He remembered the expression of serenity that had crossed her face at the moment she'd opened her eyes and looked at him, remembered her words and the fuzzy feelings they had evoked in him.

Something had passed between them—something fleeting but tangible.

There was no way Hannah could have known who he was at that moment.

One thing he did know was that she had gained a false impression of him. If she knew who he really was, he would be the last man she would make such a shameless proposition to.

Regardless, he could hardly credit how tempted he was.

He was a red-blooded male. What man *wouldn't* be tempted by such an offer?

But Hannah was a virgin, he reminded himself—despite the fact that he'd thought virgins over the age of eighteen were from the tales of mythology.

Surely this was every man's basest fantasy? A virgin begging to be deflowered.

'You have no idea who I am,' he told her flatly.

'Are you talking about the gangster thing?'

'The gangster thing?' His voice took on a hint of menace. How could she be so blasé about it? Was she so naive she didn't understand his life wasn't something watched from the safety of a television set, played by men who likely had manicures between takes?

Scrutinising her properly, her innocence was obvious. She had an air about her—the same air he saw every time he looked through his parents' wedding album. His mother had had that air when she'd married his father, believing it to be a love match, blissfully oblivious to her husband's true nature, and the true nature of his business affairs.

Hannah raised her shoulders again. 'I've read all about you on the internet. I know what it says your family are.'

'And do you believe everything you read on the internet?'

'No.' She shook her head to emphasise her point.

Deliberately, he stepped towards her and into her space. He brought his face down so it was level with hers. 'You *should* believe it. Because it's true. Every word. I am not a good person for you to know. I am the last person a woman like you should get involved with.'

She didn't even flinch. 'A woman like me? What does that mean?'

'You're a doctor. You do not belong in my world.'

'I just want *one night* in your world, that's all. One night. I don't care what's been written about you. I know you would never hurt me.'

'You think?' Where had she got this ludicrous faith in him from? He had to eradicate it, make her see enough of the truth to scare her all the way back to the safety of her hospital.

He straightened to his full height, an act capable of intimidating even the hardest of men. He breached the inches between them to reach into her thick mane of hair and tug the rabbit ears free. They were connected by some kind of plastic horseshoe that he dropped onto the floor and placed a foot on. He pressed down until he heard the tell-tale crunch.

She stared at him with that same serene look in her hazel eyes.

'Tell me,' he said, gently twisting her around so her back was flush against him, 'how, exactly, do you want me to take your virginity?'

He heard an intake of breath.

Good. He'd unnerved her.

Gathering her hair together, he inhaled the sweet scent of her shampoo. Her hair felt surprisingly soft. 'Do you want me to take you here and now?'

He trailed a finger down her exposed slender neck, over the same collarbone that had been broken less than two months before, and down her toned arm before reaching round to cup a breast flattened by the leotard she wore.

'Or do you want me to take you on a bed?' He traced his thumb over a nipple that shot out beneath his touch.

'I...' Her voice came out like a whimper. 'I...'

'You must have some idea of how you would like me to perform the deed,' he murmured, breathing into her ear and nuzzling his nose into a cheek as soft as the finest silk. 'Is foreplay a requirement? Or do you just want to get it over with?'

'I...I know what you're doing.'

'All I'm doing is ascertaining how, exactly, you would like me to relieve you of your virginity. I can do it now if you would like.' He pressed his groin into the small of her back so as to leave her in no doubt how ready he was. 'Right here, over the desk? Up against the wall? On the floor?'

Much as he hated himself for it, his body was responding to her in the basest of fashions.

He would control it, just as he controlled everything else.

He would *not* give in to temptation.

He would make the good doctor see just how wrong she was about him.

Hannah Chapman was one of the few people in the world who made a difference.

He would not be the one to taint her, no matter how much he desired her or how much she wanted it.

He was better than that. He was better than the man who had created him, who would, no doubt, have already relieved Hannah of her virginity if he'd been in Francesco's shoes.

He would not be that man. And if he had to come on heavy to make her run away, then that was what he would do. Reasoning clearly didn't work with her.

'You're trying to scare me off.'

Francesco stilled at her astuteness.

Although her breaths were heavy, he could feel her defiance through the rigidity of her bones.

It was with far too much reluctance that he released his hold and turned her back round to face him.

Hannah's hair tumbled back around her shoulders. Her cheeks were flushed, her eyes wide. Yet there was no fear. Apprehension, yes, but no fear.

'You are playing with fire, Dr Chapman.'

She gave a wry smile. 'I'm trained to treat burns.'

'Not the kind you will get from me. You'll have to find another man to do the job. I'm not for hire.'

His mind flashed to the man who'd been groping Hannah earlier—who, he imagined, would be more than happy to accede to her request. He banished the image. Who she chose was none of his concern.

All the same, the thought of that man pawing at her

again sent a sharp, hot flush racing through him. She was too...*pure*.

A shrewdness came into her eyes, although how such a look could also be gentle totally beat him.

She tilted her head to the side. 'Do I scare you?'

'On the contrary. It is you who should be afraid of me.'

'But I'm not scared of you. I don't care about your reputation. I'm not after a relationship or anything like that—the only thing being with you makes me feel is good. After everything you've done for me, how can I not trust that?'

He shook his head.

This was madness.

He should call his guards and have her escorted out of his club. But he wouldn't.

Francesco had heard stories about people who saved lives being bound to the person they'd saved, and vice versa. And while he hadn't saved her in a technical sense, it was the only explanation he could think of for the strange chemistry that brewed between them. Total strangers yet inexplicably linked.

Something had passed between them, connecting them.

It was his duty to sever that link. *His* duty. Not his guards'.

He would make her see.

'You think I'm worthy of your trust?' Unthinkingly, he reached out a hand and captured a lock of her hair.

'I *know* you are.' Reclosing the gap between them, she tilted her head back a little and placed a hand on his cheek. 'Don't you see? A lesser man wouldn't try to scare me off—he would have taken what I offered without a second thought.'

His skin tingled beneath the warmth of her fingers. He wanted to clasp those fingers, interlace his own through them....

'I'm not cut out for any form of relationship—my career matters too much for me to compromise it—but I want to *feel*.' She brought her face closer so her nose skimmed against his throat, her breath a whisper against his sensitised skin. 'I want one night where I can throw caution to the wind. I want to know what it's like to be made love to and I want it to be you because you're the only man I've met who makes me feel alive without even touching me.'

Francesco could hardly breathe. His fingers still held the lock of her hair. The desire that had been swirling in his blood since he'd nuzzled into her neck thickened.

When had he ever felt as if he could explode from arousal?

This was madness.

'If I believed you felt nothing physically for me, I would walk away now,' she continued, her voice a murmur. 'I certainly wouldn't debase myself any further.'

'How can you be so sure I feel anything for you physically?'

'Just because I'm a virgin doesn't mean I'm totally naive.'

In his effort to scare her away, he'd pressed his groin into her back, letting her feel his excitement through the layers of their clothing.

That particular effort had backfired.

Hannah had turned it round on him.

Well, no more.

Clasping the hand still resting against his cheek, he tugged it away and dropped it. He stepped back, glowering down at her. 'You think you can spend one night with me and walk away unscathed? Because that isn't going to happen. Sex isn't a game, and I'm not a toy that can be played with.'

For the first time a hint of doubt stole over her face. 'I

never meant it like that,' she said, her voice low. 'It's not just that I'm wildly attracted to you, it's more than that. I can't explain it, but when I look at you I see a life full of excitement, of travel, of so much more than I could ever hope to experience. All I want is to reach out and touch it, to experience some of it with you.'

'You think you know me but you don't. I'm not the man you think. My life is seedy and violent. You should want nothing to do with it.'

For long, long moments he eyeballed her, waiting for her to drop her eyes. But it didn't happen—her gaze held his, steady and immovable.

'Prove it.' She gave a feeble shrug. 'If you really think you're so bad for me, then *prove* it.'

He almost groaned aloud. 'It's not a case of proving it. You need to understand—once your virginity's gone you will never get it back. It's lost for ever, and who knows what else you might lose with it.'

She swallowed but remained steady. 'There's nothing else for me to lose. I'm not after a love affair. Francesco, all I want is one night.'

It was hearing his name—and the meaning she put into it—on her lips that threw him.

It made him want to find a dragon to slay just to protect her. Yet he knew that the only thing Hannah needed protecting from was herself.

He reminded himself that he did not need this aggravation. His mind should be focused on the Mayfair deal— the deal that would be the crowning glory in his empire. Hannah had compromised his concentration enough these past few days.

Maybe if he gave her some of what she wanted his mind could regain its focus without her there, knocking on his thoughts.

'You want proof of who I really am?' he said roughly. 'Then that's what you shall have. I will give you a sample of my life for one weekend.'

Her eyes sparkled.

'*This* weekend,' he continued. 'You can share a taste of my life and see for yourself why you should keep the hell away from me. By the end of our time together I guarantee you will never want to see my face again, much less waste your virginity on a man like me.'

CHAPTER FOUR

HANNAH HAD BEEN twitching her curtains for a good half hour before Francesco pulled up outside her house on an enormous motorbike, the engine making enough racket to wake the whole street.

It didn't surprise her in the least that he waited for her to come out to him. Once Francesco had agreed to a weekend together, he had wasted no time in dismissing her by saying, 'I will collect you at 7:00 a.m. Have your passport ready.'

He was taking her to Sicily. To his home.

She couldn't remember the last time she'd been this excited about something. Or as nervous.

Her very essence tingling with anticipation, she stepped out into the early-morning sun, noticing that at least he had taken his helmet off to greet her.

'Good morning,' she said, beaming both at him and, with admiration, at the bike. There was something so...*manly* about the way he straddled it, which, coupled with the cut of his tight leather trousers, sent a shock of warmth right through her. 'Are we traveling to Sicily on this?'

He eyed her coldly. 'Only to the airbase. That's if you still want to come?' From the tone of his voice, there was no doubting that he hoped she'd changed her mind.

If she was honest, since leaving his office six short hours

ago, she'd repeatedly asked herself if she was doing the right thing.

But she hadn't allowed herself to even consider backing down. Because all she knew for certain was that if she didn't grab this opportunity with both hands she would regret it for the rest of her life, regardless of the outcome.

'I still want to come,' she said, almost laughing to see his lips tighten in disapproval. Couldn't he see, the more he tried to scare her off, the more she knew she was on the right path, that it proved his integrity?

Francesco desired her.

The feel of his hardness pressed against her had been the most incredible, intoxicating feeling imaginable. She had never dreamed her body capable of such a reaction, had imagined the thickening of the blood and the low pulsations deep inside were from the realms of fiction. It had only served to increase her desire, to confirm she was following the right path.

She'd been his for the taking in his office but he had stepped back, unwilling to take advantage. Again.

Francesco was doing everything in his power to put her off, but she doubted there was anything to be revealed about him that would do that. What, she wondered, had made him so certain he was all bad? Was it because of his blood lineage? Whatever it was, she knew there was good in him—even though he clearly didn't believe it himself.

Face thunderous, he reached into the side case and pulled out some leathers and a black helmet. 'Put these on.'

She took them from him. 'Do you want to come in while I change? Your bike will be perfectly safe—all the local hoodlums are tucked up in bed.'

'I will wait here.'

'I have coffee.'

'I will wait.'

'Suit yourself.'

'You have five minutes.'

In her bedroom, Hannah wrestled herself into the tight leather trousers, and then donned the matching jacket, staggering slightly under the weight of it.

When she caught sight of her reflection in the full-length mirror she paused. Whoever said leathers were sexy was sorely mistaken—although she'd admit to feeling very Sandra Dee in the trousers.

Sandra Dee had been a virgin, too.

Hannah was a virgin in all senses of the word.

But, she reminded herself, with Francesco's help she was going to change that. Just for this one weekend. That was all she wanted. Some memories to share with Beth.

She took a deep breath and studied her reflection one last time. Her stomach felt knotted, but she couldn't tell if excitement or trepidation prevailed.

She checked the back door was locked one last time before grabbing her small case and heading back out to him.

'That will not fit,' Francesco said when he saw her case.

'You're the one whisking me away for a romantic overnight stay on a motorbike,' she pointed out. 'What do you suggest I do?'

'Let me make this clear, I am not whisking you away anywhere.'

'Semantics.'

'And I never said anything about us going away for one night only. We will return to the UK when *I* am ready.'

'As long as you get me back in time for work at nine o'clock Monday morning, that's fine by me.'

His face was impassive. 'We will return when my schedule allows it, not yours.'

'Is this the part when I'm supposed to wave my hands and say, "oh, in that case I can't possibly come with you?"'

'Yes.'

'Bad luck. I'm coming. And you'll get me back in time for work.'

'You sound remarkably sure of yourself.'

'Not at all. I just know you're not the sort of person to allow a ward full of sick children to suffer from a lack of doctors.'

His features contorted, the chocolate fudge of his eyes hardening. 'That is a risk you are willing to take?'

'No.' She shook her head, a rueful smile playing on her lips. 'I know there's no risk.' At least no risk in the respect of getting her to work on time. And as to Francesco's other concerns, Hannah knew there was no risk in the respect of her heart, either; her heart hadn't functioned properly in fifteen years.

More practically, she supposed there were some dangers. She could very well be getting into something way out of her depth, but what was the worst that could happen? Hannah had lived through her own personal hell. The worst thing that could happen had occurred at the age of twelve, and she had survived it. God alone knew how, but she had.

It was only one weekend. One weekend of *life* before she went back to her patients, the children she hoped with all her semi-functioning heart would grow up to lead full lives of their own.

'On your head be it,' said Francesco. 'Now either find a smaller case for your stuff, put it in a rucksack you can strap to you, or leave it behind.'

Her gaze dropped to her case. She didn't have either a smaller case or a rucksack....

'Give me one minute,' she said, speaking over her shoulder as she hurried back into the house. In record time she'd grabbed an oversized handbag and shoved her passport, phone, purse, clean underwear, toothbrush, and a thin sundress into it. The rest of her stuff, including some research papers she'd been reading through for the past week, she left in the case.

This was an adventure after all. Her first adventure in fifteen years.

'Is that all you're taking?' Francesco asked when she rejoined him, taking the bag from her.

'You're the one who said to bring something smaller.'

He made a noise that sounded like a cross between a grunt and a snort.

She grinned. 'You'll have to try harder than that to put me off.'

Nostrils flaring, he shoved her bag into the side case then thrust the helmet back into her hands. 'Put this on.'

'Put this on...?' She waited for a *please*.

'Now.'

How could *anyone* be so cheerful first thing in the morning? Francesco wondered. It wasn't natural.

What would it take to put a chink in that smiley armour?

With great reluctance, he reached over to help her with the helmet straps. Even through the darkened visor he could see her still grinning.

If he had his way, that pretty smile would be dropped from her face before they boarded his plane.

'Have you ridden on one of these before?' he asked, tightening the straps enough so they were secure without cutting off her circulation.

She shook her head.

'Put your arms around me and mimic my actions—lean into the turns.'

Only when he was certain that she was securely seated did Francesco twist the throttle and set off.

Francesco brought the bike to a halt in the airport's private car park.

'That was amazing!' Hannah said, whipping off her helmet to reveal a head of hair even more tangled than a whole forest of birds' nests.

If his body wasn't buzzing from the exhilaration of the ride coupled with the unwanted thrum of desire borne from having her pressed against him for half an hour, he would think she looked endearing.

His original intention had been to take advantage of the clear early-Saturday-morning roads and hit the throttle. What he hadn't accounted for was the distraction of having Hannah pressed so tightly against him.

And no wonder. Those trousers...

Caro Dio...

Behind that sensible, slightly messy exterior lay a pair of the most fantastic legs he had ever seen. He'd noticed how great they looked the night before, but the ridiculous pink tutu had hidden the best part: the thighs.

Not for a second had he been able to forget she was there, attached to him, trusting him to keep her safe.

Where the hell did she get this misplaced trust *from*?

In the end, he'd kept his speed strictly controlled, rarely breaching the legal limits. Not at all the white-knuckle ride he'd had in mind.

His guards were already there waiting for him, forbidden from following him when he was riding in the UK. It was different on the Med, especially in Sicily. The only good thing he could say about England was he never felt the need to have an entourage watching his back at all times.

In as ungracious a manner as he could muster, he pulled

Hannah's bag from the side case, handed it to her, then threw the keys of his bike to one of his men.

'What are you doing?' he asked, spotting Hannah on her phone. It was one of the latest models. For some reason this surprised him. Maybe it was because she was a virgin who dressed in a basic, functional manner that he'd assumed she'd have a basic, functional phone.

'Answering my emails,' she said, peering closely at the screen as she tapped away.

'From who?'

'Work.'

'It is Saturday.'

She peered up at him. She really did look ridiculous, with the heavy jacket clearly weighing her down. Still, those legs... And that bottom...

'Hospitals don't close for weekends.' She flashed him a quick grin. 'I'll be done in a sec.'

Francesco had no idea why it irked him to witness Hannah pay attention to her phone. He didn't want to encourage her into getting any ideas about them but, all the same, he did *not* appreciate being made to feel second best.

'All done,' she said a moment later, dropping the phone back into her bag.

Once the necessary checks were made, they boarded Francesco's plane.

'You own this?' she asked with the same wide-eyed look she'd had when she'd first walked into his club carrying a bunch of flowers for him.

He jerked a nod and took his seat, indicating she should sit opposite him. 'Before I give the order for us to depart, I need to check your bag.'

'Why? It's already been through a scanner.'

'My plane. My rules.' He met her gaze, willing her to

fight back, to leave, to get off the aircraft and walk away before the dangers of his life tainted her.

He thought he saw a spark of anger. A tiny spark, but a spark all the same.

She shrugged and handed it over to him.

He opened the bag. His hand clenched around her underwear. He should pull it out, let her see him handle her most intimate items. The plane hadn't taken off. There was still time to change her mind.

But then he met her gaze again. She studied him with unabashed curiosity.

No. He would not humiliate her.

His fingers relaxed their grip, the cotton folding back into place. He pulled out a threadbare black purse.

Resolve filled him. He opened it to find a few notes, a heap of receipts, credit and debit cards, and a photo, which he tugged out.

Hannah fidgeted before him but he paid her no heed.

She wanted him to prove in actions how bad he was for her? This was only the beginning.

He peered closely at a picture of two identical young girls with long flaxen hair, hazel eyes, and the widest, gappiest grins he had ever seen.

'You are a twin?' he asked in surprise.

Her answer came after a beat too long. 'Yes.'

He looked at her. Hannah's lips were drawn in. Her lightly tanned skin had lost a little of its colour.

'Why was she not out last night with you, celebrating your other sister's hen night?'

Her hands fisted into balls before she flexed them and raised her chin. 'Beth died a long time ago.'

His hand stilled.

'Please be careful with that. It's the last picture taken

of us together.' There was a definite hint of anxiety in her voice.

This was another clear-cut opportunity to convince her of his true self. All he had to do was rip the photo into little pieces and he guaranteed she would leave without a backward glance.

But no matter how much he commanded his hands to do the deed, they refused.

Hannah's voice broke through his conflicted thoughts. 'Can I have my stuff back now?' she asked, now speaking in her more familiar droll manner.

Without saying a word, he carefully slotted the photo back in its place, blinking to rid himself of the image of the happy young girls.

The last picture of them together?

His stomach did a full roll and settled with a heavy weight rammed onto it.

Getting abruptly to his feet, he dropped the bag by Hannah's seat. 'I need to speak with the crew. Put your seat belt on.'

Hannah expelled all the air from her lungs in one long movement, watching as Francesco disappeared through a door.

There had been a moment when she'd been convinced he was going to crush the photo in his giant hands.

If there was one thing she'd be unable to forgive, it was that.

But he hadn't. He'd wanted to, but the basic decency within him had won out. And he hadn't fired a load of questions about Beth at her, either.

It was very rare that she spoke about her twin. Even after fifteen years, it still felt too raw, as if vocalising it turned it back into the real event that had ripped her apart. People treated her differently. As soon as someone learned about it, she just knew that was how they would start referring to her. *That's the girl whose twin sister died.* She'd heard those very whispers at school, felt the curious glances and the eyes just waiting for the telltale sign of her suffering. She knew what her schoolmates had been waiting for—they'd been waiting for her to cry.

She'd cried plenty, but always in the privacy of her bedroom—the room she'd shared with Beth.

She'd learned to repel the curiosity with a bright smile, and ignore the whispers by burying herself in her schoolwork. It had been the same with her parents. And Melanie. She'd effectively shut them all out, hiding her despair behind a smile and then locking herself away.

When Francesco reappeared a few minutes later, she fixed that same bright smile on him.

'We'll be taking off in five minutes,' he said. 'This is your last chance to change your mind.'

'I'm not changing my mind.'

'Sicily is my turf. If you come, you will be bound under my directive.'

'How very formal. I'm still not changing my mind.'

His eyes glittered with menace. 'As I said earlier—on your head be it.'

'Gosh, it's hot,' Hannah commented as she followed Francesco off the steps of the plane. She breathed in deeply. Yes, there it was. That lovely scent of the sea. Thousands of miles away, and for a moment she had captured the smell of home. Her real home—on the coast of Devon. Not London. London was where she lived.

'It's summer' came the curt reply.

At least she'd had the foresight to change out of the leathers and into her sundress before they'd landed. Not that Francesco had noticed. Or, if he had, he hadn't acknowledged it, keeping his head buried so deep into what he was doing on his laptop she wouldn't have been surprised if he'd disappeared into the screen. The only time he'd moved had been to go into his bedroom—yes, he had a *bedroom on a plane*!—and changed from his own leathers into a pair of black chinos, an untucked white linen shirt, and a blazer.

A sleek grey car was waiting, the driver opening the passenger door as they approached. Another identical car waited behind, and Francesco's guards piled into it—except one, who got into the front of their own car.

The doors had barely closed before the guard twisted round and handed a metallic grey object to Francesco.

'Is that a gun?' Hannah asked in a tone more squeaky than anything a chipmunk could produce.

He tucked the object into what she assumed was an inside pocket of his blazer. 'We are in Sicily.'

'Are guns legal in Sicily?'

He speared her with a look she assumed was supposed to make her quail.

'I hope for your sake it's not loaded,' she said. 'Especially with you keeping it so close to your heart.'

'Then it's just as well I have a doctor travelling with me.'

'See? I have my uses.'

Despite her flippancy, the gun unnerved her. It unnerved her a lot.

Knowing on an intellectual level that Francesco was dangerous was one thing. Witnessing him handle a gun with the nonchalance of one handling a pen was another.

He's doing this for effect, she told herself. *Remember, this is an adventure.*

'Where are we going?' she asked after a few minutes of silence had passed.

'My nightclub.'

It didn't take long before they pulled up outside an enormous Gothic-looking building with pillars at the doors.

'This is a nightclub?'

'That's where I said we were going.'

In a melee of stocky male bodies, she followed him inside.

The Palermo Calvetti's was, she estimated, at least four times the size of its English counterpart. Although decorated in the same glitzy silver and deep reds and exuding glamour, it had a more cosmopolitan feel.

A young woman behind the bar, polishing all the hardwood and optics, practically snapped to attention at the sight of them.

'Due caffè neri nel mio ufficio,' Francesco called out as he swept past and through a door marked *Privato*.

Like its English equivalent, his office was spotless. Two of his men entered the room with them—the same two who'd been guarding the English Calvetti's when she had turned up just five short days ago.

Francesco went straight to a small portrait on the wall and pressed his fingers along the edge of the frame until it popped open as if it were the cover of a book.

'Another cliché?' she couldn't resist asking.

'Clichés are called clichés for a reason,' he said with a shrug of a shoulder. 'Why make it easy for thieves?'

Watching him get into his safe, Hannah decided that it would be easier to break into Fort Knox than into Francesco Calvetti's empire. The inner safe door swinging open, her eyes widened to see the sheer size of the space inside, so much larger than she would have guessed from the picture covering it.

Her stare grew wider to see the canvas bags he removed from it and she realised that they were filled with money.

Francesco and his two men conversed rapidly, all the

while weighing wads of notes on a small set of electronic scales and making notes in a battered-looking A4 book. When the young woman came in with two coffees and a bowl of sugar cubes, Francesco added two lumps into both cups, stirred them vigorously, then passed one over to Hannah, who had perched herself on a windowsill.

'Thanks,' she said, ridiculously touched he'd remembered how she liked her coffee.

Not that it would have been hard to remember, she mused, seeing as he took his exactly the same.

The same thought must have run through Francesco's head because his eyes suddenly met hers, a look of consternation running through them before he jerked his head back to what he was doing.

It amazed her that he would allow her in his inner sanctum when such a large amount of money was, literally, on the table. Then she remembered the gun in his jacket, which he had placed over the back of his captain's chair.

Peering less than subtly at his henchmen, she thought she detected a slight bulge in the calf of the black trousers one wore.

Unnerved by the massive amounts of money before her and the fact she was alone in an office with three men, two of whom were definitely armed, she reached for her phone to smother her increasing agitation.

Working through her messages, Hannah's heart sank when she opened an email from an excited Melanie, who had finally, after months of debate, settled on the wedding-breakfast menu. She could only hope the response she fired back sounded suitably enthusiastic, but she couldn't even bring herself to open the attachment with the menu listed on it, instead opening a work-related email.

It was the most significant event in her little sister's life and, much as Hannah wanted to be excited for her, all she felt inside when she thought of the forthcoming day was dread.

'What are you doing?' Francesco asked a while later, breaking through her concentration.

'Going through my messages.'

'Again?'

'I like to keep abreast of certain patients' progress,' she explained, turning her phone off and chucking it back into her bag.

'Even at weekends?'

'*You're* working,' she pointed out.

'This is my business.'

'And the survival and recovery of my patients is *my* business.'

She had no idea what was going on behind those chocolate-fudge eyes but, judging by the set of his jaw and the thinning of his lips, she guessed it was something unpleasant.

A few minutes later and it appeared they were done, the two henchmen having placed all the money into a large suitcase.

'Before you leave for the bank, Mario,' Francesco said, speaking in deliberate English, 'I want you to show the good doctor here your hand.'

The guns hadn't made any overt impression on her, other than what he took to be a healthy shock that he armed himself in his homeland. He felt certain the next minute would change her impression completely.

Mario complied, holding his hand with its disfigured fingers in front of her.

She peered closely before taking it into her own hands and rubbing her fingers over the meaty skin.

A hot stab plunged into Francesco's chest. He inhaled deeply through his nose, clenching his hands into fists.

She was just examining it like the professional she was, he told himself. All the same, even his mental teeth had gritted together.

'What do you see?' he demanded.

'A hand that's been broken in a number of places—the fingers have been individually broken, too, as if something heavy was smashed onto them.'

'An excellent assessment. Now, Mario, I would like you to tell Dr Chapman who broke your hand and smashed your fingers.'

If Mario was capable of showing surprise, he would be displaying it now, his eyes flashing at Francesco, who nodded his go-ahead. This was an incident that hadn't been discussed or even alluded to in nearly two decades.

'Signor Calvetti. He did it.'

Hannah looked up at Francesco. 'Your father?'

Deliberately, he folded his arms across his chest and stretched his legs out. 'No. Not my father.'

Her eyes widened. 'You?'

'*Sì*. I caught him stealing from my father. Take another look at his hand. That is what we do to thieves in my world.'

CHAPTER FIVE

Francesco kept his gaze fixed on Hannah, waiting for a reaction other than her current open-mouthed horror.

See, he said with his eyes, *you wanted proof? Well, here it is.*

She closed her eyes and shook her head. When she snapped them back open, she gave Mario's hand another close inspection.

'These scars look old,' she said.

'Nearly twenty year,' Mario supplied in his pigeon English. 'Is okay. I ask for it.'

'What—you asked for your hand to be smashed?'

'What he means is that he did the crime knowing what his punishment would be if caught,' said Francesco.

Her eyes shrewd, she nodded. 'And yet, even after what you did to him and his so-called crime, he still works for you, is trusted enough to handle large quantities of money on your behalf, and, if I'm reading this right, carries a gun that he has never turned on you in revenge.'

How did she do it?

She'd turned it round on him *again*.

'Do not think there was any benevolence on my part,' he countered harshly, before nodding a dismissal at Mario, who left the office with his colleague, leaving them alone.

Hannah remained perched on the windowsill, her hair

now turned into a bushy beehive. She'd crossed her legs, her pale blue dress having ridden up her thighs. It was one of the most repulsive articles of clothing he had ever seen: shapeless, buttoned from top to bottom, clearly brought for comfort rather than style. And yet...there was something incredibly alluring about having to guess what lay beneath it....

'What did he steal?'

'He was a waiter at one of my father's restaurants and made the mistake of helping himself to the takings in the till.'

'How much did he take?' she asked. Her former nonchalance had vanished. It pleased him to hear her troubled tone.

'I don't remember. Something that was the equivalent of around one hundred pounds.'

'So you maimed him for one hundred pounds?'

Francesco drew himself to his full height. 'Mario knew the risks.'

'Fair enough,' she said in a tone that left no doubt she meant the exact opposite. 'Why didn't you just call the police?'

'The police?' A mirthful sound escaped from his throat. 'We have our own ways of handling things here.'

'So if he stole from your father, why did *you* mete out the punishment?'

Francesco remembered that day so clearly.

He'd caught Mario red-handed. There had been no choice but to confront him. He'd made him empty his pockets. His father had walked in and demanded to know what was going on.

How clearly he remembered that sickening feeling in the pit of his stomach when Mario had confessed, looking Salvatore square in the eye as he did so.

And how clearly he remembered feeling as if he would

vomit when Salvatore had turned his laser glare to him, his son, and said, 'You know what must be done.'

Francesco had known. And so had Mario, whose own father had worked for Salvatore, and Salvatore's father before him. They'd both known the score.

It was time for Francesco to prove himself a man in his father's eyes, something his father had been waiting on for years. Something *he'd* been waiting on for years, too. A chance to gain his father's respect.

But how could he explain this to Hannah, explain that it had been an opportunity that hadn't just presented itself to him but come gift-wrapped? Refusal had never been an option.

And why did he even care to explain himself?

Francesco didn't explain himself to anyone.

He hadn't explained himself since he'd vomited in the privacy of his bathroom after the deed had been done, and only when he was certain he was out of earshot.

That was the last time he'd ever allowed himself to react with emotion. Certainly the last time he'd allowed himself to feel any vulnerability.

Overnight he'd put his childhood behind him, not that there had been much left of it after his mother had overdosed.

'I did it because it needed to be done and I was the one who caught him.'

She kept her eyes fixed on him. There was none of the reproach or disgust he expected to find. All that was there was something that looked suspiciously like compassion....

'Twenty years ago you would have been a boy.'

'I was seventeen. I was a man.'

'And how old was he?'

'The same.'

'Little more than children.'

'We both knew what we were doing,' he stated harshly. 'After that night we were no longer children.'

'I'll bet.'

'And how many more hands have you mangled in the intervening years?'

'Enough of them. There are times when examples need to be made.'

Violence had been a part of his life since toddlerhood. His mother had tried to protect him from the worst of his father's excesses but her attempts had not been enough. His first memory was looking out of his bedroom window and witnessing his father beating up a man over a car bonnet. The man had been held down by two of his father's men.

His mother had been horrified to find him looking out and dragged him away, covering his eyes. Francesco had learned only ten months ago that the bruising he often saw on his mother's body was also from the hands of his father, and not the result of clumsiness.

Francesco had spent his entire life idolising his father. Sure, there were things he'd never been comfortable about, but Salvatore was his father. He'd loved and respected him. After his death four years ago, certain truths had been revealed about aspects of his father's business that had taken some of the shine off his memories, like discovering his drug importing. That in itself had been a very bitter blow to bear, had sickened him to the pit of his stomach. But to learn the truth of what he'd done to his mother... It had sent Francesco's world spinning off its axis.

The walls of the spacious office started to close in on him. The air conditioning was on but the humidity had become stifling, perspiration breaking out on his back.

Hannah stared intently into those beautiful chocolate eyes. Only years of practice at reading her patients allowed her to see beneath the hard exterior he projected. There was pain there. A lot of it. 'What is it about me that scares you so much?'

His lips curled into a sneer. Rising from his chair, he strode towards her like a sleek panther. 'You think you scare me?'

'What other reason is there for you to try so hard to frighten me off and go out of your way to try to make me hate you? Because that's what you're doing, isn't it? Trying to make me hate you?'

He stilled, his huge frame right before her, blocking everything else out.

She reached out a hand and placed it on his chest. 'I bet you've never treated a woman like this before.'

'Like what?' he asked harshly, leaning over and placing his face right in hers, close enough for her to feel the warmth of his breath. 'You're the one with the foolish, romanticised notions about me. I warned you from the start that you didn't belong in my world, and yet you thought you knew best.'

'So this is all to make me see the real you?'

'We had a deal, Dr Chapman,' he bit out, grabbing her hand, which still rested against his hard chest, and lacing his fingers through it. He squeezed, a warning that caused no physical pain but was undoubtedly meant to impress upon her that, if he so chose, he *could* hurt her. 'I made you a guarantee that by the end of our time together I would be the last man you would want to give your virginity to.'

Squeezing his fingers in return, her mouth filling with saliva, she tilted her chin a touch. His mouth was almost close enough to press her lips to....

'If you really want to prove it, then hurt me, don't just give me a warning. You're twice my size—it would take no effort for you to hurt me if you really wanted.' Oh, but she was playing with fire. She didn't need Francesco to point that out. But no matter what she had seen in the two hours she'd been in his country, deep in her marrow was the rooted certainty that he would never hurt her, not in any meaningful sense.

If eyes could spit fire, Francesco's would be doing just that. But there was something else there, too, something that darkened as his breathing deepened.

'See?' she whispered. 'You can't hurt me.'

'Where does your faith in me come from?' His voice had become hoarse.

'It comes from *here*,' she answered, pulling their entwined fingers to her chest and pressing his hand right over her heart. 'I've seen the good in you. Why do you have so little faith in yourself?'

'I have no illusions about what I'm like. You have dedicated your life to healing sick children, whereas my life revolves around power and money, and all the seediness they attract.'

'Your power and money mean nothing to me.'

A groan escaped from his lips and he muttered something she didn't understand before snaking his free hand around her neck and pressing his lips to hers.

All the air expelled from her lungs.

She'd had no notion of what kissing Francesco would be like, could never have envisaged the surge of adrenaline that would course through her veins and thicken her blood at the feel of his firm lips hard against hers, not moving, simply breathing her in.

Returning the pressure, she placed a hand to his cheek, kneading her fingers into the smooth skin as she parted her lips and flitted her tongue into the heat of his mouth.

Francesco's breathing became laboured. His hold on her neck tightened then relaxed, the hand held against her chest moving to sweep around her waist and draw her flush against him to deepen the connection. When his own tongue darted into her mouth, she melted into him, two bodies meshed together, kissing with a hunger that bloomed into unimaginable proportions.

He tasted divine, of darkness and coffee and something else Hannah could only assume was *him*, filling her senses.

Deep inside, the pulsations she had first experienced when he had touched her in his London office began to vibrate and hum.

To think she had gone for twenty-seven years without experiencing *this*.

Brushing her hand down his cheek to rest on the sharp crease of his collar, she stroked the tips of her fingers over the strong neck, marvelling at his strength and the power that lay beneath the skin.

It wasn't the power that came from his position in the world that attracted her so much, she thought dimly, it was the latent masculine power within *him*.

Before she could make sense of all the wonderful sensations rising within her, he pulled away—or, rather, wrenched apart the physical connection between them.

His chest rising and falling in rapid motion, Francesco took a step back, wiping his mouth as if to rid himself of her taste.

'I know my power and money mean nothing to you,' he said, virtually spitting the words out. 'That's why getting involved with you is wrong on every level imaginable.'

Trying to clamp down on the humiliation that came hot on the heels of his abrupt rejection, Hannah jumped down from the windowsill. 'I don't know how many times I have to say this, but I do *not* want to become involved with you, not in any real sense. All I want is to experience some of the life every other woman takes for granted but which has passed me by.'

'And you *should* experience it, but it should be with someone who can give you a future.'

'Medicine is my future.'

'And that stops you building a future with a man, does it?'

Not even bothering to hide her exasperation, she shook her head. 'I'm married to my work, and that's the way I like it. I want to make it to consultant level and I've worked too hard and for too long to throw it all away on a relationship that would never fulfil me even a fraction as much as my job does.'

'How can you know that if you've never tried?'

She pursed her lips together. A deep and meaningful debate about her reasons for not wanting a relationship had not been on the agenda. 'I just know, okay?'

'Your job will never keep you warm at night.'

'My hot-water bottle does a perfectly good job of that and, besides, what right do you have to question me on this? I don't see a wedding ring on your finger. If the internet reports on you are true, as you say they are, you seem to have a phobia towards commitment yourself.' Hadn't that been another tick on her mental checklist, the fact Francesco appeared to steer away from anything that could be construed as permanent?

His face darkened. 'I have my reasons for not wanting marriage.'

'Well, I have mine, too. Why can't you respect that?'

Francesco took a deep breath and slowly expelled it. Why could he not just take everything Hannah said at face value? *His* body was telling him to just accept it, to take her back to his villa and take her, just as she'd asked, until she was so sated she would be unable to think.

But even if he did take her words at face value and accepted that she wasn't asking for anything more than one night, it didn't change the fact that making love to her would taint her. She deserved better than Salvatore Calvetti's son, even if she couldn't see it herself.

He would make her see.

'Let's get out of here,' he said, unable to endure the claustrophobia being shut in four walls with Hannah Chapman induced a minute longer. 'I'm taking you shopping.'

'Shopping?'

'You need a dress for tonight.'

'Why? What's happening tonight?'

'We're going to my casino. There's a poker tournament I need to oversee. I'm not having you by my side dressed as some kind of bag lady.'

Her face blanched at his cruel words, but he bit back the apology forming on his tongue.

In truth, there was something unbearably sexy about Hannah's take-me-as-I-am, comfortable-in-my-skin approach to her appearance, and the longer he was in her company, the sexier he found it.

A bag lady.

Francesco looked at her and saw a *bag lady*?

Having been dumped in a designer shop, whereby Francesco had promptly disappeared, leaving at her disposal a driver with the words, 'I'll meet you at my villa in a few hours—buy whatever you want and charge it to me,' Hannah still didn't know whether she wanted to laugh or punch him in the face.

Trying on what was probably her dozenth dress in the plush changing room, she reflected on his words.

Okay, so her appearance had never been a priority, but did she really look like a bag lady?

Her clothes were mostly bought online when the items she already owned started wearing out. She selected clothes based on suitability for work and comfort. Clothes were a means of keeping her body warm.

Her hair... Well, who had the time for regular haircuts? Not hardworking doctors fighting their way up the food chain, that was for sure. And if the rest of her colleagues managed to fit in regular visits to a salon, then good for them. Still, she had to admit her hair had become a little wild in recent years, and racked her brain trying to remember the last time a pair of scissors had been let loose on it. She came up with a blank.

She could remember the first time her mother had let her and Beth go to a proper hairdresser rather than hack at their hair with the kitchen scissors. It had been their twelfth birthday and the pair of them had felt so grown-up. How lovingly they'd attended their hair after that little trip, faithfully conditioning it at regular intervals.

She tried to think of the last time she'd conditioned her hair and came up with another blank.

Was it really possible she'd gone through the past fifteen years without either a haircut or the use of a conditioner? A distant memory floated like a wisp in her memories, of her mother knocking on her bedroom door, calling that it was time for her appointment at the hairdresser's. She remembered the knots that had formed in her throat and belly and her absolute refusal to go.

How could she get a haircut when Beth wouldn't be there to share it with her? Not that she'd vocalised this particular reasoning. She hadn't needed to. Her mother hadn't pressed her on the issue or brought the subject up again. Haircuts, make-up, all the things that went with being a girl on the cusp of womanhood were banished.

How had she let that happen?

After selecting a dress, a pair of shoes and matching clutch, and some sexy underwear which made her blush as she fingered the silken material, she handed the items to the manager, along with her credit card.

'Signor Calvetti has made arrangements to pay,' the manager said.

'I know, but I can pay for my own clothes, thank you.'

'It is very expensive.'

'I can afford it.' And, sadly, she could. She didn't drink and rarely socialised—Melanie's hen do had been Hannah's first proper night out that year. After paying off her mortgage and other household bills every month, her only expenditure was food, which, when you were buying frozen meals for one, didn't amount to much. She didn't drive. Her only trips were her monthly visits to her parents' home in Devon, for which she always got a lift down with Melanie and her soon-to-be brother-in-law.

Her colleagues, especially those around the same age as her, regularly complained of being skint. Hannah, never spending any money, had a comfortable nest egg.

How had she allowed herself to get in this position?

It was one thing putting money aside for a rainy day but, quite frankly, she had enough stashed away that she could handle months of torrential rain without worrying.

Despite her assurance, the store manager still seemed reluctant to take her card.

'Either accept my card or I'll find a dress in another shop,' Hannah said, although not unkindly. She smiled at the flustered woman. 'Honestly, there's enough credit on there to cover it.'

'But Signor Calvetti...'

Ah. The penny dropped. It wasn't that the manager was worried about Hannah's credit; rather, she was worried about what Francesco would do when he learned his wishes had been overruled. 'Don't worry about him—I'll make sure he knows I insisted. He's learning how stubborn I can be in getting my own way.'

With great reluctance, the manager took Hannah's card. Less than a minute later the purchase was complete. Hannah had spent more in one transaction than she'd spent on her entire wardrobe since leaving medical school.

'I don't suppose you know of a decent hairdresser that could fit me in with little notice, do you?'

The manager peered a little too closely at Hannah's hair, a tentative smile forming on her face. 'For Signor Calvetti's lover, any salon in Palermo will fit you in. Would you like me to make the phone call?'

Signor Calvetti's lover... Those words set off a warm feeling through her veins, rather as if she'd been injected with heated treacle. 'That's very kind, thank you—I'll be sure to tell Francesco how helpful you've been.'

Five minutes later Hannah left the boutique with a shop assistant personally escorting her to the selected salon, her driver/bodyguard trailing behind them.

Having her hair cut was one of the most surreal events she could ever recall and, considering the dreamlike quality of the day thus far, that was saying something.

The salon itself was filled with women who were clearly the cream of Sicilian society, yet Hannah was treated like a celebrity in her own right, with stylists and assistants fawning all over her and thrusting numerous cups of strong coffee into her hands.

At the end, when she was given the bill, she made an admirable job of not shrieking in horror.

Oh, well, she told herself as she handed her credit card over for another battering, it would surely be worth it.

She was determined that, after tonight, Francesco would never look at her like a bag lady again.

CHAPTER SIX

Hannah had been shopping in Palermo for such a long time that Francesco started to think she'd had second thoughts and hopped on a plane back to London.

He could have found out for himself by calling the bodyguard he'd left to watch over her, but resisted each time the urge took him. He'd stopped himself making that call for almost two hours.

Thus, when the bulletproof four-by-four pulled up within the villa's gates late afternoon, he fully expected Hannah to get out laden with bags and packages, having gone mad on his credit card. Likely, she would have changed into one of her new purchases.

Instead, she clambered her way out and up the steep steps leading to the main entrance of his villa, still dressed in that ugly shapeless dress. All she carried was her handbag and two other bags and, to top it all off, she wore a navy blue scarf over her hair.

She looked a bigger mess than when he'd left her in the boutique.

Even so, his heart accelerated at the sight of her.

Taking a deep breath to slow his raging pulse, then another when the first had zero effect, Francesco opened his front door.

Hannah stood on the step before him. 'This is your home?' she asked, her eyes sparkling.

'*Sì*.'

'It's fabulous.'

It took every ounce of restraint within him not to allow his lips to curve into the smile they so wanted. 'Thank you.'

He took a step back to admit her. 'You were a long time.' Immediately he cursed himself for voicing his concern.

'The boutique manager—a fabulous woman, by the way—managed to get me into a hairdresser's.'

'You've had your hair cut?' He caught a whiff of that particular scent found only in salons, a kind of fragrant chemical odour. It clung to her.

'Kind of.' Her face lit up with a hint of mischief. 'You'll just have to wait and see—the hairdresser wrapped the scarf round it so it didn't get wind damaged or anything.' She did a full three-sixty rotation. 'I can't believe this is your home. Do you live here alone?'

'I have staff, but they live in separate quarters.'

'It's amazing. Really. Amazing.'

Francesco's home was a matter of pride, his sanctuary away from a life filled with hidden dangers. Hannah's wide-eyed enthusiasm for it filled his chest, making it expand.

'Who would have guessed being a gangster would pay so well?' Her grin negated the sting her words induced. 'I'm just saying.' She laughed, noticing his unimpressed expression. 'You're the one trying to convince me you're a gangster.'

'You really don't believe in beating around the bush, do you?'

Her nose scrunched up a little. 'Erm…I guess not. I've never really thought about it.'

'It's very refreshing,' he surprised himself by admitting.

'Really? And is that a good thing?'

'Most refreshing things are good.'

'In that case...excellent. It's nice to know there's something about me you approve of.' Despite the lightness of her tone, he caught a definite edge to it, an edge he didn't care for and that made him reach over and grab her wrist.

'When are you going to learn, Dr Chapman, that my approval should mean nothing to a woman like you?'

'And when are you going to learn, Signor Calvetti, that I may be a doctor but I am still a human being? I am still a woman.'

He was now certain the edge he had detected was the whiff of reproach.

Surely he should be delighted she was starting to see through the layers to the real man inside. So why did he feel more unsettled than ever?

'Believe me, *Dr* Chapman,' he said, putting deliberate emphasis on her title, 'I am well aware that beneath your haphazard appearance is a woman.'

A smile flitted over her face, not the beaming spark of joy he was becoming accustomed to but a smile that could almost be described as shy. Bright spots of colour stained her cheeks.

Shoving his hands in his pockets lest they did something stupid like reach out for her again, Francesco inclined his head to the left. 'If you head in that direction you will go through several living rooms before you reach the indoor pool, which you are welcome to use, although you might prefer the outside one. If you go through the door on the other side of the pool you'll find the kitchen. If you're hungry my chef will cook something for you, but I would suggest you keep it light as we will be dining in the casino.'

'We're eating out?'

'Yes. I'll show you to the room you will be sleeping in whilst you're here as my guest.'

'Which is only until tomorrow,' Hannah stated amiably, biting back the question of whether it would be *his* room she would be sleeping in, already knowing the answer.

Francesco's villa was a thing of beauty, a huge white palace cleverly cut into the rocks of the hillside. Walking up the steps to his home, the scent of perfumed flowers and lemons had filled her senses so strongly she would have been happy to simply stand there and enjoy. If she hadn't been so keen to see Francesco, she would have done.

She'd been aware he possessed great wealth, but even so...

It felt as if she'd slipped through the looking glass and landed in a parallel universe.

She followed him through huge white arches, over brightly coloured tiled flooring, past exotic furniture, and up a winding stone staircase to a long, uneven corridor.

'Was this once a cave?' she asked.

He laughed. *Francesco actually laughed.* It might not have been a great big boom echoing off the high ceilings, more of a low chuckle, but it was a start and it made her heart flip.

'Its original history is a bit of a mystery,' he said, opening a door at the end of the corridor. 'This is your room.'

Hannah clamped a hand over her mouth to stop the squeal that wanted to make itself heard. Slowly she drank it all in: the four-poster bed, the vibrant colours, the private balcony overlooking the outdoor pool...

'Wow,' she said when she felt capable of speaking without sounding like a giddy schoolgirl. 'If I didn't have to get back to work on Monday, I'd be tempted to claim squatters' rights.'

'You're still trusting I will get you back to London in time?'

She rolled her eyes in answer.

'Let us hope your faith in me is justified.'

'If I turn out to be wrong then no worries—I'll get my own flight back.'

'And what about your passport? You will need that to leave the country.'

'My passport's in my bag.'

'You are sure about that?' At her puzzled expression, Francesco leaned over and whispered into her ear, 'A word of advice, Dr Chapman—when in the company of criminals, never leave your bag open with your passport and phone in it.'

With that, he strolled to the door, patting his back pocket for emphasis. 'Be ready to leave in two hours.'

Hannah watched him close the door before diving into her handbag.

Unbelievable! In the short time she'd been in his home, Francesco had deftly removed her passport and mobile and she hadn't noticed a thing.

She should be furious. She should be a lot of things. He had her passport—effectively had her trapped in his country—but it was her phone she felt a pang of anxiety over.

She had to give him points for continuing to try to make her see the worst in him, but there was no way in the world he would keep hold of her stuff. She had no doubt that, come the morning, he would return the items to her.

The morning...

Before the morning came the night.

And a shiver zipped up her spine at the thought of what that night could bring.

Francesco sat on his sprawling sofa catching up on the day's qualifying event for one of the many motor racing sports he followed, when he heard movement behind the archway dividing the living room from the library.

Sitting upright, he craned his neck to see better.

He caught a flash of blue that vanished before reappearing with a body attached to it. Hannah's body.

Hannah's incredible body.

His jaw dropped open.

There she stood, visibly fighting for composure, until she expanded her arms and said, 'What do you think? Do I still resemble a bag lady?'

A bag lady? He could think of a hundred words to describe her but the adjective that sprang to the forefront of his mind was *stunning*.

Where the blue dress she had changed into on his plane had been a drab, ill-fitting creation, this soft blue dress was a million miles apart. Silk and Eastern in style with swirling oriental flowers printed onto it, it skimmed her figure like a caress, landing midthigh to show off incredibly shapely legs.

Whatever the hairdresser had been paid could never be enough. The thick mop of straw-like hair had gone. Now Hannah's hair was twisted into a sleek knot, pinned in with black chopsticks. There was not a millimetre of frizz in sight. If his eyes were not deceiving him, she'd had colour applied to it, turning her multicoloured locks into more of a honey blonde.

She wore make-up, too, her eyes ringed with dark smokiness that highlighted the moreish hazel, her lips a deep cherry-red...

She looked beautiful.

And yet...

He hated it.

She no longer looked like Hannah.

'No. You no longer resemble a bag lady.'

'Well, that's a relief.' She shuffled into the room on shoes with heels high enough to make her hobble—although not as high as many women liked to wear—and stood before him, her hand outstretched. Her short nails hadn't been touched, a sight he found strangely reassuring. 'Can I have my phone back, please?'

'You can have it back when you leave Sicily.'

'I'd like it back now.'

'For what reason?'

'I've told you—I like to keep abreast of what's going on with my patients.'

'And what can you do for them here?'

'Not worry about them. No news is good news.'

'Then it seems I am doing you a favour.'

'But how am I going to know if there is no news? Now I'll worry that bad news has come and I won't know one way or the other.'

Hiding his irritation, he said, 'Do all doctors go to such lengths for their patients?'

Her lips pressed together. 'I have no idea. It's none of my concern what my colleagues get up to when they're off duty.'

'What happened to professional detachment? I thought you doctors were trained to keep your distance?'

A hint of fire flashed in her eyes. 'Keeping a check on the welfare of my patients is at odds with my professionalism?'

'I'm just asking the question.'

'Well, don't. I will not have my professionalism questioned by you or anyone.'

It was the first time Francesco had heard her sound even remotely riled. He'd clearly hit a nerve.

Studying her carefully, he got to his feet. 'I think it will do you good to spend one evening away from your phone.'

Hannah opened her mouth to argue but he placed a finger to it. 'I did not mean to question your professionalism. However, I am not prepared to spend the evening with someone who has only half a mind on what's going on. Constantly checking your phone is rude.'

Her cheeks heightened with colour, a mutinous expression blazing from her eyes.

'I will make a deal with you,' he continued silkily. 'You say you want to experience all the world has to offer, yet it will be a half-hearted experience if you are preoccupied with worrying about your patients. If you prove that you can let your hair down and enjoy the experience of what the casino has to offer, I will give you your phone back when we return to the villa.'

For the first time since she'd met him, Hannah wanted to slap Francesco. Okay, keep her passport until it was time to leave—that didn't bother her. She knew she would get it back. She knew she would get her phone back eventually, too, but she needed it *now*. She needed to keep the roots the mobile gave her to the ward.

And how dared he imply that she had no detachment? She had it. But she refused to lose her empathy. Her patients were her guiding motive in life. Never would she allow one of her young charges to be on the receiving end of a doctor who had lost basic humanity. She wouldn't. She couldn't. She'd been at the other end and, while it hadn't made the pain of what she went through any worse, a little compassion would have helped endure it that little bit better.

Eventually she took a deep breath and bestowed Francesco with her first fake smile. 'Fine. But if you want me to let my hair down and enjoy myself it's only fair you do the same, too. After all,' she added airily, 'I would say that, of the two of us, you're the greater workaholic. At least I take weekends off.'

Calvetti's casino was a titanic building, baroque in heritage, set over four levels in the heart of Palermo. Hannah followed Francesco up the first sweeping staircase and into an enormous room filled with gambling tables and slot machines as far as the eye could see. It was like stepping into a tasteful version of Vegas.

Flanked by his minders, they continued up the next set of stairs to the third floor. There, a group of men in black parted to admit them into a room that seemed virtually identical to the second floor. It took a few moments for her to realise what the subtle differences were. The lower level was filled with ordinary punters. The third floor, which had around a quarter of the number of customers, was evidently the domain of the filthy rich.

Sticking closely to Francesco, Hannah drank everything in: the gold trimming on all the tables, the beautiful fragrant women, the men in tuxedos—which, she noted, none filled as well as Francesco, who looked even more broodingly gorgeous than usual in his. After a host of conversations, Francesco slipped an arm around her waist and drew her through a set of double doors and into the restaurant.

And what a restaurant it was, somehow managing to be both opulent and elegant.

'Are the customers on the second floor allowed to dine in here?' she asked once they'd been seated by a fawning maître d' at a corner table.

'They have their own restaurant,' he said, opening his leather-bound menu.

'But are they allowed to eat in here?'

'The third floor is for private members only. Anyone can join, providing they can pay the fifty thousand euro joining fee and the ten thousand annual membership.'

She blinked in shock. 'People pay that?'

'People pay for exclusivity—the waiting list is longer than the actual membership list.'

'That's mind-blowing. I feel like a gatecrasher.'

She only realised he'd been avoiding her stare when he raised his eyes to look at her.

'You are with me.'

The possessive authority of his simple statement set her pulse racing, and in that moment she forgot all about being mad at him for refusing to hand back her phone.

'So what do you recommend from the menu?' she asked when she was certain her tongue hadn't rooted to the roof of her mouth.

'All of it.'

She laughed, a noise that sounded more nervous than merry.

A waiter came over to them. *'Posso portarti le bevande?'*

Francesco spoke rapidly back to him.

'He wanted our drink order,' he explained once the waiter had bustled off. 'I've ordered us a bottle of Shiraz.'

'Is that a wine?'

'Yes. The Shiraz we sell here is of the highest quality.'

'I don't drink wine. I'll have a cola instead.'

A shrewdness came into his eyes. 'Have you ever drunk wine?'

'No.'

'Have you ever drunk alcohol?'

'I had a few sips of champagne at Mel's hen do.' Suddenly it occurred to her that Melanie's hen party had been just twenty-four hours ago.

Where had the time gone?

It felt as if she'd experienced a whole different life in that short space of time.

'And that was your first taste of alcohol?'

She stared at him, nodding slowly, her mind racing. After all, wasn't the whole point of her being in Sicily with Francesco to begin her exploration of life? 'Maybe I *should* have a glass of the Shiraz.'

He nodded his approval. 'But only a small glass. Your body has not acquired a tolerance for alcohol.'

'My body hasn't acquired a tolerance for anything.'

The waiter returned with their wine and a jug of water before Francesco could ask what she meant by that comment.

The more time he spent with Hannah, the more intriguing he found her. Nothing seemed to faze her, except having her professionalism cast into doubt. And having her phone taken away.

He watched as she studied the menu, her brow furrowed in concentration. 'Are mussels nice?' she asked.

'They're delicious.'

She beamed. 'I'll have those, then.'

A platter of antipasto was brought out for them to nibble on while they waited for their meals to be cooked.

'Is this like ham?' she asked, holding up a slice of prosciutto.

'Not really. Try some.'

She popped it into her mouth and chewed, then nodded her approval. Swallowing, she reached for a roasted pepper.

'Try some wine,' he commanded.

'Do I sniff it first?'

'If you want.' He smothered a laugh when she practically dunked her nose into the glass.

She took the tiniest of sips. 'Oh, wow. That's really nice.'

'Have you really never drunk wine before?'

'I really haven't.' She popped a plump green olive into her mouth.

'Why not?'

Her nose scrunched. 'My parents aren't drinkers so we never had alcohol in the house. By the time I was old enough to get into experimenting I was focused on my studies. I wasn't prepared to let anything derail my dream of being a doctor. It was easier to just say no.'

'How old were you when you decided to be a doctor?'

'Twelve.'

'That's a young age to make a life-defining choice.'

'Most twelve-year-olds have dreams of what they want to do when they grow up.'

'Agreed, but most change their mind.'

'What did you want to be when *you* were twelve?'

'A racing bike rider.'

'I can see you doing that,' she admitted. 'So what stopped you? Or did you just change your mind?'

'It was only ever a pipe dream,' he said with a dismissive shrug. 'I was Salvatore Calvetti's only child. I was groomed from birth to take over his empire.'

'And how's that going?'

Francesco fixed hard eyes on her. 'I always knew I would build my own empire. I am interested to know, though, what drew you to medicine in the first place—was it the death of your sister?'

A brief hesitation. 'Yes.'

'She was called Beth?'

Another hesitation followed by a nod. When Hannah reached for her glass of water he saw a slight tremor in her hand. She took a long drink before meeting his eyes.

'Beth contracted meningitis when we were twelve. They said it was flu. They didn't get the diagnosis right until it was too late. She was dead within a day.'

She laid the bare facts out to him in a matter-of-fact manner, but there was something in the way she held her poise that sent a pang straight into his heart.

'So you decided to be a doctor so you could save children like Beth?'

'That's a rather simplistic way of looking at it, but yes. I remember walking through the main ward and going past cubicles and private rooms full of ill children and their terrified families, and I was just full of so much... Oh, I was full up of every emotion you could imagine. Why her? Why not me too? Meningitis is so contagious....' She took a deep breath. 'I know you must think it stupid and weak, but when Beth died the only thing that kept me going was the knowledge that one day I would be in a position to heal as many of those children as I could.'

Francesco expelled a breath, the pang in his heart tightening. 'I don't think it's weak or stupid.'

Hannah took another sip of her water. The tremor in her hand had worsened and he suddenly experienced the strangest compulsion to reach over and squeeze it.

'My mother was hospitalised a number of times—drug overdoses,' he surprised himself by saying. 'It was only the dedication of the doctors and nurses that saved her. When she died it was because she overdosed on a weekend when she was alone.'

He still lived with the guilt. On an intellectual level he knew it was misplaced. He'd been fifteen years old, not yet a man. But he'd known how vulnerable his mother was and yet still he and his father had left her alone for the weekend, taking a visit to the Mastrangelo estate without her.

It had ostensibly been for business, his father and Pietro Mastrangelo close friends as well as associates. At least, they had been close friends then, before the friendship between the Calvettis and Mastrangelos had twisted into antipathy. Back then, though, Francesco had been incredibly proud that his father had wanted him to accompany him, had left with barely a second thought for his mother.

While Francesco and Salvatore had spent the Saturday evening eating good food, drinking good wine and playing cards with Pietro and his eldest son, Luca, Elisabetta Calvetti had overdosed in her bed.

To think of his mother dying while he, her son, had been basking in pride because the monster who fed her the drugs had been treating him like a man.... To think that bastard's approval ever meant anything to him made his stomach roil violently and his nails dig deep into his palms.

His mother had been the kindest, most gentle soul he had ever known. Her death had ripped his own soul in half. His vengeance might be two decades too late, but he would have it. Whatever it took, he would avenge her death and throw the carcass of his father's reputation into the ashes.

'I have nothing but the utmost respect for medical professionals,' he said slowly, unfurling the fists his hands had balled into, unsure why he was confiding such personal matters with her. 'When I look at you, Dr Chapman, I see a woman filled with compassion, decency, and integrity. The world I inhabit is driven by money, power, and greed.'

'You have integrity,' she contradicted. 'A whole heap of it.'

'On that we will have to disagree.' He nodded towards the waiter heading cautiously towards them. 'It looks as if our main courses are ready. I suggest we move on from this discussion or both our meals will be spoiled.'

She flashed him a smile of such gratitude his entire chest compressed tightly enough that for a moment he feared his lungs would cease to work.

CHAPTER SEVEN

THANKFULLY, FRANCESCO KEPT the conversation over the rest of their meal light, with mostly impersonal questions about medical school and her job. His interest—and it certainly seemed genuine—was flattering. In turn, he opened up about his love of motorbikes. It didn't surprise her to learn he owned a dozen of them.

When their plates were cleared and Hannah had eaten a dark-chocolate lava cake, which was without doubt the most delicious pudding she'd ever eaten—except hot chocolate-fudge cake, of course—Francesco looked at his watch. 'I need to check in with my head of security before the poker tournament starts. Do you want to come with me or would you like me to get one of my staff to give you a tour of the tables?'

'Are you entering the tournament?'

'No. This one is solely for members. It's the biggest tournament that's held here, though, and the members like to see me—it makes them feel important,' he added, and she noticed a slight flicker of amusement in his eyes, which made her feel as if she'd been let into a private joke. It was an insight that both surprised and warmed her.

'You don't have much time for them?'

'I always make time for them.'

'That's not what I meant.'

'I know what you meant.' His lips, usually set in a fixed line, broke into something that almost resembled a lazy smile. He drained his glass of wine, his eyes holding firm with hers. 'Do you know the rules of poker?'

'Funnily enough, I do. It's often on late at night when I'm too brain-dead to study any longer and need to wind down before bed.'

'You're still studying?'

'Yes. Plus there are always new research papers being published and clinical studies to read through and mug up on.'

'Doesn't sound as if you leave yourself any time for having fun,' he remarked astutely.

'It's fun to me. But you're right—it's why I'm here after all.'

'When you said you'd spent your whole adult life dedicating yourself to medicine, I didn't think you meant it in a literal sense.'

She shrugged and pulled a face. 'It's what I needed.'

'But that's changed?'

'Not in any fundamental way. Medicine and my patients will always be my first priority, but my accident… It made me open my eyes…' Her voice trailed away, unexpected tears burning the back of her eyes. It had been so long since she'd spoken properly about Beth.

Hannah carried her sister with her every minute of every day, yet it had felt in recent weeks as if she were right there with her, as if she could turn her head and find Beth peering over her shoulder.

Blinking back the tears, she spoke quietly. 'I don't know if heaven exists, but if it does, I don't want Beth to be angry with me. She loved life. We both did. I'd forgotten just how much.'

She almost jumped out of her seat when Francesco placed a warm hand on hers, so large it covered it entirely. A sense of calm trickled through her veins, while conversely her skin began to dance.

'Would you like to enter the poker tournament?'

'Oh, no, I couldn't.'

'Think of the experience. Think of the story you'll have to tell Beth.'

With a stab, she realised how carefully he'd been listening. Francesco understood.

The sense of calm increased, settling into her belly. 'Well...how much does it cost?'

'For you, nothing. For everyone else, it's one hundred thousand euros.'

If her jaw could thud onto the table, it would. 'For one game of poker?'

'That's pocket change to the members here. People fly in from all over the world for this one tournament. We allow sixty entrants. We've had a couple drop out, so there is room for you.'

'I don't know. Won't all the other entrants be cross that I'm playing for free?'

'They wouldn't know. In any case, it is none of their business. My casino, my rules. Go on, Hannah. Do it. Enjoy yourself and play the game.'

It was the first time he'd addressed her by her first name. Oh, but it felt so wonderful to hear her name spilling from his tongue in that deep, seductive accent.

Play the game.

It had been fifteen years since she'd played a game of any sort—and school netball most certainly did *not* count when compared to this.

Straightening her spine, she nodded, a swirl of excitement uncoiling in her stomach. 'Go on, then. Sign me up.'

* * *

Francesco watched the tournament unfold from the sprawling security office on the top floor of the casino, manned by two dozen staff twenty-four hours a day. Other than the bathrooms, there wasn't an inch of the casino not monitored. Special interest was being taken in a blackjack player on the second floor—a man suspected of swindling casinos across the Continent. Of course, there was the option to simply ban the man from the premises, but first Francesco wanted proof. And banning was not enough. Once his guilt was established, a suitable punishment would be wrought.

The first round of the tournament was in full swing. On Hannah's table of six, two players were already out. Her gameplay surprised him—for a novice, she played exceptionally well, her poker face inscrutable. Of those remaining, she had the second-largest number of chips.

The dealer dealt the four players their two cards and turned three over on the table. From his vantage point, Francesco could see Hannah had been dealt an ace and a jack, both diamonds. The player with the largest pile of chips had been dealt a pair of kings. One of the table cards was a king, giving that player three of a kind. The player went all in, meaning that if Hannah wanted to continue playing she would have to put *all* her remaining chips into the pile.

She didn't even flinch, simply pushed her pile forward to show she wanted to play.

There was no way she could win the hand. Lady Luck could be kind, but to overturn a three of a kind... The next table card to be turned over was an ace, quickly followed by another ace.

She'd won the hand!

It seemed that fifteen years of perfecting a poker face,

along with too many late nights half watching the game played out for real on the television had paid off.

Hannah allowed herself a sip of water but kept her face neutral. The game wasn't over yet. No one looking at her would know the thundering rate of her heart.

The look on her defeated opponent's face was a picture. He kept staring from his cards to hers as if expecting a snake to pop out of them. Her two remaining opponents were looking at her with a newfound respect.

If she wasn't in the midst of a poker tournament, she'd be hugging herself with the excitement of it all. It felt as if she were in the middle of a glamorous Hollywood film. All that was needed was for the men to light fat cigars and create a haze of smoke.

As the next hand was dealt she noticed a small crowd forming around their table and much whispering behind hands.

She looked at her two cards and raised the ante. One of her opponents matched her. The other folded, opting to sit out of the hand. The table cards were laid. Again she raised the ante. Again her opponent matched her. And so it went on, her opponent matching her move for move.

She didn't have the best of hands: two low pairs. There was every chance that his cards were much better. All the same, the bubble of recklessness that had been simmering within her since she'd followed Francesco off the dance floor the night before grew within her.

It was her turn to bet. Both she and her opponent had already put a large wedge of chips into the pot.

Where was Francesco? He'd said he would be there socialising with the guests.

He wasn't in the room, but somehow she just *knew* he was watching her.

Her heart hammering, she pushed her remaining chips forward. *Please* let Francesco be watching. 'All in.'

Her opponent stared at her, a twitch forming under his left eye.

She stared back, giving nothing away.

He rubbed his chin.

She knew before he did that he was going to fold, hid her feelings of triumph that she'd successfully bluffed him.

The big pile of poker chips was hers.

It would appear that her long-practised poker face had become a blessing in itself.

Francesco could hardly believe what he was witnessing over the monitors.

Hannah was a card shark. There was no other way to describe the way she played, which, if you were in a position to see the cards she'd been dealt, as he was, at times verged on the reckless. Not that her opponents could see how recklessly she played. All they saw was the cool facade, the face that didn't give away a single hint of emotion.

For a woman who had never played the game before, it was masterful. And yet...

Something deep inside his gut clenched when he considered why she'd been able to develop such a good poker face. Only someone who'd spent years hiding their emotions could produce it so naturally. He should know. He'd been perfecting his own version for years.

When she'd knocked her fourth opponent out... The way she'd pushed her chips forward, the clear *simpatico* way she'd said, 'All in...'

His gut had tightened further. Somehow he'd known those two little words meant more than just the chips before her.

It didn't take long before she'd demolished her final opponent. Only when she'd won that final hand did that beautiful smile finally break on her face, a smile of genuine delight that had all her defeated opponents reaching over to shake her hand and kiss her cheeks. The mostly male crowd surrounding her also muscled in, finding it necessary to embrace her when giving their congratulations.

They wouldn't look twice if they could see her in her usual state, Francesco thought narkily. They would be so blinkered they would never see her for the natural beauty she was.

'I'm going back down,' he said, heading to the reinforced steel door. For some reason, his good mood, induced by dinner with Hannah, had plummeted.

Striding across the main playing area of the third floor, he ignored all attempts from players and staff to meet his eyes.

With play in the tournament temporarily halted so the players who'd made it through to the second round could take a break, he found Hannah sipping coffee, surrounded by a horde of men all impressing their witticisms and manliness upon her.

When she saw him, her eyes lit up, then dimmed as she neared him.

'What's the matter?' she asked.

'Nothing.'

'Ooh, you liar. You look like someone's stolen your granny's false teeth and you've been told to donate your own as a replacement.'

Her good humour had zero effect on his blackening mood. 'And you look like you're having fun,' he said pointedly, unable to contain the ice in his voice.

'Isn't that the whole point of me entering the tournament? Didn't you tell me to enjoy myself?'

Francesco took a deep breath, Hannah's bewilderment

reminding him he had no good reason to be acting like a jealous fool.

Jealousy?

Was that really what the strong compulsion running through him to throw her over his shoulder and carry her out of the casino and away from all these admiring men was?

His father, for all his catting about with other women half his age, had been consumed with it. His mother had suffered more than one beating at his hands for daring to look at another man the wrong way.

Francesco had assumed that, in his own case, jealousy had skipped a generation. The closest he'd come to that particular emotion had been in his early twenties. Then, he'd learned Luisa, a girl he was seeing, was two-timing him with Pepe Mastrangelo, whom she'd sworn she'd finished with. That hadn't been jealousy, though—that had been pure anger, a rage that had heightened when he learned she'd tricked him out of money so she could hightail it to the UK for an abortion. So duplicitous had she been, she'd no idea if he or Pepe was the father.

He'd despised Luisa for her lies, but not once had he wanted to seek Pepe out. Instead, Pepe had sought *him* out, his pain right there on the surface. But the only bruising Francesco had suffered had been to his ego, and the fight between them had been over before it started.

To learn he was as vulnerable to jealousy's clutches as the next man brought him up short, reminding him that he had Calvetti blood running inside him.

Salvatore Calvetti would never have walked away from the Luisa and Pepe debacle as Francesco had done. If Salvatore had walked in his shoes, Luisa would have been scarred for life. Pepe would likely have disappeared, never to be seen again.

But he didn't want to be anything like Salvatore.

He never wanted to treat *anyone* the way his father had treated his mother.

Raking his fingers through his hair, a growl escaped from his throat. Whether he liked it or not, Calvetti blood ran through his veins.

Just one more reason why he should never touch her.

Hannah looked as if she wanted to say something, but the gong sounded for the second round. She was placed on table one. Her chips were passed to her. Francesco watched as she stacked them into neat piles, oblivious to the crowd forming around her table.

The strength of his possessiveness had him clenching his fists. Was she really so ignorant of the admiring glances and lecherous stares?

She raised her eyes to meet his glare and gave a hesitant smile. He looked away.

A discreet cough behind him caught his attention. He turned to find his general manager standing there.

'We have the proof—the blackjack player *is* cheating us,' he said, his lips barely moving.

'Give me a few minutes.' Francesco barely bothered trying to hide his impatience.

Hannah was still looking at him, a puzzled groove in her forehead.

'I can get the ball moving...'

'I *said*, give me a few minutes.' The blackjack cheat could wait. Francesco would not step a foot away from the room until Hannah was done with the tournament. His presence was the only thing stopping the fawning men from trying their luck that bit harder.

She was done much earlier than he'd envisaged. From playing the first round like a pro and with a good dollop of luck, her game fell to pieces and she was the first player out.

She shrugged, smiled gracefully, took a sip of water, and leaned back in her chair.

He was by her side in seconds. 'Come, it is time for us to move elsewhere,' he said, speaking into her ear, ignoring the curious stares of all those surrounding them.

'I want to watch the rest of the tournament.'

'You can watch it from my security office. There are things I need to attend to.'

Hannah turned to face him. 'Go and attend to them, then,' she said with a shrug.

'But I require your company.' Or, rather, he wanted to get her away from this room full of letches.

Swivelling her chair around with exceptionally bad grace, she got to her feet.

'What is the matter with you?' he asked as they swept through the room and out of the door.

'Me?' Incredulous, Hannah stopped walking and placed a hand on her hip. 'I was having a lovely time until you came in looking as if you wanted to kill me.' Seriously, how could anyone concentrate with Francesco's handsome face glowering at them? 'You totally put me off my game, and then you dragged me out before I could enjoy watching the rest of it.'

She glared at him. She'd had such a wonderful meal, had thought he'd enjoyed himself, too, the aloof, arrogant man unbending into something infinitely more human that warmed her from the inside out. But now he'd reverted, and was more aloof and arrogant than ever.

'It wasn't you that angered me.'

She folded her arms and raised a brow in a perfect imitation of him. 'Really?'

'Did you not see the way those men were looking at you? As if you were a piece of meat.'

'They were just being friendly.' Men *never* looked at her

in that way. Not that she ever met men outside the hospital environment, she conceded.

'Take a look in the mirror, Dr Chapman. You're a beautiful woman.'

His unexpected compliment let loose a cluster of fluttering butterflies in her belly.

'And I'm sorry for putting you off your game—you're quite a player.'

'You think?' His compliment—for it was definitely a compliment coming from him—warmed her insides even further, making her forget to be cross with him.

He smiled, an honest-to-goodness smile, and reached out to touch a loose tendril of her hair. 'If you were to give up medicine, you could make a good living on the poker circuit.'

The butterflies in her belly exploded. Heat surged through her veins, her insides liquefying.

Was it her imagination, or was the longing she could feel swirling inside her mirrored in his eyes…?

Dropping his hand from her hair, he traced a finger down her cheek.

She shivered, her skin heating beneath his touch.

'Come. I need to attend to business,' she said before steering her off to the top floor, not quite touching her but keeping her close enough that she was constantly aware of his heat, of *him*.

'What are we going up here for?' she asked once she'd managed to get her tongue working again. But, oh, it was so hard to think straight when the skin on her cheek still tingled from his touch.

'A player from the second floor has been caught cheating. Stealing from us.'

'Have you called the police?'

He looked at her as if she'd asked if the moon was made of chocolate. 'That is not how we do things here.'

'How do you do things...?' The strangest look flitted over her face. 'Oh. You break hands.'

The sadness in Hannah's tone cut through him. Francesco paused to look at her properly. 'The punishment is determined by the crime.'

'But surely if a crime has been committed then the police should be left to deal with it? That's what they're paid for after all.'

'This is Sicily, Dr Chapman. The rules are different here.'

'Because that's what you were taught by your father?'

Her question caught him up short. 'It's nothing to do with my father. It's about respect and following the rules.'

'But who makes the rules? This is *your* empire, Francesco. Your father isn't here anymore. You're an adult. Your actions are your own.'

The air caught in his lungs, an acrid taste forming in his throat. 'Do you have an answer for everything?'

'Not even close.' She looked away, avoiding his gaze. 'If it's all the same to you, I'd like to wait downstairs.' Her tone had become distant.

His stomach rolled over. 'Nothing will happen to the cheating thief on these premises.'

'I don't want anything to happen to him off the premises, either. I'm a doctor, Francesco. I can't be—won't be—a party to anything that harms another person. I know this is your life and what you're used to, but for me...' She shook her head. 'I could never live with myself. Can you get one of your men to take me back to the villa?'

'Wait in the bar for me,' he said. 'I'll be with you in ten minutes.'

Not smiling, she nodded her acquiescence and walked

back down the stairs, gripping onto the gold handrail as she made her descent.

Francesco's chest felt weighted, although he knew not why.

He never made any apologies for his life and the way his world worked. Hannah knew the score—he'd never hidden anything from her. He'd *told* her what it was like. He'd warned her. In fact, it was the only reason he'd brought her here, so she could see for herself that he was not worth wasting her virginity on. It was not his fault she hadn't listened.

So why was the only thing he could see as he pushed the door open the sad disappointment dulling her eyes?

He entered the manager's office. Mario and Roberto, another of his most trusted men, were already there, along with the cheat.

Up close, he could see the cheat was a young man in his early twenties, who looked as if he should be playing computer games with an online community of other awkward young men, not systematically ripping off casinos across the Continent. He sat in the middle of the room. He looked terrified.

There was a tap on the door and the manager walked in, handing Francesco a dossier on the blackjack player's activity. It made for quick reading.

Mario watched him, waiting for the nod.

This was the part of the job Francesco liked the least. When he'd first bought into this, his first casino, three years ago, he'd employed his father's old henchmen, knowing them to be reliable and loyal. Within months, he'd paid the majority of them off when it became clear they expected to continue using the methods enjoyed by Salvatore as punishment. While he had always respected his father, Francesco had always known that when the time came for him to take over, his methods would be different, less extreme.

Mario was Francesco's man and capable of great restraint. Apart from one drug dealer who'd frequented Francesco's Naples nightclub and who they'd discovered was pimping out vulnerable teenage girls, he never made the punishments personal and never caused damage that would not heal.

When he gave the nod, Mario and Roberto would take the young man somewhere private. They would teach him a lesson he would never forget—a lesson that rarely needed to be given, as most people were not stupid enough to try to cheat a Calvetti casino. Francesco's reputation preceded him. And, really, this was the perfect opportunity to rid himself of Hannah. It was clear this whole situation had unsettled her enough to at least consider getting a flight home. If he gave the nod, he could guarantee she would be on the first flight back to England....

Yet her insinuation that he was following in his father's brutish footsteps jabbed him like a spear.

He was *not* his father. If this young cheat had tried any such behaviour in any of Salvatore's businesses, he would have disappeared. For ever.

Rules were rules, even if they were only unwritten. They were there for a reason.

His father would never have dreamed of breaking them....

Hannah nursed her strong coffee, gazing absently at the huge flat-screen television against a wall of the bar showing music videos. She didn't want to think of what was happening on the floor above her. If she thought about it hard enough she might just scream.

But when she tried not to think about it, thoughts of Melanie's wedding filled the space instead.

How could she endure it? Every morning she woke knowing the nuptials were one day closer, the knot in her belly tightening another notch.

She would give anything to get out of going, but even if an excuse came fully presented on a plate she would not be able to take it. Melanie had appointed her maid of honour, a role Hannah knew she did not deserve.

The wedding was something she would have to find a way to cope with. Whatever it took, she would try to keep smiling so her little sister could walk down the aisle without her day being ruined.

'Due bicchieri di champagne.'

Francesco's sudden appearance at her side startled her.

'Hi,' she said dully, hating that her heart thumped just to see him.

'Ciao.' He nodded. 'I've just ordered us each a glass of champagne.'

'You said you would take me back to the villa.'

'And I will. Five minutes. You look as if you need a drink.'

'I need to get my phone and my passport, and go home. To England,' she added in case her meaning wasn't absolutely clear.

Francesco had been right from the start. She really didn't belong in his world, not even on a temporary basis.

The injuries to Mario had been inflicted a long time ago and were, in effect, history. Mario's loyalty to Francesco only served to reinforce this notion of a long-forgotten event, something that had no bearing on the present.

The person they'd caught stealing tonight… This was now; this *was* the present.

Hannah was a doctor. She had dedicated her life to

saving lives. She could never be a party to someone else's injury.

'Come, Dr Chapman. You are supposed to be living a little. You are here to see something of the world and experience the things that have passed you by. You hardly touched your wine at dinner.'

'I'm really not in the mood.'

Pressing his lips to her ear, he said, 'I called the police.'

Her head whipped round so quickly she almost butted his nose. 'Seriously?'

Two glasses of champagne were placed before them. Francesco picked them up and nodded at a corner sofa. Thoroughly confused, she followed him.

Sitting gingerly next to him, she would have ignored the champagne had he not thrust it into her hand.

'Drink. You need to relax a little—you're far too tense.'

'Did you really call the police?'

'As you implied, I make the rules.' A slight smile played on his lips. 'I thought about the prison system here. When I said I was calling the police, the thief begged for a beating.'

She couldn't contain the smile that spread over her face or the hand that rose to palm his cheek. 'See? I *was* right about you.'

At his quizzical expression, she added, 'I knew there was good within you. You proved it by taking care of me so well after my accident, and now you've reaffirmed it.'

He shook his head. 'It's just for this one time, okay? And only because I respect your profession and the oath you took.'

'If you say so.' A feeling of serenity swept through her. Stroking her fingers down his cheek, she took a sip of her champagne.

'Better?'

She nodded. 'Much. I'll feel even better when I have my phone back.' She felt lost without it.

'Finish your champagne and I will take you back.'

His eyes bored into her, *daring* her to drink it. The sip she'd had still danced on her tongue, tantalising her, just as Francesco tantalised her.

This was why she was here, she reminded herself. Not to involve herself in the intricacies of his life but to experience her *own*.

Putting the flute back to her lips, she tipped the sparkling liquid into her mouth and drank it in three swallows.

A grin spread across his face, somehow making him even more handsome, a feat she hadn't thought possible.

'Good for you.' He downed his own glass before rising to his feet. 'Come. It is time to take you back.'

Hannah grabbed her clutch bag and stood. Her body felt incredibly light.

Surrounded by Francesco's minders, who'd been waiting in the corner of the bar for them, they left. When they reached the stairs, he placed a hand on the small of her back, a protective gesture that lightened her even further.

CHAPTER EIGHT

Francesco's villa was in darkness, but as soon as his driver brought the car over the foot of the driveway, light illuminated it, bathing it in a golden hue. With the stars in the moonless night sky twinkling, it was the prettiest sight Hannah had ever seen.

'Can I get you a drink?' Francesco asked once they were alone inside, his minders having left for their own quarters. 'How about a brandy?'

The effects of the champagne had started to abate a little, but did she want to risk putting any more alcohol into her system?

'Only a small one,' he added, clearly reading her mind.

'Yes, please. A small one,' she agreed, hugging herself.

She followed him through the sprawling reception and into the living room, where Francesco swept a small white object from the windowsill. 'Catch,' he said, throwing it at her.

Luckily she caught it. Before she could admonish him for the reckless endangerment of her phone, he'd continued through the huge library, through the dining room, diverted round the indoor swimming pool, stepped through huge French doors and out onto a veranda overhanging the outdoor pool.

It was like stepping into a tropical-party area where the

only thing missing was the guests. A bar—a proper bar, with flashing lights, high stools, and everything—was set up at one end. Tables, chairs, and plump sofas abounded.

'I bet you have some fantastic parties here,' she said. The perfect setting for the playboy Francesco was reputed to be, yet, she reflected, not at all the man who she was learning he was.

'Not for a long time.'

'Why's that?'

'I have different priorities now.' He raised his shoulder, affecting nonchalance, but there was no doubting the 'I'm not prepared to discuss this' timbre in his voice.

That was fine by her. She doubted she wanted to know what his new priorities were anyway.

She spotted a long white board jutting through the trellis. 'Is that a diving board?'

He nodded. 'It beats walking down the steps to reach the swimming pool.'

'You should get a slide—that would be much more fun.'

He chuckled and slipped behind the bar. 'That's not a bad idea. Do you swim?'

'Not for years.'

'I would suggest a dip now but alcohol and swimming pools do not mix well. We will have time for a swim in the morning—that is, if you want to stay the night. Or do you still want to get a flight home?'

There was no mistaking the meaning in his quietly delivered words.

A thrill of excitement speared up her spine, making her shiver despite the warmth of her skin in the balmy night air.

Dimly she recalled saying she wanted to go home. The anger that had made her say those words had gone. All that lay within her now was a longing, wrapped so tightly in her chest it almost made her nauseous.

This was what she'd wanted. It was the whole reason she was here.

She shook her head. 'I don't want to go home. I want to stay.'

His eyes held hers, heat flashing from them before he reached for a bottle and poured them both a drink, topping the smaller measure with a splash of lemonade. He handed it to her. 'I've sweetened it for you, otherwise your untried taste buds might find it a little too harsh.'

Their fingers brushed as she took the glass from him. That same flash of heat sparked in his eyes again.

'Saluti,' he said, holding his glass aloft.

'Saluti,' she echoed, chinking her glass to his.

Francesco took a swallow of his drink. 'I thought you would have checked your phone by now.'

'Oh.' Disconcerted, she blinked. 'I should, really.' After all the fuss she'd made over it, she'd shoved it into her clutch bag without even checking the screen for messages.

For the first time since she'd gained her permanent place on the children's ward, the compulsion to check her phone had taken second place to something else. And that something else was gazing at Francesco.

The more she looked at him, the more the excited nausea increased. Was it even nausea she felt? She didn't know; she had no name befitting the ache that pulsed so, so low within her.

While she stood there rooted, helpless for the first time to know what to do, all her bravado and certainty from the night before gone, Francesco finished his brandy and laid the glass on the bar. 'Time for bed.'

Bed...

Immediately the butterflies inside her began to thrash about, her heart racing at a gallop.

It was late. She'd been awake the best part of two days

after a night of hardly any sleep, yet she didn't feel the least bit weary.

But sleep wasn't what Francesco was implying with his statement.

She gulped her drink down, completely forgetting it had alcohol in it. It had a bitter aftertaste that somehow soothed her skittering nerves a touch. She felt like grabbing the bottle and pouring herself another, this time without the lemonade.

Francesco must have read what was going on beneath her skin, for he stepped out from behind the bar and stood before her. He reached out a hand and pulled her chopsticks out. After a moment's suspended animation her hair tumbled down.

'That's better,' he murmured. Before she could ask what he meant, he inhaled deeply and took a step back. 'I'm going to my room. I will let you decide if you want to join me in it or if you wish to sleep alone.'

'But…'

'I can see you're nervous. I want you to be sure. I meant what I said last night—I will not take advantage of you. My room is two doors from yours. I leave the ball in your court.' With that, he bowed his head, turned on his heel, and strode away.

After a long pause in which all the blood in her body flooded into her brain and roared around her ears, Hannah expelled a long breath of air.

What had she expected? That Francesco would take charge, sweep her into his arms, and carry her manfully all the way to his bedroom as if she weighed little more than a bag of sugar? That he would lay her on his bed and devour her, taking command of every touch and movement?

Hadn't she known he was far too honourable for that?

How right she had been that he would never do anything

to hurt her—even taking her phone had been, according to Francesco's sense of logic, for her own good. Saying that, if he ever stole it from her again she certainly wouldn't be so forgiving.... Oh, what was she thinking? After tonight he would never have another opportunity to steal her phone. Once this weekend was over she would throw herself back into her work—her life—and Francesco would be nothing but a memory of one weekend when she'd dared embrace life in its entirety.

If she wanted Francesco to make love to her, she would have to go to him....

But could she do that? Could she slip into his room and slide under his bedcovers?

Could she not?

No. She couldn't *not* do it.

She would never meet another man like him—how could she when she'd spent twenty-seven years having never met *anyone* who made her feel anything?

It had all felt so different last night, though, when she'd practically begged him to make love to her. Before she'd spent time with him and discovered the complex man behind the cool facade, the man who could be both cruel and yet full of empathy. A man who was capable of both great brutality and great generosity. He was no longer some mythological dream figure. He was flesh and blood, with all the complexity that came from being human.

Francesco stood under the shower for an age, fixing the temperature to a much lower setting than the steaming-hot he usually favoured. If he kept it cold enough it might just do something to lessen his libido.

He pressed his forehead to the cool tiles.

Hannah was his for the taking. She'd been his for the taking since she'd first strolled into his nightclub carrying a bunch of flowers for him. All he had to do was walk two doors down and she would welcome him into her arms.

It unnerved him how badly he wanted to do that. How badly he wanted her.

Would she come to him?

He honestly could not guess.

She was not one of the worldly women he normally spent time with, for whom sex was a form of currency.

Hannah was a twenty-seven-year-old virgin who'd hidden the essence of herself from the world—from herself, even—for the best part of fifteen years.

He'd seen the hesitation in her eyes when he'd said it was time for bed. All the boldness from the night before had vanished, leaving her vulnerability lying right there on the surface.

He would not be the man to take advantage of that vulnerability, no matter how easy it would be and no matter how much she would welcome it.

Francesco could pinpoint the exact moment when the determination to keep her out of his bed had shifted. It had been when he'd looked at that cheating thief, a man so like all those other men who'd been fawning over her during the poker tournament. Now that Hannah's sexuality had awoken, it wouldn't meekly lie back down when she returned to London and return to its former dormancy. Eventually she would meet another man she wanted enough to make love to. It could be any of those men. It could be any man, not one of whom could be trusted to treat her with the tenderness she deserved.

Hannah wanted *him*.

And, *caro Dio*, he wanted her, too, with a need that burned in the very fabric of his being.

But he knew that this final step had to come from her

and her alone, however agonising the wait for her decision would be.

Stepping out of the shower, he towelled himself dry, brushed his teeth, and wandered naked through the doorway of the en suite bathroom into his bedroom....

While he'd showered, Hannah had crept into his room. She stood before the window, her eyes widening as she took in his nude form.

'You've taken your make-up off,' he said, walking slowly towards her. She'd showered, too, her hair damp, her body wrapped in the thick white bathrobe kept in the guest room.

She raised a hand to a cheek, which, even in the dim light, he could see had flushed with colour.

He covered her hand with his own. 'This is better. You're beautiful as you are.'

She trembled, although whether that was down to the hoarseness of his voice or a reaction to his touch he could not say.

Slowly he trailed a hand down the swan of her neck to the V made by the bathrobe, slipping a finger between the bunched material to loosen it, exposing the cleavage of her creamy breasts. Slower still, he slid down to the sash and, using both hands, untied it before pushing the robe apart, exposing her to him.

Hannah's breaths became shallow. Her chest hitched. She stood as still as a statue, staring at him with a look that somehow managed to be both bold and shy. He pushed the shoulders of the robe so it fell softly to the floor.

His own breath hitched as he drank her in.

Her body was everything he'd imagined and more—her breasts fuller and higher, her belly softly toned, her hips curvier, her legs longer and smoother.

He swallowed, the ache in his groin so deep it was painful.

He forced himself to remember that she was a virgin. No matter how badly he wanted to go ahead and devour her, he needed to keep the reins on himself.

Hannah had never felt so exposed—had never *been* so exposed—as she was at that moment. Her heart thundered, her blood surged, but none of it mattered. The hunger in Francesco's eyes was enough to evaporate the shyness and quell any last-minute fears, although, when she dared cast her eyes down to his jutting erection, she experienced a different, more primitive fear that was accompanied by a wild surge of heat through her loins.

Naked except for the gold cross that rested at the top of his muscular chest, Francesco was truly glorious. For such a tall, powerful man he had a surprising grace about him, an elegance to his raw masculinity that tempered the powerhouse he was.

Moisture filled her mouth. She swallowed it away, her eyes captured by the heat of hot chocolate fudge that gleamed.

She wanted to touch him. She wanted to rake her fingers through the whorls of dark hair covering his chest, to feel his skin beneath her lips.

Except she was rooted to the spot on which she stood, helpless to do anything but receive his study of her naked form.

'We'll take it very slowly,' he said, his words thick.

She couldn't speak, could only jerk a nod, aching for it to start, yearning for it to be over, a whole jumble of thoughts and emotions careering through her. Out of the fear and excitement, though, it was the latter that rose to the top.

This was it....

And then she was aloft, clutched against Francesco's hard torso as he swept her into his arms and carried her over to the enormous four-poster bed, her private fantasy coming to life.

Gently he laid her down on her back before lying beside her. He placed a hand on her collarbone—the same bone that had been broken during the moment that had brought him into her life—before slanting his lips on hers.

The heat from his mouth, the mintiness of his breath, the fresh oaky scent of him...sent her senses reeling. His kiss was light but assured, a tender pressure that slowly deepened until her lips parted and his tongue swept into her mouth.

Finally she touched him, placing a hand on his shoulder, feeling the smoothness of his skin while she revelled in the headiness evoked by his increasingly hungry kisses.

He moved his mouth away, sweeping his lips over her cheek to nibble at her earlobe. 'Are you sure about this?'

'You have to ask?' In response to the low resonance of his voice, her own was a breathless rush.

'Any time you want to stop, say.'

She turned her head to capture his lips. 'I don't want to stop.'

He groaned and muttered something she didn't understand before kissing her with such passion her bones seemed to melt within her.

His large hand swept over her, flattening against her breasts, trailing over her belly, stroking her, moulding her. And then he followed it with his mouth. When his lips closed over a puckered nipple she gasped, her eyes flying open.

Always she had looked at breasts as functional assets, understanding in a basic fashion that men lusted after them. Never had it occurred to her that the pleasure a man took from them could be reciprocated by the woman—by *her*. She reached for him, digging her fingers into his scalp, silently begging him to carry on, almost crying out when he broke away, only to immediately turn his attention to the other.

It was the most wonderful feeling imaginable.

At some point he had rolled on top of her. She could feel his erection prod against her thigh and moaned as she imagined what it would feel like to actually have him inside her, being a part of her...

Oh, but she burned, a delicious heat that seeped into every inch of her being, every part alive and dancing in the flames.

It was as if Francesco was determined to kiss and worship every tiny crevice, his mouth now trailing down over her belly whilst his hands...

Her gasp was loud when he moved a hand between her legs, gently stroking his fingers over her soft hair until he found her—

Dear God...

He knelt between her legs, his tongue *there*, pressed against her tight bud.

What was happening to her?

Never in her wildest imaginings had she dreamed that the very essence of her being could ache with such intensity. Nothing. Nothing could have prepared her.

Oh, but this was incredible—*he* was incredible...

Right in her core the heaviness grew. Francesco stayed exactly where he was, his tongue making tiny circular motions, increasing the pressure until, with a cry that seemed to come from a faraway land, ripples of pure pleasure exploded through her and carried her off to that faraway land in the stars.

Only when all the pulsations had abated did Francesco move, trailing kisses all the way back up her body until he reached her mouth and kissed her with a savagery that stole her remaining breath.

He lifted his head to gaze down at her. The chocolate in his eyes had fully melted, his expression one of wonder. 'I need to get some protection,' he said, sounding pained.

She didn't want him to leave her. She wanted him to stay right there, to keep her body covered with the heat of his own.

He didn't go far, simply rolling off her to reach into his bedside table. Before he could rip the square foil open, she placed her hand on his chest. Francesco's heart thudded as wildly as her own.

Closing her eyes, she twisted onto her side and pressed a kiss to his shoulder. And another. And another, breathing in his musky scent, rubbing her nose against the smoothness of his olive skin.

With trembling fingers she explored him, the hard chest with the soft black hair, the brown nipples that she rubbed a thumb over and heard him catch a breath at, the washboard stomach covered with a fine layer of that same black hair that thickened the lower she went, becoming more wiry...

She hesitated, raising her head from his shoulder to stare at him. How she longed to touch him properly, but there was a painful awareness that she didn't know what she was doing. How could she know what he liked, how he wanted to be touched? It wasn't that she had minimal experience—she had *no* experience. Nothing.

'You can do whatever you want,' he whispered hoarsely, raking his hands through her hair and pressing a kiss to her lips. 'Touch me however you like.'

Could he read her mind?

Tentatively, she encircled her hand around his length, feeling it pulsate beneath her touch. Francesco groaned and lay back, hooking one arm over his head while the other lay buried in her hair, his fingers massaging her scalp.

His erection felt a lot smoother than she'd expected, and as she moved her hand up to the tip, a drop of fluid rubbed in her fingers.

A rush of moist heat flooded between her legs, a sharp pulsation, the same ache she had experienced when Francesco had set her body alight with his mouth. To witness his desire for her was as great an aphrodisiac as anything she had experienced since being in his room.

So quickly she didn't even notice him move, he covered her hand with his. 'No more,' he growled. 'I want to be inside you.'

She couldn't resist wrapping an arm around his neck and kissing him, pressing herself against him as tightly as she could.

Hooking an arm around her waist, Francesco twisted her back down, sliding a knee between her legs to part them.

With expert deftness, he ripped the foil open with his teeth and rolled it on before manoeuvring himself so he was fully on top of her and between her parted thighs, his erection heavy against her.

He pressed his lips to hers and kissed her, his left hand burying back into her hair, his right sliding down her side and slipping between them.

She felt him guide the tip of his erection against her and then into her, and sucked in a breath. Francesco simply deepened the kiss, murmuring words of Sicilian endearment into her mouth. He brought his hand back up to stroke her face and thrust forward a little more, still kissing her, stroking her, nibbling at the sensitive skin of her neck, slowly, slowly inching his way inside her.

There was one moment of real discomfort that made her freeze, but then it was gone, her senses too full of Francesco and all the magical things he was doing to dwell on that one thing.

And then he was there, all the way inside her, stretching her, filling her massively, his groin pressed against her pubis, his chest crushing against her breasts.

'Am I hurting you?' he asked raggedly.

'No. It feels...good.' It felt more than good—it felt heavenly.

'*You* feel so good,' he groaned into her ear, withdrawing a little only to inch forward again.

His movements were slow but assured, allowing her to adjust to all these new feelings and sensations, building the tempo at an unhurried pace, only pulling back a few inches, keeping his groin pressing against her.

The sensations he'd created with his tongue began to bubble within her again but this time felt fuller, deeper, more condensed.

Her arms wrapped around his neck, her breaths shallow, she began to move with him, meeting his thrusts, which steadily lengthened. And all the while he kissed her, his hands roaming over the sides of her body, her face, her neck, her hair...everywhere.

She felt the tension increase within him, his groans deepening—such an erotic sound, confirmation that everything she was experiencing was shared, that it was real and not just a beautiful dream. The bubbling deep in her core thickened and swelled, triggering a mass of pulsations to ripple through her. Crying out, she clung to him, burying her face in his neck at the same moment Francesco gave his own cry and made one final thrust that seemed to last for ever.

CHAPTER NINE

FRANCESCO STRETCHED, LOOKED at his bedside clock, then turned back over to face the wall that was Hannah's back. When they'd fallen into sleep she'd been cuddled into him, their limbs entwined.

The last time he'd had such a deep sleep had been his birthday ten months ago. That had been just two days before he'd discovered his mother's diaries.

For the first time in ten months he'd fallen asleep without the demons that plagued him screwing with his thoughts.

Only the top of Hannah's shoulder blades were uncovered and he resisted the urge to place a kiss on them. After disposing of the condom, he'd longed to make love to her again. He'd put his selfish desires to one side. She'd had a long week at work, little sleep the night before, and her body was bound to ache after making love for the first time. Instead he'd pulled her to him and listened to her fall into slumber. It was the sweetest sound he'd ever heard.

He rubbed his eyes and pinched the bridge of his nose, expelling a long breath.

If someone had told him just twenty-four hours ago that making love to Hannah Chapman would be the best experience of his life, he would have laughed. And not with any humour.

To know he was the first man to have slept with her

made his chest fill. To know that he'd awoken those responses... It had been a revelation, a thing of beauty.

Francesco had never felt humble about anything in his life, yet it was the closest he could come to explaining the gratitude he felt towards her for choosing him.

Hannah hadn't chosen him for his power or his wealth or his lifestyle—she'd chosen and trusted him for *him*.

To think he'd dismissed her when she'd blurted out that she wanted him to make love to her. She could have accepted that dismissal. Eventually she would have found another man she trusted enough...

It didn't bear thinking about.

The thought of another man pawing at her and making clumsy love to her made his brain burn and his heart clench.

Suddenly he became aware that her deep, rhythmic breathing had stopped.

His suspicion that she'd awoken was confirmed when she abruptly turned over to face him, her eyes startled.

'*Buongiorno,*' he said, a smile already playing on his lips.

Blinking rapidly, Hannah covered a yawn before bestowing him with a sleepy smile. 'What time is it?'

'Nine o'clock.'

She yawned again. 'Wow. I haven't slept in that late for years.'

'You needed it.' Hooking an arm around her waist, he pulled her to him. 'How are you feeling?'

Her face scrunched in thought. 'Strange.'

'Good strange or bad strange?'

That wonderful look of serenity flitted over her face. 'Good strange.'

Already his body ached to make love to her again. Trailing his fingers over her shoulder, enjoying the softness of her skin, he pressed a kiss to her neck. 'Are you hungry?'

His lust levels rose when she whispered huskily into his ear, 'Starving.'

A late breakfast was brought out to them on the bar-side veranda. Their glasses from the previous evening had already been cleared away.

Wrapped in the guest robe, her hair damp from the shower she'd shared with Francesco, Hannah stretched her legs out and took a sip of the deliciously strong yet sweet coffee. Sitting next to her, dressed in his own dark grey robe, his thigh resting against hers, Francesco grinned.

'You are so lucky waking up to this view every morning,' she sighed. With the morning sun rising above them, calm waves swirling onto Francesco's private beach in the distance, it was as if they were in their own private nirvana.

Breakfast usually consisted of a snatched slice of toast. Today she'd been treated to eggs and bacon and enough fresh rolls and fruit to feed a whole ward of patients.

Yes. Nirvana.

'Believe me, this is the best view I've had in a *very* long time,' he said, his eyes gleaming, his deep voice laced with meaning.

Thinking of all the beautiful women she'd seen pictured on his arm, Hannah found that extremely hard to believe.

Her belly twisted.

It was no good thinking of all those women. Comparing herself to them would be akin to comparing a rock to the moon.

For the first time in her life she wished she'd put some make-up on, then immediately scolded herself for such a ridiculous thought. All those women who had the time and inclination to doll themselves up…well, good luck to them. Even after the make-up lesson she'd been given in the salon, painting her face for their night out had felt like wasted time. Looking at her reflection once she was done had been like looking at a stranger. She hadn't felt like *her*.

She supposed she could always look at it as practice for Melanie's wedding, though—a thought that brought a lump to her throat.

'You do realise you're the sexiest woman on the planet, don't you?' Francesco's words broke through the melancholy of her thoughts.

'Hardly,' she spluttered, taking another sip of her coffee.

'I can prove it,' he murmured sensually into her ear, clasping her hand and tugging it down to rest on his thigh. Sliding it up to his groin, he whispered, 'You see, my clever doctor, you are irresistible.' As he spoke, he nibbled into the nape of her neck, keeping a firm grip on her hand, moving it up so she could feel exactly what effect she was having on him.

A thrill of heady power rushed through her. Heat pooled between her legs, her breath deserting her.

They'd already made love twice since she'd awoken. She'd thought she was spent, had assumed Francesco was, too.

With his free hand he tugged her robe open enough to slip a hand through and cup a breast, kneading it gently. 'You also have the most beautiful breasts on the earth,' he murmured into her ear before sliding his lips over to her mouth and kissing her with a ferocity that reignited the remaining embers of her desire.

'What…what if one of your staff comes out?' she gasped, moving him with more assurance as he unclasped her hand and snaked his arm round her waist.

'They won't.' Thus saying, he slid his hand under her bottom and lifted her off the chair and onto the table, ignoring the fact that their breakfast plates and cups were scattered all over it.

Francesco ached to be inside her again, his body fired up beyond belief, and such a short time after their last bout. It was those memories of being in the shower with her, when she'd sunk to her knees and taken him in her mouth for the first time....

Just thinking about it would sustain his fantasies for a lifetime.

Dipping his head to take a perfectly ripe breast into his mouth, he trailed a hand down her belly and slipped a finger inside her, groaning aloud to find her hot and moist and ready for him.

Diving impatiently into his pocket, he grabbed the condom he'd put in there as an afterthought and, with Hannah distracting him by smothering any part of his face and neck she could reach with kisses, he slipped it on, spread her thighs wide, and plunged straight into her tight heat.

Her head lolled back, her eyes widening as if in shock.

Silently he cursed himself. Such was his excitement he'd totally forgotten that until a few short hours ago she'd been a virgin.

'Too much?' he asked, stilling, fighting to keep himself in check.

'Oh, no.' As if to prove it, she grabbed his buttocks and ground herself against him. The shock left her eyes, replaced with the desire he knew swirled in his own. 'I want it all.'

It was all he needed. Sweeping the crockery this way and that to make some space, he pushed her back so she was flat on the table, her thighs parted and raised high, her legs wrapped around his, and thrust into her, withdrawing to the tip and thrusting back in, over and over until she was whimpering beneath him, her hands flailing to grab his chest, her head turning from side to side. Only when he felt her thicken around him and her muscles contract did he let himself go, plunging in as deep as he could with one final groan before collapsing on top of her.

It was only when all the stars had cleared that he realised they were still in their respective robes, Hannah's fingers playing under the Egyptian cotton, tracing up and down his back.

She giggled.

Lifting his chin to rest it on her chest, he stared at her intently.

'That was incredible,' she said, smiling.

He flashed his teeth in return. 'You, *signorina*, are a very quick learner.'

'And you, *signor*, are a very good teacher.'

'There is so much more I can teach you.'

'And is it all depraved?'

'Most of it.'

She laughed softly and lay back on the table, expelling a sigh of contentment as she gazed up at the cobalt sky. He kept his gaze on her face. That serene look was there again. To think he was the cause of it...

A late breakfast turned into a late lunch. Francesco did not think he had ever felt the beat of the sun so strongly on his skin. For the first time in ten months he enjoyed a lazy day—indeed, the thought of working never crossed his mind. The rage he felt for his father, the rage that had boiled within him for so long, had morphed into a mild simmer.

In the back of his mind was the knowledge that at some point soon he would have to arrange for his jet to take Hannah back to London, but it was something he desisted from thinking about too much, content to make love, skinny-dip, then make love again. And she seemed happy, too, her smile serene, radiant.

Kissing her for what could easily be the thousandth time, he tied his robe around his waist and headed back indoors and to his bedroom for more condoms.

The box was almost empty. He shook his head in wonder. He'd never known desire like it. He couldn't get enough of her.

When he returned outside, Hannah had poured them both another cup of coffee from the pot and was curled up on one of the sofas reading something on her phone.

'Everything okay?' he asked, hiding the burst of irritation that poked at him.

This was the third time she'd gone through her messages since they'd awoken.

She's a dedicated professional, he reminded himself. Her patients are her priority, as they should be.

For all his sound reasoning, there was no getting around the fact he wanted to rip the phone from her hand and stamp on it. After all, it was the weekend. She was off duty.

She looked up and smiled. 'All's well.'

'Good.' Sitting next to her, he plucked the phone from her hand and slipped it into his pocket.

'Not again,' she groaned.

'Now you have satisfied yourself that your patients are all well, you have no need for it.'

'Francesco, give it back.'

'Later. You need to learn to switch off. Besides, it's rude.'

'Please.' Her voice lowered, all her former humour gone. 'That's my phone. And I wasn't being rude—you'd gone to the bedroom.' She held her hand out, palm side up. 'Now give.'

'What's it worth?' he asked, leaning into her, adopting a sensuous tone.

'Me not kicking you in the ankle.'

'I thought you didn't believe in violence.'

'So did I.' A smile suddenly creased her face and she burst out laughing, her mirth increasing when he shoved her phone back into the pocket of her robe. 'Now I get it—threats of violence really do work.'

He kissed her neck and flattened her onto her back. 'The difference is I knew you didn't mean it.'

Raking her fingers through his hair, she sighed. 'I guess you'll never know.'

'Oh, I know.' Hannah healed people. She didn't hurt them.

But he didn't want to think those thoughts. The time was fast approaching when he'd have to take her home, leaving him limited time left to worship her delectable body.

'I'm going to be in London more frequently for a while,' he mentioned casually, making his way down to a ripe breast. 'I'll give you a call when I'm over. Take you out for dinner.' With all the evidence pointing to Luca Mastrangelo still sniffing around the Mayfair casino, Francesco needed to be on the ball. If that meant spending more time in London, then so be it. The casino would be his, however he had to achieve it. He would secure that deal and nothing would prevent it.

Hannah moaned as he circled his tongue around a puckered nipple.

At least being in London more often meant he could enjoy her for a little longer, too.

It never occurred to him that Hannah might have different ideas.

Hannah opened the curtains and stepped into the cubicle, pulling the curtains shut around her. She smiled at the small girl lying in the bed who'd been brought in a week ago with encephalitis, inflammation of the brain, then smiled at the anxious parents. 'We have the lab results,' she said, not wasting time with pleasantries, 'and it's good news.'

This was her favourite part of the job, she thought a few minutes later as she walked back to her small workspace—telling parents who'd lived through hell that their child would make it, that the worst was over.

Clicking the mouse to get her desktop working, she opened the young girl's file, ready to write her notes up into the database. Her phone vibrated in her pocket.

She pulled it out, her heart skipping when Francesco's name flashed up.

Time seemed to still as she stared at it, her hands frozen.

Should she answer?

Or not?

It went to voicemail before she could decide.

Closing her eyes, she tilted her head back and rolled her neck.

Why, oh, why had she agreed to see him again? Not that she had agreed. At the time she'd been too busy writhing in his arms to think coherently about anything other than the sensations he was inducing in her....

She squeezed her eyes even tighter.

Francesco, in all his arrogance, had simply assumed she'd want to see him again.

An almost hysterical burst of laughter threatened to escape from her throat.

There was no way she could see him again. She just couldn't.

Their time together in Sicily had brought him, her dream man, to life—the good and the bad. Being with him had been the most wonderful, thrilling time imaginable. She had felt alive. She had felt *so much*.

She had felt *too* much.

All she wanted now was to focus on her job and leave Francesco as nothing but a beautiful memory.

She would carry on seeking out new experiences to share with Beth for when the time came that they were together again. But these experiences would be of an entirely different nature, more of a tick box—*I've done that, I've parachuted out of an aeroplane*—experience. Nothing that would clog her head. Nothing that would compromise everything she had spent the majority of her life working towards.

But, dear God, the hollowness that had lived in her chest for so long now felt so *full*, as if her shrivelled heart had been pumped back to life. And that scared her more than anything.

It was easier to shatter a full heart than a shrivelled one.

'Hannah, you should go home,' Alice, the ward sister said, startling her from her thoughts. Alice looked hard at her. 'Are you okay?'

Hannah nodded. Alice was lovely, a woman whose compassion extended from the children to all the staff on the ward. 'I'm fine,' she said, forcing a smile. 'I'll be off as soon as I get these reports finished.'

'It'll be dark soon,' Alice pointed out. 'Anyway, I'm off now. I'll see you in the morning.'

Alone again, Hannah rubbed her temples, willing away the tension headache that was forming.

She really should go home. Her shift had officially finished two hours ago.

The thought of returning to her little home filled her with nothing but dread, just as it had for the past three days since she'd returned from Sicily.

Her home felt so empty.

The silence…how had she never noticed the silence before, when the only noise had been the sound of her own breathing?

For the first time ever, she felt lonely. Not the usual loneliness that had been within her since Beth's death, but a different kind of isolation. Colder, somehow.

Even the sunny yellow walls of her little cubbyhole felt bleak.

Francesco's phone rang. *'Ciao.'*

'That young drug dealer is back. We have him.'

'Bring him to me.'

Francesco knew exactly who Mario was on about. A young lad, barely eighteen, had visited his Palermo nightclub a few weeks ago. The cameras had caught him slipping bags of powder and pills to many of the clubbers. As unlikely as it was, he had slipped their net, escaping before Francesco's men could apprehend him, disappearing into the night.

He rubbed his eyes.

No matter how hard he tried to remove the dealers, there was always some other cocky upstart there to fill the breach. It was like trying to stop the tide.

The one good thing he could say about it was that at least he was making the effort to clean the place up, to counter some of the damage his father had done.

Salvatore had been responsible for channelling millions of euros' worth of drugs into Sicily and mainland Europe. How he had kept it secret from his son, Francesco would never understand; he could only guess Salvatore had known it was the one thing his son would never stand idly by and allow to happen. If Francesco *had* known, he would have ripped his father apart, but by the time he'd learned of his involvement, it had been too late to confront him. Salvatore had already been buried when he found out the truth.

It occurred to him, not for the first time, that his father had been afraid of him.

Slowly but surely, he was dismantling everything Salvatore Calvetti had built, closing it down brick by brick, taking care in his selection of which to dismantle first so as not to disturb the foundation and have it all crumble on top of him. Only a few days ago he had taken great delight in shutting down a restaurant that had been a hub for the distribution of arms, one of many in his father's great network.

While he'd been paying off Paolo di Luca, the man who'd run the restaurant on his father's behalf for thirty years, he had seen for the first time the old man Paolo had become. A man with liver spots and a rheumy wheeze. The more he thought about it, the more he realised all the old associates were exactly that—old.

When had they got so ancient?

These weren't the terrifying men of his childhood memories. Apart from a handful who hadn't taken kindly to being put out to pasture, most of them had been happy to be paid off, glad to spend their remaining years with their wives—or mistresses in many cases—and playing with their grandchildren and great-grandchildren.

There was a knock on the door, and the handle turned.

Mario and two of his other guards walked in, holding the young drug dealer up by the scruff of his neck.

With them came a burst of music from the club, a dreadful tune that hit him straight in his gut.

It was the same tune Hannah had been dancing to so badly in his London club, when he'd threatened the fool manhandling her.

The same Hannah who'd ignored her phone when he'd called and, in response to a message he'd sent saying he would be in London at the weekend, had sent him a simple message back saying she was busy. Since then…nothing. Not a peep from her.

It wasn't as if she never used her blasted phone. It was attached to her like an appendage.

There was no getting around it. She was avoiding him.

He looked at the belligerent drug dealer, but all he could see was the look of serenity on Hannah's face when he'd told her of calling the police on the casino cheat.

Hannah saved lives. She'd sworn an oath to never do harm.

What was it she'd said? *Who makes the rules?*

'Empty your pockets,' he ordered, not moving from his seat.

He could see how badly the drug dealer wanted to disobey him, but sanity prevailed and he emptied his pockets. He had two bags of what Francesco recognised as ecstasy tablets and a bag full of tiny cellophane wraps of white powder. Cocaine.

A cross between a smirk and a snarl played on the drug dealer's lips.

Francesco's hands clenched into fists. He rose.

The drug dealer turned puce, his belligerence dropping a touch when confronted by Francesco's sheer physical power.

Who makes the rules?

'You are throwing your life away,' he said harshly before turning to Mario. 'Call the police.'

'The police?' squeaked the dealer.

It was obvious that the same question echoed in Mario and his fellow guards' heads.

First the stealing, cheating gambler and now a drug dealer? He could see the consternation on all their faces, could feel them silently wondering if he was going soft.

Naturally, none of his men dared question him verbally, their faces expressionless.

'Yes. The police.' As he walked past the dealer, Francesco added, 'But know that when you're released from your long prison sentence, if I ever find you dealing in drugs again, I will personally break your legs. Take my advice—get yourself an education and go straight.'

With that, he strode out of his office, out of his nightclub, and into the dark Palermo night, oblivious to the cadre of bodyguards who'd snapped into action to keep up with him.

CHAPTER TEN

HANNAH BROUGHT HER bike to a stop outside her small front gate and smothered a yawn. She felt dead on her feet. The Friday-evening traffic had only compounded what had been a *very* long week.

She dismounted and wheeled her bike up the narrow path to her front door. Just as she placed her key in the lock, a loud beep made her turn.

A huge, gleaming black motorbike with an equally huge rider came to a stop right by her front gate.

No way...

Stunned, she watched as Francesco strode towards her, magnificent in his black leathers, removing his helmet, a thunderous look on his face.

'What are you doing here?' Her heart had flown into her mouth and it took all she had not to stand there gaping like a goldfish.

'Never mind that, what the hell are you doing back on that deathtrap?'

He loomed before her, blocking the late sun, his eyes blazing with fury.

Hannah blinked, totally nonplussed at seeing him again. Only years of practice at remaining calm while under fire from distressed patients and their next of kin alike allowed her to retain any composure. 'I don't drive.'

Breathing heavily through his nose, he snapped, 'There are other ways of getting around. I can't believe you're still using this...thing.'

'I'm not. It's a new one.'

'I gathered that, seeing as your old one crumpled like a biscuit tin,' he said, speaking through gritted teeth. 'I'm just struggling to understand why you would still cycle when you nearly died on a bicycle mere weeks ago.'

'I don't like using public transport. Plus, cycling helps shift some of the weight from my bottom,' she added, trying to inject some humour into her tone, hoping to defuse some of the anger still etched on his face. Her attempt failed miserably.

'There is nothing wrong with your bottom,' he said coldly. 'And even if there were—which there isn't—it's hardly worth risking your life for.'

The situation was so surreal Hannah was tempted to pinch herself.

Was she dreaming? She'd had so little sleep since returning from Sicily five days ago that it was quite possible.

'Like every other human on this planet, I could die at any time by any number of accidents. I'm not going to stay off my bike because of one idiot.' She kept her tone firm, making it clear the situation was no longer open for discussion. She was a grown woman. If she wanted to cycle, then that was her business. 'Anyway, you're hardly in a position to judge—do you have any idea the number of mangled motorcyclists I had to patch back together when I was doing my placement in Accident and Emergency?'

A cold snake crawled up her spine at the thought of Francesco being brought in on a trolley....

She blinked the thought away.

'My riding skills are second to none, as you know perfectly well,' he said with all the confidence of a man who knew he was the best at what he did. 'In any case, I do not ride around on a piece of cheap tin.'

'You can be incredibly arrogant, did you know that?'

'I've been called much worse, and if being arrogant is what it takes to keep you safe then I can live with that.'

His chocolate eyes held hers with an intensity so deep it almost burned. Her fingers itched to touch him, to rub her thumb over the angry set of his lips.

No matter how…shocked she felt at his sudden appearance, there was something incredibly touching about his anger, knowing it was concern for her safety propelling it.

She looked away, scared to look at him any longer. 'I appreciate your concern, but my safety is not your responsibility.'

Suddenly aware her helmet was still attached to her head, she unclipped it and whipped it off, smoothing her hair down as best she could.

God, since when had she suffered from vanity? Last weekend notwithstanding, not in fifteen years.

And why did she feel an incomprehensible urge to burst into tears?

It was a feeling she'd been stifling since she'd walked back into her home on Sunday night.

'What are you doing here?' she asked again, her cheeks burning as she recalled the two phone calls she'd ignored from him.

'That's not a conversation I wish to have on your doorstep.'

When she made no response, he inclined his head at her door. 'This is the point where you invite me into your home.'

Less than a week ago she'd invited him into her house, only to have him rudely decline.

Then, her heart had hammered with excitement for what

the weekend would bring. Now her heart thrummed just to see *him*...

'Look, you can come in for a little while, but I've had a long, difficult week and a *very* long, *very difficult* day, and I want to get to bed early.' Abruptly, she turned away and opened the door, terrified he would read something of her feelings on her face.

The last word she should be mentioning in front of Francesco was *bed*.

She could hardly credit how naive she'd been in sleeping with him. Had she seriously thought she could share a bed with the sexiest man on the planet and walk away feeling nothing more than a little mild contentment that she'd ticked something off her to-do list?

What a silly, naive fool she'd been.

Francesco thought he'd never been in a more depressing house than the place Hannah called home. It wasn't that there was anything intrinsically wrong with it—on the contrary, it was a pretty two-bedroom house with high ceilings and spacious rooms, but...

There was no feeling to it. Her furniture was minimal and bought for function. The walls were bare of any art or anything that would show the owner's tastes. It was a shell.

Hannah shoved her foldaway bike in a virtually empty cupboard under the stairs and faced him, a look of defiance—and was that fear?—on her face. Her hair had reverted back to its usual unkempt state, a sight that pleased him immeasurably.

'I need a shower,' she said.

'Is that an invitation?' he asked, saying it more as a challenge than from any expectation.

She ignored his innuendo. 'I've been puked on twice today.'

He grimaced. 'So not an invitation.'

'Give me five minutes, then you can tell me whatever it is you came all this way to discuss. While I'm gone, you can make yourself useful by making the coffee.' Thus saying, she headed up the wooden stairs without a backward glance, her peachy bottom showing beautifully in the functional black trousers she wore....

Quickly he averted his eyes. Too much looking at those gorgeous buttocks might just make him climb into that shower with her after all.

Besides, a few minutes to sort their respective heads out would probably be a good idea.

Hannah's reception had not been the most welcoming, but what had he expected? That she would take one look at him and throw herself into his arms?

No, he hadn't expected that. Her silence and polite rebuff by text message had made her feelings clear. Well, tough on her. He was here and they would talk whether she wanted to or not.

Yet there had been no faking the light that had shone briefly in her eyes when she'd first spotted him. It had been mingled with shock, but it had been there, that same light that had beamed straight into his heart the first time she'd opened her eyes to him.

Then he'd ruined it by biting her head off over her bike.

He cursed under his breath. If it took the rest of his life, he'd get her off that deathtrap.

He heard a door close and the sound of running water. Was she naked…?

He inhaled deeply, slung his leather jacket over the post of the stairs, and walked into the small square kitchen. He spotted the kettle easily enough and filled it, then set about finding mugs and coffee.

As he rootled through Hannah's cupboards, his chest slowly constricted.

He had never seen such bare cupboards. The only actual food he found was half a loaf of bread, a box of cereal, a large slice of chocolate cake, and some tomato sauce. And that was it. Nothing else, not even a box of eggs. The fridge wasn't much better, containing some margarine, a pint of milk, and an avocado.

What did she eat?

That question was answered when he opened her freezer.

It wasn't just his chest that felt constricted. His heart felt as if it had been placed in a vice.

The freezer was full. Three trays crammed with ready meals for one.

The ceiling above him creaked, jolting him out of the trance he hadn't realised he'd fallen into.

Experiencing a pang of guilt at rifling through her stuff, he shut the freezer door and went back to the jar of instant coffee he'd found and the small bag of sugar.

No wonder she had wanted to experience a little bit of life.

He'd never met anyone who lived such a solitary existence. Not that anyone would guess. Hannah wasn't antisocial. On the contrary, she was good company. Better than good. Warm, witty... Beautiful. Sexy.

Before too long she emerged to join him in the sparse living room, having changed into a pair of faded jeans and a black T-shirt.

'Your coffee's on the table,' he said, rising from the sofa he'd sat on. He would bet the small dining table in the corner was rarely used for eating on, loaded as it was with medical journals and heaps of paper neatly laid in piles.

'Thank you.' She picked it up and walked past him to

the single seat, leaving a waft of light, fruity fragrance in her wake. She curled up on it, cradling her mug.

Now her eyes met his properly, a brightness glistening from them. 'Francesco, what are you doing here?'

'I want to know why you're avoiding me.'

'I'm not.'

'Don't tell me lies.'

'I haven't seen you to avoid you.'

'You said you were busy this weekend, yet here you are, at home.'

Her head rolled back, her chest rising and falling even more sharply. 'I've only just got back from work, as you well know, and I'm on the rota for tomorrow's night shift. So yes, I am busy.'

'Look at me,' he commanded. He would keep control of his temper if it killed him.

With obvious reluctance, she met his gaze.

'Last weekend… You do realise what we shared was out of this world?'

Her cheeks pinked. 'It was very nice.'

'There are many words to describe it, but *nice* isn't one of them. You and me…'

'There is no you and me,' she blurted, interrupting him. 'I'm sorry to have to put it so crassly, but I don't want to see you again. Last weekend *was* very nice but there will be no repeat performance.'

'You think not?' he said, trying his hardest to keep his tone soft, but when she dug her hand into her pocket and pulled out her phone, the red mist seemed to descend as if from nowhere. 'Do *not* turn that thing on.'

Her eyes widened as if startled before narrowing. 'Don't tell me what I can and can't do. You're not my father.'

'I'm not trying…'

'You certainly are.'

'Will you stop interrupting me?' He raised his voice for the first time.

Her mouth dropped open.

'It's a bit much feeling as if I'm in competition with a phone,' he carried on, uncaring that she had turned a whiter shade of white. He knew without having to be told that there was no competition, because the phone had won without even trying. Because as far as Dr Hannah Chapman was concerned, her phone was all she needed.

He rose to his feet, his anger swelling like an awoken cobra, his venom primed. 'You hide behind it. I bet you sleep with it on your pillow.'

His comment was so close to the mark that Hannah cringed inwardly *and* outwardly. Dear God, why had he come here? Why hadn't he just taken the hint and kept away?

She hadn't asked for any of this. All she'd wanted was to experience one night as a real woman.

She'd ended up with so much more than she'd bargained for.

'Do you really want to spend the rest of your life with nothing but a phone to keep you warm at night?'

'What I want is none of your business,' she said, her tongue running away as she added, 'but just to clarify what I told you in your nightclub, I do *not* want a relationship—not with you, not with anyone.'

He threw his arms out, a sneer on his face. 'Of course you don't want a relationship. Your life is so fulfilling as it is.'

'It is to me.' How she stopped herself screaming that in his face she would never know.

'Look at you. Look at this place. You're hiding away from life. You're like one of those mussels we ate in the casino—you threw yourself at me to experience some of what you'd been missing out on, got what you wanted, then retreated right back into your shell without any thought to the consequences.'

She didn't have a clue what he was talking about. 'What consequences? We used protection.'

'I'm not talking about babies—I'm talking about what you've done to me!' If he'd been a lion he would have roared those last few words, of that she had no doubt. Francesco's fury was a sight to behold, making him appear taller and broader than ever, filling the living room.

She should be terrified. And there was no denying the panic gnawing furiously at the lining of her stomach, but it wasn't fear of him...

No, it was the fear of something far worse.

And this fear put her even further on the defensive.

Shoving her mug on the floor, she jumped to her feet. The calmness she had been wearing as a facade evaporated, leaving her jumbled, terrified emotions raw and exposed. 'I haven't done *anything* to you!'

'You've changed me. I don't know how the hell you did it—maybe you're some kind of witch—but whatever you did, it's real. I let a drug dealer escape without a beating last night, had my men turn him over to the police.'

'And that's a bad thing?'

'It's not how I work. That's never been how I work. Drugs killed my mother. Drug dealers are the scum of the earth and deserve everything they get.' Abruptly he stopped talking and took a long breath in. 'You gave me the best night of my life and I know as well as you do that you enjoyed every minute of it, too. You can deny it until you're blue in the face but we both know what we shared was special. *You* forced that night on *me*. It was what *you* wanted, and it's me that's paying the price for it.'

'You knew it was only for one night.'

'A one-night stand is never that good. Never. Not even close. But now you're treating me as if I'm a plague carrier, and I want to know why.'

'There's nothing to tell. I just don't want to see you again.'

'Will you stop lying?'

'I can't have sex with you again. I just can't. You've screwed with my brain enough as it is.'

'*I've* screwed with *your* brain?' His tone was incredulous. 'Do you have any idea what you've done to *me*?'

'Oh, yes, let's bring it all back to you,' she spat. 'The poor little gangster struggling to deal with his newly found conscience while I…'

Hannah took a deep breath, trying desperately to rein all her emotions back in and under her control. 'After my accident, you filled my mind. You were all I could think about. When I met you it only got worse. I came to you partly because I thought doing something about it would fix it. I thought we would have sex and that would be it—my life would return to normal, I'd be able to go back to concentrating on my job without any outside influences…'

'Didn't it work out exactly as you envisaged?' he asked, his tone mocking.

'No, it did not! I thought it would. But you're still there, filling my head, and I want you gone. My patients deserve all my focus. Every scrap of it. I want to experience more of life, but not to their detriment. This is all *too much* and I can't handle it.'

'I warned you of the consequences,' he said roughly. 'I told you a one-night stand wasn't for a woman like you.'

Something inside Hannah pinged. Taking three paces towards him, she pushed at his chest. 'You are a hypocrite,' she shouted. 'How many women have you used for sex? Double figures? Treble? How many lives have *you* ruined?'

'None. All the women before you knew it would only ever be sex. It meant nothing.'

'Ha! Exactly.' She shoved him again, hard enough to knock him off balance and onto the sofa. 'The minute the tables are turned, your fragile ego can't deal with it...'

She never got to finish her sentence for Francesco grabbed hold of her waist and yanked her onto the sofa with him, pinning her down before she could get a coherent thought in her head.

'You know as well as I do that what we shared meant something,' he said harshly, his hot breath tickling her skin. 'And contrary to your low opinion of my sex life, I am not some kind of male tart. Until last weekend I'd been celibate for ten months.'

She wanted to kick out, scream at him to get off her, but all the words died on her tongue when his mouth came crashing down on hers, a hard, furious kiss that her aching heart and body responded to like a moth to a flame.

That deep masculine taste and scent filled her senses, blocking out all her fears, blocking out everything but him. Francesco.

Just five days away from him, and she had pined. Pined for him. Pined for this.

She practically melted into him, winding her arms around his hard body, clinging to him, pressing every part of her into him.

And he clung to her, too, his hands roaming over her body, bunching her hair, his hot lips grazing her face, her neck, every available bit of flesh.

Being in his arms felt so *right*. Francesco made the coldness that had settled in her bones since she'd returned from Sicily disappear, replacing it with a warmth that seeped through to every part of her.

In a melee of limbs her T-shirt was pulled over her head

and thrown to the floor, quickly followed by Francesco's. Braless, her naked breasts crushed against his chest, the last remaining alarms ringing in her brain vanished and all she could do was savour the feel of his hard strength flush against her.

His strong capable hands playing with the buttons on her jeans, her smaller hands working on the zip of his leathers, somehow they managed to tug both down, using their feet to work them off to join the rest of their strewn clothing, in the process tumbling off the sofa and onto the soft carpet.

Only when they were both naked did Francesco reach for his leathers, pull out his wallet and produce a now familiar square foil.

In a matter of seconds he'd rolled it on and plunged inside her.

This time her body knew exactly what to do. *She* knew exactly what to do. No fears, no insecurities, just pure unadulterated pleasure.

The feel of him, huge inside her, his strength on the verge of crushing her, Hannah let all thoughts fly out of the window, giving in to this most wonderful of all sensations.

Later, lying in the puddle of their clothes on the floor, Francesco's face buried in her neck, his breaths hot against her skin, she opened her eyes and gazed at the ceiling. Hot tears burned the back of her retinas.

'Am I squashing you?' he asked, his breathing still ragged.

'No,' she lied, wrapping her arms even tighter around him.

Francesco lifted his head to look at her. There had been a definite hitch in her voice. 'What's the matter?'

'Nothing.'

'Stop lying to me.'

To his distress, two fat tears rolled down her cheeks.

'I'm so confused. *You* confuse me. I'd told myself I would never sleep with you again and look what's happened. You turn up and I might as well have succumbed to you the moment I let you in the door.'

Rolling onto his back, taking her with him so she rested on his chest, he held her tightly to him. 'All it proves is that we're not over. Not yet. Neither of us wants anything heavy,' he continued. 'For a start, neither of us has the *time* for anything heavy. But we enjoy each other's company, so where's the harm in seeing each other? I promise you, your patients will not suffer for you having a life.'

There was no room for Hannah in his life. Not in any meaningful way. The more he got to know her, the more he knew that what they shared could never be anything more than a fling.

Ever since he'd reached adulthood he'd assumed he would never meet a woman to settle down with. Even before he'd discovered his mother's diaries and learned of his father's despicable behaviour towards her, he'd known how badly she struggled to cope with his father's way of life.

His mother had been a good woman. Kind and loving, even when she was doped to her eyeballs on the drugs his father fed her by the trough. Not that he'd known his father fed them to her—back then he'd believed his father to be as despairing and worried about her habit as he was.

Elisabetta Calvetti had no more fitted into his father's world than Hannah fitted in his.

The women who did fit into Francesco's world and thrived were like poison. The rarer women—women like Hannah who did not fit in—he'd always known should never marry into such a dangerous life. To marry into it would destroy them, just as it had destroyed his mother.

Deep down, he knew he should have accepted her rebuffs and left her alone, but the past few days…

How could he concentrate on anything when his mind was full of Hannah?

The wolves, in the form of Luca Mastrangelo, were circling the Mayfair casino and Francesco needed to be on the ball. Otherwise the deal that would symbolise above all others that Salvatore Calvetti's empire was over, his legacy shrivelled to dust, would be lost.

He wasn't ready to let her go. Not yet. Knowing Hannah was in his life meant he could focus his attention entirely on the purchase of the casino and not have his mind filled with her.

'Okay,' she said slowly, pressing a kiss to his chest. 'As long as you promise not to make any demands on my time when I'm working, we can see each other.'

His arms tightened while the constriction in his chest loosened. He ignored the fact that her condition for seeing him—a condition he was used to dictating to his lovers and not the other way round—made his throat fill with bile.

CHAPTER ELEVEN

THE MAYFAIR CASINO was a lot shabbier than the ones Francesco owned, but the decoration was not something that concerned him. That was cosmetic and easily fixed. Even the accounts, usually his first consideration when buying a new business, mattered not at all. All he craved was what the business symbolised.

Tonight, though, symbolism and everything else could take a hike. He'd finally managed to drag Hannah out for the night.

Naturally, she'd been too busy to buy a new dress and had changed into the same dress she'd worn three weeks before in Sicily, confessing with an embarrassed smile that it was the only suitable item in her wardrobe.

He'd bitten back the offer of buying her a whole new wardrobe. He knew without having to ask that she would refuse. He was man enough to admit that it had been a blow to his pride when he'd learned she'd paid for the dress herself in Palermo. And her haircut. It surprised him, though, how much he respected her for it. She'd had free rein in that boutique. She could have easily racked up a bill for tens of thousands of euros, all in his name.

Tonight she looked beautiful. In the ten minutes she'd taken to get changed, she'd brushed her hair, but all this had done was bush it out even more. She'd applied only a little make-up. All she wore on her feet were her black ballet slippers.

In Francesco's eyes she looked far more ravishing than she had three weeks ago when she'd gone the whole nine yards with her appearance. Now she looked real. She looked like Hannah.

An elderly man with salt-and-pepper hair ambled towards them, his hand outstretched. 'Francesco, I didn't know you would be joining us this evening.' There was a definite tremor in both his hand and voice.

'I wanted to show my guest around the place,' he replied, shaking the wizened hand before introducing him to Hannah. 'This is Dr Hannah Chapman. Hannah, this is Sir Godfrey Renfrew, the current owner of this establishment.'

'Doctor?' Godfrey's eyes swept her up and down, a hint of confusion in them.

'Lovely to meet you,' Hannah said, smiling. Did Francesco *have* to keep referring to her by her title?

'The pleasure is mine,' he said quickly, before fixing his attention back on Francesco. 'I have some of your compatriots visiting me this evening.'

So that was the reason for Godfrey's discomfort.

Francesco glanced around the room, homing in on two tall men leaning against a far wall drinking beer.

So his spies had been onto something when they'd reported that Luca Mastrangelo was trying to usurp the deal. And it seemed as if Pepe was in on it, too.

If Francesco was in Sicily, all he would have to do was whisper a few well-chosen words into Godfrey's ear and the casino would be his.

But he wasn't in Sicily. And Godfrey had already proved himself immune to Sicilian threats, and much worse.

'I see them,' Francesco confirmed, keeping his tone steady, bored, even. 'They're old acquaintances of mine.'

'Yes…they said you had…history.'

That was one way of describing it. Smiling tightly, he bowed his head. 'I should go and say hello.'

Now wishing he hadn't brought Hannah out with him, Francesco bore her off towards the Mastrangelo brothers.

'Who are we going to say hello to?' she asked, surprising him by slipping her fingers through his.

Apart from when they were lying in bed together, she never held his hand. Not that they'd ever actually been out anywhere to hold hands, all their time together over the past fortnight having been spent eating takeaway food and making love.

'Old acquaintances of mine,' he said tightly, although the feel of her gentle fingers laced through his had a strangely calming reaction.

By the time they stood before the Mastrangelo brothers, his stomach felt a fraction more settled.

'Luca. Pepe.' He extended his hand. 'So the rumours are true,' he said, switching to Sicilian.

'What rumours would they be?' asked Luca, shaking his hand with a too-firm grip. Francesco squeezed a little tighter in turn before dropping the hold.

'I'd heard you were interested in this place.'

Luca shrugged.

'I thought you'd got out of the casino game.'

'Times change.'

'Clearly.' Francesco forced a smile. 'Does your little wife know you're going back into forbidden territory?'

Luca bared his teeth. 'You leave Grace out of this.'

'I wouldn't dream of bringing her into it, knowing how much she hates me.' Here, he looked at Pepe. 'I do believe your sister-in-law hates me more than you do.' Not giving either of them the chance to respond, he flashed his own teeth. 'I suggest the pair of you rethink your decision to try to buy this place. The documents for my ownership are on the verge of completion.'

Pepe finally spoke. 'But they're not completed yet, are they?'

'They will be soon. And if either of you try anything to stop the sale going through, you will live to regret it.'

'Are you threatening us?'

'You sound surprised, Luca,' he said, deliberately keeping his tone amicable. 'You should know I am not a man to deal with threats. Only promises.'

Luca pulled himself to his full height. 'I will not be threatened, Calvetti. Remember that.'

Only the gentle squeeze of Hannah's fingers lacing back through his stopped Francesco squaring up to his old friend.

He shook himself. He didn't want to be having this conversation in front of her, regardless of the fact that they were speaking in their native tongue and not in English.

'Don't start a war you'll never win, Mastrangelo.'

'I remember your father saying exactly the same thing to me when my father died. Your father thought he could take control of the Mastrangelo estate.' Luca smiled. 'He didn't succeed in getting his way. And nor will you.'

Baring his teeth one last time, Francesco said, 'But I am not my father. I have infinitely more patience.'

'Are you okay?' Hannah asked as soon as they were out of earshot.

'I'm fine. Let's get out of here.'

'But we've only just arrived.'

Expelling air slowly through his nose, he stopped himself from insisting they leave right now. He could insist and she would have no choice but to follow, but to do so would upset her, and that was the last thing he wanted to do.

Strangely enough, Hannah's presence tempered the

angry adrenaline flowing through him—not by much, but enough to take the edge off it.

Having promised to teach her how to play Blackjack, he found seats at a table for them to join in. Unlike at the tournament in Sicily, where her remarkable poker face was her biggest asset, there was no bluffing needed when playing against the dealer. She still picked it up like a pro. At one point he thought she would finish with more chips than him.

Watching her have fun eased a little more of his rage, enough so that there were moments he forgot the Mastrangelos were there, trying to muscle in on his territory. It pleased him enormously to watch her drink a full glass of champagne. She really was learning to switch off.

His driver was ready for them when they left. As soon as they were seated in the back, the partition separating them from the driver, Hannah squished right next to him and reached for his hand. Pulling it onto her lap, she rubbed her thumb in light circular motions over his inner wrist.

The breath of air he inhaled went into his lungs that bit easier.

'How do you know those two men?' she asked after a few moments of silence.

He could only respect her reticence in waiting until they were alone before starting her cross-examination. 'Luca and Pepe?'

'Is that their names?' she said drily. 'You forgot to introduce us.'

He sighed. 'I apologise. They're old friends. Were old friends. At least, Luca was.'

'Was?'

'Their father used to work for my father. And then he quit.'

He felt her blanch.

'Don't worry. My father didn't touch him—they'd been

childhood friends themselves, which saved Pietro from my father's vengeance. But the fact my father didn't put a bullet through him didn't mean the perceived slur could be forgotten. Once their professional relationship finished, family loyalty meant any friendship between Luca and I was finished, too. It's all about respect.' In his father's eyes, everything had been about respect. Everything.

How he'd envied the easy affection the two Mastrangelo boys shared with their father. It was the kind of relationship he'd longed for, but for Salvatore Calvetti a sign of affection for his only child consisted of a slap on the back if he pleased him.

'Have you not seen Luca since then?'

'He came to my father's funeral.' He looked away, not wanting her to see the expression on his face reflecting what he felt beneath his skin whenever he thought of his father's funeral. While a tiny part of him had felt relief that he could break free from Salvatore's shadow, he'd mourned the man. Truly mourned him.

If he'd known then what he knew now, he would have lit fireworks by his open graveside in celebration.

'My father's death freed me. It freed Luca and me to resume our old friendship. When we were kids we often used to play cards together, and always said that when we grew up we would open a casino together. We opened our first one three years ago, but then last year he decided he wanted out.'

'Why was that?'

He met her eyes. 'His wife thought I was bad for him.'

Her forehead furrowed. 'He said that?'

'Not in so many words. But it was obvious. She hates my guts.'

Still her forehead furrowed. 'But why?'

'Because I'm a big bad gangster.'

'No, your father was a big bad gangster,' she corrected.

'Even after everything you've witnessed, you still refuse to see it.' He planted a kiss on the end of her nose.

'No, I *do* see it. You are who you are, but you're nowhere near as bad as you like people to think.'

She wouldn't say that if she could read the thoughts going through his mind. Thoughts of revenge, not just against his father but against Luca Mastrangelo. And Pepe.

He would not allow the Mayfair casino to fall into Mastrangelo hands. It was *his* and he would do whatever was needed to ensure it.

'Do I take it that those men are also interested in buying the casino?' Hannah asked, swinging her legs onto his lap.

'I'd heard rumours they were after it. Being there tonight confirmed it.'

'And do I take it you threatened them?' At his surprised glance, she grinned ruefully. 'I might not speak Sicilian, but I can read body language.'

'And you think I have *good* in me?' Rubbing his hand absently over her calf, he couldn't help but notice the little bags that had formed under her eyes. Those little bags made his heart constrict.

This was a woman who worked so hard for such a good purpose she hardly slept. And *she* saw good in *him*?

'You won't hurt them,' she said with simple confidence.

He didn't answer. The one thing he would never do was lie to her. He'd lived a lifetime of lies.

Before she could question his silence, her phone vibrated. Dropping his hand, she reached into her bag.

'Is it work?' he asked, trying hard to keep the edge from his voice. The only time Hannah lost her sweet humour was when he mentioned her excessive use of her phone. On those occasions her claws came out.

She shook her head absently. 'Melanie.'

'She's back from her work trip?'

'Yep. She wants to know if I'm free tomorrow for the last fitting. For my bridesmaid dress,' she added heavily.

'Are you not going to answer?' When it came to work she would fire off a reply the second she read them.

'I suppose I should.'

Before he could question her reluctance, they pulled up outside his hotel.

'Shall we have a bath together?' he asked once they were safely ensconced in his suite.

Hannah's nose wrinkled. She felt all…out of sorts. Right then she needed something sweet to counteract the acidity that had formed in her throat. 'Can we have chocolate-fudge cake first?'

'Hot?'

She smiled. Already he knew her so well. Especially with regard to her hot chocolate-fudge cake addiction, which was fast becoming usurped by her Francesco addiction.

Was this how drug addicts started out? she wondered. A little fix here, a little fix there, then swearing never to do it again? But then temptation was placed right under their nose and they were too weak to resist? Because that was how she felt with him. Unable to resist.

Why did she even need to keep resisting? Addictions were bad things. How could Francesco possibly be classed as bad for her? Her work hadn't suffered for being with him.

The only reason to resist now was for the sake of her heart, and she'd already lost that battle. In reality, she hadn't stood a chance.

She looked at him, her big bear of a man.

What would he say if he knew that, despite all her protestations over not wanting a relationship, she'd fallen for him?

She'd watched him square up to those two men in the

casino and she'd wanted to dive between them and kung fu them into keeping away from him.

The strength of her protectiveness towards him had shocked her.

It was how she used to be with Beth. If you messed with one twin you messed with the other.

And like it had been with Beth, when she was with Francesco she felt safe. She felt complete. It was a different completeness but every bit as powerful.

'Will you come to Melanie's wedding with me?' She blurted out the words before she'd even properly thought of them.

Her heart lurched to see the palpable shock on his face.

'Sorry. Forget I said anything,' she said quickly. 'It's a silly…'

'You took me by surprise, that's all,' he cut in with a shake of his head. 'You want me to come to your sister's wedding?'

'Only if you're not too busy. I just…' She bit her lip. 'I just could do with…'

Francesco didn't know what she was trying to tell him, but the darting of her eyes and the way she wrung her hands together pierced something in him.

'Will there be room for me?' he asked, stalling for time while he tried to think.

A sound like a laugh spluttered from her lips. 'If I tell them I'm bringing a date they'll make room, even if it means sitting one of the grandparents on someone else's lap.'

'Okay,' he agreed, injecting more positivity than he felt inside. 'I'll come with you.'

The gratitude in her eyes pierced him even deeper.

It wasn't until midmorning they got into the enormous bath together. After a night of making love and snatches of tortured sleep, Hannah was happy to simply lie between Francesco's legs, her head resting against his chest, and enjoy the bubbly water.

Her phone, which she'd placed on the shelf above the sink, vibrated.

'Leave it,' he commanded, tightening his hold around her waist.

'It might be important.'

'It will still be there in ten minutes.'

'But…'

'Hannah, this can't continue. You're using your phone as an emotional crutch and it's not good for you.' There was a definite sharpness to his tone.

Since they'd started seeing each other properly, she'd been acutely aware of his loathing for her phone. Not her work, or the research papers or her studying; just her phone.

'I think it's a bit much you calling it an emotional crutch,' she said tightly. 'If one of my patients dies when I'm not on shift, then I want to know—I don't want to get to work and come face-to-face with bereaved parents in the car park or atrium or café or wherever and not know that they've just lost the most precious thing in their lives.'

The edge to his voice vanished. 'Is that what happened to you when Beth died?'

She jerked a nod. 'When Beth was first admitted, the doctor was very clinical in his approach, almost cold.' She fixed her gaze on Francesco's beautiful arms, adoring the way the water darkened the hair and flattened it over the olive skin. 'Beth died in the early hours of the morning, long after that first doctor had finished his shift. Luckily, she was in the care of some of the loveliest, most compassionate doctors and nurses you could wish for. They let us stay with her body for hours, right until the sun came up. I remember we had to go back to the children's ward as we'd left Beth's possessions there when she'd been taken off to Intensive Care. We got into the lift and that first doctor got in with us.'

She paused, swallowing away the acrid bile that formed in her throat.

'He looked right through us. Either he didn't recognise us as the family of the young girl he'd been treating twenty-four hours before, or he did recognise us and just didn't want to acknowledge us. Either way, I hated him for it. My sister was dead and that man didn't even care enough to remember our faces.'

'Do you still hate him?'

She shook her head. 'I understand it now. There are only so many times you can watch a child die before you grow a hard shell. We all do it. The difference is, he let his shell consume him at the expense of the patient. I will *never* allow myself to become like that. I never want any of my patients or their loved ones to think I don't care.'

'That must take its toll on you, though,' he observed. Francesco had only watched one person die: his mother. He'd made it to the hospital in time to say goodbye, but by that point the essence of *her* had already gone, her body kept alive by machines.

It had been the single most distressing event of his life.

To choose a profession where you were surrounded by illness and death... He could hardly begin to comprehend the dedication and selflessness needed to do such a job.

She shrugged, but her grip on his arms tightened. 'We send hundreds more children home healed than we lose. That more than makes up for it.'

He found himself at a loss for what to say.

Hannah had suffered the loss of the most precious person in her life—her twin—and she'd turned her grief into a force for good.

Hadn't he known from the start that she was too good for him? He still knew it, more than ever.

'Beth's death broke something inside me,' she said quietly. 'My parents tried very hard to comfort me, but they were grieving, too, and in any case I pushed them away. Melanie was desperate to comfort me, but I pushed her away, too. Since my accident I can see how badly I've treated my family. I've kept myself apart from them. I've kept myself apart from everyone…until you.'

His chest tightened. 'Your family was happy for you to isolate yourself?'

'No.' Her damp hair tickled his nose. 'They weren't happy. But what could they do about it? They couldn't *make* me.' Her voice became wistful. 'I think I wanted them to force the issue. I was so lost but I couldn't find the way out.…'

There was so much Francesco wanted to say as her words trailed away. None of it would help.

'You're probably right about my phone,' she muttered. 'I guess I have been using it as a crutch. It's easier for me to interact with an object than a human. At least that was the case until I met you.'

She turned her head, resting her cheek on his shoulder as she stared at him. 'I'm so glad you're coming to the wedding with me.'

The very mention of the *W* word was enough to make his stomach roil.

'I've been dreading it for so long now,' she confessed.

'Is Beth the reason you're so anxious about it?' He dragged his question out. 'Because she can't be there?'

Her nails dug into his arms. 'This is the first real family event we've had since she died.' She placed a kiss to his neck and inhaled. 'With you by my side, I think I can endure it without ruining Melanie's day. The last thing I want is to spoil things for her, but I don't think even my poker face will be able to hide my feelings.' She swallowed. 'It's all feeling so raw again.'

Francesco cleared the sourness forming in his throat.

He hadn't bargained on this. None of it was part of his plan, whereby he would see her whilst spending lots of time in London finalising the Mayfair deal, after which they would head their separate ways.

None of this was in the script.

He hadn't for a minute imagined she would start needing him, not his self-sufficient doctor who didn't rely on anyone but herself.

Something gripped at his chest, a kind of panic.

If it wasn't for the tears spilling down her cheeks and the confidences she'd just entrusted him with, he would have dreamed up a good excuse not to go there and then.

But Hannah crying? In his mind there was no worse sight or sound. He would promise her anything to stop it.

Francesco slammed his phone down in fury.

The purchase agreement he'd spent months working on had been blown out of the water, with Godfrey Renfrew admitting he wanted time to 'consider an alternative offer'.

The Mastrangelos were standing in his way.

He picked the receiver up and dialled his lawyer's number. 'I want you to arrange a meeting between me and Luca Mastrangelo,' he said, his words delivered like ice picks. 'Tell him that unless he agrees to meet tomorrow, he will only have himself to blame for the consequences.'

The second he put the phone down, his mobile rang. It was Hannah. *'Ciao,'* he said, breathing heavily through his teeth.

'What's the matter?' she asked, picking up on his tone even though she was in London and he in Palermo.

'Nothing. I'm just busy. What can I do for you?' Looking at the clock on his wall, he could see it was lunchtime. She must be calling him on her break.

'I haven't heard from you in a couple of days. I just wanted to make sure you're okay.' There wasn't any accusation in her voice. All he heard was concern.

'I'm busy, that's all.'

Silence, then, 'Any idea what time you'll be over tomorrow?'

He rubbed his eyes. He'd promised he'd be back in London early Friday evening so they could head straight down to Devon. She'd even booked him a hotel room.

'I'll confirm tomorrow morning,' he said, wishing he could relieve the sharp pain digging in the back of his eyes. He would ensure his meeting with Luca and Pepe took place in the morning. That would give him plenty of time to get to her.

More silence. 'Are you sure you're okay?'

'Go back to your patients, Dr Chapman. I'll see you tomorrow.'

Hannah checked her watch for the umpteenth time. Her bags were all packed, butterflies playing merry havoc in her belly.

She felt sick with nerves and dread. Knowing Francesco would be by her side throughout it all dulled it a little but not as much as it should.

He'd sounded so distant on the phone. The plentiful text messages from him had whittled away to nothing.

Something niggled in her stomach, a foreboding she was too scared to analyse.

Twitching her curtain, relief poured through her to see the large black car pull up outside.

Her relief was short-lived when she opened the door

and saw the serious look on his face. 'You're not coming with me, are you?'

He stepped over the threshold and pushed the door shut behind him. 'I apologise for the short notice, but I have to meet with Luca and Pepe Mastrangelo tomorrow lunchtime. The sale of the Mayfair casino is under threat.'

For long moments she did nothing but stare at him. 'You bastard.'

He flinched, but a cold hostility set over his features. 'I do not have the power to be in two places at once. If I could then I would.'

'Liar,' she stated flatly, although her chest had tightened so much she struggled to find breath.

This could not be happening.

'You could have arranged the meeting for any time you like. Your life doesn't revolve around a set schedule.' Francesco's time was his to do as he pleased. One of the very things she'd been so attracted to had turned around and bitten her hard.

Francesco could do as he liked, and what he liked was to avoid her sister's wedding.

He was asking her to face it alone.

After everything she had confided and all the trust she'd placed in him, he was leaving her to face the wedding on her own.

'It has to be tomorrow.' He raked his hands through his hair. 'I wanted to organise it for today but tomorrow is the only day the three of us can be in the same country at the same time. Time is of the essence. I won't allow the Mastrangelos to steal the casino away from me. I've worked too long on the deal to let it slip through my fingers—it's far too important for me to lose. I've arranged for Mario to drive you to Devon.'

'Don't bother. I'll make my own way there.' She'd

rather cycle on her pushbike. She'd rather walk. 'You can leave now.'

'Hannah, I know you're disappointed. I've gone out of my way to tell you personally—'

'Well, that makes everything all right, then,' she snapped. 'You're blowing me out of the water so you can kneecap some old friends but, hey, no worries, *you told me to my face.*'

'I have spent the best part of a year demolishing my father's empire, eradicating the streets from the evils he peddled,' Francesco said, his voice rising, his cool facade disappearing before her eyes. 'The only business he wanted that he couldn't have was this casino. He did everything in his power to get it, including abducting Godfrey's son, and still he didn't win. But *I will*. It's taken me *months* to gain Godfrey's trust and I will not allow the Mastrangelos to snatch it away from me.'

His father? Hannah had known his relationship with his dead father had been difficult, had seen the way he tensed whenever Salvatore was mentioned, but she'd never suspected the depths of Francesco's animosity towards him.

He paused, his eyes a dark pit of loathing, his malevolence a living, breathing thing. 'You live your life imagining Beth watching over you. Well, I imagine mine with my father watching over me. I like the thought of him staring down watching me destroy everything he built, but more than anything I want him to see me succeed where he failed. I want him turning in his hellish coffin.'

Hannah didn't think she had ever witnessed such hatred before, a loathing that crawled under her skin and settled in the nauseous pit of her belly.

This was the Francesco he had warned her about right at the start. The Francesco she had refused to see.

And now she did see, all she felt was a burning anger that made her want to throw up.

'Go and take your vengeance. Go ruin your old friends. Go and show your dead father how much *better* you are than him by purchasing the very casino he could never have. Let it symbolise how *different* you are to him.'

Shoving him out of the way, she opened the front door. 'Now leave, and don't you *ever* contact me again.'

His chest heaving, he stared at her before his nostrils flared and he strode past her.

'Enjoy your vengeance, Francesco,' she spat. 'Try not to let it choke you.'

He didn't look back.

CHAPTER TWELVE

Hannah fixed the back of her pearl earrings into place, trying desperately hard to contain her shaking hands. Since that awful confrontation with Francesco the night before, it had been a constant battle to stop the tremors racking through her. The long last-minute train journey to Devon had been a constant battle, too—a battle to stop any tears forming for the bastard who'd abandoned her when she needed him most.

She didn't want to think about him. Not now. Not when she was minutes away from leaving for the church to watch her little sister get married.

There was a tap on the door, and Melanie walked into the room carrying a small box.

'How do I look?' she asked, putting the box on the floor, extending her arms and giving a slow twirl.

'Oh, Mel, you look beautiful.' And she did, an angel in white.

'You look beautiful, too.' Careful not to crease each other's dresses—Hannah wore a baby-pink bridesmaid dress—they embraced, then stepped back from each other.

'The cars are here and our bouquets are ready,' Melanie said. Her eyes fixed on Hannah's bedside table, on which rested a photo of Hannah and Beth, aged eight. 'I've got a bouquet for her, too.'

'What do you mean?'

'Beth. I've got her a bouquet, too.'

Hannah had to strain to hear her sister's voice.

'If she was still here she'd be a bridesmaid with you.' A look of mischief suddenly crossed Melanie's face. 'The pair of you would probably follow me down the aisle trying to trip me up.'

A burst of mirth spluttered from Hannah's mouth. She and Beth together had been irrepressible. 'We were really mean to you.'

'No, you weren't.'

'Yes, we were. We hardly ever let you play with us and when we did it was to torment you. I remember we convinced you to let us make you into a princess.'

'Oh, yes! You coloured my hair pink with your felt tip pens and used red crayon as blusher. You treated me like a doll.'

'I'm sorry.'

'Don't be. I was just happy you wanted to play with me.'

'It must have been hard for you, though,' Hannah said, thinking of all the times Melanie had been desperate to join in with their games, how their mum would force them to let her tag along and they would spend the whole time ignoring her. Unless they found a good use for her.

Melanie didn't even pretend not to understand. 'It was hard. I was very jealous. You had each other. You didn't need me.'

Silence rent the room as they both stared at the photo. Despite all her vows, hot tears stung the back of Hannah's eyes. How desperately she wished Beth was there. And how desperately the pathetic side of her wished Francesco was there, too....

Thank God Melanie hadn't grilled her about the latest sudden change to the seating plan, simply giving her a quick hug and a 'No problem.'

Melanie cleared her throat. 'We should get going before we ruin our make-up.'

Looking at her, Hannah could see Melanie's eyes had filled, too, a solitary tear trickling down her cheek.

She reached over to wipe it away with her thumb, then pressed a kiss to her sister's cheek. 'You do look beautiful, Mel. Beth would be insanely jealous.'

Melanie laughed and snatched a tissue from the box on Hannah's bedside table. She blew her nose noisily, then crouched down to the box she'd brought in and removed the lid. 'Here's your bouquet, and here's the one for Beth. I thought you might like to give it to her.'

Hannah sniffed the delicate fragrance.

She looked at her sister. Melanie had been nine when Beth died. A little girl. Now she was a woman less than an hour away from marriage.

How had she missed her own sister growing up? It had happened right before her eyes and she'd been oblivious to it. Melanie had followed Hannah to London. She had been the one to keep the sisterly relationship going—she'd been the one who'd kept the whole family going. Unlike their parents, who still took Hannah's reclusiveness at face value, Melanie at least tried. It was always at her suggestion that they would go out for lunch. It was always Melanie who organised their monthly visits back to Devon, carefully selecting the weekends Hannah wasn't on shift. Melanie, who had never wanted anything more than the company of her big sister.

Her sister. The same flesh and blood as herself and Beth.

Hannah took another sniff of the flowers. 'Do you want to come with me and give them to her?'

'Really?' Melanie was too sweet to even pretend to fake nonchalance.

When it came to visiting Beth, Hannah preferred solitude. Alone, she could chat to her and fill her in on all the family and work gossip.

Since the funeral she had never visited with anyone else.

She had done far too many things alone.

All those wasted years hiding herself away, too numb from the pain of her broken heart to even consider letting anyone in—not her parents, not her sister. No one. And she hadn't even realised she was doing it, pretending to be content in her little cocoon.

She hadn't meant to let Francesco in. If she'd known the risk to her heart, she would have taken his advice at the first turn and found a safer method to start living her life.

But she had let him in. In return he'd dumped her in the cruellest of fashions.

She didn't care about his reasons. He'd left her to face this day alone and she would never forgive him.

Except she wasn't alone....

Her heart had opened for him, but it had also opened for her poor neglected family, who wanted nothing more than to love her. All those years spent hiding her heart from them had been wasted years, she could see that now.

She didn't want to hide any more. She couldn't. She needed them. She *loved* them.

Ironically, Francesco's rejection had helped in an unexpected fashion. She would *not* allow Melanie's big day to be ruined by *him*.

Fixing her old practised smile to her face, she took Melanie's hand in her own and gave it a squeeze. 'Why don't we leave now? We can do it before the ceremony starts.'

Melanie's eyes shone. 'I would really like that.'

'Beth would, too. And so would I.'

* * *

Francesco checked his watch. It was bang on half past one.

In thirty minutes Melanie Chapman would walk down the aisle, followed by her doctor sister.

He swatted the thought away.

Now was not the time to be wondering how Hannah was holding up.

Now was the time for action.

With Mario and Roberto by his side, he strolled through the lobby of the neutral hotel both parties had agreed upon and headed up in the lift to the private suite hired for the occasion.

Two men, equally as large as his own minders, guarded the door.

'Wait here,' he said to his men.

This conversation was private.

Sweeping past them, he stepped into the room and shut the door.

He could taste the malice in the air in his first inhalation.

Luca sat at the long dining table, his black eyes fixing on him.

Pepe leant against a wall, his arms folded.

Hannah would be on her way to the church...

Where had that thought come from?

He'd successfully pushed Hannah out of his mind since he'd left her home. He'd cut her out. He would *not* allow himself to think of her. Or the pain on her face. Or the words she'd said, her implication that he was exactly like his father.

He was not like his father.

If he was anything like his father, Luca and Pepe would both be long dead by now—Pepe when he'd tried to fight him all those years ago, Luca when he'd broken their partnership. He hadn't just broken their partnership, he'd severed their friendship, too.

'Well?' said Luca, breaking the silence. 'You're the one who wanted this meeting. What do you want, Calvetti?'

He'd thought he'd known. The casino. The final piece in the obliteration of Salvatore Calvetti's legacy.

His revenge against the man Francesco had learned too late had used his mother as a punchbag.

As hard as he tried to push her out, the only image in his head was Hannah, lying on the cold concrete and opening her eyes, that serene smile that had stolen his breath.

Stolen his heart.

'Well?' Luca's voice rose. 'What do you want?'

Francesco looked at the two brothers. His old friends. He looked at Pepe, the man whose girlfriend he'd stolen all those years ago. He hadn't known she was still seeing him, but he'd known damn well Pepe had been serious about her.

No wonder Pepe hated him.

He looked back at Luca. His oldest friend. A man who'd found that rare kind of love he would do anything to keep.

The rare kind of love he could have with Hannah.

Could have had if he hadn't abandoned her on the one day she needed him.

He'd known the second she'd asked him to go to the wedding with her that she'd fallen for him.

And he, stupid fool that he was, had thrown it back in her face so cruelly, and for what?

Vengeance against a man who was already rotting in hell.

His heart beat so loudly a drum could have been in his ear.

Hannah wasn't his mother. She wasn't a young, suggestible girl. She was a professional woman with more backbone than anyone he knew.

More important, he wasn't his father, something she'd known from the off.

Only two people in his entire life had looked at him and seen *him*, Francesco, and not just Salvatore's son. One of those had given birth to him. The other was at that very moment bleeding with pain for her dead twin who couldn't be there to celebrate their sister's marriage.

What had he done?

He took a step back and raised his hands. 'It's yours.' At their identical furrowed brows, he allowed the tiniest of smiles to form on his lips. 'The casino. If you want it so badly, you can have it.'

They exchanged glances, their bodies straightening.

'I'm serious. It's all yours. I'll call Godfrey and withdraw my offer.' When he reached the door he looked straight at Pepe. 'I was very sorry to hear about the loss of your baby.'

Pepe's eyes flickered.

Turning back to Luca, Francesco continued, 'Send my regards to Grace. She's far too good for you, but I think you already know that.'

He turned the handle of the door.

'Calvetti.' It was Luca's voice.

Francesco turned one last time.

'The casino's yours. Not ours.'

'Sorry?'

A rueful grin spread over Luca's face. 'Grace and Cara were already furious at us for looking at buying a casino, and they're just about ready to kill us for instigating a war with you. We've already told Godfrey to accept your offer.'

In spite of the agonies going on within him, Francesco managed a grin. 'See? I said Grace was too good for you.'

Just as Hannah was too good for him.

He looked at his watch again. At any moment the bridal party would start their slow walk down the aisle.

'I need to be somewhere.'

Hannah followed Melanie up the aisle, trying very hard to keep a straight face, a hard job considering the train of Melanie's dress was streaked with grass and mud.

Beth was buried in the cemetery attached to this very church, and the pair had left the rest of the bridal party to say a few words to her and leave the bouquet by her headstone.

All those years when she'd refused to visit Beth's grave with anyone... How selfish she'd been.

How glad she was that Melanie had found a man who put her first, who loved her enough to compensate for all the neglect she had suffered at the hands of her big sister. Not that Melanie saw it as neglect. Bless her heart, Melanie understood. It hadn't been said, not in so many words, but it didn't need to be.

In all the years Hannah had been grieving the loss of her twin, she had neglected to recognise there was another person in her life grieving, too—a young woman who was a part of her, just as Beth was. Sure, it wasn't exactly the same—how could it be? But then, what two relationships were ever the same? Their parents loved them equally but the relationships between them all were different. Hannah's relationship with them couldn't be any more different.

She looked at her father, walking with Melanie's arm tucked inside his. She might not be able to see his face but she could perfectly imagine the radiant smile on his face. And there was her mother, on her feet in a front pew, still a beautiful woman, looking from her beloved husband to her two surviving daughters, tears already leaking down her cheeks.

And there was the groom, his legs bouncing, his nerves

and excitement palpable. When he knelt before the priest by the side of his fiancée, titters echoed throughout the church at the *HE* written in white on the sole of his left shoe, and the *LP* on the right.

So much love. So much excitement for a new life being forged together.

As they exchanged their vows, the tears she'd successfully kept at bay since that terrible argument with Francesco broke free.

According to Francesco's satnav, the route from London to Devon should take three hours and forty-five minutes by car. By motorbike, he estimated he could make it in two hours.

What he hadn't accounted for was stationary traffic as hordes of holidaymakers took advantage of the late English summer to head to the coast.

This was a country of imbeciles, he thought scathingly as he snaked his way around motionless cars. Why couldn't they all be sensible like Hannah and travel down on the Friday night when the roads were empty?

The ceremony would be over by now, the wedding breakfast in full swing.

Hannah needed air. Her lungs felt too tight.

She'd tried. She really had. She'd smiled throughout the ceremony and wedding breakfast, held pleasant conversations with countless family members and old friends she hadn't seen in years. The number-one question she'd received was a variant of 'Have you met a nice man yet?' While she'd answered gracefully, 'Not yet, but I'm sure I will one day,' each time she was asked it felt as if a thorn were being pressed deep into her heart.

Now all the guests had congregated at the bar while the

function room was transformed for the evening bash, she saw her opportunity for escape.

She stepped out into the early-evening dusk and sat on a bench in the hotel garden. She closed her eyes, welcoming the slight breeze on her face.

Five minutes. That was all she needed. Five minutes of solitude to clamp back down on her emotions.

'Can I join you?'

Opening her eyes, she found her mother standing before her.

Unable to speak, she nodded.

'It's been a beautiful day,' her mum commented.

Hannah nodded again, scared to open her mouth lest she would no longer be able to hold on.

How could Francesco have left her alone like this?

How could she have got him so wrong?

She'd been so convinced he would never hurt her.

She'd been right about the physical aspect. In that respect he'd given her nothing but pleasure. Emotionally, though... he'd ripped her apart.

For the first time in fifteen years she'd reached out to someone for help. He'd known what a massive thing that was for her and still he'd abandoned her, and for what? For revenge on someone who wasn't even alive to see it.

Had she been too needy? Was that it? How could she know? She had nothing to compare it to. Until she'd barged her way into his life, she'd had no form of a relationship with anyone. Not even her family. Not since Beth...

'Why did you let me hide away after Beth died?' she asked suddenly. Francesco's probing questions about her relationship with her parents had been playing on her mind, making her question so many things she'd never considered before.

She felt her mother start beside her.

A long silence formed until her mum took Hannah's hand into her own tentatively, as if waiting for Hannah to snatch it away. 'That's a question your father and I often ask. When Beth died, we knew, no matter the pain we were going through and Mel was going through, that it was nothing compared to what you were living with. You and Beth... you were two peas in a pod. She was you and you were her.'

Hannah's chin wobbled.

'When you said you wanted to be a doctor, we were happy you had something to focus on. When you first hid yourself away, saying you were studying, we thought it was a good thing.' She rummaged in her handbag for a tissue and dabbed her eyes. 'We should have handled it better. We were all grieving, but we should never have allowed you to cut yourself off. At the time, though, we couldn't see it. It was so gradual that by the time we realised how isolated you'd become, we didn't know how to reach out to you anymore. To be honest, I still don't. I wish I could turn the clock back to your teenage years and insist you be a part of the family and not some lodger who shared the occasional meal with us.'

'I wish I could, too,' Hannah whispered. She gazed up at the emerging stars, then turned to look at her mother. 'Mum, can I have a hug?'

Her mum closed her eyes as if in prayer before pulling Hannah into her embrace, enveloping her tightly in that remembered mummy smell that comforted her more than any word could.

Hannah swallowed the last of her champagne. The bubbles playing on her tongue reminded her of Francesco. The optics behind the bar reminded her of Francesco. The man who'd just stepped into the function room, where the dancing was now in full swing, also reminded her of Francesco.

Unable to bear the reminder, she turned her attention back to the party surrounding her. The women from Melanie's hen party had hit the dance floor, dragging her dad up there with them. She couldn't stop the grin forming on her face as she watched his special brand of dad dancing. At least she knew where she got her rhythm from.

Why wasn't she up there with them?

Why was she hiding by the bar, observing rather than joining in?

She'd made it through the day with what was left of her shattered heart aching, but she'd *made* it. She'd come through the other side and she was still standing. She hadn't fallen apart at the seams.

A record that had been hugely popular when she was a kid came on. Her grin widening, Hannah weaved through the tables to the dance floor and grabbed her father's hands. His answering smile was puzzled, shocked, even, but delighted all the same.

Their special brand of nonrhythmic dancing took off, a crowd quickly forming around them, the bride and groom hitting the floor, too.

She could do this. She could be a part of life. She didn't have to sit alone on the sidelines.

One of her sister's hen party tapped Hannah on the shoulder. 'Isn't that the man from Calvetti's?' she yelled above the music, pointing across the room.

Following the pointing finger, Hannah's heart jolted to see the tall figure she'd spotted leaning against the wall watching the dancing. Watching *her*.

She gave an absent nod in response, tuning out everything around her—everything except him.

Francesco.

Her stomach lurched heavily, feeling as if it had become detached from the rest of her.

He began to move, snaking his way round the packed tables, revellers parting on his approach in a manner that evoked the strongest sense of déjà vu.

Her heart flipped over to see him so groomed and utterly gorgeous in a snazzy pinstriped suit, the top buttons of his crisp blue shirt undone, exposing the top of his broad chest and the cross he wore around his neck....

Up close he looked in control and terrifying, the intent in his eyes showing he could eat her alive if she refused him anything.

Francesco crossed the dividing line onto the dance floor.

After the road trip from hell, he'd finally made it to her.

Nothing had come easy that day, the puncture on his tyre the last straw. By the time the helicopter had illegally landed to collect him, he'd been ready to rip someone's head off.

At last he stood before her. She'd frozen on the spot, her eyes big hazel pools of pain and bewilderment.

What had he done to her?

He had no idea what was being played by the DJ and nor did he care. When he placed his hands on Hannah's hips and pulled her to him, the sound tuned out and he moved her in a rhythm all their own.

She looked so vulnerable in her traditional bridesmaid dress. She trembled in it, rigid in his arms yet quivering.

He could feel eyes from all directions fixed on them.

'What are you doing here?' she asked, not looking at him.

'I want us to talk.'

'I don't want to be anywhere near you.'

'I know.' He breathed her scent in. 'But *I* need to be near *you*.'

She moved to escape his arms but he tightened his hold, continuing to move her around the floor. 'I'm not letting you go anywhere, not until you've given me the chance to speak.'

'I'm not speaking to you here,' she hissed into his ear, her warm breath sending completely inappropriate tingles racing over his skin. 'This is my sister's wedding. These guests here are my family and my sister's friends.'

'And I should have been with you today, getting to know them, instead of leaving you to face it on your own, but I'm the bastard who let his thirst for revenge cause pain to the one person in the world he loves.'

He stopped dancing and looked at her. The pain in her eyes had gone, only stark bewilderment remaining.

'You,' he emphasised. 'I love *you*. I should have trusted fate when it brought you to me.'

'I don't want to hear it.' Her voice was hoarse, her cheeks flushed.

Her resistance was nothing less than he deserved. He released his tight hold and stepped back, keeping his hands on her arms so she couldn't run.

'Remember when I gave you five minutes of *my* time?' he said, reminding her of that time a month ago when she'd first begged for five minutes. If he'd known then what those five minutes would lead to, he would have locked himself away in his office without a second thought. What an arrogant fool he had been. 'Now I am asking for five minutes of *your* time.'

Had it really only been a month ago that she'd propositioned him?

How could his entire world transform in such a small timeframe?

'Believe me, if I could have that time again I would do everything differently,' she said, wriggling out of his hold. 'Let's go sit in the garden. But only because I don't want to have a scene in front of my family.'

* * *

The breeze had picked up since Hannah had sat in the garden with her mother. Now the evening party was in full swing, the peace she'd found then had gone, music and laughter echoing through the windows.

She sat on the same bench. A bunch of kids had escaped the party and were having a game of football with an empty can.

Francesco sat next to her, keeping a respectable distance. All the same, she could feel his heat. How she wished she didn't respond to him so physically. Her emotional reactions to him were bad enough without her treacherous body getting in on the act, too.

'Go on, then, what did you want to talk about?' she said, making a silent vow to not say another word for the duration of the next five minutes. If he started spouting any more nonsense about loving her she would walk away.

If he loved her he would never have let her face this day on her own.

'I want to tell you about my father,' Francesco said, surprising her with his opening thread.

Despite her vow to remain mute, she whispered, 'Your father?'

He breathed heavily. 'I always knew what a bastard he was, but he was my father and I respected him. God help me but I loved him. All I ever wanted was his respect. I turned a blind eye to so many of his activities but turned the blindest eye to what was happening right under my own roof.'

His eyes held hers, the chocolate fudge hard, almost black.

'I always knew my father was a violent man. To me that was normal. It was our way of life. I knew he craved respect. Again, that was normal. What I did not know until after his death four years ago was that he was one of mainland Europe's biggest suppliers of drugs. That was a blow, enough to make me despise him, but not enough to destroy all my memories of the man. But what I learned just a year ago when I discovered my mother's diaries was that he beat her throughout their marriage, cheated on her, and fed her the drugs that eventually killed her.'

When he reached for her hand she didn't pull away, not even when he clasped it so tightly she feared for her blood supply.

'She was seventeen when they married, an innocent. He was twenty-three years older and a brute from the start.' He practically spat the words out. 'He forced himself on her on their wedding night. He beat her for the first time on their honeymoon. I wish I'd known, but my mother did everything in her power to protect me from seeing too much. As a child it was normal for my mother to be bruised. We would laugh at how clumsy she was, but it was all a lie.'

He shook his head and dragged his fingers through his hair. 'I spent three days reading her diaries. When I finished I was filled with so much hate for the man. And *guilt*—how could I have been so blind? The man I hero-worshipped was nothing but a drug-peddling wife beater. He *wanted* her hooked—it was a means to control her. I swear if he hadn't been dead I would have killed him myself using my bare hands.'

Hannah shivered. Oh, poor, poor Francesco. She'd known he hated his father, but this? This was worse than she could ever have imagined.

Suddenly he let go of her hand and palmed her cheeks. 'I have spent the past eleven months eradicating everything that man built. Everything. The parties stopped, the womanising stopped. All I wanted was vengeance for my mother and, even though my father was rotting in hell, I was determined to destroy what was his. I'd already closed his drug dens, but I resolved to annihilate everything else—the armouries, the so-called legitimate businesses that were in fact a front for money laundering—every last brick of property. The one thing I wanted above all else, though, was the Mayfair casino.'

Here, his eyes seemed to drill into hers. 'Years ago, my father tried to get that casino. It was the only failure of his life. He tried everything to get his hands on that place, but Godfrey Renfrew refused to sell it to such a notorious gangster. That failure was a large thorn in my father's side. For me to purchase that same property would mean I had succeeded where he had failed, proof that I was a better man than him.'

'So you've won,' she said softly. 'You've got your vengeance.'

'No.' He shook his head for emphasis. 'I walked into that room with the Mastrangelos today and knew I had lost. I had lost because I had lost *you*. How could I be a better man than him when I had let the most important person in my world down for the sake of vengeance?'

He brushed his lips against hers, the heat of his breath filling her senses, expanding her shrivelled heart.

'After speaking with the Mastrangelos, I called Godfrey earlier and withdrew my offer for the casino,' he whispered. 'I don't want it anymore. It's tainted. All I want is you. That's if you'll have me. I wouldn't blame you if you didn't.' He sighed and nuzzled into her cheek. 'You asked me once if you scared me. The truth is you did—you scared me because you made me feel, and because I knew I wasn't worthy of you. The only real relationship I have as a reference is my parents', and witnessing that was like living in one of Dante's circles of hell. You deserve so much better.'

'Not all marriages and relationships are like that.'

'Intellectually, I know that. Emotionally, though, it's

taken me a lot longer to accept it. I wanted to protect you from me. I looked at you and saw the innocence my mother had before she married my father. I didn't want to taint you.'

'How could you do that? You are not your father, Francesco. You're a mixture of both your parents and the uniqueness that is *you*. You're just you. No one else.'

He almost crushed her in his embrace. 'I swear I'll never hurt you again. Never. *You* make me a better man. Even if we leave here and head our separate ways, I will still be a better man for having known you.'

Tears pricked her eyes. Her heart felt so full she now feared it could burst.

Head their separate ways? Was that really what she wanted?

'I know how important your work is to you and I would never want to get in the way of that. Medicine is your life, but what I want to know—*need* to know—is if you can fit me into your life, too. Forget what I said about you not fitting into my world—it's *your* world *I* need to fit into. Let me in, I beg of you. I'm not perfect, not by any stretch of the imagination, but I swear on my mother's memory that I will love and respect you for the rest of my life.'

Hannah's chin wobbled. But she kept it together, refusing to let the tears fall. All the same, her voice sounded broken to her own ears. 'I love that you're not perfect.'

He stilled and pulled away to look at her. His eyes glittered with questions.

'Neither of us is perfect but…' She took a deep breath, trying to keep a hold of her racing heart. If Francesco, her big, arrogant bear of a man, could put his heart and pride on the line… She cupped his warm cheek. 'I think you're perfect for me.'

She'd barely got the words out before his mouth came

crashing down on hers, a kiss of such passion and longing that this time the tears really did fall.

'Don't cry, *amore*. Don't cry.' Francesco wiped her tears away and pressed his lips to her forehead. He wrapped his arms around her and she nestled her cheek against his chest.

He gave a rueful chuckle. 'I can't believe I worried about *you* getting burned. I should have known from the start—deep down I think I did—that, of the two of us, I was the more likely to be.'

'Oh, no, but you were right,' she confessed. 'And I'm glad I was so blasé about your concerns because if I'd known how badly you *would* burn me I would have run a mile.'

She tilted her chin back up to look at him. She felt light, as if the weight that had been compressing her insides for what felt like for ever had been lifted. 'You've brought me back to life and let colour back into my world. You make me whole and I want to be in your life, too. Your past, everything you've been through has shaped you into the man you are today and that's the man I've fallen in love with.'

'You really love me?'

For the first time Hannah saw a hint of vulnerability in Francesco's cool, confident exterior.

'More than anything. I didn't think I needed anyone. You've shown me that I do. Not just you, but my family, too.' She kissed his neck then whispered into his ear, 'You've also weaned me off my addiction to my phone. I've only checked it three times today.'

He threaded his long fingers through her hair, a deep laugh escaping his throat that deepened when he snagged a couple of knots. 'If I could trust myself not to break every bone in his body, I would pay another visit to that bastard who knocked you off your bike and thank him.'

'For bringing us together?'

'The stars aligned for us that morning.'

'Shame about my broken collarbone and concussion.'

'Not forgetting your poor finger.'

She giggled. She hadn't thought of her finger in weeks. 'I'm surprised you let him walk away without any injury.'

'He took one look at me in his doorway and virtually wet himself. I didn't need to touch him. If the same thing were to happen to you now, I doubt I would be so restrained.'

'Yes, you would,' she chided, rubbing her nose into his linen shirt.

'And you know that how?'

'Because you would never hurt me, and to cause physical injury to another human, especially in my name, would be to hurt me.'

'You still believe that? After what I did to you last night, you still believe in me?'

'I believe it more than ever.' And she did. She, more than anyone, knew the hold the past had on the present. All that mattered was that they didn't allow the past to shape their futures. 'In any case, I bet he'll spend the rest of his life having nightmares that you'll turn up on his doorstep again.'

'Good. He deserves it.' He gave a humourless chuckle. 'We should invite him to our wedding.'

'Why, are we getting married?'

'Too right we are. I love you, Dr Chapman, and I will love you for the rest of my life.'

'I love you, too, Signor Calvetti.'

He kissed her again. 'Dottore Hannah Calvetti. It has a nice ring to it.'

'Hmm…' Her lips curved into a contented smile. Francesco was right. It had a wonderful ring to it.

EPILOGUE

HANNAH WALKED CAREFULLY up the steep steps to the front door of the villa, happily inhaling the scent emitted by the overabundance of ripe lemon trees.

Francesco opened the door before she got to the top.

'Buonasera, Dottore Calvetti,' he said.

'Good evening, Signor Calvetti,' she replied, before slipping into fluent Sicilian-Italian. 'How has Luciano been today?'

'An angel. Well, he's been an angel since I relieved the nanny. I think he might have given her an extra grey hair or two today. He's definitely worn himself out—he fell asleep fifteen minutes ago. But enough of the small talk—how did you do?'

She couldn't hide the beam that spread across her face. 'I got the job!'

Francesco's face spread into an identical grin. He drew her to him and kissed her, then rubbed his nose to hers. 'I knew you could do it, you clever lady. In fact, Tino is at this moment preparing your favourite meal to celebrate.'

'Mussels in white wine?'

He nodded with a definite hint of smugness. 'Followed by hot chocolate-fudge cake.'

'I love you!' Tino, their chef, made the best chocolate-fudge cake in the world.

He laughed and tapped her bottom. 'Go shower and get changed. I'll open a bottle of wine.'

This time it was she who kissed him, hard.

'Before I forget, Melanie messaged me earlier,' she said. 'They can definitely come for the weekend.'

'Great. Let me know the times and I'll get the jet over to England for them.'

With a spring in her step, Hannah climbed the stone staircase and headed down the uneven corridor to their bedroom. As she passed their eighteen-month-old son's nursery, she poked her head through the door to find him in deep sleep. He didn't stir when she lowered the side of the cot to press a gentle kiss to his cheek. 'Night, night, sleep tight,' she whispered before slipping back out.

She opened her bedroom door and there, on her dressing table, was the most enormous bunch of roses she had ever seen, huge even by Francesco's standards.

His faith in her never ceased to amaze her.

Luciano had come into their lives more quickly than either had anticipated. Within two months of their marriage she'd fallen pregnant, which hadn't been all that surprising considering the laissez-faire approach to contraception they'd adopted.

When it came time for Hannah to take maternity leave, they'd uprooted to Sicily. It had been agreed that when her maternity was up they would move back to London. Except…she'd fallen in love with Sicily, with the people and the language. Besides, it was easier for Francesco to run his empire from there, so she saw more of him during the week than she had in London, and they hated having to spend nights away from each other.

Full of determination, she'd set about learning the language. She'd employed a tutor and within weeks had refused to answer Francesco or any of his staff unless they spoke in their native tongue. She had been determined to master it. And they had all been determined to help her.

'I got the job, Beth,' she said, speaking aloud in English, just in case Beth hadn't bothered to learn Italian with her. Now that she couldn't visit her grave so regularly, she had taken to simply talking to her whenever the mood struck. Sometimes, in her dreams, her twin spoke back. 'I'm going to work at the hospital on the children's ward here in Palermo and train for my consultancy here, too.'

All the pieces had come together.

She could not be happier.

* * * * *

KING'S RANSOM

JACKIE ASHENDEN

To the cat. For absolutely no reason at all.

CHAPTER ONE

Ajax

I WAS TEN years old the first time I suspected my father was a criminal.

At thirteen he showed me the truth.

That's when I decided I was going to take him down. But if you want to take down a man like Augustus King you have to do it right. You can't leave anything behind. A crime empire is like a Hydra—cut off the head and twenty more sprout.

It took me nearly two decades to cut off every single head. Yet I did. And I put that prick in jail once and for all.

But surviving decades of being the oldest son of the biggest crime lord in Sydney doesn't leave a man without scars, and mine ran deep.

That was okay, though. Scars were reminders of the big picture and my big picture involved keeping my brothers and my city safe. Staying vigilant for danger. Always on the lookout for threats.

Threats such as William goddamn White, my father's enemy and the last head of the Hydra.

Dad had been in jail five years and I'd been legit

ever since, running one of the fastest growing property development companies in Sydney, and, as much as I wanted to, I couldn't simply cut that head off the way I preferred. Not if I wanted to avoid jail myself.

No, I had to use other methods.

I leaned against the wall of the ballroom of one of Sydney's top hotels, studying the glittering, couture-wearing crowd all gathered to celebrate the formation of a new charity.

I hadn't been invited—no one would invite a King to a swanky charity ball like this one—but I'd shown up anyway and they'd been too afraid of me to turn me away.

The King past was something my two brothers and I were trying to overcome, but it came in handy at times. And I wasn't above using it, especially when it came to driving home to the cream of Sydney society that the King brothers were up-and-coming and they couldn't ignore us any more.

But that wasn't the only reason I was here.

That other reason was sitting across the ballroom from me, at a table surrounded by goons in suits trying hard not to look like goons in suits and failing.

Miss Imogen White, William White's daughter and the most guarded heiress in the entire city.

The chick was like Rapunzel in her tower—no one was getting inside. Both figuratively *and* literally. She was the apple of her father's eye and he made sure she stayed pure and pristine, his perfect Princess.

Sadly for White, I was about to storm his daughter's pretty little castle and sully the fuck out of it.

He'd managed somehow to stay out of the law's reach following the collapse of Dad's empire and he'd been waiting in the shadows ever since. Not drawing attention, quietly trying to resurrect Augustus King's filthy legacy.

A legacy I was going to destroy once and for all.

That motherfucker was going *down* and I was going to use his daughter to do it.

I tilted my head, studying her as she sat on her chair, all alone apart from her goons.

Five foot nothing, long blonde hair the colour of pale corn silk. Big green eyes that watched the rest of the room and the people in it like they were a cage full of tigers and she was a goat tethered to a stake.

Interesting that her father had managed to get her an invite and that she was attending without him. Almost made me think that she *was* playing the part of a goat tethered to a stake.

Bait. To lure someone out.

Me, perhaps? But then, probably not. As far as White was concerned, I was too busy running King Enterprises, my property empire, to worry about him—an illusion I'd worked hard to cultivate to hide my real motivations.

Whosever bait she was, Imogen was pretty in her plain white cocktail frock. A perfect little doll. Pale and virginal and pure. Except not totally pure, not with the kind of sulky pink mouth that would look great wrapped around a man's cock.

Yes, she was lovely, but she was also nothing but leverage.

Her father's weapon that I was going to turn back on him, using her to ensure that whatever he was doing in those shadows, whatever plans he was hatching, he needed to stop immediately and get the hell out of Sydney.

Only then would I release his daughter.

And if he didn't? I'd take that carefully guarded virginity of hers and make her mine. Because if there was one thing I knew about William White, it was that he'd rather slit his own throat than have a King touch his daughter.

Especially me. As far as he was concerned, I was still rough and brutal, still only a few steps away from the violence that had made me.

He wouldn't want his daughter anywhere near me.

As plans went it wasn't all that subtle, but I'd been searching for some legal way to take that bastard down and hadn't managed to find anything I could use against him.

No, his daughter was it. My plan to protect everything I'd built.

Ten years ago, I could have headed over to her and slung her over my shoulder and no one would have stopped me. Even the police would have given me a wide berth—they didn't want to mess with a King.

But it wasn't ten years ago. It was now, and even though I'd never have considered using Dad's kind of tactics—I was, after all, a different man—the stakes were too high to risk failure, which meant the end justified any means.

Such as kidnapping William White's daughter from a ballroom full of people.

Oh, yeah, and not get caught.

I glanced away from the scaredy-cat Princess and looked towards the bar area of the ballroom. Sure enough, there was my younger brother Leon, along with his wife, Vita. They were commanding a lot of attention, which was the reason I'd demanded the pair of them attend the ball with me.

They could take the heat while I did my thing unnoticed.

Leon would be pissed if he knew what I was planning, especially given his own past, but what he didn't know wouldn't hurt him. This was my idea and not telling him would allow all the responsibility to fall on me if it turned to shit.

The only person who'd get hurt here was William fucking White.

I shifted against the wall, checking on Imogen again.

She was sitting up so straight and still, her hands clasped in her lap, holding herself rigid, except for one little white-satin-covered foot that was tapping to the music that filtered through the ballroom. Then it stopped and she looked down at herself, colour staining her pale cheeks. As if she'd only just realised what she was doing and caught herself. As if tapping her foot to the music was a bad thing.

Another man might have felt sorry for her sitting there all by herself, not even able to enjoy the music. But I didn't. I couldn't afford to. She was a tool for me to use. That was all.

On the table near her was a glass of iced water that I'd paid one of the waiters to keep refilled. Eventually, given the amount of times she'd emptied the thing, she'd need to visit the bathroom and when she did…

Right on cue, she glanced at her bodyguards and slid off the chair, gesturing towards the exit to the bathrooms. One of them nodded and jerked his head at the man standing next to him, the two of them then falling into place behind her as she moved towards the exit.

Good.

Taking on five of them would be tricky, but two? Easy.

I stepped away from the wall and ducked out through a nearby doorway that led to the same corridor where the bathrooms were located, reaching the ladies' bathroom in time to see her vanish into it. The two guards stationed themselves outside.

Giving them a minute or two, I took out the cap I had in the back pocket of my suit pants and put it on, pulling it down to hide my face, then I moved in for the kill.

I took them down as quickly and as quietly as possible then shoved their unconscious bodies into the empty men's bathroom, pulling shut the door behind me and breaking the handle so they couldn't get out.

That done, I moved over to the ladies' and stepped inside.

Luckily it was empty, apart from White's little Princess, standing at the bank of sinks opposite the door. She was in the process of washing her hands, her head bent.

I closed the door silently behind me and locked it for good measure, then I leaned back against it, watching her, waiting to see how long it would take her to notice me.

A good minute as it turned out.

She was humming something under her breath, a cheerful-sounding pop song, completely distracted. And it wasn't until she'd dried her hands and had leaned forward to study her reflection that her gaze met mine in the mirror.

The humming stopped, her green eyes going big and filling with shock.

'Don't scream,' I said calmly. 'I'm not going to hurt you. However, I might change my mind if you try to call for help. Is that understood?'

Her eyes widened even further, her mouth in a soft pink O. But she gave a very slight nod to show me that she did, staring at me in the mirror all the while as if I was the devil himself.

I stared back.

Her skin was pale, like cream, and her eyelashes were tipped with gold. She had a conventional prettiness that was saved from being bland by that quite frankly carnal mouth and the delicate little mole sitting just above it.

There was an energy to her, an electricity that reminded me of a live wire about to spit sparks.

Somewhere deep inside me, interest tightened.

What would it feel like to put my hands on her and touch that electricity for myself? Would it shock the dead parts of me back to life?

Shit, touching her wasn't the point of the kidnapping, no matter the threat I was going to deliver to her father. Besides, pure princesses—live wires or not—had never been my type. I liked a woman who knew her way around a man's cock and who didn't mind getting rough with it, not a wide-eyed virgin like this one.

I dismissed the thoughts. Right now, getting her out of here with the minimum of fuss was my priority.

'W-where are my bodyguards?' Her voice was clear with an inexplicably sexy roughness to it.

'I dealt with them.' I stepped away from the door-frame and straightened to my full height, her gaze following every move I made.

The shock had begun to drain from her pale face, leaving behind it an expression I didn't recognise. '*Both* of them?' She sounded incredulous, as if I'd done something incredibly difficult.

'Yes. They're in the men's room with the door locked.' I took a step towards her. 'They're not coming to save you, little one.'

She didn't move. 'You're Ajax King.'

'You've heard of me.' I took another step.

'Of course. My dad hates you.'

'The feeling's mutual.' I was close now, standing right behind her, watching her face in the mirror.

Her lashes lowered. Then she turned around, her head tipping back, looking straight up at me.

She was very small, the top of her head barely reaching my shoulders, and the pale skin of her cheeks had gone pink, deepening the vivid green of her eyes. They were glowing. They were full-on fucking glowing.

Maybe that's when I recognised her expression, the one that wasn't fear or shock or anger, or any of the other emotions I'd expected when I'd first stepped inside.

No. What I saw in her face was unconcealed awe.

Not the reaction I normally got. People were either afraid of me or they loathed me. But not this green-eyed virginal Princess. She looked at me like I was the second coming of Christ.

For some reason, my cock liked that very much indeed.

Fuck. That was all I needed. Desire wasn't supposed to be part of this plan and I didn't want it to be. The goal was protecting my city and my brothers, not screwing a wide-eyed little ingénue.

Ignoring my disreputable dick, I gave her the stare I usually gave to those who thought they could argue with my decisions. 'Okay, here's the deal,' I began. 'You're going to need to—'

'Why are you here?'

I blinked at her interruption. Another thing that people knew better than to do. 'What?'

'I mean, why are you here? In the women's bathroom?'

'Well, I—'

'You *do* know it's the women's bathroom, don't you?'

'Yeah, I know it's the—'

'Are you here for me?'

I gritted my teeth. 'You're going to have to stop interrupting me.'

A line appeared between her pale silky brows, the electric energy of her intensifying somehow. 'Sorry, I didn't mean to. I just really need to know.'

Hell, what was I doing, standing here letting her pepper me with pointless questions? I was supposed to be kidnapping her, for fuck's sake.

'Yeah,' I growled, taking another step closer, looming over her, hoping she'd get the idea she was supposed to be scared and not keep looking at me like I was Captain fucking America. 'I'm here for you.'

Her eyes glowed even more and she'd gone even

pinker, as if I was the man of her dreams and I'd just asked her out.

'Don't look so fucking pleased,' I said harshly. 'I'm not asking you to dance. I'm here to kidnap you.'

That gorgeous mouth of hers dropped open. 'Kidnap me?' she echoed, looking astonished. Then, before I could speak, she grinned. 'Oh, my God, that's excellent!'

CHAPTER TWO

Imogen

'What do you mean, "excellent"?' Ajax King's mesmerising blue eyes had narrowed into shards of ice and there was offence in his deep, rough voice.

Weird. You'd have thought he'd be happy that I wanted to go with him without making a screaming fuss.

Obviously not.

Then again, I didn't have time to be thinking about whether he'd be offended or not. All I was conscious of was finally—freaking finally!—here was the opportunity I'd been searching more than two years for.

The opportunity to get away from my bloody father.

My shuddering heartbeat was going hell for leather, adrenaline pulsing through me.

'There's no time,' I said hurriedly, tilting my head to the side so I could see past his massive, broad figure to the door. 'Dad's other guys will notice I haven't come back and they'll come after me. So if we're going to leave, we have to leave now.'

'Now wait just a fucking minute—'

But I had no fucking minutes to waste.

I reached for his hand and pulled him over to the door. Or at least I tried to. Bit difficult when he wouldn't let himself be pulled.

Dammit.

I turned back, fear beginning to thread through my excitement. 'Please. If you're going to kidnap me then you have to do it now. Come on!' I tugged on his hand again.

He didn't move, only pinned me with those icy blue eyes. 'You actually *want* me to kidnap you?'

Seriously? He was asking me stupid questions now?

'Would I be asking you to do it if I didn't want you to?' I pulled on his hand yet again. 'Come *on*.'

But it was like trying to pull on a mountain. The damn man wouldn't budge.

Fear tightened inside me. If we didn't leave now the rest of my bodyguards were going to come looking and they'd find me. And then they'd try to stop me, and my chance of escape would be gone.

I'd be back to living in my gilded cage, where I couldn't move a muscle without five guards springing into action. Where I had to watch my behaviour so assiduously that it was easier to stay in than go out. It was a cage I hadn't noticed get smaller and smaller as the years progressed. Not until the day I'd realised exactly what kind of man my father was and that if I stayed in the cage any longer I was going to get crushed.

I'd go back to being powerless. Back to being used. Back to being so lonely it made my soul ache.

No, I couldn't do it. I wouldn't.

Right here was my opportunity to escape and I was taking it.

Ajax King was my father's greatest enemy so who

better to help me? He'd been watching me all evening—I'd noticed since I'd nothing else to do—and now I knew why.

It couldn't have been more perfect.

Right then, someone knocked on the door and I froze, fear an iceberg floating in the centre of my chest.

'Miss White?' a male voice asked. 'Are you in there?'

Shit. It was Colin, one of my guards.

I turned back to Ajax, standing near the vanity unit, so tall his head almost brushed the ceiling. He stared at me from underneath the cap he wore, his expression impassive. His rough features were intensely compelling. A sharp, hard jaw and strong blade of a nose. High cheekbones. Those deep set, amazing blue eyes. Not typically handsome. Very, *very* masculine, and the look he was giving me…

I felt an odd flash of something. A crackle over my skin, like electricity. It was unexpected and strange so I ignored it, too worried about what he was going to do to pay attention to it.

Would he change his mind? Give me back to them?

I swallowed, my mouth dry, and I gave him a pleading look. *Please help me. Please.*

'Miss White?' Colin asked again, sharper this time. 'Are you in there?'

Ajax shot a glance at the door then back at me.

Then suddenly he pulled me towards him so I was only inches away from his massive, muscular figure. He lowered his head, his mouth near my ear. 'Do as I say,' he murmured. 'And I'll get you out of here.'

I blinked at the wall of white cotton in front of me. I hadn't been this close to a man in years. Possibly I hadn't been this close to a man *ever*.

It was weird. He was very, *very* warm and he smelled good. A spicy, woody scent that for some reason made the iceberg in my chest start to melt and calmed my rising panic.

'Now, put your arms out. And don't say a word.'

His breath on my skin made goosebumps rise along my neck and shoulders, that crackling sensation getting more intense.

I didn't have time to think about it so I put my arms out obediently. Quickly, he shrugged out of his black suit jacket and, before I could figure out what he was going to do with it, he'd put it on me.

Nearly forgetting that I wasn't supposed to speak, I opened my mouth to ask him what he was doing. But he whipped the cap off his head and put it on mine, then, with surprising skill for a guy, he coiled my hair up underneath so it wasn't showing.

I blinked up at him. Way, *way* up at him.

His eyes were the most incredible blue. The pupils had a dark ring of midnight around them before lightening up towards the iris, a shade that was exactly the same as the sky on a perfect winter's day. They were made even more noticeable by the straight black brows and thick black lashes that framed them.

My heart gave a weird thump.

I didn't know much about him, only that my father hated his guts because Dad and Augustus King had been rivals until Augustus had finally gone to jail. Dad had been hoping that once Augustus had gone he'd be able to grab what was left of his empire and take it for himself—he was nothing if not opportunistic.

But apparently Ajax King kept getting in the way.

Maybe that was why I hadn't screamed when Ajax

had appeared in the bathroom. Why I'd believed him when he said he wouldn't hurt me.

He might have once been the heir to the biggest crime empire in Sydney, but he wasn't now and any enemy of my father was a friend of mine.

Of course, I hadn't been thinking straight when he'd appeared in the doorway and clearly I wasn't thinking straight now if all it took to make my heart thump was one look into his eyes.

Forgetting that I'd promised not to speak, I opened my mouth to ask him what was going on but, before I could, he bent and picked me up in his arms.

My stomach dropped away, the world lurching around me; every question I'd been going to ask vanished from my head.

I'd never been held by a man. Couldn't remember the last time I'd been held, full stop.

Had it been this hot? Because that's all I was conscious of. An intense, stunning heat surrounding me. From the hard torso I was lying against and the strong arms locked around me. It made something restless and antsy inside me go utterly still.

I caught my breath.

'Hide your face against my chest,' Ajax murmured before heading straight to the door.

My brain didn't seem able to process the instruction. Hide my face? Why? And what was he doing? Didn't he know that—

There was a sudden crash as he kicked the door open and I caught one glimpse of Colin and the other guy—a new guard whose name I could never remember—and instinctively I turned away, hiding my face against Ajax's broad chest, just like he'd told me to.

The cotton of his shirt had been warmed by the hot skin beneath it and his scent filled my senses. Sandalwood, maybe, and…cedar? I'd taught myself about perfumes once and remembered the scents. Anyway, it was amazing. I pressed my cheek against the fabric, feeling firm muscle beneath it, and inhaled, the smell of him going straight to my head.

'What?' Ajax demanded, his deep voice making his chest vibrate against my cheek. 'Get the fuck out of my way.'

Silence.

I should have been paying attention to what was happening, but being in his arms was way too distracting.

The warmth of his body was soaking through the stupid white cocktail frock Dad had insisted I wear tonight, and I was conscious of how hard he was. Like he'd been carved out of rock, not muscle and bone.

The restless thing inside me had curled up and gone to sleep, as if it felt safe. As if it knew that he would protect me if anything went wrong, which was strange since I knew that men in general weren't particularly safe to be around.

'We're looking for Miss Imogen White,' Colin was saying. 'She was in the—'

'Don't know, don't give a fuck,' Ajax said casually, continuing to walk with me in his arms down the corridor. 'Go check the damn bathroom yourself. There's no one in there now.'

'But you must have—'

'If you hadn't noticed, I'm busy.'

There was more silence after that and, given that Ajax hadn't stopped, it must have meant my guards hadn't realised it was me in his arms. The suit jacket and cap now made sense; he'd been trying to hide my identity.

I'd relaxed totally against him, but curiosity stole through me and I began to turn my head, only to have him say gruffly, 'Keep your head where it is. We're not out of the building yet.'

I nodded and closed my eyes, inhaling warmth and spice and the faint smell of laundry powder from his shirt. His heart was beating beneath my ear and I could hear the rhythm of it, steady and strong and sure.

Like him.

Odd thing to think about a man I'd only just met and didn't know. Maybe I was drunk. Maybe I was high. On him and his magical scent. Whatever, I accepted the thought without protest.

Not that it mattered. He could have been Jack the Ripper and I would have been okay with it if he could get me out of the building without being seen.

The thought of freedom being so close made excitement surge through me and if I hadn't been held so securely in his arms I would have wriggled.

Keeping still was something I found difficult at the best of times, but most especially when I was excited or angry or sad.

A fidgety chatterbox, all the nannies had said about me.

A mess, said my father, looking at me with the disapproval that used to cut me so badly when I was a kid and longing for his attention.

My mother had died when I was born and if she hadn't, things would have been different. Dad would have been different. But she had and he wasn't, and all I remember wanting was his love.

He didn't like my insatiable curiosity or the way I couldn't stop moving. I used to try to stay still, to not piss him off by jogging my leg or humming or asking questions, or any of the other things I did that irritated him, but it had always been a constant battle.

But it wasn't until I was eighteen that my inability to check myself had consequences. Terrible consequences.

Since then I'd tried to stay in the box Dad had put me in, but the fight against my restless nature was never-ending and quite frankly exhausting.

I didn't feel exhausted now, though. Now I could have lain quiet and still in Ajax's arms all day.

I rubbed my cheek absently against the cotton of his shirt, wanting to get closer to him, and he made a growling sound. 'Fuck's sake, don't move until I tell you. Your hair will come down and people will see it and they'll guess who you are.'

I stilled obediently. 'Who do they think I am now then?'

'Some girl I'm carrying back to my cave to screw.'

The words travelled down my spine like an electric shock. 'Really? Do you often carry girls out of balls to screw?'

'You can stop talking now.'

'But what about—'

'Quiet.'

There was a note of deep authority in his voice that calmed me, not that I needed extra calming right now. I was so calm I was nearly catatonic, lulled by his heat and the feeling of being held gently and carefully. As if I was something precious he didn't want to drop.

A large group of people passed by us, their conversation loud, and then cooler air brushed against my bare legs, the glare of neon and streetlights illuminating the white of Ajax's shirt.

We must be outside.

It felt like we were walking down some steps and I could hear cars.

Regret gripped me. Being outside meant he was going to put me down and I would lose his heat and that blissful sense of peace.

I didn't want to. I wanted to stay here, in his arms, against his hard chest, listening to the certainty of his heartbeat.

There was the sound of a car door opening and his arms were loosening, and sure enough I was being let go and bundled into the back of a featureless black van.

'Go,' Ajax ordered the driver as he climbed in behind me, slamming the door closed. Then he pushed me down onto one of the bench seats, grabbed a seat belt and buckled me in as the van took off in a screech of tyres.

I clutched the seat belt as the van lurched, while Ajax sat down himself and did his own belt up.

The warmth that had held me so safe and still was seeping away, making me feel cold, the restless part of me stirring to life again.

'Please tell me that's it.' I stared out the window as the building receded behind us, my heart racing, waiting for my guards to come spilling out. 'Please tell me they're not going to come after us.'

'Oh, they might come after us,' Ajax replied with

infuriating calm. 'But locating us is going to be a different matter.'

I turned to find his gaze on mine, satisfaction gleaming in his icy blue eyes.

My breath caught again.

He was sitting in a casual, arrogant sprawl, long legs outstretched, the material of his shirt pulled tight across his muscled shoulders and chest, as if he didn't care that he was taking up as much room as possible. As if he was expecting *me* to move if I didn't like it, but he certainly wasn't going to.

He was like a king on his throne, staring at me as if I was a new country he'd just conquered.

Through the remains of the warmth left over from his touch, a shiver shot through me.

And all of a sudden it crashed down on me what had just happened and what it meant.

I was free of my father, but I wasn't free. Not when I'd been kidnapped by Sydney's baddest billionaire.

And I had no idea what he was going to do with me.

CHAPTER THREE

Ajax

I saw the moment the realisation hit her. The realisation of exactly what she'd got herself into. And, for the first time, wariness crept into her gaze.

It wasn't fear, but I'd take wariness and about fucking time.

She'd been curled up in my arms, all warm and soft, relaxing as if I was her own personal hero all set to save her. And that shit wasn't happening. Not when I wasn't anyone's goddamn hero.

Especially not when all I could think about was that tempting mouth of hers with that fascinating little mole just above her top lip. I wanted to kiss it. I wanted to lick it. I wanted to bite her bottom lip then suck gently on it, watch it get even redder and fuller than it was already.

Not that I would. She might be proving to be unexpectedly tempting, but I had a plan and I wasn't going to deviate from it. Not when her continued virginity was such an important part.

She stared at me, that mesmerising energy she threw off still crackling all around her.

It was good that she was wary. Because I *was* dangerous.

Everyone treated me with caution, the more nervous giving me a wide berth. It was a reputation I cultivated because if there was one thing Dad had taught me, it was that fear kept people in line better than being nice ever did.

And people had to fear me. I didn't want another Augustus King rising in this city and fear of what I might do to any pretenders to Dad's empty throne kept the more ambitious at bay.

'So,' Imogen said, her long delicate fingers clutching at her seat belt. 'This is fun.' Then she had the gall to smile—a bit uncertain but a smile nonetheless. 'Do I get to know where you're taking me? And what you want with me? What about Dad? Won't he be—'

I put a finger across her velvety pink mouth, silencing her, purely because I could.

Her eyes widened.

She looked ridiculously cute swamped by my jacket, with the cap pulled down over her pale hair, staring at me with those big green eyes.

I could still feel the imprint of her in my arms, the warmth of her body nestled against my chest. She'd rested there so quietly, yet I'd felt that live wire quality to her, a subtle vibration that had somehow crawled under my skin and stayed there. It made me think that she wasn't the fragile little thing she'd first seemed. Certainly, when she'd pulled at my hand back up there in the bathroom, there had been a surprising strength to her grip. And even now, after I'd kidnapped her, I could see a glimmer of determination beneath the wariness in her gaze.

Curiosity flickered into life inside me, smouldering alongside the undeniable physical attraction. But I crushed both. Hard. She was a tool, a means to an end, and I couldn't afford any distractions, not now.

'We're going to my house.' I let my finger linger on her lips a fraction, to show her I meant business. Nothing to do with how soft they felt. 'And I'm going to keep you there a little while.'

Her mouth turned up, giving me a smile that had no hesitancy in it whatsoever, the wariness draining from her clear gaze.

And for a second I didn't quite know what to do with that. I was her father's mortal enemy. She had to know who I was—*what* I was. She should be cringing in fear, not giving me bright smiles like I was her best friend.

'Yay.' Her lips moved against my finger, brushing against my skin, the warmth of her breath making me catch mine. 'I was hoping you'd say that. Where do you live?'

Yay? What the fuck? And why the hell was I breathless? Luckily, physical attraction was the easiest appetite to control so I controlled it.

I dropped my finger. 'That doesn't concern you right—'

'What kind of house do you have? Does it have a pool? Is it by the sea?'

'It's not—'

'Can I go outside? Does it have a view?'

'You're not going to—'

'How long can I stay? Will you be there?' Her eyes were glittering with excitement and there was a flush in her pale cheeks, the live wire spitting sparks.

You'd think I'd just promised her the trip of a lifetime, not that I was going to hold her prisoner until her father did what I wanted.

Losing patience, I stared hard at her. 'Interrupt me again and there'll be hell to pay.'

Her lips pressed together obediently, but her eyes didn't lose that excited sparkle. She didn't even have the grace to look ashamed of herself. 'I'm sorry. I always talk when I'm nervous.' Then, clearly picking up on my irritation, she added, 'I didn't interrupt this time.'

'This is a kidnapping. You do understand that, don't you?'

She laughed. 'I know. And?'

Laughing. She'd been kidnapped and now she was *laughing*. And, even worse, the husky, joyful sound sent a hot pulse down my spine, jump-starting something inside me. Something that had been dead a long time.

Shit. Just what I *didn't* want.

I ignored the feeling and scowled. 'You should be frightened of me.'

An arrested expression crossed her face, as if the thought had never occurred to her. 'Should I? I mean, I was a bit unsure a moment ago. But…' Her forehead creased. 'Do you want me to be?'

The thing that had sprung to life inside me burned, her complete lack of fear for some reason more powerful than any aphrodisiac.

Dammit. I wasn't looking to be attracted to her, for fuck's sake. That kind of shit only got in the way and I was *not* looking for distractions right now. Not that I ever had. My own desires were irrelevant when I had a goal in mind and I let nothing distract me from that goal.

Including the bolt of electricity in human form sitting next to me.

I fixed her with a 'don't fuck with me' look. 'Anyone ever tell you that you ask too many questions?'

The colour in her cheeks deepened. 'Kind of.'

'Listen. You know who I am. You must have heard the rumours. They're all true, understand? And yes, you should be scared. Because you have no idea what I'm going to do with you when I get you home.'

'What are you going to do with me?' She didn't sound as if it worried her. At all.

Christ. If ever a woman needed a lesson in proper kidnapping etiquette, it was this one.

I leaned forward fractionally, letting my physical size intimidate her. 'I'm going to ruin you, little one. That's what I'm going to do.'

Or at least I would if her father didn't do what I wanted.

Far from being intimidated, though, Imogen only frowned. As if I'd handed her a fascinating puzzle to work out. 'Ruin me? Like…how?'

This was ridiculous. Did I really have to explain a sexual threat?

'Like this…' I reached out again and this time I brushed my thumb along her lower lip to illustrate my point, because the day I had to explain myself was the day I'd hand in my scary motherfucker badge.

Her mouth was just as soft and warm as it had been when I'd touched it not a minute or so earlier, and the burning thing in my gut flamed like a fucking firework.

Mistake. You shouldn't touch her.

Bullshit. I didn't make mistakes and I wasn't a damn

fifteen-year-old boy touching a woman for the first time. I could control myself. She had a pretty mouth but that was all. Pretty mouths were a dime a dozen and if I wanted one that badly, I'd find one. Later.

Her eyes went huge as I touched her. 'Oh...' The word was warm, exhaled against my skin. '*That* kind of ruin.'

So she understood. Good.

Yet she still didn't look scared. Wary, yes, but there was definitely no fear in her expression.

Hell. What did I have to do? Pull a gun? A knife? A fucking bomb?

'So how exactly do you ruin someone sexually these days?' she went on, her eyes alight with interest. 'It's a bit nineteenth century, if you know what I mean. Virginity isn't the big thing it used to be.'

'That's it?' I dropped my finger from her mouth, ignoring the warmth that lingered on my skin. 'That's your response?'

'Should it be different?' A crease appeared between her brows. 'If you're going to ruin me or whatever—' she waved her hand as if the 'whatever' was negligible and not the threat it very much was '—I'd like to know how you're going to do it. Seeing as how I have a vested interest and all.'

'Screwing you, that's how I'll do it,' I growled, my patience starting to run even thinner than it was already, hoping that would quell her.

'Oh, sure.' She shrugged, very much unquelled. 'Screwing goes without saying. But I'd still like to know how that ruins me.'

Shit, this woman was either simple or...she was playing me.

I was beginning to suspect it was the latter and if that was the case, she'd regret it. I could play that game better than she ever could.

'You're a virgin—'

'Hey, how do you know that?'

'Interrupt me one more time and I'll give you back to your father's men.'

Her mouth closed up tight. Interesting. She really didn't want to go back. I filed that fact away for future reference.

'As I was saying,' I went on. 'You're a virgin and your father has been guarding that very jealously for a long time. You may not think it's important, but it is for him because if he wants to make alliances with potential friends, he's going to use you and your pretty hymen to do it. But how will that work when his virginal daughter has been in the hands of his enemy? Make no mistake. The ruin I'm talking about will make you mine and mine completely, and once you're mine you'll be useless to anyone else, including him.'

Emotion shifted in her eyes, gone so fast I wasn't sure what it was. Not fear, something more complicated than that.

This girl seemed open and sincere, but maybe she wasn't. Maybe there was more to her than there appeared.

The curiosity I thought I'd crushed earlier smouldered back into life, making me want to know exactly *what* more there was.

I'd always enjoyed a complicated woman—I was a man who got bored easily—and I hadn't had complicated for longer than I cared to remember.

But no. This wasn't about what *I* wanted and never had been.

Imogen took a soft breath, the fabric of her strapless white dress pulling tight across a pair of quite frankly beautiful little tits. The dress moulded to her generous hips too, outlining her rounded thighs.

Nice. Very nice. Not usually my type—tall, athletic women handled me better than small kittens like this one. But she was soft and strokeable, and undeniably sexy. What would she be like in bed?

Fucking wildfire.

Another pulse of heat burned through me, making my cock twitch.

'So what does that mean exactly?' She frowned. 'Am I a threat or a tool for you?'

'Both.' I ignored the heat in my groin. 'I want your father to leave Sydney. Only when he's gone will I let you go.'

She glanced down at where her hands clutched at her seat belt, a lock of pale hair falling out from underneath the cap I'd put on her head and down over her shoulder. It gleamed like watered silk in the light coming through the windows. Pretty.

What would it feel like coiled around your finger?

Nothing. Because I wasn't going to touch it.

'That still doesn't really explain this ruin thing,' she said. 'And you haven't said what it involves exactly.'

'What do you want? A fucking diagram?'

A flash of green glinted from underneath her pale lashes. 'Actually, that would be super helpful. Especially since I don't know anything about fucking.'

The heat I was trying to ignore burned a little hotter. Was she…flirting with me? Toying with me? If so, she was playing a dangerous game.

This wasn't a date and I wasn't some harmless boy desperate to kiss her hand. I was the oldest and most feared son of one of Sydney's worst criminals, and I had things in my past that would wipe that expression off her face. That would make her look at me as if I was the devil himself.

Maybe it was time she learned that this wasn't a fun night out and that I wasn't some tame house cat she could stroke, who'd curl up in her lap. I was a wolf and I'd eat this Red Riding Hood alive.

'You really want to know?' I leaned right into her space, getting a kick out of the way she had to press herself against the window to keep the distance between us. 'Are you sure?'

Her eyes went wide, her sulky, pouty mouth opening. And for a second I thought I saw fear there, but then it was gone and something else glittered in the green depths of her gaze.

Yet more excitement.

Shit.

'Seriously, I am *so* sure.' Her voice was on the edge of husky. 'Tell me, Ajax. I'd really like to know how you're going to ruin me.'

CHAPTER FOUR

Imogen

He was very close, inches away. His broad shoulders blocked out the streetlights coming through the opposite window of the van, his body in that pristine white shirt and black suit trousers, a hard wall of muscle in front of me.

And his eyes. Electric blue, so vivid against his olive skin. Fascinating in a way I couldn't describe.

He was so compelling. He made my heart shudder behind my ribs for reasons I didn't understand.

This talk of being ruined… It was all I could think about.

Since I'd been taught at home by tutors, I'd never gone to high school, never dated. I'd never had a teenage crush, except once, on a guy I'd seen through the window of the car while I was on my way somewhere. I'd constructed a whole set of dreamy fantasies around him for at least a week until I'd lost interest in the whole idea.

If I'd had any girlfriends I'd have discussed my lack of a sex life with them. But I didn't even have girlfriends.

What I did have, though, was an insatiable curiosity about pretty much everything, including all the things I wasn't allowed to have.

Such as sex.

I'd learned how to get around the blocks Dad had put on my Internet years ago and I'd looked stuff up. Sexy stuff. Enough to have an idea of what I might like when it came to men.

One thing I hadn't realised, though, was that looking at sex on a computer screen was *very* different to having an actual man right in front of you, looking at you so intently it made you want to burst into flames.

Like me, right now, with him.

'S-so,' I stuttered, unable to keep quiet, my heart racing. 'You know, how does it happen? Do I have to take my clothes off? Do you touch me or—'

'I don't have to touch you to ruin you, little one,' he said in that dark, deep voice I felt right down low inside me.

Okay, wow. That was…intense.

My heartbeat ratcheted up another notch. 'That's a bit patronising, you know. The whole *little one* thing.'

God knows why I was arguing with him. Probably stupid given my situation and the fact that me not being afraid of him clearly annoyed him.

But too bad. I wasn't afraid. He might think that all of this would frighten me, but what he didn't understand was that I didn't see this as a kidnapping. No, this was a rescue.

He'd bloody well *saved* me.

And, for all his talk of ruining me, I knew he wouldn't hurt me. Not a man who'd carried me so gently; close to his chest; holding me as if I were precious.

He was scowling now, not liking that I was arguing, and maybe I was completely crazy but I loved how growly and fierce he was, though I didn't really know why. Maybe it was simply the fact that I could get a reaction from him. Me. The sheltered virgin who could never sit still. Who was of no use to anyone except as a tool.

You're Ajax's tool now.

Yeah, but it felt different somehow. For a start, Ajax was a complete stranger. Unlike my dad, he wasn't supposed to love me and I wasn't supposed to love him. I could push back at him with impunity and it wouldn't matter.

'I don't give a shit whether it's patronising or not,' he said. 'You're my prisoner and I'll call you whatever the fuck I want.' He paused, his gaze like a searchlight finding all my secrets, all my hidden desires. 'Besides,' he added, 'I think you like it.'

I went red. Sadly, I *did* like it. I'd never had anyone refer to me as anything but Imogen and being called *little one* made me think of being curled up in his arms, safe.

Not knowing what to say, I frowned instead.

He smiled, all satisfied like he'd won a point off me. 'Of course you do. But that's not what you wanted to talk about, is it?'

'You were going to tell me how you can ruin me without touching me,' I reminded him. 'How does that work? Is it possible to screw someone without touching them? Do you just talk at me? I mean, maybe I don't know how these things go, but—'

He leaned forward even more, making the rest of what I'd been going to say catch in my throat.

The glass of the window was cold against the back of my head, the door handle jabbing my spine painfully. Yet those sensations seemed quite distant, even irrelevant.

There was only Ajax and his electrifying blue gaze.

'It's very simple.' His voice brushed over my skin like soft black fur. 'First I'd get you to lift up your dress. Then I'd tell you to spread your legs and pull your knickers to the side.' The words became even deeper, even rougher. 'Then I'd get you to slide your fingers over your pussy, rubbing that little clit in exactly the way I tell you to, and not stopping until you come. Hard. While I watch.'

All my breath had vanished, my heartbeat out of control. I couldn't tear my gaze away from his. My cheeks had to be scarlet and there was a definite pressure between my thighs. A pulse. An ache.

Those things he said were shocking and yet…they made me hot and restless and I…wanted to do them.

Except I had a suspicion that he hadn't said them to get me off. He'd said them to frighten me.

Unfortunately for him, fear was the last thing I felt right now.

And it hit me in that moment that Ajax King wasn't a choice my father would *ever* have made for me. It was why I'd been at that stupid ball in the first place, to meet a guy that Dad had decided might be a potential ally. To charm him, be the bait in the honey trap Dad had set up.

Ajax telling me that Dad was using me wasn't anything I didn't know. I'd figured out what my purpose was for Dad after what had happened with Cam, and it wasn't simply to be his treasured daughter.

I was the Princess, the prize he'd use to set various people off against each other, and whom he'd award to whoever was the strongest.

It was like a medieval marriage bargain, where I got no say and my feelings on the subject were irrelevant.

Dad didn't care whether I wanted to be used like that or not. The only aspect of me he cared about was the debt I owed him for being the cause of Mum's death.

A debt I had no choice but to try and repay, even though it wasn't my fault.

But I had a choice now.

I could try and escape, or I could choose to be ruined by Ajax King, Dad's most hated enemy.

Dad would be *so pissed*.

It was perfect.

'Okay,' I said thickly. 'Do you want me to do those things now? Or should I wait till we get to your place?'

He blinked. Rapidly. 'You did hear what I said, didn't you?'

'Uh, yeah. A bit difficult *not* to hear, to be honest.'

'And you understood what I wanted you to do?'

'Of course. I'm not stupid.' I swallowed, my throat dry. Oh, I wanted to touch him. Feel that hard chest I'd been held against, test all that delicious muscle with my hands.

I had a whole folder of hot guys on my computer at home, inspiration pics for when I got too lonely. But having the reality right in front me…

He was so intent, studying me as if he'd never seen anything like me in all his life. 'This doesn't frighten you at all, does it?'

'No,' I said honestly. 'I'm sorry, but it doesn't.'

His straight black brows drew down. 'Why not? It should.'

'Well, it might if I didn't want to do it. But…' I stopped, belatedly self-conscious about what I was admitting to. I was attracted to him, but he might not feel the same way about me. After all, he didn't know me from a bar of soap. 'It's okay, you know,' I went on in a rush. 'You don't have to ruin me if you don't want to. I mean, you might not actually want me and I don't have any experience and—'

'Quiet,' Ajax said for the second time that night, the note of authority in his voice making me fall silent. 'You really have no idea what the fuck you're talking about. If you think playing with a man like me is a good—'

'Playing with you?' I interrupted yet again, shocked. 'I'm not playing with you. I just don't know—'

Ajax took my chin in one hand, his thumb silencing me the way he had earlier. And, just like earlier, I swear I could feel every single whorl of his thumbprint on my lips. As if I were a lock and he the only key.

'Listen,' he said quietly. 'First, you need to shut up and do as you're told. Second, I'm not ruining anyone in the back of a bloody van. I'm not fifteen any more. And third, if you think I don't want you then you're very much mistaken.'

I ignored everything he said but the last part.

He *did* want me.

I shouldn't have done it but, next thing I knew, my hands had let go of their death grip on my seat belt and were reaching out for him, my lips parting so I could taste his thumb pressed against them, the flavour of his skin salty and sharp on my tongue.

My fingertips made contact, pressing against his chest. So warm, so hard...

Ajax made a sound and I felt the vibration of it in my fingertips. And I looked and saw flames. Blue flames.

'Little virgin.' His voice was very soft. 'What the fuck do you think you're doing?'

Oh...

I looked at my hands on his chest, the heat of him burning through my fingertips. Perhaps touching him had been a mistake.

Damn. I'd been trying so hard to modify my behaviour and *not* simply do the first thing that came into my head. I was supposed to think things through, restrain myself, because I knew what happened when I didn't. I'd seen the consequences. And they were terrible.

My cheeks were burning as I snatched my hands away, a combination of shame and embarrassment gripping me. 'I'm sorry,' I muttered against his thumb. 'I didn't mean to. I just...wanted to t-touch you.'

His grip on my chin tightened.

And, before I knew what was happening, his head bent, his mouth brushing lightly over mine.

I'd never been kissed on the lips before, and for a second my brain simply ceased to function. There was softness, a fleeting pressure and heat. Lots and lots of heat.

A current of electricity crackled over my skin, goosebumps following along in its wake, and my hands were lifting once again, reaching for him, but he was gone, my fingers closing on empty air.

Panting, I realised that the sudden darkness meant

my eyes were closed, so I opened them to find his wintry blue gaze staring into mine.

'You kissed me,' I said stupidly. 'Why?'

His beautiful mouth quirked. 'How else was I going to shut you up?'

'I wasn't—'

'And to get a taste of what we're working with here.'

I couldn't think. What was he talking about? 'I don't understand.'

'Of course you don't.' That quirk became a smile, satisfied and somehow very male. 'But you'll find out.'

'What do you mean?'

He didn't answer. He merely straightened up and sat back in his seat, getting out his phone and looking down at the screen.

Dismissing me.

A million questions swarmed but, perhaps for the first time in my life, it was easy to stay quiet. Because I could still feel that kiss, the imprint of his lips on mine, tingling, burning…

I'd only known him half an hour. God.

Turning away, I stared sightlessly out the window of the van at the neon of the city outside, not even thinking about how cool it was that I was out without an entourage, on my own for the first time in my life.

Out from under my father's thumb.

My own woman at last.

No, all I could think about was Ajax bloody King and that kiss.

And, for the second time that night, I wondered if maybe I was in way over my head.

CHAPTER FIVE

Ajax

I SAT BACK in my chair on the big stone terrace that looked out over the sea, nursing an espresso. The sun was warm on my face, the ocean busy throwing itself against the rocks below the house I'd claimed after Dad had gone to jail.

Last night I'd shown Imogen to the bedroom I'd set aside for her and she'd gone quietly, without peppering me with any more questions.

Satisfied she was secure for the night, I'd then sent texts to my two brothers, telling them that I wouldn't be around for a week or so and that they were to handle any emergencies that might crop up.

Luckily their personal lives had settled down recently with two lovely women keeping them on the straight and narrow. God knows it was about time someone other than me stayed on top of things, and I was appreciative.

It certainly helped me now when I had to concentrate all my attention on a lovely woman of my own.

A strangely fascinating young woman, who was not in any way what I'd anticipated.

The virgin part, yes. The questions and the excitement and the sheer vibrating energy of her, not so much.

I hoped that wouldn't become a problem.

But that was an issue for later. First I had to contact White, let him know I had Imogen, and deliver my ultimatum.

I picked up my phone and pressed a button, waiting until the contact I'd been given answered the call.

'Yeah, who is this?' It was one of White's thugs.

'Ajax King,' I said curtly. 'Tell your boss I have his daughter. If he wants to see her safe and sound, get him to call me at this number.'

I didn't wait for a response, cutting the call then putting the phone back down on the table and ignoring it as it began to ring almost immediately.

I wasn't going to answer him right away. He could stew for a couple of hours.

Glancing down at my watch, I checked the time.

Nine-thirty in the morning.

Jesus Christ, just how long was Imogen going to sleep?

Kidnapped women were not supposed to have long lie-ins when their captors were waiting to inform them of the rules of their captivity.

In spite of my satisfaction with how easily my plan had come together, a thread of annoyance wound through me.

I couldn't believe how unafraid of me she'd been in the van last night, even when I'd deliberately been explicit, thinking that would scare the shit out of her.

But the bloody woman only seemed to find that even more exciting. And then she'd touched me, laid those delicate little fingers on my chest, pressing lightly, *feeling* me.

As if she had no idea about the chemistry flaring between us.

As if I was no fucking threat to her at all.

That touch shouldn't have affected me in the slightest.

But it had.

Given that, I shouldn't have kissed her and Christ knew why I had. Perhaps it was simply the way she'd looked at me, as if she'd never seen anything so fascinating in all her life, and then the assumption that I didn't want her, like she'd be disappointed if I didn't…

Nice justifications. You just wanted her.

But since when had what I wanted ever mattered?

Except her lips had been as soft as I'd known they would be, and she'd smelled of something sweet, something that had made my heart twist inside my chest. Roses. My mother's favourite flower.

Ah, fuck, what was wrong with me? It was just a kiss from a wide-eyed virgin. Nothing to get wound up about.

Whatever my own feelings on the subject, though, one thing was clear: her virginity was the only leverage I had and so it had to remain intact.

I had to stay focused on my end game, because that was all that mattered.

Even if some other things get broken?

Yes, even then. Years ago, I'd had to stand by while my middle brother, Leon, had been kidnapped and tortured at the hands of my father's enemies, and let my youngest brother, Xander, be used as some kind of evil financial genius to grow Dad's empire.

That was my fault, my responsibility.

But my goal had always been to take Dad down, to save my city, and that outweighed everything. Even if it meant pretending I was on board with everything Dad did, no matter how it had sickened me.

The end justified any means.

And even now that end had been accomplished, the story wasn't done. We still had enemies. And I would keep protecting my brothers.

I'd do the hard things so that no one else had to.

I sipped my coffee, gazing out at the sea, white-capped and with a few boats sailing here and there. It was a peaceful view and one I'd always loved when I was a kid, imagining I could just get in one of those boats and sail the fuck away, escape my father and his legacy for good.

A dream.

Despite the small yacht I kept in the boathouse at the foot of the cliffs, I'd never escaped and I was never going to.

Dad might be in jail, but he wasn't the only one with a life sentence. That was fine, though. It was something I'd accepted long ago.

I glanced down to check the time again.

Quarter to ten.

Time for my prisoner to get the hell up.

I put my coffee down on the table and went back into the house, making my way into the wing that had once housed my stepsister and Dad's second wife, and which I'd had renovated as guest quarters.

There was room enough to house an entire football team, though right now there was only the one occupant.

The unexpected little virgin I'd kidnapped the night before.

I strode down the hall that ran the length of the wing, the polished floorboards shining in the sunlight coming through the windows.

Arriving at Imogen's door, I stopped outside it and knocked lightly.

There was no response.

Jesus, she'd better still be in there. Not that she'd be able to escape even if she wanted to, not given the security I'd surrounded the house with. The place was a fortress. Nothing got in or out. Including her.

Still, it was better to be safe than sorry so I didn't wait, pushing the door open and stepping inside.

The room faced the ocean, one wall just glass to enhance the view. A king-sized bed had been pushed up against the wall at right angles to the glass, and in the centre of the bed, all curled up like a sleepy cat, was Imogen.

Sunlight fell over the bed, her long, silky pale hair tangled across the white linen of the pillowcases, a sheet wrapping around her middle, leaving the rest of her uncovered. She hadn't even bothered to undress, and was still wearing her white dress.

Her hands were tucked under her chin, her pale lashes lying motionless on her cheeks, deeply asleep. A smile curved that pretty mouth I'd kissed the night before, as if she was tucked up in her own bed and having a lovely dream, not a prisoner of Sydney's most infamous King.

Lust flickered to life inside me, dark and dirty. I wanted to go over to the bed, pull away her dress, uncover her satiny, strokeable skin and ravage her carnal mouth. Find out whether she'd be as wild and electric with my dick inside her as I thought she'd be. Whether she'd shock those long dead parts of me back into life with a touch...

Ignoring the lust, I leaned against the doorframe instead, taking a moment to study her uninterrupted.

Last night she'd been happy that I'd kidnapped her and even though her lack of fear of me had been annoying, it did tell me one thing: being captured by me was preferable to being her father's prisoner.

I wondered why. Her father had his own fledgling crime syndicate going on, extortion and violence the means he used to keep his followers loyal, and being related to someone like that wasn't exactly going to be a picnic. Hell, I should know. I was related to a prick like that myself.

But why was being *my* prisoner preferable to being his? I didn't use violence, not these days, but I was going to use her the way he had—for my own ends. The only thing that distinguished me from him was that my goal was ultimately to protect people.

Pushing myself away from the doorframe, I moved over to the side of the bed. She slept on, completely unaware that her kidnapper was standing beside her, staring at her.

Hell. The woman had no sense of danger whatsoever.

You like that. You like that a lot.

Imogen shifted, making a sexy noise and snuggling into the pillow. The top of her strapless dress had pulled down, her rounded breasts pushing against it.

My cock, the predictable fuck, hardened at the view. I ignored it.

'Wake up, little one.' I couldn't keep the growl out of my voice. 'I'm getting tired of waiting for you.'

She made another of those noises, then her lashes fluttered and she sighed, a sliver of green appearing as she opened her eyes.

Automatically, I searched her face for any signs of fear but there were none. Apparently, waking up to find me standing beside her bed wasn't frightening or even all that surprising.

In fact, as her gaze found mine, that delicious velvety mouth turned up in a slow and sleepy smile.

She's delectable.

The heat I'd been fighting tightened its grip.

'Oh,' she said, the word exhaled on a long, relieved-sounding breath. 'Thank God. I was afraid you were a dream.'

'I'm not a dream,' I said flatly. 'I'm a nightmare.'

She grinned then threw her arms above her head, stretching unselfconsciously in the sunlight like a sleepy cat. 'No, you're not. And it was definitely *not* a nightmare.'

The top of her dress dipped even lower, revealing lots of pale silky skin, and, despite myself, I couldn't stop staring. My hands itched to tug that fabric down, to see what colour her nipples were and what they might taste like if I sucked on them.

'Are you sure?' I finally dragged my gaze from her chest, but looking into her eyes wasn't any better. They were wide, the colour of new grass, and I caught a hint of her scent—roses and heat…

Delicious.

'Oh, I'm sure.' She blinked at me, apparently unaware of how close to the knife-edge I was. 'I can even tell you about it if you want.'

'I do not want.' I kept my voice cold, trying to force away the ache in my groin. 'What I would like is for you to listen. I have some things I need to say to you.'

'Really?' Her tongue crept out, small and pink, touching her top lip. The move wasn't flirtatious but I was riveted anyway. 'What things?'

I knew I should turn away, look at something other than that small pink tongue and soft mouth; that tiny mole near her upper lip; the pulse at the base of her pale throat.

But that would be to admit I wasn't in control of this situation, that somehow she had the power here, and there was no way in hell I was doing that.

So I continued to stare at her. 'Your father. I've told him I have you.'

Her gold-tipped lashes swept down, veiling her gaze. 'Oh. I see.' Slowly she pushed herself up so she was sitting on the bed, tugging up the top of her dress as she did so, which was probably a good thing considering the state of my damn cock. 'And what did he say?'

'I didn't give him a chance to say anything. Once he's got the message he'll call me.'

She sat with her head bent, looking down at her hands twisted in her lap. Her pale hair lay over her shoulders and streamed down her back, gleaming in the sun like new minted gold.

There was a stillness to her now, that vibrating energy muted. 'So what's going to happen now then?'

'What do you mean, what's going to happen now?'

I frowned. 'Nothing's going to happen now. You're my prisoner and you stay here. End of story.'

'I don't care about that.' She lifted her head. 'What I want to know is when you're going to ruin me. I mean, that's what you said you were going to do.' Something that looked a lot like disappointment glittered in her eyes. 'Or did you not mean it?'

CHAPTER SIX

Imogen

Yes, I was disappointed and, even though I tried, I couldn't hide it.

Last night when he'd shown me to my room and told me there was no point escaping because the whole house was surrounded by his men, I'd been expecting him to continue what he'd started with that kiss.

But he hadn't. He'd pointed out the en suite bathroom then left.

It was a bit of an unhappy surprise after I'd decided that he was the perfect way to get my revenge on Dad.

I'd decided not to argue about it, though. I was tired anyway and consoled myself with the thought that maybe I could ask him about it the next day.

So I'd lain down on the bed fully dressed, shut my eyes and had gone out like a light.

It had been the best sleep I'd had in years, and that dream I'd had about him had really helped.

My very *naughty* dream.

I'd had sex dreams in the past, usually involving faceless men who would touch me and then walk away, leaving me hot and aching and restless with feelings I didn't understand.

But not last night. Last night I'd dreamed I'd stayed in that van and this time the man wasn't faceless. He had rough, blunt, handsome features and eyes the colour of a winter sky. And he'd watched me as I pulled up my dress, telling me what to do in his deep, harsh voice...

God, so *hot*. And now there was an ache between my legs, a throbbing heat. I wanted him to touch me, to make good on all the threats he'd delivered the night before, but, given the way he was standing there, the expression on his face utterly impassive, it was obvious he had no intention of doing so.

Dammit.

Did that mean that my one and only chance for getting back at Dad, of having any kind of choice about being with a man *I* wanted, was gone?

To make matters worse, Ajax looked unbelievably good in the white T-shirt and jeans he had on, the short sleeves exposing heavily muscled arms and inked olive skin. I hadn't realised he was tattooed and I could barely drag my gaze from all those black lines snaking around his biceps and forearms. That and his beautiful mouth. And the way the cotton pulled over his broad chest...

I could barely drag my gaze from him, full stop.

He was just taunting me now, wasn't he?

'No.' He crossed his arms across that incredible chest. 'I didn't mean it.'

It was strange to feel the hurt so personally, but I did.

'So you lied,' I said, only just stopping myself from crossing my arms too.

Ajax frowned, the mesmerising blue of his eyes sharpening. 'I'm not sure I like your tone.'

I should have stopped arguing, but I wasn't good at hiding my feelings and the disappointment was biting unexpectedly deep. 'You told me you wanted me. Was that a lie?'

'You should be more worried about the fact that you're my prisoner, not whether or not I'm going to fuck you.'

I lifted my chin. 'You know, for an ex-criminal mastermind, or whatever you are, you're not very smart. I don't care about being kidnapped or about being your prisoner.'

'You should care.'

'Why? I just wanted to get away from Dad and you helped me do that.'

'I did *not* help you.'

I sniffed. 'Whatever, dude. As far as I'm concerned, you got me away from Dad and that's the only thing that matters to me.'

A muscle leapt in the side of his impressive jaw. 'You don't care that all you've done is swap cages?'

'No. Anyway, you told me last night you'd let me go when Dad leaves Sydney.' At least Ajax's cage wouldn't end up crushing me. Probably.

He stared at me for a minute, not saying anything. As if he couldn't quite figure me out. Which I liked. Especially considering I got nothing but dismissal from Dad.

'If he doesn't,' Ajax said, 'I'm going to take your virginity. You do understand that, don't you?'

Seriously? He thought I didn't understand? Maybe I should have told him what I'd decided, but if he was grumpy now, he'd definitely be grumpy about the fact that I wanted to use him purely as a way to get back at Dad.

I gave him an exasperated look. 'And do *you* understand that I'm okay with you taking my virginity? I mean, why do you think I didn't mind any of what you said to me last night in the van?'

'Little one, you barely know me. And you've certainly got no fucking idea what losing your virginity to me even means.'

'Okay, first, like I told you last night, I'm not stupid. I have some idea what losing my virginity means. Second, I've read about you. I know about your reputation.'

He remained motionless beside the bed, his eyes glittering strangely, his big body radiating tension. 'Whatever you heard about my reputation, just know that it's twice as bad and twice as fucked up as any of the rumours. I'm not a man you want anywhere near your bed, Imogen.'

That didn't sound like a 'no'. More like a…warning.

Too bad I didn't care about warnings.

'Why not?' I asked. 'The rumours said you once took down a drug ring all by yourself and that you broke the kneecaps of—'

'Enough.' His voice was as hard and cold as the look in his eyes. 'You'll remain my prisoner until your father leaves Sydney. That's all.'

I bit my lip, trying to hold my tongue and hide my disappointment.

Except I could see my chance for revenge slipping further and further away and a question came out all the same. 'So all those threats last night were empty ones?'

His scowl became thunderous. 'Don't push me.'
Another warning. Which I also ignored.

If I couldn't change his mind now, then I'd be returned to Dad like an unwanted present, free to be handed to whomever pleased him the most.

And I would never, ever have this chance, this choice again.

'Why not?' I asked. 'What are you going to do to me? I know you won't hurt me—'

'You don't know that.'

'Yes, I do. You didn't last night when you kidnapped me, which means you're not going to now. I mean, you could have used my life to get Dad to do what you want, but you didn't. You used my virginity. Which is a whole lot friendlier than, say, actual murder.'

His expression shifted, the look in his eyes sharpening. 'Tell me why you were so pleased to be kidnapped by me.'

The change of subject caught me off guard. Should I tell him everything? Maybe I shouldn't.

It said something about me that I hadn't realised how prescribed my life had become until I was eighteen, and I was a bit of ashamed of that. And then there was the fact that it had almost taken a man's life to make me see it.

Yeah, I wasn't too keen to share that with him.

I'd had one attempt at a normal life, where I'd tried to have friends, a job, go to uni—all the things a girl my age should have. And it had been great—until I'd impulsively asked a guy I liked out for coffee, only to have poor Cameron beaten half to death in an alleyway.

Dad had called me into his office afterwards to inform me that it had been him who'd ordered it and that I needed to be more careful with whom I associated. That had been a wake-up call for me about how far he was prepared to go to keep me out of anyone's reach.

I'd wanted to leave ever since, but the opportunity had never presented itself until Ajax had showed up.

'I was tired of being a prisoner,' I said, deciding to keep some of the truth to myself. 'I'd been trying to figure out how to get away from him for ages and you came along at just the right time.'

His gaze roamed over me and I felt it like the sunlight falling on my skin. No, hotter than that. Way hotter. 'You don't act like a woman who's been a prisoner for years.'

'How is a woman who's been a prisoner for years supposed to act?' I shifted on the bed, restless all of a sudden.

I didn't want to sit here and talk about Dad and how he'd curtailed my life. Or about how I'd been so desperate for his approval that I'd let him. Or about Mum and the constant reminder of the debt I had to pay.

You can't pay it now.

And I never would. But surely that didn't mean I wasn't allowed to have a life? I wanted to have a taste of all the stuff I'd missed out on. Stuff like exploring having sex with Ajax King.

Surely that was allowed?

Except Ajax completely ignored my slightly pissy tone. 'Did he hurt you?'

'Who? Dad?' I moved to the side of the bed and slipped off it. Not physically.' Emotionally, yes. Another thing I didn't want to talk about.

I walked past Ajax and went over to the massive

windows that looked out over the sea. It was so beautiful. The only thing I'd seen from the windows of Dad's isolated house in the Blue Mountains, where I mainly lived, was trees and paddocks and yet more trees.

'Wow,' I breathed, staring at the ocean and white-capped waves and the yachts sailing on it. 'What an amazing view. Can I go outside and see it? Do you have a boat?'

'No, you can't go outside, not yet. And yes, I have a boat.'

I could feel the pressure of his stare against my back but I didn't turn around, keeping my gaze on the sea, enjoying the way he was looking at me. 'Oh, good. Can I go out—?'

'What did he do?' Ajax's deep voice cut through mine like a hot knife through cold butter.

The damn man had a one-track mind.

'Can we not talk about that?' Slowly I turned around. 'Can't we talk about what you promised me in the van last night?'

Ajax had remained by the bed, but was now facing me, his arms folded across his chest. The expression on his hard features was difficult to read, but something steely glinted in his eyes. 'I'm not sleeping with you, Imogen. I've already made that clear.'

He said it so…flatly. As if that kiss he'd given me, that small taste of pleasure, didn't mean a thing.

Of course it didn't. He just told you he didn't mean it. The real question is: why does it mean so much to you?

Wasn't that obvious? Dad had told me what to do my entire life and now I had a chance to do what *I* wanted for a change, I couldn't—wouldn't—give it up.

'You're not going to sleep with me *yet*,' I amended for him. 'But why can't we do it now? Dad will never know.'

'He will if he demands a doctor's examination.'

My face went hot because, knowing Dad, that's exactly what he would demand.

How humiliating.

'As it stands now,' Ajax went on ruthlessly, 'he's going to have to take my word that I haven't touched you.'

'You could…lie, maybe?' I tried not to sound too hopeful.

But that was clearly the wrong thing to say because the blue of his eyes became ice. 'My word as a King means something to men like him. And I won't put that at risk with a lie simply because you want to lose your virginity.'

I blinked, feeling like he'd thrown a bucket of cold water over me, with an extra helping of shame following along behind it. I'd gone full Imogen on him last night, not even bothering to try and contain myself. Asking questions and interrupting. Touching him without asking and then getting annoyed when he told me to stop.

I'd made it all about me. I hadn't even thought about him.

'I'm sorry.' I shoved away my disappointment, trying to regain my dignity. 'You don't want to sleep with me and that's fine. I respect that.'

But something in my tone must have given me away because the muscle in the side of his jaw leapt again. 'You're a sexy woman, Imogen. And it's not about your lack of attractiveness, understand? But nothing gets in the way of me achieving a goal, and that includes any personal distractions.'

I didn't take offence at being lumped under the heading of 'personal distractions'. I was too curious.

'The goal being to get Dad out of the city?' I asked. 'Why?'

'Why do you think? Your father is trying to set himself up as a pretender to Dad's empty throne and that's not happening. Not while I can still fucking breathe.'

A whisper of cold swept through me. I knew who my father was. I knew that the money we had didn't come from him working hard. I understood that my mother's death had left a hole inside him that he'd been struggling to fill. I'd once wanted to be the one who helped him fill that hole, but that had been before he'd made it clear that I could never be that for him.

He didn't want the child his wife had died giving birth to.

He preferred money. He preferred power.

Of course he'd want to be the new Augustus King.

At that moment, Ajax's phone started buzzing.

He pulled it from his pocket and checked the screen then he hit the answer button and raised it to his ear. 'King.'

Silence fell as whoever was on the other end of the call talked.

Ajax simply stared at me. 'Listen,' he said eventually, his voice ice-cold. 'Here's what's going to happen. The only way you'll get your daughter back is if you get the fuck out of Sydney and stay out. And if you don't? Then I'll take her precious virginity and make her mine.'

Another silence fell, Ajax's gaze burning.

Was it weird to find the way he'd said that hot? Not that I cared if it was weird or not. It *was* hot. Especially the way he'd said 'make her mine'.

Calm down. You've known him approximately twelve hours or less.

So? It wasn't like I was going to fall in love with him or anything. This was all about attraction.

'Yes,' Ajax went on. 'She's alive.' He held out his phone towards me. 'Say something to your father, Imogen.'

I looked at the phone and everything I'd been thinking vanished from my head as a wave of dread swept through me.

I didn't want to talk to Dad. He'd be disgusted with me for allowing myself to be taken. And it would be my fault. Everything was my fault.

Why do you still care what he thinks?

I didn't know. But that didn't change the fact that I cared.

Ajax's blue gaze narrowed then, as abruptly as he'd pointed the phone at me, he lifted it back to his ear. 'She'll speak to you later. Remember what I said.' Then he disconnected the call without another word.

I cleared my throat, feeling like an idiot, but Ajax spoke before I could say anything. 'Take a shower if you like—I've asked my housekeeper to leave you some clothes. There's breakfast on the terrace for you when you're done. You're allowed to go anywhere in the house including outside, but the top floor is off limits.' He paused, giving me a look that pinned me where I stood. 'I'm going to be out the rest of the day, but don't worry. You're safe here. Understand?'

'Yes,' I croaked. 'But where are you—?'
'Later,' he said. 'We'll talk more later.'
And, before I could ask him any more questions, he turned and walked out.

CHAPTER SEVEN

Ajax

I ABSENTED MYSELF from the house over the next couple of days, using the time to have meetings with people who should have known better than to fuck with me. Meetings that involved gentle reminders of who was boss…and that wasn't William White.

The reminders weren't of the violent kind—it wasn't necessary when threatening people's money worked just as well—but that didn't mean I was kind. I'd ruin every last son of a bitch in this town if they even so much as kept White's name in their contact list, and they knew it.

I also tried not to think about Imogen, an impossible task seemingly.

My brain kept returning to the look on her face when I'd handed her the phone that morning. She'd stared at it like I'd handed her a snake, making every one of my protective instincts sit up and take notice.

She'd told me her father hadn't hurt her physically, yet she *really* didn't want to talk to him. In fact, the only time I'd seen her scared was when I'd given her that phone.

Why? What had he done to her?

Knowing what the story was between her and White didn't affect my overall goal and technically it could be called a distraction. But I couldn't stop thinking about it.

I couldn't stop thinking about what a delicate thing she'd seemed that morning either, with the light falling on her hair, turning her from white and pale into sun-drenched gold. She was fragile and vulnerable, a woman in need of protection.

Yet that's not all she was. There had been a demanding element to her, flashes of a strong, stubborn will, plus an honesty I hadn't experienced in a long time. The world I moved in—even now it was totally legit—was full of bluffs and façades and gambles and trade-offs. Games. That's what doing business was all about.

But Imogen didn't appear to have a façade at all. She didn't strike me as a game-player either. There was no artifice to her, no guile. She wanted me and she'd been totally straight up about that.

Hot.

It was probably a good thing I'd stayed out of the house. God knew my dick could sure as hell use some time out.

Two days later I stepped out of the building where I'd had my last meeting, heading to the featureless black sedan where Andy, my assistant, was waiting for me.

Getting into the car, I settled myself then slammed the door shut behind me.

As Andy pulled into the traffic, my thoughts drifted back to my little captive. I hadn't seen her for the past couple of days, though my housekeeper had been giving me daily updates, which consisted of Imogen roaming around my house being bored, apparently.

Too bad. Then again, Imogen kept asking my housekeeper questions which annoyed Mrs Jacobs because I'd forbidden her to answer them.

I probably needed to give Imogen a few more things to do.

You could think of a couple of things.

I scowled at the traffic. Yeah, there were a lot of things I could think of for her to do. Particularly things involving a bed.

Sadly, that wasn't happening. I had to keep my eye on the big picture, that's what I'd always been about. I couldn't get obsessed with the details and, right now, Imogen White was merely a detail.

Like your brothers were details?

Shit, my brothers had never been details. No, I hadn't been able to stop what had happened to them, not when I'd had to keep up the façade of the loyal first son to Dad, but it had been vital that Dad thought I was on his side. That way he wouldn't see me working in the background to take him and his filthy empire down.

Yes, Leon and Xander had got caught in the crossfire, but they were better now. They had the lives they'd always wanted and all because Dad was no longer in the picture.

It had all been worth it in the end.

My phone buzzed in my pocket.

I hauled it out and looked down at the screen. Yet another call from White. Should I answer it this time or leave the prick to stew a little longer?

I hit the answer button but didn't say anything.

'King?' White's voice vibrated with fury. 'You'd better be answering this time, you piece of—'

'Are you ready to give me what I want?' I interrupted. 'Or am I going to have to disconnect yet again?'

There was a silence, White evidently trying to get himself under control. 'I'll call the police. Tell them you have my daughter.'

'No, you won't. You can't afford to have the police getting into your business and we both know it.'

He muttered a curse. 'I'm not leaving this city. It's impossible.'

'Then I'll make sure your pure Princess isn't so pure any more.'

'You can't. She won't let you touch her.'

I laughed. 'Oh, you'd be surprised. She seems to quite like the idea.'

'If you've even so much as—'

'Relax, I haven't done anything to her.' Apart from a kiss, but that didn't count. 'Her virginity is quite safe.'

'I've only got your word for that.'

I watched the city moving past my window. 'And my word is all you'll get.'

'The word of a King.' He spat the words down the phone, my name dripping with contempt.

'You respected my father's,' I said coldly. 'You'll respect mine.'

'What makes you think I care enough about her virginity to pack up my life and go somewhere else anyway?'

'Because you need it. Once she's mine, she'll be useless to you. And you don't have anything else of value to get people on your side, do you?'

'You have no idea—'

'I've done my research, White. Believe me. You don't have the finance, not these days. All you have is your daughter.' I leaned back against the seat. 'Except you don't even have her now, do you? I could make her mine, get a couple of kids on her. What do you say to having a couple of King grandchildren, hmm?'

'Fuck you.' His voice was bitter. 'I'll leave and when you free her I'll take her somewhere else. A new city. Melbourne, maybe.'

'Fine. I don't care where you go.' And I didn't. There was only one thing that mattered to me. 'Just stay the fuck away from what's mine.'

There was silence from the other end of the phone, though I could feel his fury.

'I want proof of life,' he said eventually. 'In person.'

Something inside me tightened. 'A meeting?'

'Yes. Alone.'

'No.' I didn't even need to think about it. 'There will be no meeting.'

'Listen. You let me talk to her for five minutes, just so I know she's okay and unhurt. And if she's fine I'll leave Sydney. I'll even take a few people with me so they're out of your hair.'

Interesting. He was clearly desperate to have her back if he was prepared to negotiate. And I'd certainly be happy with fewer troublemakers to worry about. 'That could work,' I allowed.

'Once I've gone, you can let her go and we'll go elsewhere. But only on condition that wherever it is I go, you stay out of it.'

My smile widened. 'Like you can tell me what to do. I dictate the terms here, White. Not you. But I'm feeling magnanimous. I'm sure a five-minute meeting with your daughter can be arranged.'

'Good. Tonight. Bring her to—'

'As I was saying. *I* dictate the terms. Which means I'll be in touch.' I didn't wait for him to launch into yet another round of protests, I simply disconnected the call then put my phone back in my pocket.

Good. This was proceeding much more smoothly than I'd planned. If all he wanted was a meeting with his daughter, then that was easy enough to arrange. Of course, he might want to meet with Imogen in order to steal her back, but I'd make sure that didn't happen.

Will Imogen agree, though?

I thought back to the way she'd frozen up when I'd tried to hand her the phone and the fear in her face…

Yeah, her agreement might be a problem.

Perhaps it was time I asked her what the deal with her father was. Directly.

I finished up the last of my meetings then headed back to the King mansion in Vaucluse, darkness beginning to fall.

A kick of excitement hit me as the car approached the gates, which was strange since I'd never particularly enjoyed coming home before. I'd had the place renovated to the highest standards, but it was little more than a hotel room. Too many shit memories basically.

But not tonight. Tonight there was someone waiting for me.

Except when I got inside I couldn't find her.

She wasn't in the kitchen I almost never used, with all its stainless steel and white tiles. Or in the cavernous lounge with the windows that faced the ocean and the black leather sectional sofas. She wasn't in any of the bedrooms on the first floor, or in the gardens outside. Or by the pool on the terrace that looked out over the sea. Or in the massive bathroom with the bath big enough to be a hot tub all on its own.

Mrs Jacobs had gone home so I snapped questions at my security staff, but they swore she hadn't left the building.

Which meant only one thing.

She was upstairs. Where I'd told her she wasn't allowed to go.

Bad little one. That was where my bedroom and office were, my private space.

I stormed up the stairs, taking them two at a time but soundlessly. Because if she was up there after I'd explicitly told her not to, then she was up there for a reason. And if that reason was something I didn't want her to fucking do, then I wanted to catch her in the act.

My office was empty, same with the other couple of rooms, which left only my bedroom.

Silently I stepped inside.

One wall was glass, as was most of the side of the house that faced the ocean, and the light shining through it showed me nothing but an empty room, except for my bed that faced the huge windows.

I waited, barely breathing, allowing myself to become aware of the space around me, the breath of air on my skin, any change in temperature, the slightest of sounds. It was a trick I'd learned from Dad's old Head of Security and it had helped me on more than one occasion.

I moved through the room slowly, expanding my awareness outwards, listening.

Nothing.

I stopped by the big walk-in closet. The door was half open, exactly the way I'd left it this morning.

But there was the faintest of scents in the air.

Roses.

CHAPTER EIGHT

Imogen

I LEANED IN to the suit that hung from the rail in front of me and sniffed, the warm scent of sandalwood and cedar filling my senses.

It was such a delicious smell. I wanted to bury my nose in the lapels of Ajax's jacket and spend the rest of the evening breathing it in.

Okay, so it was a little weird, me being in his closet and sniffing his clothing, and I did feel bad about poking around in his private space.

It was only that after two days of being alone with nothing to do I was going stir-crazy.

After he'd left me that morning, I'd decided that the only way to figure out how to get him on board with the whole losing my virginity thing was to explore as much of his house as I could, see what I could discover about him. And then perhaps use it to my advantage.

Unfortunately, there wasn't much to discover. He had an industrial, minimalist aesthetic which seemed to involve no clutter anywhere and absolutely nothing personal, including no knick-knacks or family photographs.

So I'd asked what I could of his housekeeper, Mrs Jacobs, but she wouldn't give me any answers, getting annoyed when I attempted to press the issue.

So I'd tried to wait him out.

I swam in the pool. I walked around the gardens. I watched TV and a few movies. I peered through his library and the bookshelves full of books.

But I couldn't settle. Every passing hour was another hour of my freedom gone. Another hour closer to going back to my father and a life of no choices about anything.

It put me in a foul mood.

This wasn't just about sex and my stupid hymen. Or even revenge against my dad. This was about life. *My* life. And what was missing from it. Choice. That was what was missing.

And I wanted the very first choice that I made to be about Ajax. Learning more of his secrets. Discovering more of his touch, more of *him*. And the longer he stayed away, the hungrier for him I became.

That's why I was up here on the forbidden second level of his house. Because my curiosity had morphed into frustration and I hadn't been able to contain it. I couldn't stop obsessing about what was up there, thinking that if he'd told me to stay away, it must mean that there was something he didn't want me to see.

So on the third day I'd crept up the stairs.

The second level had been quiet, with the same kind of uncluttered, minimalist vibe that the downstairs had.

There was an office and a bedroom that both faced the ocean and made the most of the awesome view.

His office was a plain white room with a polished wooden floor and a huge slab of black wood that served as a desk, with a sleek silver computer on it. Bookshelves lined two walls, all stacked with business texts and filing boxes. But, unlike downstairs, there was a piece of art on the wall above his desk: a painting of a yacht on the ocean, sailing towards the horizon. The picture was simple and clean and beautifully done. I could almost smell the salt coming from it, feel the wind in my hair.

Why had he hung this picture here? What was it that he liked about it?

I was tempted to look at his books or have a nosey at his computer, but I did have a few scruples and decided not to in the end, moving into his bedroom instead.

That was a nice space, the only furniture a massive bed that faced the wall of glass and a dresser. There were two photos on it, who I assumed were his brothers, Leon and Xander.

There wasn't much else in the bedroom but, since the door to the closet was open, I put my head in and had a quick look inside. That's when his scent hit me and that's when I stepped inside, moving to where one of his suits hung, wanting more of it and the warm feeling it gave me.

Yes, I was an idiot and sniffing his clothes was ridiculous. But that scent reminded me of how he'd made me feel the night he'd kidnapped me. Safe. Peaceful. Yet excited too.

You should probably leave before he catches you here.

I straightened reluctantly. I really didn't want him to catch me on the second level, especially not in his closet with my nose in his suit.

Abruptly, fingers closed around my upper arm.

I froze, a burst of panic exploding through me.

The fingers tightened in an irresistible grip and I found myself being pulled gently but firmly out of the closet then pushed with the same irresistible gentleness against the closet door.

An expanse of white cotton was in front of me, a T-shirt pulled tight over a broad, muscled chest.

Oh, hell.

I went from panic to excitement in seconds as it slowly penetrated whose fingers were wrapped around my upper arm. And the scent that I'd been inhaling only moments before was now coming direct from the source.

'Little one,' Ajax rumbled. 'What the fuck are you doing in my closet?'

Embarrassment set fire to my cheeks and I wanted to sink straight through the floor.

Going through his things had turned out to be a really stupid idea.

'I'm sorry.' I stared at his chest because I couldn't bear to look up at him. 'I was just…uh…bored.'

'Bored,' he echoed. 'So bored that you had to come upstairs, where I explicitly told you *not* to go, and start looking around my fucking closet?'

He sounded pissed and he had every right to be. Being found intruding on his privacy didn't exactly reflect well on me.

'I… I'm sorry,' I repeated. 'I know I shouldn't have. But there wasn't anything else to do. I swam in the pool and watched all the movies. And I don't have a computer, and I—'

'Look at me when you're speaking to me.'

I didn't want to, but staring at his chest was stupid so I gritted my teeth and looked up.

His electric-blue gaze slammed into mine and all the air vanished from my lungs, sending my heartbeat tumbling over itself.

In the two days he'd been away, I'd told myself that surely I'd overstated his attractiveness; that he couldn't possibly have been as gorgeous and compelling as I'd made him in my head.

But I was wrong. If anything, I'd *understated* it.

He stood very close, looking down at me, and his fingers on my skin were warm, sensitising all the places that he wasn't touching.

Bloody man.

'That doesn't explain what you're doing up here.' He said each word very quietly, anger gleaming in his eyes. 'After I told you not to.'

My own anger rose, fuelled by my helpless response to him, not to mention a fair amount of embarrassment.

I should have locked it down, but I couldn't. I'd been trapped in his house for two days, with the timer on my brief window of freedom from Dad slowly ticking down, and I didn't have the emotional resources to get myself under control.

'I was curious,' I snapped, lifting my chin. 'And look, if you leave me alone for two days, you're going to have to give me something to do or else I'll find something on my own that you may not like.'

'What are you, a toddler?' His expression turned thunderous. 'This area is private and I told you it was out of bounds. What made you think you could just come up here and start looking around?'

Another wave of defensive anger went through me,

his tone reminding me of the way Dad would berate me for my behaviour, telling me I was an insult to my mother's memory.

It never failed to hurt me.

'You patronising asshole,' I said, stung. 'Don't call me that.'

'I'll call you anything I damn well please. Especially if you're poking about in places that don't concern you.'

'Yeah, I know,' I shot back. 'I said I was sorry. I was just curious about you, okay?'

He went quite still, like a big predator spotting prey, a kind of electricity gathering around him that made something inside me pulse with excitement despite my anger. 'Curious about me?'

My mouth had gone dry, my quicksilver emotions changing in response, the anger beginning to fade, excitement building. 'I wanted to find out more about you.'

'What more?'

'I don't know.' Another blush heated my cheeks. 'Anything really.'

He leaned down, his face inches from mine, his astonishing blue eyes filling my vision. And I could smell his scent again, warm and sexy and masculine. 'If you've gone through my stuff, there'll be hell to pay.' He moved his muscled body closer, his heat surrounding me. 'I'm sorry about the toddler thing, but understand me: I wouldn't allow my brothers up here, let alone the daughter of my enemy.'

My breath hitched.

He was so beautiful and I stared, my anger forgotten.

The sharp angle of his jaw was made even sharper

by the faint black line of his beard and his cheekbones were to die for. The blade of his nose was straight, though I could see a few faint scars bisecting one eyebrow, scar tissue pulling at the corner of one eye.

It was a fascinating face. One that contained secrets and mysteries.

His black lashes were thick, a perfect frame for those startling pale blue eyes and the anger glowing in the depths of them.

I didn't look away. I couldn't. 'I didn't go into your things, I promise.' God, I wanted to touch him again. To feel his hot skin and the prickle of his beard against my fingertips. 'I only looked and then I…had to go smell your clothes a little.'

He blinked. 'Smell my clothes?'

I wasn't embarrassed any more, not now he was right in front of me, overwhelming me with his physical nearness. A bomb could have gone off behind him and I wouldn't have noticed. 'What can I say? You smell nice.' Somehow, without my conscious control, my hand was lifting, my fingers brushing along his jaw, the delicious prickle of his whiskers against my fingertips. 'And…you feel nice too.'

Ajax became statue-still. You'd think I'd shot him rather than simply touched him.

I shouldn't be doing this. I should control myself better, especially when I'd already made him angry by intruding on his privacy.

But I couldn't make myself stop. My fingertips grazed the sharp plane of his jaw, the feel of his skin sending short, intense pulses of excitement through me. This was so new, so different. It was wondrous.

The anger in his eyes changed, becoming something

hotter. Brighter. 'What are you doing?' His voice was strange, deep and oddly husky.

'Touching you.' Helplessly, my gaze dropped to his fascinating mouth and I brushed the curve of his bottom lip. My God. It was so soft. Who knew there could be something soft about Ajax King? 'Is that okay?'

He was so still and he was staring at me so fixedly. Perhaps he didn't want this. Perhaps he didn't like it.

Control yourself, girl. You're an embarrassment.

Dad's voice echoed in my head like a warning and a part of me curled up in shame. Yet that wasn't enough for me to take my hand away.

He was fascinating, addictive. A temptation too great for me to resist and it had been so long since I'd touched another person, so long since I'd had any physical contact with anyone at all, and I ached. I'd been so isolated and I was so lonely.

This was my chance to take something for myself.

Every other woman got to choose their own partner so why couldn't I?

'Stop,' Ajax said in that strange voice.

Remember what happened the last time you made a choice.

Yes, I remembered. Cam.

The shame inside me grew larger. 'I'm sorry.' I snatched my hand away and looked at the floor. 'I didn't mean to touch you. I should have asked or something. I'm not very good at—'

'Look at me, Imogen.'

I took a breath and looked, the note of command in his voice irresistible.

The heat in his gaze nearly flattened me.

Desire burned in his eyes. He liked me touching him. I could tell.

My breath caught.

'It's not that I don't want you to touch me,' he said roughly. 'It's that you shouldn't. And you know why.'

Of course I did. The whole virginity thing.

'But…you can kiss me, right?' I stared up at him. 'Dad wouldn't know if you did.'

'No,' Ajax murmured. 'No, he wouldn't.' His attention drifted, falling to my mouth. 'But what I want doesn't matter.'

That puzzled me. Why would he think that what he wanted didn't matter? And what did he want anyway?

'Doesn't it?' I asked. 'Why not?'

Somehow he was closer than he had been a moment ago, though I hadn't seen him move. He still had his hand wrapped around my arm and I was so aware of it I was sure I could feel every line of his fingerprints on my skin.

He didn't answer, his gaze lifting to clash with mine again.

There was a pressure in the air around us, the relentless build of attraction getting stronger and stronger.

'Please,' I heard myself say. 'I've never been kissed before. Not properly. And I… I'd like my first proper kiss to be with someone I want.'

He stared at me another long, aching second.

Then he closed the gap between us and covered my mouth with his.

Shock held me motionless.

I'd thought he wouldn't do it, but he had, and now Ajax King was kissing me. Those beautiful lips I'd traced with my finger mere moments ago were now on mine and they felt…oh, God, *amazing*.

He must have been drinking coffee at some point, the taste dark and rich, combining with a heady flavour that was all Ajax. It was delicious. I couldn't get enough.

The kiss was hard and yet somehow soft at the same time, his tongue tracing the seam of my mouth, getting me to open for him. And I shuddered in helpless reaction, lightning striking all over my skin, sending goosebumps racing everywhere, leaving me helpless to do anything but give him what he wanted.

This was nothing like the brief brush of his lips in the car a few days earlier. This was as similar to that as a candle flame was to a forest fire.

His tongue pushed into my mouth, beginning to explore me slowly and deliberately, and with so much heat I began to shake.

I pressed my palms to his hard chest, gripping onto the warm cotton of his T-shirt, holding on tight. A deep moan of pleasure escaped me.

I didn't know what had made him change his mind, but I didn't want to question it. I just wanted more.

And he seemed to understand, moving so I was pinned between him and the closet door, deepening the kiss, controlling it with such effortless mastery I nearly swooned.

Correction, actual swooning was already happening, my knees weak, my hands clenching even tighter in the cotton of his shirt just to stay upright.

I couldn't control myself any more. It had become impossible. I'd been without physical closeness for so long, thinking about him constantly for two days straight, craving his touch so badly I couldn't stop.

I tipped my head back, opening my mouth to give him greater access, at the same time as I tried to kiss him in return, wanting more of his heat and intoxicating flavour. Wanting more of his touch and his scent and the feel of him against my skin.

But I had no idea how to get it.

I tried to pull him closer, tugging on his T-shirt, but he wouldn't move, making me groan in frustration.

But then he cupped my jaw in one of his big, warm hands and kissed me harder, deeper, nipping at my bottom lip, changing the angle, turning the kiss into something so unbearably erotic I wondered if it was possible to come from kissing alone.

It wasn't enough, though. I arched my back against the closet door, trying to press myself into his hard body.

He ignored me, lifting his mouth from mine and, when I tried to follow, his fingers on my jaw tightened, holding me in place.

I was panting and I didn't care. 'Don't stop.' My mouth felt deliciously swollen and a little bruised from that kiss. 'Please.'

The electricity in his gaze crackled over my skin, the heat burning in the depths of all that winter blue undeniable. There was a flush to his high cheekbones, a slash of red that told its own story, and I could hear his ragged breathing.

He wanted me. It was obvious.

'No,' he said.

CHAPTER NINE

Ajax

IMOGEN WAS LOOKING up at me, her eyes wide and dark, her delectable mouth all red from my kiss. Her hands were gripping the front of my T-shirt so tightly it was like she was afraid to let me go, her chest rising and falling fast and hard. The scent of roses and the faint musk of feminine arousal were winding tight around me, making my breath catch.

I shouldn't have kissed her. Why the fuck had I?

All I'd meant to do was ask her why the hell she was in my room after I'd explicitly told her she wasn't allowed up here.

But then she'd touched me. Despite my very real anger, she'd simply put up her small hand and those delicate fingers had run along my jaw, lightly, gently. And she'd looked at me as if she'd never seen anything like me before in all her life. As if I was fascinating to her.

People were afraid of me. They were never fascinated by me.

For some women my reputation was a turn-on and I was a trophy. Bedding the most dangerous man in Sydney had a certain status factor.

Yet there was no fear in Imogen, either of me or my anger, and it got me hard. The way she'd begged me to kiss her, because her first kiss should be with someone she wanted…

Hell, how could I deny her?

You wanted to kiss her. Two days and she still affects you as badly as she did the night you kidnapped her.

She did. That was a fact. And fuck, I *did* want to kiss her. So why shouldn't I?

It was only a kiss…

Except now I was hard as a rock and the scent of her was driving me crazy. And there was a part of me that had forgotten about the goddamn big picture. That wanted nothing more than to lift her against the closet door and fuck us both into the middle of next week.

Except her virginity was the leverage I needed against her father and if I took it, that leverage would be gone.

There are other methods you can use to get rid of him.

Sure there were. But those were Dad's methods and I didn't use them. I was better than that.

So what? You can fake a doctor's certificate if need be.

Yeah, but I'd given my word as a King that I wouldn't touch her and that still meant something.

You know White doesn't give a shit about your word.

He might not, but I did. The King name was mud in this town and my brothers and I wanted that to change. And that meant standing by our promises, keeping to the agreements we'd made.

And going back on my word would make me no better than Dad.

'No? Okay then.' The disappointment in her voice caught at me. 'I'm sorry. I shouldn't have asked for a kiss. I just...'

The skin of her jaw beneath my fingertips was very warm and her hair brushing the back of my hand where I held her was very soft. It felt silky, and I caught a faint suggestion of what it would feel like spread over my chest.

I couldn't lie, couldn't tell myself I didn't want her. But those big picture goals were more important than what I wanted for myself and always would be.

I couldn't sacrifice them for a couple of hours in bed with a woman, no matter how lovely she was.

'You just what?' I prompted, trying not to let myself become mesmerised by her pink mouth and the little mole just above it. She'd tasted sweet when I'd kissed her, and yet tart at the same time, the flavour lingering on my tongue. What would the rest of her taste like?

There was a worried look in her eyes, as if she couldn't decide on what to say. Then her mouth firmed. 'Okay, the truth is that I was hoping for some revenge on Dad. You know what he's been using me for, a trophy for his friends to build alliances. And he doesn't care how I feel about it. And I'm pissed off, Ajax. When I lose my virginity, I want it to be with someone who's my choice, not his. Someone I'm attracted to.' She kept her gaze on mine as she turned her cheek into my palm, nuzzling into it like a little cat. 'Someone like you.'

There was determination in those green eyes of hers. A hint of the strength that I'd seen when I'd first come up behind her in the bathroom at the ball. This woman wasn't only wide-eyed questions and restless energy.

She was more complex than that, which was both fascinating and intensely sexy at the same time.

'I'm your father's enemy, though,' I murmured. 'He's not going to like it.'

'I know. That's kind of the whole point. That's what makes it perfect.'

Revenge. Hell, that was a concept I could relate to.

I kept my hand where it was, against her cheek. 'But your virginity is vital to my plan working, remember?'

Disappointment flashed across her expressive face. 'In that case, you'd better let me go.'

I didn't want to. She could have her revenge, couldn't she? And maybe I could get a little something for myself too. Such as her, all silky and strokeable beneath me.

It's a slippery slope. You know this.

Fuck, I did know. It was the tiny slips that led to greater ones. Small actions that didn't seem like massive deals, that eventually brought you down. That's how I'd finally managed to bring my father down, after all.

And if I took Imogen, if I got rid of the only thing I could use against White, what would I have left?

The only other language he understood was violence and I could *not* go down that road again.

The disappointment in Imogen's eyes was loud and clear. But there was also something else under that, something that hooked into my chest and twisted hard.

'What?' I asked roughly, my hand still against her cheek, even though I knew better than to keep it there. 'Don't look at me like that.'

'You're the only one.' Her voice was hoarse. 'You're the only one who's ever made me feel like this.'

Ah, Christ. What was she doing saying shit like that to me? 'I'm not special, Imogen. How many men have you even met?'

'Enough.' She lifted her hand and put it over mine, holding my palm to her warm skin. 'Enough to know it's you, Ajax. It's all you.'

The sensation in my chest twisted even tighter. 'I can't.'

'Then let me go.' Her hand dropped away.

Yes, I should let her go. I *should*.

And yet there was a part of me that refused. A part that was sick of having to sacrifice everything I wanted all the damn time. After everything I'd done so far for my brothers and my city, wasn't I fucking owed something for myself?

You can't have it and you know that.

'I'm not any girl's first time.' My voice had roughened further, turning dark and gritty, and I didn't even know why I was saying it when I wasn't going to be doing anything with her. 'Not if you're after sweet and nice.'

'Who said I wanted sweet and nice?' Her gaze searched mine. 'What if I wanted…rough? And kind of dirty?'

As if she even knew what that meant. Christ, why was I standing here? Why was I *still* touching her?

'Do you?' I asked, as if I was going to go through with it, throwing away the only leverage I had.

'I've watched a few videos.' She nuzzled against my palm again and this time the edge of her teeth grazed the base of my thumb. Then she bit me gently, watching my reaction with undisguised interest.

I felt that small nip like she had her teeth against

the head of my dick, short, sharp and electric. 'A few videos don't mean shit, little virgin,' I growled, angry at myself that I couldn't seem to do what I should and let her go. 'If you haven't done it, you don't know what it means.'

Her cheeks flushed, but determination glowed in her bright eyes. 'Why don't you show me then?'

Step away from her.

'Imogen...'

'Is that a yes?'

The smell of roses was laced through with the scent of her arousal, the heat of her body so close, bleeding into mine. I'd got my housekeeper to get her some clothes the night I'd kidnapped her and clearly she'd helped herself to them, wearing a green T-shirt and grey yoga pants. When she sucked in a breath the fabric stretched tight across her perfect little tits, her nipples pressing hard against the cotton.

You're going to do this, aren't you?

I'd had to put aside all the things I'd truly wanted. A home. A woman I loved and who loved me. A family that wasn't rotten to the core.

I'd accepted that those things weren't for men like me. Not when association with me would turn them into targets for my enemies. I couldn't allow anyone to take that risk, nor could I allow myself any vulnerabilities.

I couldn't allow myself to slip down the slope that would lead me back to my father and all I'd done in his name.

But...this girl wanted me. I was *her* choice. And the way she looked at me, like I was a dream come true...

You'll put everything at risk just to fuck her?

I could make it work. Doctors' certificates could be faked. And if I could bring down Augustus King, then surely one afternoon with a beautiful woman wouldn't put anything at risk.

Somehow my thumb was brushing lightly over her cushiony lower lip, then easing into her mouth. The heat of her lips closing around my skin made my breath catch.

Green fire glittered in her eyes. She bit me again.

Electricity arced directly to my aching cock and it was all I could do not to slam her against the door, rip those goddamn yoga pants off her and sink straight into her hot little pussy.

'A couple of hours,' I growled, making a decision that I knew I'd regret but making it anyway. 'That's all I can give you.'

She nodded frantically, her breathing turning ragged.

'Good. Now listen, this is important.' I leaned down a fraction more, looking deep into her eyes, watching the flames in them leap higher. 'You need to tell me if anything doesn't feel good or if you don't like it. And especially if something is—'

Imogen bit me harder, cutting off everything I'd been going to say.

Fuck it.

I pulled my thumb from her mouth and covered it with mine, taking what I wanted for once in my fucking life.

Something for me.

And the moment my lips touched hers, she opened for me, hot and sweet, her tongue touching mine at first hesitantly and then with more demand. Then her hands opened on my chest and slid up, winding her arms around my neck, her small curvy body arching into me. A soft moan escaped her and I found myself putting one palm onto the closet door beside her head while I cupped her jaw with the other, leaning in as she tried to pull me closer.

She was raw demand and passionate heat, holding nothing back. And she tasted so fucking sweet. So fucking hot.

Beneath those wide eyes and painful honesty, she was primal.

Just like me.

Any resistance I had left burned to ashes right where I stood.

I let go of her jaw and slid my hand into her pale silky hair, curling my fingers through it and gripping on tight, pulling her head back so I could kiss her deeper.

She didn't protest, moaning as I nipped her lower lip, licking into her mouth and taking possession once again. Jesus, she was delicious.

Her arms around my neck tightened, pulling me even closer, and then she began to climb me like a goddamn tree, winding her legs around my waist, arching her spine, pressing her tits against my chest and tilting her hips so my dick was rubbing up against her clit through her clothes.

She stole my breath.

I pulled her hands from around my neck, pinning them back against the closet door above her head. Then I lifted my mouth from hers. 'If you don't want this to be over right here, right now, you need to slow down.'

She was panting, her chest heaving, her luscious

mouth pink and swollen from my kisses. 'But I don't want to go slow.' Her hips rolled against mine, her heat soaking through the yoga pants she wore and through the denim of my jeans. 'Oh... Ajax...' Her voice was husky and breathless. 'I need you...please.'

It wouldn't have taken much to rip all that material out of my way and get inside her. But I wasn't an animal. I'd take my own sweet time and give us both as much pleasure as I could.

So I settled my hips between her thighs and rocked against her, watching as her face became even more flushed, her eyes luminous. She moaned as I made sure the ridge of my hard-on hit her clit, grinding on it, making her shudder and tremble and pull against the hold I had on her wrists.

'Oh, God. That feels amazing.' She writhed slowly, moving her hips in response. 'But aren't you...? I m-mean, don't you...? Oh...'

'Stop talking and let me concentrate.' I changed my angle, rubbing my aching dick against her.

She tipped her head back, her eyes half closing in pleasure. 'But I think...' Her chest heaved. 'Oh... I might...c-come. And I don't want to, not yet.'

I leaned down and pressed my mouth to her throat, licking the salt from her skin, feeling her shudder in response. 'There's no limit to the number of orgasms you can have, sweetheart. So feel free.'

'But...don't... Oh, Ajax... *Ajax*...'

The sound of desperation in her voice was unbelievably fucking hot. So was the way she writhed and panted, arching her back, wanting more.

So I gave it to her.

Keeping one hand wrapped around her wrists above

her head, I pulled her T-shirt up with the other, exposing a delicate white lace bra. It was pretty, especially the way her pink nipples showed through the fabric. I took a second to admire it, then dragged one of the cups to the side, baring her. Then I bent to her hard nipple and licked it.

She jerked in my arms, gasping.

I licked her again, the salty-sweet taste of her skin as delicious as her kiss. Jesus, this woman. I could eat her up.

Hell, I would. Right now.

I drew her nipple into my mouth and sucked, feeling her body stiffen and hearing her breath catch. Then I nipped her at the same time as I began to grind against her once again, trying to go slow, to tease her, to draw out the pleasure as long as I could.

But she wouldn't let me.

Her legs tightened around my waist as she lifted her hips against mine and arched her spine again, encouraging me to suck on her harder, deeper.

'Yes,' she gasped thickly. 'Oh, Ajax, yes…'

She was so fucking sexy. That taste of her was in my mouth, her wet little pussy soaking my goddamn jeans.

Jesus, she was going to make me come like a bloody teenage boy.

I teased her nipple with my teeth until the words she was muttering became incoherent cries. Until she went suddenly stiff in my arms, calling my name as she came.

CHAPTER TEN

Imogen

I SHUDDERED IN Ajax's arms, mind-blowing pleasure ripping through me, making me feel like I was glowing, lit up from the inside by the sheer ecstasy of his touch.

Hell, if I'd known sex would be like this, I'd have tried a lot harder to escape Dad.

It's not just the sex. It's Ajax.

I had my head tipped back against the closet door and my eyes were closed, but now I opened them a crack, half afraid to look at him, yet at the same time half desperate too.

His eyes were cobalt with desire, his expression feral with possessive hunger.

My soul shivered in instinctive response.

I'd told him just before that it was him, that he was different, and that had been instinct. But now I knew for certain. This feeling inside me, this pleasure. It was all because of him.

For a second I tried imagining doing this with anyone else and I...couldn't. I'd wanted him from the moment I'd first seen him, on a visceral level, but he also made me feel safe and protected.

Yet he wasn't a safe man. He was dangerous. And that excited me for reasons I didn't understand. There was a physical energy that drew me to him, yet it was about more than that.

I affected him. I'd seen him trying to resist me and being unable to. I liked that. I liked that a *lot*. It made me feel powerful and strong, and it had been too long since I'd felt either of those things.

'Still with me?' His voice was rough black velvet brushing over my skin, dark and sensual with a husky edge.

And this time my body shivered along with my soul.

I still had my legs wrapped around his lean waist, the ridge of his cock nudging my throbbing clit. The pressure of his fingers around my wrists was getting me off too, as if part of me enjoyed being held helpless like this.

I should have been embarrassed by the way I'd clawed at him and climbed him, losing control of myself in a way my father would have despised. But the way Ajax was looking at me made all my embarrassment fade away.

'Um...yes.' God, I sounded croaky. 'Unless those videos were wrong, we haven't finished, though, right?' I couldn't quite hide my uncertainty, a part of me worried that this was all he was going to give me. That he might change his mind and leave me here, sated yet still starving.

He shifted, the hard ridge between my thighs brushing against my sensitive sex, sending a shockwave of pleasure through me, his free hand cupping my bare breast.

His palm was hot, searing against my skin, and

when he brushed his thumb over my nipple, still slick from his mouth, I groaned.

'No, we're not finished.' He watched me, gauging my reactions. 'After all, you're still a virgin.'

'Well, right?' A weird reaction was starting to set in, a burst of intense emotion sweeping over me, making me feel like crying.

Okay, now *this* was embarrassing.

I never cried. Not ever. Not even the day Dad had informed me that I'd killed my mother by being born and he'd never forgive me for it. And that if I ever wanted even a crumb of attention from him, I'd have to work for it.

Not that I'd ever think about that day again.

'I mean, this hymen isn't going to break itself,' I babbled, trying to talk away the vulnerability that was getting wider and larger inside me. 'And it's not going to be much of a revenge if—'

Ajax lifted his hand from my breast and laid his thumb against my mouth, stopping the flow of words. His gaze narrowed, focusing intensely on me. 'Little one, are you okay?'

To my horror, I felt my lower lip wobble.

This wasn't how it went in the videos. The women all moaned and gasped like they were enjoying themselves, but no one cried afterwards. No one talked about feelings.

I knew that wasn't the point—porn didn't have feelings attached—but my reaction still caught me by surprise.

Why was this happening? A combination of his physical closeness and the unstoppable pleasure he'd given me? The realisation that this was all centred around him somehow? Or was it something else?

Whatever it was, I didn't like it. I didn't want it.

'What's wrong?' Ajax took his thumb from my mouth. 'And give me the truth this time.'

I swallowed, trying to get rid of the lump in my throat.

Dad would be appalled.

He would. He hated my tears. He thought I didn't deserve to cry.

'Nothing.' Desperately, I tried to salvage the situation. 'I'm fine.'

But of course Ajax knew I was lying.

'You're not fine,' he said flatly. 'You were honest with me before, Imogen. Why are you lying now?'

Shit. I was such a failure. This was why I'd wanted to get away from Dad in the first place, because I could never be what he wanted me to be. I could never earn a place in his heart. And my inability to do any of that only got people hurt in the process.

'Okay, so you're right. I'm not fine,' I croaked pathetically, not even trying to hide it because what was the point? 'I feel…weird. Like I want to cry. But it's not you. It's nothing you've done. It's just…'

He didn't say anything, simply stared at me.

'Don't think that this means I don't want you to keep going,' I added, angry with myself for ruining the moment. 'I still need you to take my virginity, okay? I want my damn revenge.'

He remained silent.

Great, so I'd screwed up. I'd been too full-on. Too honest. Too emotional. Too…everything.

I should have remembered that there were always

consequences when I didn't keep myself under control. Consequences such as what had happened to Cameron, the poor guy beaten within an inch of his life.

My fault. I'd never even thought that asking him out would be a problem, I'd simply gone ahead and asked him, too caught up in my attraction to him. And he'd got hurt because of me.

Failing. I was always failing.

Ajax lowered my arms from over my head, chafing my wrists gently. Then he eased me down his body until I was standing on the floor.

His gentleness made the emotions crashing around inside me somehow even worse. I felt like a hurt child in need of comfort.

How humiliating.

I tried to muster up some anger but, before I could get good and worked up, he picked me up in his arms and carried me over to the huge bed that faced the ocean, putting me down on the edge of the mattress before crouching in front of me.

'It's okay,' I muttered. 'You can leave now.'

'Leave?' He frowned. 'Why would I do that?'

'Uh, because I'm being pathetic and emotional?'

He shrugged one powerful shoulder as if that didn't matter at all to him. 'You're not being pathetic. Emotional yes, but what you're feeling is normal. Sometimes it happens when sex is particularly intense.'

Well, it *had* been intense, that was for sure.

I swallowed past the lump in my throat. 'Has it happened to you? Wanting to cry after sex, I mean?' The question sounded stupid as soon as it came out of my mouth. Ajax King wanting to cry after an orgasm?

The idea was as ludicrous as Dad suddenly becoming Prime Minister.

Ajax didn't laugh, thank God. 'No, but I know it happens to some people.'

'Well, I don't want it to happen to me.' And I didn't. Not crying was about the only thing I'd managed to succeed at, the only thing that Dad didn't criticise me for.

Crying now would be one failure too many.

I blinked hard and looked down at my hands. 'I don't blame you if you don't want to do this any more. I didn't mean to ruin the mood.'

Strong fingers caught my jaw, tipping my face up.

He'd risen to his feet and was bending over me, his intense blue gaze blazing into mine. 'You're not ruining anything. Cry if you want to. Scream if you want to. Emotion doesn't scare me, Imogen. I'm going to fuck you either way.'

The words shot down my spine like shocks. His expression was uncompromising and it came to me all of a sudden that of course my emotions didn't scare him. They didn't matter to him *at all*.

Because he didn't care.

Something tight in my chest, something I hadn't realised was there, suddenly eased. Like a heavy stone being lifted away.

I could cry. I could scream. I could ask too many questions. Be too restless. Talk too much. Do whatever I wanted.

I could be myself and it wouldn't matter.

Because Ajax didn't care and that meant I didn't need to either.

There is no way you can fail, not here, not with him.

A tear slid down my cheek without my conscious control. Then another and another and, for the first time in years, I didn't try to repress them or swallow them back, or talk to distract myself from the ache in my heart.

I let them fall.

There was no judgement in Ajax's face, that I'd seen so often in Dad's. None of the distaste or the active contempt. He simply…watched, expressionless, giving me some time and a quiet space to cry.

Then, after a while, his grip on my chin tightened and he bent down over me and kissed me.

I tasted the salt of my tears and that rich, dark flavour that was all him, and I was suddenly hungry. Hungrier than I'd ever been in my entire life.

Opening my mouth, I let him in, reaching out to pull him to me. But he was already pushing me back onto the bed and following me down onto it. His body was heavy, solid with muscle and so hot it felt like I was lying directly under a furnace.

He felt so good.

I arched up, pressing myself against him, spreading my thighs so he could lie between them and curling my arms around his neck. I kissed him harder, deeper; kissed him like there was no tomorrow and no yesterday, only now. Salt and Ajax in my mouth, the taste of him imprinting on me so I'd never get it out of my head and never want to.

He kissed me back, demanding, pushing his tongue deep into my mouth. Nipping my lower lip, sucking on it. Licking and taking, conquering. And I let myself be conquered.

Our kisses became more desperate, the sound of our breathing ragged.

Abruptly, he pushed himself off me, going up on his knees, straddling my hips, and he reached for the hem of his T-shirt, dragging it up and over his head. The movement was sexy and when his T-shirt came off I nearly gasped.

He was a work of art. Not only was every muscle from his pecs to his abs cut and sharply defined, they were highlighted by the most incredible tattoos I'd ever seen. Thick black abstract lines running all over his torso, trailing down over the broad plane of his chest and curling around his lean hips, outlining every dip and hollow, every flex and contraction.

I pushed myself up, my breath already short and getting shorter, reaching for him, my palms landing on his stomach. He was smooth and hot, the muscle beneath rock-hard. And I could feel the tightening of his abs beneath my fingertips, the merest hint of the power contained in his magnificent body.

Desperate to touch as much of him as I could, I ran my palms up from his stomach to his pecs, the prickle of hair an added excitement. God, he felt incredible. I leaned in, nuzzling against his abdomen, loving his heat and the woody, spicy scent of him. Then I licked him, tasting salt.

He shuddered, his reaction firing my desire even higher. I tried licking him again, but he caught me underneath my arms and pushed me back down onto the mattress. And then I couldn't do anything but lie there as he virtually ripped my clothes off.

In the hundreds of romance novels I'd read, I'd always thought that the ripping of the clothes was figurative. Apparently not with Ajax King.

He tore my T-shirt clean down the middle and got rid of the fabric, pulling apart my lacy white bra with the same ease. Then he jerked away my yoga pants and knickers along with them, so I lay naked in the middle of the bed.

He paused a moment, his gaze electric, scorching me every place it touched. And it touched *everywhere.*

If I'd thought about it I might have been embarrassed. No one had seen my naked body since I was a child. But it didn't even occur to me. All I wanted was him, naked as I was, his skin against mine.

'Ajax,' I said hoarsely. *'Please.'*

He said nothing, watching me with those intense, unfathomable eyes. Then his hands slowly moved to the buttons of his jeans.

Too slowly.

I sat up and reached for them myself, but he knocked my hands away.

'Lie down.' His voice was full of authority and darkness. 'Lie down and wait patiently, and you'll get what you want.'

A frustrated sound escaped me, but I did what I was told.

I didn't like to stay still for long and lying there, my breathing fast and hard, the need inside me like an animal tearing at me in its hunger, felt like the most difficult thing I'd ever done.

Slowly, achingly slowly, Ajax undid the buttons of his jeans and pulled down the zip, spreading the fabric. I could see the long, hard length that pressed against the material of his black boxers…

My pulse began to accelerate, my mouth was watering, my breath catching hard in my chest.

Holy crap. He was huge.

I began to push myself up again, wanting to touch him and unable to keep still for much longer, but he got off the bed suddenly, jerking down his jeans and getting rid of the rest of his clothes.

I blinked, staring at him, utterly mesmerised by the sheer masculine beauty of him. All that muscle and power. All that strength.

And his cock too, big and thick and hard, curving up towards his flat stomach. I wanted to touch it, wanted to see what it felt like and whether it would be as hard as it looked, or as smooth.

But I didn't get a chance to touch because he was back on the bed, sliding his arms beneath me and gathering me up before covering me with his body, pressing me back down onto the mattress.

The slide of his bare skin over mine made me shiver and the weight of him… I didn't feel crushed or suffocated. I felt anchored. Safe.

I put my arms around him, smoothing my palms over his broad back, feeling his muscles flex as I stroked down his spine, glorying in the feel of him. His hips were positioned between my thighs, his cock lying against my throbbing sex.

So. Good.

His mouth found mine and he was kissing me again, deeply, hungrily. I tried to kiss him back but he'd moved on, kissing a path along my jaw and down my throat, licking and nipping at me like I was his favourite ice-cream and he was making a meal out of me.

I panted as he found my breasts, teasing my nipples

with his tongue then sucking hard on each one, making me groan and arch up into him. His mouth was so hot and the graze of his teeth on my skin made me moan.

His big hands glided over my hips, scorching, then over my thighs and between them, pushing them apart with an irresistible strength that I found shockingly erotic. And then his breath moved over my stomach, his mouth brushing the sensitive skin of my inner thighs.

Oh, God. He could not be doing what I thought he was doing. Could he?

I pushed myself up on my elbows, looking down the length of my body. He was kneeling between my legs, the predatory hunger on his face making me lose my train of thought.

'What are you doing?' I gasped, shuddering as he slid his palms under my butt, lifting me.

He merely pinned me with his mesmerising stare, one corner of his mouth turning up in the wickedest, sexiest smile I'd ever seen. Then he buried his face between my legs and the entire world exploded into flame.

I cried out, sensation swamping me as his tongue pushed deep into my pussy, licking and exploring. I'd seen this in the videos but I'd honestly never thought the pleasure would be quite this intense. And then his hold on me shifted, his thumb finding my clit, an added pressure that made me arch back on the mattress in ecstasy.

Oh, God. Oh, God. Could something be *too* good? Because this was. I had no idea how I was going to survive it.

Gently, he separated the folds of my sex with his fingers so his tongue could explore me deeper, the hungry sounds of masculine pleasure filling the room, making me go hot all over.

I reached down blindly and tangled my fingers in his hair, needing something to hold onto as he pushed me higher and higher. Every lick was a brush of fire, the pressure of his tongue inside me and his thumb on my clit almost unbearable.

The orgasm hit without warning, pleasure detonating like a bomb, making me cry out as the raw ecstasy of it overwhelmed me.

Then I lay there trembling with the aftershocks, my mind completely blown, feeling him move on the bed. The sound of a drawer being opened came and then the crinkle of foil.

A condom. Which meant…

I felt the brush of his skin, hot and smooth, on mine and then his body coming back to cover me again. I forced my eyes open to find him staring down at me, his gaze an intense electric blue.

And he kept on staring at me as he positioned himself, the head of his cock nudging at the entrance of my sex. Sliding his hand under my thigh, he hooked my leg up and around his waist, opening me up for him. Then he slowly pushed into me and I felt myself stretch around his huge cock, the unfamiliar sensation making me gasp and clutch at his shoulders.

I was expecting pain, but there was none. Only a strange pinch that made me stiffen momentarily before the feeling vanished. And then there was nothing but him inside me, thick and hard, sliding deeper, filling me up so completely I could hardly breathe.

His head was bent, his mouth at my throat, his teeth

finding the sensitive place between my shoulder and neck and biting down. At the same time he sunk himself into me as far as he could go and I lay there panting and shaking at the intense pressure.

It was unbearable. It was amazing.

He bit me again, his hips pulling back, making me feel every inch as he slid his cock out, then he was pushing back in, a slow, relentless glide.

My eyes rolled back in my head, moans coming out of my throat without my conscious control.

He was everywhere. Inside me. Around me. The taste of him in my mouth, the scent of him in my nostrils, the feel of him in my sex. I was drowning in him and, quite honestly, I didn't want to be saved.

He ravaged my throat as he began to thrust, deep and hard, taking no account of my inexperience.

Apparently he hadn't been kidding when he'd said he didn't do sweet and nice.

But that was okay. Because I'd told him that maybe I wanted rough and dirty and if this was rough and dirty, I liked it.

No, I *loved* it.

All I was conscious of was the intense pressure and the slow lick of pleasure that began to build. I lifted my other leg and wrapped that around his waist too, instinctively trying to meet his thrusts, grinding to increase the friction.

He growled into my neck, answering my unspoken need by upping the pace.

I dug my nails into his back, gasping as the pleasure began to intensify, wrapping my legs tighter around him.

There was nothing in all the world but this feeling.

Nothing in the world but him and what he was giving me. It was heaven.

He got faster, driving himself deeper, and I clawed at his back, desperation pulling tighter.

'Ajax.' I twisted under him, blind to everything but the need inside me, the pleasure almost frightening in its intensity. 'Please… God…please…'

'Look at me,' he ordered, heated darkness edging his tone. 'Look at me, Imogen.'

My eyes flicked open and I felt the collision as his sky-blue gaze met mine, an impact that shook me right to my core.

He moved harder, ecstasy winding tight around my soul, making me feel helpless and treasured and powerful all at the same time.

Then he pushed his fingers between us, finding my aching clit and pinching gently.

The jolt of delicious pain was all the ignition I needed.

The pressure inside me released in an incandescent burst of pleasure that swamped me, drowned me.

And the blue of his eyes was the only thing that kept me from being swept away.

CHAPTER ELEVEN

Ajax

I WATCHED THE moment her climax hit, a brilliant flare of emerald in her eyes, and I bent my head, kissing her again, taking her desperate cry of release into my mouth.

Then I moved hard and deep, her slick little pussy clenching around my cock and blowing my goddamn mind. She was so soft and hot against me, all roses and musk and husky pleas.

I should have been careful with her, but the way she was clawing at me, her thighs clamped tight around my waist, made me think she could handle what I was giving her.

So I let go, driving her into the mattress as I chased the orgasm that was just out of reach. But my little ex-virgin wouldn't let me go without her. She moved restlessly, panting and writhing, letting me know in no uncertain terms that she was building up to yet another climax.

But I didn't know how long I could hold out.

My cock was aching, every slide into her wet heat

making me grit my teeth not to blow it right there and then.

I'd never had this problem before, could always put off my orgasm for as long as I wanted to, but not with this woman.

The way she gripped me, digging her nails into my back so hard they were going to leave marks. The way she moved under me, clearly hungry for more. The way she looked at me, her iris a thin emerald circle around her dilated pupils, staring at me as if I was the centre of her universe.

She wasn't afraid and she wasn't wary. There was no hesitation or doubt. She didn't care about my reputation or my past. She was with me, hiding nothing. Giving everything.

I had no idea why that was so fucking hot, but it was.

Perhaps it was her responsiveness, how she was so into it. Into my touch and all the new feelings she was experiencing. Because, of course, this was all new to her.

I didn't remember my first time, though I'd been young. I only remembered Julie, another stripper who worked at one of the lounges Dad went to. She'd liked me and I'd liked her and she took me to bed. Showed me what I liked and how to please a woman.

But none of it had felt new.

Not like it was new to Imogen.

And there was something about that, something that got to me even though I didn't want it to.

So I tried to hold back, because I wanted to make her come again, but the feel of her satiny skin and the way her pussy was clenching around my aching dick was too much.

The orgasm burned like wildfire up my spine, a conflagration of pleasure that made me roar against her throat and sink my teeth into her shoulder, shuddering as it blinded me.

I lost myself for a while, only coming back when I felt her hands on my skin, stroking over my shoulders as if she couldn't get enough of touching me.

What the hell had happened? I'd never had an orgasm that intense before, not with anyone.

Imogen made an impatient sound, her breath soft against my throat, so I shifted, pulling out of her and adjusting my weight so I wasn't lying fully on her. Then I looked down.

Her face was deeply flushed, her eyes grass green. A sheen of sweat was up near her hairline and gleaming in the hollow of her throat, her pale golden hair tangled and spread all over the black linen of the bed cover. Her lovely mouth was pouty and full from my kisses…

She looked thoroughly seduced and so beautiful my breath caught.

'You okay?' I asked, my voice gritty and rough.

'Omigod, *so* okay.' Her face was full of awe, no trace of those earlier tears now. 'That was just…wow. Is it always like that?'

'Sometimes.' I ignored the fact that it had never been like that, at least not for me. 'Not always.'

'Lucky for me I got the "sometimes" then.' Her hands moved from my back to my chest, stroking over my pecs and down further, tracing my abs, her touch delicate and light. 'That's probably all because of you. You're amazing, did you know that?'

Jesus, she'd better not put me on a fucking pedestal just because I'd let her cry then made her come a couple of times.

'It's just sex, little one. It's not like I cured cancer.'

I hadn't moderated my tone, but she didn't seem to care, her full mouth turning up into a smile. 'You don't know. Sex like that *could* cure cancer. You might have a magic dick and not even know.'

This woman…

She'd cried earlier, those tears telling a story that I knew I wasn't going to like, yet now she was lying here beneath me, looking sexy and sweet and flirting with me as if she'd done this a thousand times before.

As if she'd never been kept a prisoner by her father or screwed, and screwed hard, by the son of her father's enemy, with no care given for the fact that she was a virgin.

Yeah, she was trouble.

And if you're not careful you'll get in deep.

Ignoring that thought, I pushed back a couple of golden strands of hair that had stuck to her forehead. 'Did you ever think that maybe it's got nothing to do with my dick? It might be that you have a magic pussy.'

Her smile got wider and she spread her hands on my chest, pressing her palms against me, making it obvious she liked the feeling of my skin on hers. 'Hey, that's true. I might. Still, me and my magic pussy are going with my original "you're amazing".' Her fingers made another journey over my abs. 'Can we do it again, please?'

I was getting hard again, her hands on me so good. A couple of hours only I'd promised her and hell, maybe I could stretch it out longer. Especially since I was only just getting started.

The consequences of what I'd done and everything that came with them could wait.

'I don't know—are you up for it?' I stroked my hand down her body, lingering on the soft curve of her tits and the flare of her hips, down to the heat and wetness between her thighs. 'You might be sore.'

She shuddered, parting her thighs to give me access. 'No, I'm not sore. *Oh*...' Her breath caught as I found her clit, brushing lightly over it with the tip of my finger, teasing her. Her lashes swept down and she arched her back. 'Ajax…that feels so good…'

The way she said my name and the way she gave herself utterly to what I was doing to her was like a drug. I couldn't get enough.

'Wait there for me,' I muttered, moving off the bed and crossing over into the en suite bathroom to get rid of the condom.

A minute later I was back and she opened her arms to me like we'd been lovers for years and not a mere half an hour.

For some inexplicable reason, it made my chest get tight.

Refusing to examine the feeling, I ignored it, coming back down onto the bed beside her before getting her beneath me once again. Her hands settled on my shoulders and she began to stroke me as if she had every right to touch me however she liked.

Yeah, and that was hot too.

'What's going to happen about your plan?' she murmured. 'I mean, now that I've been de-virginised.'

'I'll deal with it,' I said shortly, not wanting to think about it right now.

There was a silence.

She began to trace the lines over my left pec. 'Your tattoos are incredible. What do they mean?'

I'd got them when I was much younger, the lines outlining my muscles, highlighting my strength. Dad had hated them and so I'd loved them, a secret declaration that I wasn't my father's puppet, the way he seemed to think I was.

But I wasn't going to explain that to her, so all I said was, 'Nothing in particular. A tattoo artist friend designed them for me.'

'I love them.' Her fingers moved down my left side, a look of fascination on her face. 'Did it hurt? Do you think I could get one done one day? Where's the least painful place to get one?'

'You ask a lot of questions. What's up with that?'

Her exploring fingers slowed, her lashes sweeping down and veiling her gaze. 'I'm...not very good at keeping quiet when I'm curious about something.'

I looked down at her lovely face. 'Why should you be quiet when you're interested in something?'

'It's not only that. I find it difficult to sit still and I often don't think before I speak. I'm trying not to be so impulsive all the time and I know I need to control myself better, but it's...hard.' She paused, her attention on the black lines of my ink under her fingers. 'Dad doesn't like it and I try not to do stuff he doesn't like.'

I watched her face, saw the expression on it close down, the lovely green of her eyes darken.

'Why not?' The protective instinct inside me growled deep and low and it echoed in my voice. 'I thought you said your father didn't hurt you.'

'He didn't. But there are always consequences for not doing what he wants.'

'What consequences?' It came out as a demand, but I didn't bother to soften it. William White may not have laid a finger on his daughter, but he'd clearly hurt her in other ways.

Imogen sighed. 'A couple of years ago I tried to have something of a normal life, or as much of one as you can with twenty-four-seven guards. I signed up for a course at uni, joined a few clubs to meet people, that kind of thing. Anyway, there was this guy in my history class and I liked him. I'd never been on a date before so I asked him if he'd come out for coffee with me. He said he would, except…he never turned up for it. The next day I read in the paper about a man who'd been beaten and left for dead in an alley near where we were supposed to be meeting.' She dropped her gaze, staring ferociously at her finger following the line of my tat to my hip. 'I knew it was Cam. Just like I knew it was Dad who'd hurt him. He'd always warned me that I needed to be careful who I associated with and who I spoke to, but… I don't know. I guess I never thought he'd actually do anything.' A flicker of pain crossed her expressive face. 'It was my fault Cam got hurt. I should have remembered Dad's warning. I should have thought more about the consequences of asking him out.' Her tracing finger came to a stop. 'But I was so thrilled to have a conversation with a cute guy and I…forgot.'

My protective instinct sank its claws deeper, responding to the note of pain in her voice. 'It wasn't your fault,' I growled. 'It was your father who beat him up, not you.'

'I know that. But Cameron didn't. It was my responsibility not to put him in harm's way, because I know what Dad's like.' She swallowed. 'And it's not like Dad hasn't told me for years that I need to learn how to control myself.'

I shouldn't have cared what her father had told her. She was my prisoner, nothing more.

Yet the pain that threaded through each word caught at something inside me like an anchor catching on a rock.

Did this have anything to do with the way she'd cried earlier? With how she'd tried to repress it, seemingly angry at herself for getting emotional?

I'd have bet the whole of King Enterprises that it did.

'You're going to have to explain to me why your father thinks you need to control yourself,' I ordered, not caring that my voice had got rough and uncivilised. 'And then you're going to have to explain why you believed him.'

Her mouth got a stubborn look to it. 'Why? I don't have to if I don't want to.'

I caught her chin with my finger, tipping her gaze back to mine. 'Because I'm curious, Imogen. And you know what it's like to be curious, right?'

She let out an annoyed breath, flickers of anger in her green eyes.

Good. Let her be angry. That was better than her being hurt.

'Okay, fine,' she said after a minute. 'My mother died when I was born and Dad never got over it. He told me that it was my fault she died and that I'll never be like her. Never measure up to her. I'm too emotional, too impulsive. I didn't…deserve her.'

Jesus.

'Of course you deserved her,' I said fiercely. 'Don't tell me you believed all that bullshit?'

The stubborn line of her mouth softened, became more vulnerable. 'I didn't want to. But he's my Dad. He's the only person I've got.' A shadow shifted in her green eyes. 'I don't have anyone else.'

Sound familiar?

Yeah, it did. But my isolation had been self-imposed, while hers had been forced on her, the bright, inquisitive spirit I'd seen behind those green eyes compelled to get what it needed from a man who didn't give a shit about crushing it.

Poor little one. No wonder she hadn't cared about being kidnapped. Her mother was dead and her father had denied her the connection she was hungry for. A connection she needed.

I stroked my thumb along her jaw. 'You have me. And I don't care if you're impulsive or emotional or curious or any of that other bullshit, understand? You can be yourself with me, Imogen.'

Emotions shifted and changed like quicksilver in her eyes. 'Because I don't matter to you, right?'

I didn't miss the half-desperate note in her voice. It sounded a hell of a lot like she didn't want to matter, which was pretty much the opposite of what I usually got from women.

'You don't want to matter to me?' I asked, curious. 'Why not?'

'I don't want to have to live up to anyone else's expectations. I don't want to worry about disappointing anyone.'

The way she'd disappointed her father, clearly.

'You won't disappoint me,' I said. 'Not in any way.'

Colour rose in her cheeks and her gaze flickered. 'You were disappointed that I wasn't afraid of you.'

'Apart from that.'

'And that I got into your stuff.'

'Yeah, apart from that as well.'

'And I ask a lot of annoying questions.'

'I can handle your questions.'

She let out a breath. 'Just don't care about me, Ajax. Caring makes people do things they shouldn't.'

Hell, I couldn't argue. I'd had front row seats to that particular shit show. There were a lot of things I'd done that I shouldn't have.

Such as leaving your brothers to get hurt?

Ah, fuck, I didn't need that thought in my head.

'Don't worry,' I said. 'Caring about you is the last thing I'm going to do.' I tightened my grip on her chin. 'Don't forget, little one, I'm a monster. And monsters don't care about anyone.'

CHAPTER TWELVE

Imogen

I STARED INTO Ajax's eyes and something gripped tight in my chest.

Did he really think he was a monster?

But the answer was there in his stunning blue gaze.

Denial shifted inside me. I knew monsters—at least I knew one, my father—and Ajax wasn't like him. Not in any way.

The night he'd kidnapped me, instinct had told me that Ajax King wasn't a man I should be afraid of, and so far he'd done nothing to disprove that.

And, anyway, I wouldn't have let him touch me if I'd been afraid. I wouldn't be sitting here, lying on his magnificent naked body and tracing his tattoos if he'd been the same kind of monster my father was.

He radiated protective energy; I could feel it in my bones. In my heart. He might be hard and pitiless, with a violent, fearsome reputation, but he wasn't a man who'd hurt vulnerable people.

I was the daughter of his father's enemy and, despite catching me poking around in his personal things, all he'd done was tell me off.

Hardly the actions of a monster.

You don't know him. He could be just a different type of monster.

He could be. But if he was a different type, then it was a type that I found completely fascinating and utterly compelling.

And what made him think he was a monster anyway? What was in his past that made him think he was so dangerous? There were rumours about him, about how ruthless he was as a businessman. Many had expected that, as heir to his father's throne, he'd go down along with Augustus, yet he hadn't. In fact, he'd been the one who'd taken Augustus down, seemingly escaping the charges that had caught his father.

Curiosity gripped me, winding tighter and tighter.

How had he escaped the law? When he'd supposedly been his father's true heir? Had he been granted immunity of some kind in return for betraying Augustus?

What kind of man are you touching right now?

I stared into his eyes, looking deep, and he didn't flinch away. Blue fire blazed there, burning hot and strong. A man of conviction, determination. A man of strength and power, who'd given me space to cry. Who'd told me I wasn't a disappointment.

He was no monster.

I lifted my hand and touched his cheek. 'What makes you think that? You haven't done anything particularly monstrous to me.'

'I kidnapped you. And I'm going to use you against your father to get what I want.' His mouth curved in a predatory smile that didn't reach his eyes. 'And I don't give a damn about your feelings on the subject.'

I let my fingers trail down to the sharp line of his

jaw and then lower, down the side of his strong neck. 'But I told you I didn't want you to give a damn.'

'There are worse things than not caring about people's feelings, little one. You must know that. Especially considering your own father.'

I brushed my fingers over his throat, moving down the hard expanse of his chest, crisp hair rough against my fingertips. 'Have you beaten up people and left them for dead?'

'Yes.'

It didn't surprise me. The son of Augustus King wasn't going to be as pure as the driven snow.

I didn't look away, kept my gaze on his. 'Innocent people?'

A muscle leapt in the side of his jaw. 'Yes.' A slight hesitation.

I focused on him, all my attention zeroing in on his winter-sky eyes. 'Why?'

He reached for my hand and pushed it down, curling my fingers around his hardening cock. 'My father needed to be taken down so I did what I had to do.' His voice was like iron and just as cold. 'Are we done?'

It was clear he didn't want to talk any more, but that only made me even more curious. He'd done what he had to do. What did that mean?

'No,' I said. 'I want to—'

'Because I'd prefer you to concentrate on something else.' His fingers tightened around mine, pressing my fingers against his hard flesh. 'Like my cock, for example.'

Dammit. I wanted to push, but having him in my hand, hot and smooth and firm, was distracting. Too distracting.

'Why can't we talk about you?' I looked down, at where my hand and his were wrapped around his hard-on. God, he felt good. 'I told you about me.'

'Because I said so.' His tone was flat, no room for argument. 'If you disagree, you know where the door is.'

Frustration needled at me, making me want to let him go and sweep grandly out. But I couldn't quite bring myself to do so. When would I get this opportunity again? To hold him like I was doing now, explore him the way he wanted me to? Maybe I wouldn't.

I glared at him. 'That's not fair.'

He looked back, his gaze uncompromising. 'That's it. Get angry with me. Show me what a pissed-off Imogen looks like.'

'A pissed-off Imogen might look like me leaving you alone with your hard-on.'

'Do it then.' Challenge burned in his eyes. 'If you think you can.'

And it hit me again in that moment—truly hit me—that I *could* get pissed off if I wanted to. I could get angry. I could get really, *really* angry. And there would be no consequences, because there was no one to get hurt and no one to disappoint.

There was only Ajax and he didn't care.

The weirdest rush of exhilaration swept through me. Was this what freedom felt like?

I met Ajax's stare, squeezing him at the same time as I brushed my thumb over the head of his dick, not knowing what I was doing and not giving one single damn. 'You really want to test me?'

'Fuck,' he hissed, his body tensing, every one of

those carved muscles contracting deliciously under his skin.

Oh, crap. Had I hurt him? 'Sorry,' I muttered. 'Was that too hard?'

'Hell, no.' The flame in his eyes burned even brighter. 'Do it again. And harder. And never fucking apologise to me again.'

The breath went out of me. Did I apologise too much?

Of course you do. But you don't need to worry about that with him. He can handle it. Because he doesn't care.

My hand tightened around him, my gaze riveted to his face, watching pleasure draw his features tight and set the blue of his eyes blazing even hotter.

And when I rubbed my thumb over the head of his cock again, I discovered his skin was slick and getting slicker. Interesting. I took my hand away and put my thumb in my mouth. He tasted of salt and something masculine and indefinable, delicious.

His gaze followed every movement I made, his lips drawing back in a snarl, and I felt it again, my power over him, at the same time as I could feel and see his strength.

Nothing could hurt this man, not even me.

I could do anything to him, tell him anything, and he would let it slide off him. He would remain untouched.

The adrenaline rush was back and I was moving before I could think better of it, straddling him, putting my hands on his shoulders and gripping him. Then I covered his mouth with mine, kissing him with all the passion I could feel expanding inside me.

'Yes,' he growled against my lips, his voice so rough I could barely understand him. 'Unleash yourself on me, woman. I dare you to.'

So I did.

I let the passion unfurl and along with it my power. And I touched him everywhere. Tasted him everywhere. I found out what he liked, which was pretty much everything, and what his boundaries were: he didn't have a single one.

His control seemed to be limitless, even though I tested the hell out of it. I made him growl and I made him curse. I made him shake and pant and grit his teeth, but he didn't restrain me and he didn't stop me from doing anything I wanted.

I felt free. Drunk on him and the feel of his body, the taste of his skin.

It was the most incredible experience I'd ever had in my life.

We were both shaking by the time I ripped the condom packet open and rolled it down on him, drawing more guttural curses from him.

But he didn't move as I straddled him, putting his hands on my hips only to steady me as I slowly eased myself down onto his hard cock.

Then I sat there, loving the stretch and burn of him inside me and the way his blue eyes stared into mine, his jaw clenched and his body beneath me as tight as a wound spring.

'Ride me, woman,' he growled, low and deep. 'Ride me like you mean it.'

Woman. Yes, that's what I was. I was a woman. Not a child.

His woman.

I tossed my head back and I rode him, and he showed me the way. And then he gave me my head and I galloped, riding wild and free, until our skins were slick with sweat and the rough sounds of earthy, masculine pleasure mingled with my own gasps of delight.

Until finally he gripped me hard between his hands, making me scream as he roared my name, our voices echoing off the walls of his bedroom.

Then when we were done he rolled over, tucking me close to his chest. 'Sleep,' he murmured roughly in my ear. 'You've earned it.'

He was warm and his big body wrapped around me made me feel safe. And, even though I didn't want to, I found myself falling into sleep all the same.

I slept like the bloody dead.

So deeply that when I finally opened my eyes again I wasn't sure where I was. At least not until I reached for the big masculine body that I somehow knew would be beside me, only to find it gone.

I cracked open an eye, wondering why I was so annoyed.

The other side of the bed was empty. And then I remembered.

Ajax.

Pleasure swept through me, a sweet, sensual ripple that reminded me of the night before and all the things we'd done. All the things *I'd* done. My body felt like it had been put through its paces, muscles aching in unusual places and most especially between my legs.

But it wasn't a bad hurt. In fact, I wouldn't have minded more because I was even hungrier for him now than I had been the night before.

Was it normal to want someone like that, even after a night of having sex with them? Or was that just him?

You already know the answer to that one.

I scowled at the thought, just as Ajax walked out of the en suite bathroom wearing nothing but a pair of low-slung jeans and carrying a black T-shirt in one hand.

'Good morning, little one,' he said in that deep, husky voice of his. 'Or is it not so good, judging by that scowl?'

I lay there for a moment, staring at him. He must have had a shower because I could see the moisture on his skin, a drop sliding down one pec and slowly over the cut lines of his abs.

My mouth watered. I wanted to lick that drop off his skin and then lick the rest of him as well.

'You weren't here,' I said. 'That's what I was scowling about.'

A flame glowed in his eyes as he took in my obvious appreciation. 'I had a shower. Some of us have things to do today.'

'I could have joined you.' Only just missing a pout, I sat up. 'You should have woken me up.'

'I didn't want to wake you.' He moved over to the side of the bed and reached out, gently pushing a strand of my hair behind my ear, making me shiver as his fingertips brushed my skin. 'Stay here and I'll bring you breakfast.'

Oh, yes. Breakfast. Suddenly I was starving.

'Breakfast in bed?' I asked hopefully.

'Of course.'

'With you?'

The flame in his eyes flickered, his hand dropping away. 'Not this morning.'

Disappointment gathered inside me. 'It would just be for half an hour. Not long. I could eat really fast—'

'Your father wants to see you, Imogen.'

The words cut across me like a whip.

Suddenly I wasn't hungry any more.

'Oh.' All the good feelings I had were slipping away, leaving me with nothing but a core of ice.

I didn't want to see Dad. He was going to be so angry and that anger wouldn't be directed at Ajax. It would be directed at me. For shirking my duty, for the debt I owed to my mother's memory.

Why do you care? What can he do to you anyway?

I couldn't help caring; that was the problem. Dad was one thing, but I cared about my mother too. She'd died to give birth to me and that was a sacrifice I could never repay. It hurt. Every day, it hurt.

'I'm sorry,' Ajax said, watching me. 'I should have told you last night, but we got…distracted. He wants to make sure that you're okay and that I haven't touched you.'

'Uh, well, you kind of have now.' Restlessness filled me, the need to move becoming almost overwhelming. I shifted, hauling the sheet around me, but Ajax was suddenly there in front of me, his hand reaching out, a finger beneath my chin, tipping my head back.

'What are you afraid of?' he asked. 'I won't let him take you.'

I swallowed, my throat gone tight. 'I'm not afraid.'

It was a lie and we both knew it.

'He can't touch you, Imogen. I'll make sure of it.

All you have to do is tell him you're okay, and we're out of there.'

But being taken by Dad wasn't what I was afraid of. It was that I'd let him make me feel like shit again, let him use me again, and all because I couldn't bear the weight of the debt I owed.

'What about a video of me or something?' At least in a video I wouldn't have to see that contempt in his eyes. 'Would that be enough?'

'Talking to you was a condition of him leaving the city and taking some of his friends with him.'

Oh. Damn.

'So, hypothetically, what would happen if I *don't* see him?' I tried to sound casual, to not make it into a big deal.

The look on Ajax's face hardened. 'He might make himself difficult. Which means I'll be forced to take more extreme measures.'

My heart caught. 'What "extreme measures"?'

His expression become even more wintry, his eyes pale as frost. 'That all depends on how difficult he turns out to be.'

Okay, perhaps I didn't want to know what his 'extreme measures' were, nor did I want to put him in the position of having to take them.

'You don't need to do that,' I said quietly.

But the ice in Ajax's gaze glittered. 'Your father is a liability, Imogen, make no mistake. He's a threat to this city. And the safety of this city and the people in it come before everything.'

Conviction vibrated in his voice and I found myself staring at him, unable to look away. 'What do you mean, the safety of this city?'

He lifted his head, somehow becoming taller, broader. Stronger. 'My father hurt a lot of people. He murdered them, stole from them. It took me years to bring that motherfucker down and I've spent the last five mopping up the rest of the mess he left.' Beneath the ice in his eyes, a ferocious belief burned. 'No one else is going to take his place. Believe me, I will *never* allow another Augustus King to rise.'

The words were more than a promise. They were a vow.

'Wow, you're kind of like Batman,' I said, not a little impressed. 'Why?'

His expression twisted and for a second I glimpsed a terrible rage burning deep inside him. 'Why? Why do you think? It was *my* father who nearly ruined it.'

'So? That doesn't mean you have to clean it up.'

His expression became shuttered. 'Someone has to.'

'But why you?' I wasn't arguing with him. I genuinely wanted to know.

'Because there is no one else.' Turning away, he pulled on his T-shirt, covering up all those beautiful muscles and ink. 'Stay in bed,' he ordered as he stalked towards the door. 'Breakfast will be here in ten.'

Then he was gone, leaving me alone.

CHAPTER THIRTEEN

Ajax

'AJAX?' LEON'S VOICE sounded sharp on the voicemail message. 'What the fuck is going on? There are rumours going around that you've done something with William White's daughter. If so, you owe me a goddamn explanation.' There was some muffled cursing in the background and I could hear Xander murmuring something. 'Yes, I know that,' Leon said curtly, obviously to Xander. 'Call me, you bastard,' he added to me, then cut the message abruptly.

I flung the phone down onto the coffee table in front of me, fighting irritation.

I'd let them know I was going to be out of commission for the next week and that I wasn't to be disturbed, and yet here they were, disturbing me.

Did they really think I was going to call them up and explain myself? I never had before and I wasn't going to start now, especially when I knew the pair of them would disagree with my methods.

What they didn't know wouldn't hurt them and the responsibility would remain with me, the way it always had.

Protecting them was what I did. After all, my brothers were the reason I'd taken my father down in the first place.

And they got hurt. You let them get hurt.

I'd had to. I hadn't been able to go to Leon's rescue when he'd been kidnapped and tortured, or tell Xander the financial games he was playing were real. I'd had to let all that shit happen, because I'd have blown my cover and taking Dad down had been more important and I'd known it would save more lives in the end.

Yeah, sure. Nothing to do with the fact that maybe you're a monster just like him and always have been.

Ice twisted in my veins but I ignored it.

What if I was like Dad? What did it matter? My city was safe and so were my brothers. That was worth any price, wasn't it?

My phone vibrated on the table where I'd flung it, announcing another voicemail from White about when to bring Imogen to see him. My silence on the subject was obviously annoying the shit out of him.

Good. He could stay annoyed a little longer. Considering Imogen's response to the thought of meeting him, I wasn't in any hurry to set it up quite yet.

At some point I would have to, though. I wanted him gone and with the least amount of fuss, which meant getting this proof of life nonsense out of the way.

I could have denied him his request to see Imogen, but then he'd make leaving Sydney a problem and I didn't have either the time or the patience for pissing around with problems. In the kind of mood I was in, I'd likely do something I'd regret later, which wasn't a good idea either.

Music drifted from outside, a driving, thumping beat.

Imogen must be in the pool again.

It had been a couple of days since I'd left her in my bed and since then I'd busied myself with monitoring the situation with her father and his various cronies, organising the fake doctor's certificates that would confirm her virginity, checking with my contacts about White's movements, and reviewing the security surrounding my brothers and their wives, not to mention keeping tabs on what was happening with King Enterprises.

I hadn't had time to see her, but I'd made an effort to ensure she had plenty to do, instructing my housekeeper to organise a laptop for her so she could use the Net since apparently a home cinema, a gym and a library weren't enough.

Though it seemed that what Imogen liked best to do was swim.

I turned automatically to the windows, the side of the pool visible from the lounge area where I stood.

She was standing on the diving board in a green bikini that she must have found in those clothes I'd got my housekeeper to leave for her.

Her pale skin gleamed like a pearl in the sunlight, her hair a gilded skein of silk down her back.

She was poised on the edge of the board like a dancer or a bird about to take flight, her small curvy body graceful and lithe.

I'd told myself that the few hours we'd had in bed was all we'd needed. She'd had her revenge on her father, losing her virginity to a man of her choice, while I'd got a little something for myself for once.

It hadn't ended up being a big drama, not now the

virginity issue was being handled by those fake certificates.

I didn't need to go back for more.

Yet that didn't stop my stupid cock from hardening at the mere thought of those few hours or at the idea of reliving them.

Repeatedly.

When she'd unleashed herself on me, her curiosity and passion had combined into a force that was as unstoppable as it was irresistible. It had blown my fucking mind.

I'd never thought that a virgin exploring a man's body for the first time could be so erotic.

She'd started hesitantly then had gained confidence, becoming utterly fearless. Watching her bloom had been the hottest thing I'd ever seen. And knowing that I was a part of that had only made it hotter.

I stared out the windows, my goddamn cock getting harder at the sight of her and the memories that kept unreeling in my head.

I should go to a bar. Find a woman. Fuck away the need.

But the idea left me cold.

I didn't want just any woman. I wanted her.

On the diving board Imogen leapt but, instead of a graceful dive, she drew her legs up under her and wrapped her arms around them, bombing into the pool like a teenager, water going everywhere.

Then she surfaced a moment later, grinning like she was having the time of her life.

I moved before I could think better of it, shoving the huge sliding glass door open so I could step outside, the sound of the music deafening.

She had her back to me, gripping the tiled edges of the pool then pulling herself out.

A wooden sun lounger sat nearby, the speaker and laptop she was using to stream the music sitting on it.

I bent and hit a button on the laptop, cutting off the sound.

Imogen, who was now standing on the side of the pool, water streaming down her lovely body, turned around. 'Hey, who did—' She broke off, blinking as she saw me.

Colour rushed into her face and a smile like the sun coming out turned up her mouth. Then just as quickly the smile vanished and she frowned. 'You've been avoiding me.'

That fleeting smile, bright and instinctive, hit me in a place I wasn't expecting, a place I hadn't realised was vulnerable.

Fuck.

I scowled. 'Why would I avoid you?'

She shrugged then raised her hands to her hair, squeezing the water from it. 'I don't know—you tell me.'

The movement lifted her breasts, the thin fabric of her bikini pulling tight, drawing attention to those sweet little nipples. They were hard, the wet material outlining them perfectly.

I'd tasted them, rolled them in my mouth, tugged on them with my teeth. She'd liked that. I could still hear her cries of delight in my ears…

Christ, I could not be thinking shit like that. There was no need for a repeat. I had other, more important things to do with my time.

'I've been busy,' I growled, irritated both with my stupid cock and the need I felt to explain myself to her.

'Too busy to even say hi?' Her arms dropped and she wandered over to where I stood, apparently not caring that her bikini was very small, very wet, and I was getting very hard. 'That's kind of a dick move, Ajax.' Mercifully she folded her arms. 'I mean, I'm not asking for flowers and chocolates and love songs. A "hi, how are you doing" would be fine.' Her brows drew down. 'Or is vanishing usual for guys after they've taken a girl's virginity?'

She called you, asshole.

Yeah, and I did not like it. Not one fucking bit.

'You're my prisoner,' I said flatly. 'Prisoners are lucky to get food and water, let alone computers, libraries, pools and loud music.'

'No need to be a bastard.'

'I'm your kidnapper. What the fuck do you expect?'

She stared at me, her green eyes sharp. 'I know why you're angry. You're annoyed because you wanted me to come and say hi to you, right?'

Caught off guard, I couldn't think of a single response.

'Because all you had to do was say,' Imogen charged on, not waiting for me to speak anyway. 'I was around. It's not like I'm going anywhere.'

Holy shit. The bloody woman thought I'd been hanging around waiting for *her* to approach *me*?

She's right though.

No. Why would I do that? If I wanted something and it didn't interfere with my plans I went the hell out and got it. I didn't wait.

But you wanted her and did nothing.

'Like I said, I've been busy.' I gave her a hard stare.

'And I still am so turn your fucking music down so I can concentrate.'

She searched my face, her expression turning into something like…understanding. 'It's okay, I get it,' she said, even though I had no idea what she was talking about. 'But you told me not to hold back and I didn't. So why are you doing the same thing now?'

'Holding back?' I shoved my hands into my pockets, the need to grab her needling at me like an itch I couldn't scratch. 'What the fuck are you talking about?'

She let out a sigh, like I was being particularly dense, then closed the distance between us, reaching out to brush her fingers over the fly of my jeans. 'You're hard, Ajax.'

I stilled, her touch electric, stealing my breath. It took every ounce of will I had not to take my hands out of my pockets and take her on the pool tiles.

You can't. You can never have what you want.

'I told you all I'd give you was a couple of hours,' I forced out between gritted teeth, ignoring the voice in my head. 'And I fucking meant it.'

'I know. But…you still want me.'

I couldn't deny it, not when the evidence was pressing hard against the front of my jeans. 'I told you that what I want doesn't matter.'

A crease appeared between her brows. 'And I told you that it does. Seriously, Ajax. How does us having sex interfere with the safety of this city? My virginity is gone and you're dealing with the medical proof. Dad's never going to know. So what's the problem?'

The problem was the catch, and there was always a catch. I'd learned that particular lesson in my time as my father's heir and learned it well.

I'd wanted to protect my brothers, but doing so would have exposed me and then Dad would have taken me down instead of vice versa. More people would have got hurt. And he would have ruled Sydney unchecked.

Sacrifices had to be made and I was the one who'd make them.

There was no room for selfishness in my plans.

It's great how noble you can make yourself sound.

My jaw tightened.

Imogen shrugged. 'Oh, well, your loss.' Reaching around behind herself, she tugged at the tie of her bikini top and I wasn't sure what she was doing until the whole thing loosened. 'But you know where I'll be if you change your mind.' Pulling the fabric free, she dropped the top on the ground, her perfect little tits bare. 'I'll be in the pool.' Pushing her bikini bottoms down, she stepped out of them then straightened, giving me a look from underneath her lashes. 'Naked.'

Then she strolled to the side of the pool and dived in.

Every muscle in my body tensed.

The gall of the woman. Stripping naked and swimming in my pool like she didn't give a fuck. Like I wasn't standing there aching to get my hands on her and hadn't been aching for the past two days straight.

Like I hadn't been using bullshit excuses to stay away from her, when all I really wanted was to take her to bed and keep her there for the next week straight.

You think a prick like you can ever have what he wants?

I shoved the thought from my head, stalking over to the pool, drawn relentlessly by the woman in it.

She was floating on her back with her arms out, her

hair moving like silky golden kelp around her head. Her eyes were closed, her naked body the most beautiful thing I'd ever seen. Pale skin, golden hair, soft pink nipples...

Shit, if there was a catch, I couldn't find it. And since when had I ever made sex into such a big deal?

Her arms moved lazily in the water and she hummed a song I didn't recognise, oblivious to me standing on the side of the pool wrestling with my fucking conscience.

It was just sex. No big deal. Her virginity was gone and I was handling that. Taking her to bed wasn't the start of that slippery slope, the one that led back to the violence of the days I'd left behind. Anyway, she wanted me and who was I to deny her what she wanted? What we *both* wanted?

I couldn't. I wouldn't.

I took a moment to kick off my shoes, then I dived in after her.

CHAPTER FOURTEEN

Imogen

I HEARD THE SPLASH, felt the spray over my face and the movement of the water as Ajax dived in. And my heartbeat accelerated, adrenaline coursing through me.

Yes. My gamble had paid off.

For the past couple of days I'd been hanging out by the pool, hoping he'd come. Hoping that seeing me in my bikini might make him do...something.

Because ever since he'd walked out the morning after we'd slept together, he'd been avoiding me. And I hadn't been able to get him out of my head.

I hadn't expected that. I'd thought that once I'd got my little piece of revenge, that would be it. I'd be satisfied. But apparently that's not how it worked with Ajax.

One night had done nothing to put out the fire of my curiosity.

He hadn't been around so I'd used the laptop he'd provided to distract me, but all I found myself doing was surfing the Net looking for anything I could find on him. There were old news stories about his father's arrest and how they'd eventually caught Augustus due to some dodgy financial business dealings. Ajax had been involved with the takedown and I obsessively read everything about it, watched all the interviews that featured him. There weren't many, but in each one his expression was hard, his eyes glittering. He looked dangerous and mean, and said virtually nothing.

I couldn't stop watching.

The media viewed him with suspicion and, to be fair, he hadn't done anything to change their viewpoint. But I wondered why not. Because the man the media had painted him as—the violent heir who'd somehow managed to avoid conviction—was *not* the man who'd cupped my face as I'd cried, who'd held me close while I'd slept. Who'd insisted that protecting his brothers and his city came before anything else, including himself.

I wanted to know that man quite desperately. It consumed me.

I'd had intense passions like this before—the tropical fish I'd been obsessed with once as a kid that I'd lost interest in a couple of weeks after Dad had bought me a tank. Or when I'd suddenly been desperate to learn calligraphy, fascinated by the black curves and elegant straight lines, getting lots of pens and different inks, practising for a day before putting everything aside and never picking up a pen again.

Ajax was the adult version of my interest in tropical fish. Or my calligraphy. He was the Mandarin I'd tried to teach myself once, the astronomy I'd been obsessed with for a whole month.

He was a puzzle that only got more complex and more interesting the closer I examined him, and I suspected that sex was merely scratching the surface of who he was.

Whatever, I knew myself. I knew that my obsession with him wasn't going to ease until I'd satisfied my curiosity and the only way I was going to do that was to figure out a way to get close to him.

And obviously the best way to get close to him was through more sex.

I hadn't been able to stop thinking about the hours I'd spent in his bed. About how free he'd made me feel and how accepting he'd been of me and my quirks. How he'd actively encouraged me to be curious about his body and how it had fit with mine.

No one had ever made me feel as if it was okay to be myself the way he had.

So, after the first day or so of obsessing, I'd decided that I had to do something about it. Such as convincing him to take me to bed again.

Unfortunately, for that to work, he had to be around and he wasn't. Which meant I had to try something different—getting him to come to me.

I'd been thrilled when my little ploy of hanging out by the pool in my green bikini and playing loud music had worked. But then he'd been a dick, giving me all sorts of crap about how busy he was, all the while staring at me like he wanted to eat me alive and pretending he wasn't as hard as a rock.

So, to give him some incentive, I'd taken my bikini off. And, judging by the way he'd launched himself into the water, that was all the push he'd needed, which thrilled me down to the bone.

Still, I wasn't sure why he'd been denying himself what we both wanted and I'd already decided I was going to find out.

I was going to find out everything.

But maybe *after* I let him catch me.

I turned over on my front, making an attempt to swim away, but his fingers closed around my ankle and he jerked me towards him. I took a breath as I went under, then his hands closed around my hips and I was out of the water again, being pulled against his hot, hard body and held there, face to face with him.

'Tease.' The hunger in his eyes blazed.

'You can talk.' I spread my palms out on his chest, loving the contrast of his heat with the cool press of the water on my skin. 'I've been in agony for two whole days.'

'Agony?' His hands slid over my butt as he fitted my hips against his, the denim of his wet jeans rough against my sensitive bare flesh. 'You should have come to me.'

'I would have. If you'd been around.'

'I'm around now.' He squeezed me, not gently.

I gasped, the slight bite of pain adding to the rub of his wet clothing on my tender skin, the friction maddeningly erotic.

The feral look on his face intensified, as if he liked the sound very much. 'What's wrong, little one?' His fingers shifted under me, finding the folds of my pussy and brushing over them. 'Am I too much for you?'

'N-no.' Excitement made me stutter as I shifted restlessly in his grip. 'I can handle you. But I'm not sure you can handle me.'

He gave a low growl and suddenly I was being kissed—and kissed hard.

I shuddered with pleasure, winding my arms around his neck, holding on tight as his tongue pushed into my mouth, the dark addictive taste of him flooding through me. His kiss was raw, with an edge of danger to it that I found absolutely intoxicating.

Yes, God, *this* was what I wanted. What I needed. Not movies or books or calligraphy or astronomy, or any of the thousand things I'd spent the last fifteen years of my life using to fill the void inside me. The void I hadn't even realised was there until Ajax had touched me. Let me cry. Let me explore. Made me aware of what I was missing.

Him. I'd been missing him.

I tried to kiss him back, but he was having none of it, wrenching his mouth from mine.

'Ajax, please.' Disappointment crowded in my throat. 'I want—'

'No.' His voice was so rough it was almost unrecognisable, his gaze incandescent with blue fire. 'We've done what you want. Now it's time to do what *I* want.'

A couple of days ago he'd taken my virginity, let me make a choice and take my revenge. That night had been all about me.

Now he wanted it to be about him.

I could not wait.

'Y-yes.' Excitement burned in my blood. 'Show me.'

He smiled, ferocious and predatory. Then, without a word, he turned and carried me to the edge of the pool and set me on the tiles. Gripping the edge, he pulled himself out in one fluid, immensely powerful movement.

My mouth dried, my heartbeat going into overdrive as I watched him.

He stood there for a second, dripping water, then he began to pull his wet clothes off, dropping them negligently on the ground. His body gleamed in the sunlight, slick with water, the ink of his amazing tattoos stark against his olive skin.

I'd never wanted to touch anything as badly as I wanted to touch him.

I got to my feet and stretched out my hands like he was a fire I wanted to warm myself against, but he took a long, loping step towards me, a wolf on the hunt.

Adrenaline rushed through my veins, my excitement electric.

Slowly, he began to stalk me and I let him, backing away in the direction he wanted me to go, towards the nearest sun lounger. Then, when the frame pressed against the back of my legs, he picked me up and sat down on it with me in his lap, both of us facing the pool, my spine against his broad chest, his hard cock pressing between my thighs.

I trembled at the feel of him, at all that heat and coiled power in the taut muscles beneath me.

His hands urged me to lie back against him, my head on his shoulder, and then he smoothed his palms down my arms to my hips. They rested there a moment before easing lower, to my knees, sliding inwards to grip my thighs and gently pull my legs apart, spreading them on either side of his. He bent his legs at the knee, widening them, so his knees were holding my thighs open.

The position was exposing, the slight stretch of the sensitive tissues of my sex so hot I could hardly breathe.

He stroked over my stomach, one hand grazing the sensitised flesh between my thighs, the other lazily toying with my nipple, pinching it lightly.

I groaned, arching into his hands, desperate for his touch. But it was too light. I wanted more, harder.

'Ajax.' His name was a prayer in my mouth. 'Ajax, *please.*'

But he ignored me, turning his mouth into my hair and nuzzling against my ear. The press of his knees was hard against my thighs as his fingers stroked unhurriedly through my folds, getting me hot, getting me wet.

He pinched my nipple harder then found my clit with his other hand and pinched that too. 'You're mine, woman,' he said roughly in my ear. 'You want to play this game with me, then that makes you mine for the duration. And you do whatever I want, understand?'

Oh, yes, I understood. And I was totally on board.

'Okay,' I panted. 'I'm fine with that. Just…more, please.'

His fingers spread possessively over my pussy and he pinched my nipple yet again, making me groan. 'That's not up to you. Not now.' His teeth grazed my earlobe. 'I'm going to give you something and you're going to put it on me.'

I nodded quickly, the intense pressure between my thighs an ache I was desperate to relieve, his light touches only maddening me further.

He pressed something into my palm—a foil packet still wet from the pool. He must have got it out of his wallet before he'd stripped.

I sat up and with shaking hands ripped it open, taking out the condom. Then I leaned forward to put it on him—or at least I tried. He made it difficult by toying with my other breast and teasing my clit with his finger, making me pant and tremble with the brutal, wicked ecstasy of his touch.

Eventually I got the condom on and then he was taking over again, holding me open with one hand while he gripped himself with the other, fitting the head of his cock against my slick flesh.

He pushed inside me and I cried out at the stretch of him, the slow, aching slide of his flesh into mine. Then he gripped me, holding me still, his hips pushing upwards, forcing himself deeper, his knees pressing my thighs wider apart.

Pleasure cut like a knife and I arched again, writhing helplessly against him, my hips jerking against the relentless push of his.

But he held me there, not letting me move, making me feel every inch of his cock as he slid it out then back in, driving upwards in a hard, brutal motion that had me shuddering.

My hands tried to find something to hold onto, settling on his forearms, my nails digging into his skin as he thrust harder, deeper.

The angle meant I couldn't quite get the friction I wanted and I'm sure he knew that. And took complete advantage of it, every thrust driving me further and further towards madness.

I could feel the orgasm approaching, so close and yet just out of reach. Moans escaped me, desperate cries for him to relieve the growing pressure.

But he didn't. He made me wait. Pushing and pushing and pushing, until I clawed at him, twisting in his grip. Then his fingers at last found my clit and he stroked me in time with his thrusts, the pressure firm, his cock inside me achingly hard.

I exploded around him, stars shooting behind my closed eyelids, my cries echoing around the pool. It was only then that he withdrew from me and flipped me over so I was lying face down on the lounger. Then he came behind me, gripping my hips and pulling me up on my knees, sliding into me from behind.

I buried my burning face against the linen cover of the lounger and groaned, my pussy oversensitive and still pulsing with the aftershocks. But he didn't stop and I didn't want him to.

That first time, up in his bedroom, he'd been holding back and it was only now that I understood how much. Because he certainly wasn't holding back any more.

He drove into me hard and fast, low guttural sounds of pleasure coming from him as he thrust, and I gripped tight onto the cushions, more stars exploding behind my eyes, a second orgasm barrelling down on me.

I loved it. I loved how he simply took what he wanted from me without asking. It meant I couldn't fail or disappoint him, because I didn't have to try to be something I wasn't, or make up for something I didn't do.

It was enough to be myself.

And then his hand slid around my hip and down between my thighs, finding my clit and stroking relentlessly, and I stopped thinking.

The orgasm broke over me, making tears sting behind my lids and sobs choke in my throat with the intensity of the sensation.

'You're mine, woman,' Ajax growled from behind me, shoving me rhythmically into the cushions as he fucked me harder. 'Understand? Only mine.'

Then his big body slammed into mine one last time before stiffening, his roar buried against my skin as he bit my shoulder.

CHAPTER FIFTEEN

Ajax

IMOGEN RELAXED BENEATH ME, her luscious body hot and pliant. She'd turned her head on the lounger cushions, her cheek flushed, strands of hair stuck to it. Sunlight struck gold sparks from those strands and the thick, soft lashes that rested against her skin.

She was panting.

Her pussy was clenching tight around my cock and I could taste her from where I'd bitten her shoulder, her skin salty and sweet. I could see the mark my teeth had left there too, a small bruise already darkening her pretty skin.

A dark, possessive satisfaction spread out inside me.

I'd marked her. She was mine. I wasn't listening to that fucking voice in my head telling me that I didn't deserve her. That she was somehow the start of the slippery slope I was going to fall down.

It didn't matter. I'd have to let her go eventually but, until then, she was completely and utterly mine. And it felt good. It had been a long time since I'd had anything that was mine. If I ever really had.

I eased out of her then put a hand on the back of

her neck, pressing lightly. 'You okay?' I'd been rough and demanding and she was, after all, extremely inexperienced.

'Yes,' she said in a scratchy voice. 'In fact, I don't think I've ever been better.'

I smiled. My little one was as insatiable as I was.

'Good.' I pressed a little harder. 'Wait there.'

I got off the lounger and went into the house, getting rid of the condom in the downstairs bathroom. Then I went back outside.

Imogen was curled up on the lounger cushions and as I approached she turned her head, looking up at me from underneath her lashes. She smiled, green eyes dancing in the sunlight.

That thing that kept catching me in the chest caught me again. Harder.

She turned over, lying on her back, then she flung her arms up over her head and stretched, her back arching, her toes pointed like a dancer.

So fucking sexy. I was hard again, instantly.

'Little one,' I murmured. 'Are you trying to kill me?'

She opened one eye, clearly pleased. 'Is it working?'

'Maybe.' I grinned. 'Are you up for more? Because I'm not finished.'

Her eyes glittered, the hunger in them in no way diminished by the two orgasms I'd already given her. 'Good. I was hoping you'd say that.' She rolled onto her side, facing me. 'Tell me what you want next.'

Perfect. She was absolutely goddamn perfect.

I put her onto her back next then came over her on my hands and knees, my head between her legs so I could eat her out. Then I had her suck me at the same time, telling her she couldn't come unless I did.

She managed the task pretty well considering I had my tongue in her pussy the whole time, proving that the woman could clearly concentrate extremely well when given the right incentive.

After we'd recovered, I gathered her up into my arms and took her inside to the en suite bathroom next to my bedroom. Pulling her into the shower, I washed her, running my hands all over her satiny skin before lifting her up and fucking her slowly against the tiled wall until she sobbed with pleasure.

By that stage the day was edging into late afternoon and she was starving, and so was I. So I took her down to the kitchen, where I made us both a BLT.

She insisted on watching me closely as I cooked the bacon, her bright eyes alight with interest. Then she demanded to have a turn pushing the bacon around in the pan so I handed the spatula to her and let her try.

'Please tell me you've at least cooked something,' I commented as she poked at the bacon.

'Nope,' she said, completely unashamed. 'Not a thing. Dad had a lady who came and cooked for us. I never even thought about doing it myself.' She gave the bacon another poke then looked at me, her pretty face beautifully flushed. 'Can I cook something tonight? Like…an egg or something? I've never even boiled one.'

I leaned against the kitchen counter. 'You didn't learn how to do it in school?'

'No. I didn't go to school. Or high school. Dad hired tutors for me.'

Of course she hadn't. She'd been kept isolated and deliberately so.

I studied her face as she gave the bacon the same

fierce attention she'd given to my dick not an hour earlier.

Poor little one. She'd been alone for a long time yet she hadn't let it crush her spirit entirely. She was still curious, still interested, still alive to the possibilities of the world.

Unlike you.

Yeah, I knew what the possibilities of the world were. Violence. Murder. Torture. Pain. Betrayal. At least that's what they'd been for me.

She should have better.

The thought was like a meteor streaking across the front of my mind, blazing, full of light. And I had no idea why.

It wasn't my job to make her life better. She was my prisoner and now maybe my toy, but nothing beyond that. I'd keep her in my bed for a few more days and then I'd let her go.

'What did you want to be when you grew up?' she asked me suddenly. 'Like, when you were a kid?'

It was such an out-of-the-blue question that I answered without thinking. 'A sailor,' I said, memories of watching those boats on the water coming back to me. 'I always wanted to sail over the edge of the horizon, see what was on the other side.'

She smiled. 'That sounds so cool. Did you ever get the chance?'

'No.' I managed to keep the word casual and not full of any dark undertones. 'What about you? What did you want to be when you grew up?'

Her expression shifted, rippling with something that I thought was curiosity, and I tensed, waiting for her to push.

But she didn't. Instead she looked back down to the pan. 'What didn't I want to be? A nurse. A fairy. A princess. A firefighter. An ambulance driver. A doctor. A painter. An astronomer. A historian.' Her mouth turned up. 'I was interested in everything, which basically meant that I could never decide.'

That seemed to fit her quicksilver mind.

'You never found the one thing you really wanted to do?' I asked.

'Part of the problem is that I want to try everything.' She gave a little sigh. 'But then, once I figure it out, I lose interest.'

She was bright and I suspected there was an intelligence to her that her curiosity only hinted at. What would she be like if she didn't lose interest? If she found that one thing and concentrated on it?

She would be...formidable.

Yes. She bloody well would be.

'Why do you lose interest?' I asked.

She lifted a shoulder. 'I don't know. I just get obsessed by something and then, once I've found out all there is to know about it, it's like I'm...not interested any more. Or something else catches my attention.' Her small white teeth sunk into her lip. 'It's frustrating, to be honest.'

'Maybe you simply haven't found the thing that'll hold your interest yet,' I said. 'You're still young. The world is a big place.'

'You say that like you're eighty years old.'

'I feel eighty years old.' I found myself staring into her eyes. 'Especially when I look at you.'

Her mouth, with its tiny, adorable birthmark, curved. 'I know I'm young, or at least younger. And

Dad is always accusing me of behaving like a child, but…' The smile faded, darkness flickering in her eyes. 'I'm not. I'm Dad's daughter. And no kid should ever have a childhood like mine.'

That strange tightness caught in my chest again, harder this time. All I could think about was how different we were—light years apart in life experience—and yet how similar we were too.

Our fathers, hers and mine, enemies. Our childhoods twisted by the same kind of monsters. She'd been sheltered from it more than I had, but she hadn't escaped. It had touched her too.

I wanted to ask her how she'd coped, but I suspected I already knew; that quicksilver mind of hers had protected her, always moving, always finding something new to concentrate on, distracting her from the truth of her existence.

I'd had the protectiveness that lived in me, that I cursed sometimes for the way it drove me, the way it denied me.

But in the end it had been the thing that had saved me too.

'No, they shouldn't.' I reached out to cup her cheek. 'And you shouldn't have either.'

'He hurt other people worse. He never touched me.'

'Hurt doesn't have to be physical—you know that, right?'

She looked away, her skin soft against my palm. 'He had his reasons.'

Something stilled inside me. 'What reasons were they?'

'I mean, he was right—I'm not that great at controlling myself even now. And besides, he said I owed it to her.' She let out a shaky breath, staring down unseeing at the pan. 'My mum.' Another pause and I waited, because I knew there was more.

Her gaze lifted, the green sharp as glass. 'I killed her, you know.'

It took effort to keep the shock from my face. 'You killed her? What do you mean?'

'I told you, remember? She died having me. And Dad...never forgave me for that. He told me that if I hadn't been born, Mum would still be here, and that I owed him for her loss. That I...owed her too.'

Jesus. Her dad had laid that on her? The bastard. The *fucking* bastard.

I stroked her cheek with my thumb, the tightness in my chest aching at the pain in her eyes. 'You don't owe him anything, Imogen, not a damn thing. And you didn't kill her either.'

Her mouth got that vulnerable look. 'Dad thinks I did. If I hadn't been born, she wouldn't have had that haemorrhage and she'd still be alive.'

'He's wrong. Grief makes people do odd things and blame others when they shouldn't.' I'd seen enough of that in my lifetime. 'I'm sorry your mother died, but...' I paused. 'I think she would have wanted you to be born.'

Imogen had gone very still. 'She wouldn't have wanted to die.'

I stroked her again, feeling the softness of her. 'No, but she would have been glad that you're alive. That you're here.'

'You don't know that.'

'I know what it's like to want to protect the people you love. To sacrifice things for them.' I didn't understand what was making me say this stuff to her, not when she wasn't supposed to matter to me, but I couldn't stop myself. 'Your mother loved you, Imogen. And she would have sacrificed everything for you to make sure you existed. Even her life.'

A tear ran down her cheek and then another. 'But... why?' She looked at me as if she genuinely didn't have any idea. 'She didn't even get a chance to know me.'

'Why? Because you're beautiful.' I wiped away the tear with my thumb. 'And you're very brave. You're strong. And you're fiercely intelligent. Why wouldn't she?'

'But I... I'm not any of those things.'

'Bullshit. You've done nothing but be resolutely unafraid of me since I kidnapped you. Hell, no one talks to me the way you do—no one would fucking dare. Then there's how you took everything I had to give you in bed, all the while screaming for more. And now... I want to see what that amazing mind of yours can accomplish when you find something you want to focus on.' I brushed away another tear. 'Because I have a feeling that when you do you're going to work miracles.'

Shock rippled over her face, along with something else I didn't recognise. She stared at me like she'd never seen me before in her entire life.

'How...?' Her voice was scratchy. 'How do you know all this stuff?'

'My mother died when I was young too, but I had brothers,' I said quietly. 'And I would have done anything for them.'

Behind her, the oil in the pan began to smoke.

'The bacon, little one,' I reminded her gently. 'It's burning.'

CHAPTER SIXTEEN

Imogen

I ROLLED OVER and blinked as the early-morning sunlight fell over my face.

Ajax wasn't in bed with me, but that seemed to be normal with him. He hadn't been there the past couple of days when I'd woken up either, though I hadn't woken this early before.

He must have been up even earlier.

I slipped out of bed, finding one of his T-shirts on the floor and pulling it on over my head. The cotton was cool against my bare skin and it smelled of the dark, delicious male scent that was all him.

It gave me a little shiver of pleasure.

I couldn't have put into words how happy the past couple of days with him had made me.

After that day in the kitchen, when he'd said those things to me about Mum and sacrifices, I'd felt lighter than I had in years. And in the days that followed I felt lighter still.

It wasn't as if we did anything major. Just…spent a lot of time in bed, talking. Or watching TV. Or swimming in the pool. One evening I'd curled up in his lap in the library, his hand stroking through my hair as we read books together. I hadn't wanted to move, not once.

Being with him eased something frenetic inside me. With him it quietened, as if his presence lulled it.

He still hadn't talked about himself in any meaningful way, though, apart from that one comment about his brothers. His past and his thinking processes were still as much of a closed book to me as ever.

Which naturally made me even hungrier to know about them.

I crept out of the bedroom and paused in the hallway outside, glancing through the open doorway into the office next to the bedroom.

Ajax sat at the computer, leaning back in his chair, his long legs outstretched. He wore nothing but a pair of running shorts, as if he'd just come back from a workout. His skin gleamed, those incredible tattoos outlining the muscles I'd explored with my hands and my tongue for hours the night before.

He was so delicious. My palms itched, wanting to touch him.

You're never going to stop wanting him.

I shook my head at the thought. Of course I would. I always lost interest after a while. Sex with him was new and fresh and so it was fascinating to me. Once I'd explored everything he had to offer I'd be ready to move on, the way I moved on with everything.

Trying not to make a sound, I crept into the room and sneaked up behind him, hoping to surprise him.

Leaning in, I whispered, 'Caught you,' in his ear.

He didn't move and he didn't look round. 'If you want to catch me, you'll have to use something to mask your scent. I could smell you the moment you stepped into the hallway.'

'You could smell me?' I wound my arms around his neck. 'Seriously?'

'I'm used to people creeping up on me, little one. I've developed a few instincts to stop them from surprising me.'

That made sense. I didn't imagine he'd had a peaceful life.

'But didn't your father have guards to protect you?' I nuzzled against his neck. 'Like, lots of security? Mine did. I can't go anywhere without my guards.'

He was sitting there, apparently relaxed. But I could feel the sudden tension in his body. 'My father thought I needed to protect myself.'

There was a note in his deep voice that I couldn't identify.

I shut my eyes, brushed my mouth across his powerful shoulder, wanting to ease that tension somehow. 'Why? Isn't that what guards are for?'

He didn't say anything and it felt like the tension in him was seeping into the silence of the room, pressing in around us.

This was a painful subject.

Abruptly I wanted to talk about something else, ask him questions, distract him. I didn't want to hurt him.

But, before I could open my mouth, he said, 'I had to learn what it meant to be Augustus's son early. I'd always suspected he was a monster, but I had it shoved in my face when I was thirteen.'

A chill crept down my spine.

'You don't have to say anything,' I murmured. 'Not if you don't—'

He put his hand over mine where they rested on his chest and the rest of what I'd been going to say vanished from my brain. It wasn't a move meant to hold me still. It was almost as if he wanted the touch of my skin against his as a comfort.

'Dad took me to an old warehouse one day after school,' Ajax said, the words toneless. 'There was nothing in it but a man tied to a chair. I had no idea what was going on or what the man was doing there, but as soon as Dad walked in the man went white.'

The chill down my spine solidified into ice.

I might have been sheltered, but I wasn't stupid. I knew where this was going.

'I asked Dad what was happening and he said that the man in the chair was an employee of his who'd disobeyed him and then tried to leave. I asked Dad what he meant by "leave", but Dad told me it would all become clear.' Ajax paused, his grip on my hand tightening. 'Then he made me watch while he beat the man half to death.'

The ice filtered into my bloodstream, chilling me despite the warmth of his hand over mine and the heat of his bare chest.

His father had made him watch… At thirteen.

I laid my cheek against his shoulder, fighting the sick feeling in my stomach. My father might have hurt and manipulated me emotionally, but he'd never shown me his violent side. At least not until he'd hurt Cam.

'Dad told me that I needed to see what happened to people who disobeyed him,' Ajax went on expressionlessly. 'And those who wanted out. Then he said that I was a King and I'd be one for life, and if I ever betrayed him or escaped, he'd kill me. And my brothers too.'

I had no idea what to say. Because what could I say? To something as horrific as that?

So I did the only thing I could. I tightened my arms around him and spread my palms out on his chest, pressing down. Then I turned my face into his strong neck, put my mouth to his skin.

He'd been just as much a prisoner of his father as I had of mine, hadn't he? Dad had used my mother's death against me, while Augustus had taken Ajax's inherent protectiveness and used that against him.

And of course it had worked, because if I'd learned anything about Ajax it was that protectiveness lay at the very heart of him.

It was why he'd kidnapped me. To keep his city safe.

And by threatening his brothers his father had ensured Ajax's loyalty.

It turned my stomach.

'I hate him,' I said fiercely against his neck. 'He's a bastard for using your brothers against you like that. Jail is too good for him. I would have beaten him up first.'

Strangely, the tension suddenly bled out of Ajax's shoulders and he shifted, swivelling the chair around and pulling me into his lap.

'You're fierce, woman.' His sky-blue eyes met mine, direct and uncompromising. 'I approve.'

I settled myself against his chest, in the crook of his arm, and looked up at him. 'Well, it's true. And I'm glad you took him down in the end.'

An expression that I thought was regret flickered over his face. 'It took me too long.'

'But you had to be careful, right? I mean, otherwise he would have hurt your brothers.'

'It still took longer than it should. And I had to stand by while...'

I put my hand on his bare chest, feeling the strong beat of his heart, knowing that whatever had made him stop, it was painful. 'You don't need to say it.'

He searched my face for a long time. 'I had to stand by while Leon was kidnapped and tortured. While Dad used Xander to steal people's money. I couldn't do a thing for them, not without betraying myself and all the plans I'd put in place. Taking down my father was more important and I sacrificed my brothers to do it.' He stared at me as if I had the answer to a question he'd been dying to know the answer to. 'What kind of man does that?'

Grief twisted in my heart, for him and the childhood he'd had. For how his father had used him.

Was this why he thought he was a monster?

I lifted my hands to his face, holding him gently. 'You wanted to save people,' I said fiercely. 'Not just your brothers, but all the people your father hurt. All the people your father could potentially hurt too if he wasn't stopped.'

A shadow moved over his face. 'I'm not looking for forgiveness, Imogen.'

I dropped my hands, unexpectedly stung. 'I wasn't giving it.'

'That's not why I told you.'

I pushed the prick of hurt away. This wasn't about me. It was about him. 'So why did you tell me then?'

'So you understand. The end justifies the means. Every time.'

I swallowed. 'Yes, I get it.'

The hard look in his eyes softened. He brushed my

cheek with one finger. 'I'm not saying this to hurt you and I'm sorry if I did. I just want to be straight with you. You can't get too comfortable with me. I'm a man with only one goal and I won't change it. Not for you. Not for anyone.'

Hearing it shouldn't have made the hurt go deeper. He was being honest and I appreciated it. Not that I was going to get too comfortable with him in any case.

'That's good.' I tried to make my voice light. 'Because you know I'm going to lose interest in you soon in any case. I always do.'

His eyes gleamed, though whether it was amusement or something else I wasn't quite sure. 'You want to see something?'

'What?' Automatically I looked down at his shorts.

This time there was no mistaking his amusement, his laugh deep and rough and sexy. 'No, it's not that, not today.'

My hurt began to ebb, pleased by how I'd made him laugh. I flicked him a glance from underneath my lashes. 'Is there anything else as interesting?'

'Look at my computer screen and then tell me.'

I sighed and turned to look at the screen.

I saw what looked to be a 3D rendering of a building. 'What's that?'

'A new apartment block my sister-in-law is designing.' He leaned forward, gripping the mouse and shifting it, his bare skin and heat teasing my hyper-alert senses.

The building tilted and turned in response, giving a three-hundred-and-sixty-degree viewpoint.

Of course. He was in the property development business, wasn't he?

I sat up, my curiosity starting to kick in. 'Is your company going to be building that?'

'Yes. Eventually. If we get the returns we want on the luxury apartment complex that's going up soon.'

I reached out towards the mouse. 'Can I have a look?'

He nodded and sat back, letting me take control.

I studied the building from different viewpoints, zooming in, pleased when the inside plans opened up and I could see all the apartments. Simple, elegant spaces, designed to take advantage of the light.

I knew nothing about buildings, still less about architecture, but this building looked like somewhere I'd want to live myself.

'It's amazing,' I said, staring fascinated at the screen. 'Who's it for?'

'Families who don't have homes.'

I turned sharply to look at him.

His gaze was as uncompromising as it had been when he'd talked about his brothers. 'There are a lot of homeless people out there, families with nowhere to go. I've been liaising with the state housing officials and we're working something out. This building is as eco-friendly as it's possible to get and cost efficient to build, and hopefully will serve as a prototype for more.'

Saving his city. That's what he'd said he was trying to do, and not only from people who might threaten it. He was trying to make it a better place for the people who lived in it too.

'Who's going to pay for it?' I asked, trying to cover the giant lump in my throat.

'I will. I have plenty of money.'

'You're not a monster,' I said bluntly. 'You're like…

Batman and Captain America and Thor all rolled up into one.'

He lifted a hand to my face, brushing my cheek. 'Look at the building again. I want to know if you think there's anything more I need to do to it, anything I could add.'

I shivered at his touch. 'But I don't know anything about buildings.'

'You have an amazing mind, though.' His mouth turned up. 'Time to put it to good use.'

CHAPTER SEVENTEEN

Ajax

As I'd hoped, Imogen became totally engrossed in the apartment building that Poppy, Xander's new wife, had designed for me.

So much so that she barely looked at me when I finally left the room to go and do a few other things.

I took her coffee and toast an hour later, and this time she didn't even turn, merely muttering thanks as she frowned at the article she was in the middle of reading.

I smiled and left her to it, having a shower then going downstairs, yet another message on my phone from her father burning a hole in the pocket of my jeans.

There were a lot of those, each message more and more pissed-off sounding, demanding I let him see his daughter.

You've been putting it off.

I pulled open the massive sliding window in the lounge that led to the pool and stepped outside, making sure it was shut behind me. Then I walked over to where the tiled pool area met the cliff that plunged down into the sea. A small stone parapet marked the edge of the cliff and I stood near it, staring out over the sea as I took the phone from my pocket.

Yes. For the last two days I *had* been putting this off.

Because something was holding me back from granting White's request. And I wasn't sure what it was.

It wasn't the danger factor, not when I'd make sure her security would be airtight. In fact, I couldn't put my finger on exactly what was bugging me about it.

Whatever the issue was, I had to ignore it and luckily the conversation we'd had just now, up in my office, had reminded me of where my priorities lay.

Another thing puzzled me. Why had I told her about Dad and the beating I'd witnessed? About how I'd had to stand by and watch my brothers get hurt? Her comments about her own guards and the artless questions about why I hadn't been given the same treatment had somehow got under my skin.

Or perhaps it had simply been the way she'd put her arms around me, her soft lips against my neck. How she'd nuzzled against me, her breath on my skin and her hands on my bare chest. Her warmth and familiar scent had eased a tension I hadn't known was there. A tension that had nothing to do with sex.

It made me fucking uncomfortable. Maybe that's why I'd told her what I had. To make her as uncomfortable as she made me. So she knew I wasn't a man she could throw her arms around whenever she pleased or treat like someone safe. Who wouldn't hurt her if she got between him and his goal.

Like you hurt your brothers?

The truth shifted inside me, digging in, sharp like a knife.

Yeah, I wasn't that man and she had to understand that.

Hitting the button that would call her father, I waited as it rang once and then White's furious voice was answering.

'King, you bastard! I've been trying to—'

'Next week,' I cut him off curtly. 'Wednesday night. I'll send through the details of where and when to meet.'

'But I—'

'There will be no negotiation. You wanted proof of life, you'll get it. That's all.'

I hit the disconnect button before he could argue further.

There. It was done.

Next week she'd meet her father and once he'd ascertained that I hadn't hurt her or touched her, he'd leave Sydney.

And take her with him.

That had always been the deal. I'd never intended to keep her. My threat to make her mine had extended to her virginity only to ensure White's obedience.

I'd let her go and her father would take her to Melbourne or wherever he intended to set himself up, continuing to use her as his tool to build his pathetic little empire.

You're really going to give her back to him? What will happen to her if he finds out you touched her?

I lifted my head, stared out at the sea, at the yachts in the harbour, sailing to places I could never go.

He wouldn't find out I'd touched her; I'd made sure

of that. But as to letting her go... What other choice did I have? If I kept her, White would make things difficult. My investigations had discovered that he'd built quite the web and I didn't have the time to take it apart. Not when I had a whole lot of other projects on my plate. Especially that social housing project. It had been on the backburner for a while and I wanted to get it front and centre. Protecting my city was one thing, but doing something good for it was quite another.

Apart from anything else, I'd spent years dismantling my father's empire and frightening off other challengers. I wanted to do something meaningful, that wasn't about banging heads together.

Putting more distance between him and you? Yeah. Sure.

I ignored the thought.

No, I couldn't keep Imogen. She had to go back to her father in the end.

I'd tell her about the meeting with her father tonight, and ease the sting by taking her somewhere private, where she could enjoy being out of the house for a change.

I watched one of the yachts tacking slowly against the wind and smiled.

I had the perfect place.

A couple of hours later it was all organised, then I busied myself with finally dealing with my brothers.

I sent them a couple of texts reminding them I was out of contact and busy. The situation with White's daughter was being dealt with and they weren't to concern themselves with it. On pain of me being severely pissed with them.

Of course, within moments of the messages being

sent, both Xander and Leon tried to call me. I ignored them. I didn't want to talk to them. Once Imogen and her father were gone, then I'd tell them, but not before.

It wasn't till the late afternoon that I realised I hadn't seen Imogen.

I went upstairs to check if she was still in my office and she was, sitting in the same position I'd left her in that morning, staring hard at the computer screen. Some official-looking document was open on it and she was frowning at it.

There was something different about her and it took me a moment to figure out what it was. She was sitting still. Her foot wasn't jiggling and she wasn't humming. She wasn't shifting around or doing any of the other things I'd watched her do over the past couple of days.

Her attention was focused so fiercely on the screen it was as if she was trying to see inside to the electronics themselves.

I leaned against the doorframe. 'Little one.'

She didn't even look at me.

'Little one.'

She twitched, but didn't look away from the screen.

'Imogen,' I finally said, amused.

She glanced at me, blinked, then grinned. 'Oh. Sorry. Did you want something?'

'You've been sitting there all day. Did you even have lunch?'

'No,' she said slowly. 'I don't think I did. But I had a good look at your building and a whole lot of social housing stuff, what's available in New South Wales and the rules and regulations—that kind of thing.' Her eyes were shining. 'It's quite complicated. Lots of things to figure out. I mean, I guess you've done all that?'

I couldn't help smiling. 'I've done some things. Haven't had a chance to investigate others.'

'Do you want me to tell you what I discovered?' She turned back to the computer, hit a button and the printer whirred into life. There was already quite a stack of paper beside it.

Clearly, she'd been busy.

'Yes,' I said. 'But you can tell me tonight over dinner.'

'Okay. Let me know if you want me to do anything, because I might just stay here and—'

'No,' I interrupted. 'I'm taking you out.'

'Out? As in out of the house out?'

'Yes, out of the house out.'

She smiled the most beautiful smile. 'Seriously?'

There was an unfamiliar warmth in my chest that hadn't been there before, somehow called into life by her smile.

It had been a long time since I'd done anything to make anyone happy. The big picture didn't include individuals.

Certainly not individuals like this one, who smiled at me as if I'd handed her the fucking moon on a plate.

'Where are we going?' she went on. 'To a restaurant? Like, Asian food? I love Japanese. Or Indian—I love Indian too. Thai is pretty cool. But I don't really mind. If we have steak, though, it must have fries with it, because you can't have steak without chips, right?'

Adorable. Delightful. Exuberant. Full of interest and questions and excitement. And, despite how she'd been trapped in the prison her father had created for her, there was an optimism to her that I didn't have and probably never would.

She was everything I wasn't. Everything that was missing from my life.

Everything you need.

The thought sat there for one long moment and, no matter how hard I tried to ignore it, the damn thing wouldn't go away.

And the warmth in my chest just sat there too, getting bigger and bigger the more she smiled at me.

It was so easy to make her happy.

That's what you want. You want to make her happy.

'Ajax?' She was giving me a slightly concerned look now. 'Everything okay?'

Christ, how long had I been standing there staring at her?

'Be ready in an hour,' I said, my voice sounding a lot rougher than I'd intended.

'Yay.' She frowned. 'But where are we going?'

'It's a surprise.'

'Omigod, I love surprises! Do I wear a dress? I mean, there is a dress in those clothes you got me, right? What about shoes? Heels or flats? Do I need a jacket?'

I couldn't stand it.

Pushing myself away from the doorframe, I strode into the room and over to the chair, bending to take her flushed face in my hands. Then I kissed her hard, stopping her stream of questions.

Instantly her mouth opened under mine, warm and generous, and hungry. If I wasn't careful I was going to have her right here in this chair and, since I had a few things to do before we went out, that probably wasn't the best idea.

Releasing her, I stepped back. 'Wear whatever you feel beautiful in. I'll take care of everything else.'

'Can I bring those printouts? I promise I won't talk at you too long.'

'Yes. Bring them all. And you can talk at me as long as you want.' I didn't think I could say no to her. Not now.

What I did need to do was get out of this room and figure out where the fuck I'd put my distance.

Because one thing was for sure; I was going to need it if I was ever going to give her back to her father.

CHAPTER EIGHTEEN

Imogen

I WAS RIDICULOUSLY EXCITED.

Ajax still hadn't told me where we were going but, sitting next to him in the plain black car as it slid easily through the Sydney streets, I knew that, wherever it was, it was going to be fantastic.

I was out of his house. Outside. And sure, it wasn't like I was completely alone and able to do what I wanted, but I didn't mind that. In fact, having him beside me, all tall, dark, muscular and hot, made it even better somehow.

Knowing he'd organised this for me made it better too.

I'd tried to make an effort with my clothes since he'd obviously made an effort to organise this and, even though I didn't know where we were going, I thought I'd wear something sexy that we'd both enjoy.

A pretty green silk shift dress with spaghetti straps that felt nice against my skin. The look he'd given me when I'd come out wearing it had thrilled me.

He liked it. A lot.

Well, the feeling was mutual.

He was in his usual jeans—he never seemed to wear the suits hanging up in his closet—along with a black T-shirt and battered black leather jacket. Casual clothing that fitted him like a second skin, highlighting his height and powerful muscularity, making him look deliciously dark and broody.

I could hardly drag my gaze away.

His mouth curved as he caught me staring. 'Feel free to stare at me, little one,' he murmured. 'I don't mind.'

I flushed. 'I was wondering why you never wear all those suits in your closet.'

'Because I don't like suits.'

'So why did you buy them?'

Dark humour glittered in his gaze. 'Leon thought they would make me more…accessible.'

I grinned. 'He's right. You were very accessible the night you kidnapped me and you were wearing a suit then.'

'I'm not sure kidnapping you was me being accessible.'

'Well, I didn't mind it.'

'I'm glad.' There was a blue flame burning in his eyes now. 'Because I'm pretty fucking happy I kidnapped you.'

My cheeks heated, something inside me glowing at how blatantly appreciative the look he gave me was. 'I hope I won't be too overdressed,' I said breathlessly. 'Or underdressed. Or whatever.'

'You're perfect.' His smile was hungry and a touch feral. 'Completely perfect.'

It made me shiver in the best way.

I hoped we'd be somewhere private, where we could

maybe indulge our mutual hunger, but then the car pulled up and Ajax looked out the window.

'We're here,' he said.

Here turned out to be a marina with a lot of expensive sleek boats moored on long jetties that stretched out across the dark water. The place was brightly lit and there were a number of people moving among the boats, either unmooring or tying them up.

I peered curiously out the window. 'What are we doing here?'

Ajax's smile turned enigmatic. 'You'll see.'

My surprise turned out to be one of those sleek yachts that sat low in the water. It had a covered deck and an interior like a five-star hotel. Low, soft couches, gleaming wooden floors and windows on all sides. A table was set up on the deck outside, complete with silverware, crystal glasses, candles and a spray of roses. A wine bottle stood waiting to be opened.

I stared around in wonder. 'It's a boat,' I said after Ajax returned from talking with the yacht's captain, coming around the table to pull out my chair. 'A bloody boat.' I sounded ridiculous but I couldn't help it. 'I've never been on a boat before. Is it yours? Where are we going? Are we really going to have dinner here?'

'Sit down and I'll tell you,' Ajax said, amused.

Obediently I did, biting down on my questions, looking around at the marina. There were yachts with graceful sails and huge super-yachts—basically a rich man's playground.

Ajax had said he'd wanted to sail away over the horizon as a kid, so this boat had to be his, right? And now he was inviting me out on it. So cool.

His gaze was full of warmth as he sat down opposite me and it made my heart beat faster.

'It's not my boat,' he said, reaching for the wine bottle and opening it, pouring white wine into both our glasses. 'But I'm considering buying it. This is a test drive.' His blue gaze caught mine. 'And, as to where we're going, we're going on a tour of the harbour while we have dinner.'

Oh, I was up for that. *So* up. I'd been to the harbour, of course, but never without guards. Never on my own with someone I liked for company.

And I *did* like Ajax. Sure, he was uncompromising, not to mention arrogant and bossy. But his heart was in the right place. And he made me feel good. And he was really interesting. I liked the way his mind worked. He saw the whole, while I tended to focus on the different parts.

Such as him, for example. I was seeing different parts of him, but I had the sense he was only showing me the parts that he wanted me to see.

Not the whole of him.

And I wanted to see that very much.

Maybe I would tonight.

Ten minutes later we were cruising over the water, the bright crescent of the harbour bridge and the neon of the city skyline in front of us.

I couldn't stop staring. The city was beautiful and the scent of salt, the openness of the water around us and the warmth of the night pressing in made me feel alive in a way I hadn't before. As if there were possibilities in the air. Possibilities I hadn't thought about before because they were things I couldn't have.

Correction, things I thought I didn't deserve, such

as a normal life. A job. A place that was mine. Friends. A man I loved.

The thought sent a hot pulse of emotion through me. A man I loved…

Such as the man sitting opposite?

The man who'd kidnapped me, saved me. Who'd not only shown me pleasure, but shown me that I was worthy of it. Who'd allowed me to be myself and liked me despite it.

Or maybe because of it.

The man who'd told me that my mother's sacrifice had been worth it if it had allowed me to exist.

You're in love with him. You have been since the moment you met him.

My eyes filled with the stupidest tears.

'You look sad.' His deep voice wound around me, encompassing me in its rough warmth. 'What's wrong? I thought you'd like the yacht.'

I blinked furiously. God, I did *not* want to cry. I didn't even know why I was crying.

Sure, you do.

Yes. I was in love with Ajax King and I couldn't have him. Because if he didn't release me back to Dad, then Dad would stay, continuing to threaten Ajax and his family. Continuing to threaten the city Ajax had sworn to protect.

And I couldn't ask him to keep me. I couldn't ask to be put before everyone he cared about. That would be selfish.

I forced myself to smile, my heart aching. 'Oh, I'm just…happy to be outside and here,' I lied. Then, because I couldn't help myself, I added, 'With you.'

Something in his gaze shifted, his smile fading. 'I have to tell you something, Imogen.'

I swallowed. I knew what he was going to say; don't ask me how, but I did. Maybe it was simply the timing of me discovering I was in love and realising I could never have it.

'You're going to tell me that you've spoken to Dad and that I have to meet him,' I said. 'And then you're going to give me back to him.'

He was silent, staring at me.

Of course he was going to give me back to Dad. And that shouldn't have disappointed me in the slightest. I'd told him I didn't want him to care about me, after all.

'No,' Ajax murmured slowly. 'I'm not going to give you back to him.'

The shock was a hard jolt, like I'd curled my fingers around a bare electrical wire. 'W-what?'

'I changed my mind.' The intensity in his eyes burned. 'I'm keeping you.'

I'm keeping you...

A hot ball of emotion pushed against my ribs, constricting my lungs, making breathing hard.

I had *not* been expecting this.

'You can't,' I forced out. 'You can't keep me. Dad will—'

'I'll deal with your father.' For a second the warmth in his eyes was replaced with something cold. 'But you're not going back to him, end of story.'

'B-but where will I go?' I stammered. 'What will I do? How can I—'

'Did you miss the part where I said I'm keeping you?'

'No,' I managed. 'I just…thought you might be joking.'

'I'm not. I'm deadly serious.'

The hot ball of emotion got bigger, wider. 'But why?'

'Because he's a prick and he hurt you. And I want to make sure he never hurts you again. Plus...' a familiar flame leapt in his gaze '...I haven't finished with you yet.'

'What will happen to me when you do?' My brain was already leaping to the next thing. Because of course he wouldn't want to keep me for ever. 'When you finish with me, I mean. Dad's not going to go away just like that.'

'Leave him to me.'

'But I thought you said nothing was going to get in the way of you protecting your city? Not even me.'

He pinned me with that relentlessly blue gaze. 'I've never been able to have what I want. At least, I never thought I'd be able to. You were the first thing I allowed myself. And I want more. I want both. To protect my city *and* have you, and fuck, I don't see why I can't.'

The emotion in my chest was crushing. Like hunger magnified a thousand times, multiplied by need, turning into something so intense I couldn't breathe.

I loved him. But to ask for it in return was too much to ask of a man like Ajax. He was too driven, too focused on his goals, and he'd told me himself how important they were to him. Far more important than I'd ever be.

Dad never loved you. Why would Ajax King?

He wouldn't. And that was the truth.

'Why?' I asked, unable to help myself. 'If it's just about the sex—'

'It's not just about the sex. I want to keep you because you wanted me. Because I haven't had a woman look at me the way you do for years, if ever. Because you're the first person I've met who wasn't instantly afraid of me. Because you're beautiful. Because I'm fascinated by the way your mind works.' The blue flame in his eyes leapt higher. 'Because you're challenging as hell and because your optimism is so fucking bright it's blinding.'

My throat closed up. He'd told me similar things that day in the kitchen, when I'd burned the bacon. But I hadn't taken them in, not until now. Not until I saw the truth burning in his gaze.

I tried to swallow. Failed.

'I couldn't have what I wanted,' he went on, 'because anything I claim will be a target. But I can protect you. I *will* protect you.' The look on his face was naked with need. 'I want you, Imogen. Do you want me?'

Emotion burned behind my ribs, a bonfire of it.

How long will he want you for? And what will you do when it's over?

But the future had never been something I wanted to think about and I wanted to think about it even less now.

Now was all that mattered.

Now was all I had.

'Yes.' I couldn't lie, not even to protect myself. 'I want you *so* much.'

His eyes were a deep, endless blue, like that horizon he'd told me he wanted to sail over to see what was on the other side.

I wanted to sail over it too. With him. Because,

whatever was on the other side, I knew it would be endlessly fascinating. Endlessly challenging. I would never lose interest. Never.

'Stay.' Ajax looked at me as if the rest of the world didn't exist. 'Stay with me, Imogen.'

How could I resist?

'Okay.' My voice cracked. 'I'll stay.'

A look of intense satisfaction crossed his face. 'I told your father he could see you next week. Instead, I'll take the opportunity to tell him you'll be remaining with me.'

I wanted to ask him how he'd keep Dad off my back and protect his city as well, but I didn't. That was another thing I didn't want to think about.

'Okay,' I repeated shakily.

'Be sure, little one.' He looked so fierce. 'I'm very similar to your father in a lot of ways.'

No, he wasn't. Sure, he was a man who'd been brought up with a monster. And in order to take down the monster he'd had to become one. And that had been a heavy price.

He'd isolated himself. Denied himself. But that hunger for someone had never gone away—I saw it in his eyes every time he touched me. And I recognised it because I felt it myself every day.

I couldn't tell him how I felt, not without making it ten thousand times harder, but I wanted to give him something back.

I wanted to give him everything he'd given me.

'You know why I want to stay?' I said huskily. 'Because you're protective. Because you'd do anything for the people you care about. Because you're unselfish. Because you give me great orgasms and make me feel treasured. Because you're honest and you challenge me in a way no one else does.' I stared into his eyes, into the heart of him. 'And because I think you're as lonely as I am. And that you need someone as badly as I do.'

CHAPTER NINETEEN

Ajax

She saw right through me. She saw *me*.

I didn't know how, but she did.

Her steady green gaze didn't flicker, seeing the truth that lay underneath my armour. The vulnerability I'd tried to protect and keep hidden.

Not all that noble hero stuff—that was bullshit and I knew it even if she didn't—but she was right about one thing.

I did need someone. I'd *always* needed someone.

But it hadn't been until the moment she'd boarded the boat and smiled at me like I was everything she'd ever dreamed of that I'd accepted that the someone I needed was her.

I'd been trying for distance, but distance with Imogen was impossible.

Giving her back to White was impossible.

Keeping her was not only possible, it was the only thing that made sense.

It would piss White off and no doubt he'd retaliate, but I couldn't let her go back. I couldn't let that bastard use her or hurt her the way he'd been doing, making her feel like shit, like she had some debt to repay.

My city was important to me and the safety of my brothers too, but somehow Imogen had become important as well.

Having her was addictive and it wasn't something I wanted to give up. Fundamentally, she understood that, deep down, we were the same. Both of us hungry for something we'd never been allowed to have. So why couldn't we have it now?

It was wrong to keep her, because she would find no freedom with me. Simply through being mine, she'd become a target and those guards of her father's she'd hated would soon be her King security detail.

She would only ever be alone with me or at my house.

It wasn't the life she should have, but there was no other choice. It was either that or give her back.

You could let her go.

Every part of me tightened in instinctive denial.

Let her go back to what? She'd always be at risk from her father and, anyway, she was mine. Keeping her would ensure she stayed mine.

Imogen's eyes glittered like emeralds, green fire in the depths, a flame I'd never seen go out, not once. Her face was pale in the night yet it glowed with the strength of her emotion.

For me.

I wanted to tell her all the different ways she was right, that I did need someone, but that would take too long. What I really needed was to show her.

So I shoved my chair back and got to my feet, stalking around the table to where she sat.

She watched me come and when I bent and swept her up in my arms she took my face between her small palms and kissed me like she was dying of thirst and I was a cold glass of water.

The dinner I'd organised was forgotten.

I carried her into the cabin and down into the main stateroom, where there was a bed, and then I stripped that pretty green dress off her and laid her down onto it. I took all her sweet demand and gave it back to her, my hands on her skin, my mouth on hers, making the connection we were both desperate for and couldn't get enough of.

It felt easier after that.

We couldn't be bothered getting dressed so I brought dinner into the stateroom and we ate sitting on the bed, her printouts scattered on the sheets, Imogen talking nineteen to the dozen about everything she'd discovered on social housing.

I could have listened to her talk all night. Her mind was a beautiful thing, jumping from topic to topic, looking at every angle and analysing each one in greater depth than I ever had. I kept her on track, helping her gather all the various parts of her subject into a whole so she could see the big picture, while she gave me insight into smaller aspects I hadn't seen or had dismissed as being unworkable.

'You should manage the housing project,' I said, the idea gripping me and refusing to let go. 'You'd be good at it.'

Her eyes opened wide. 'Me? But I don't know what I'm talking about.'

She was sitting cross-legged on the bed, the sheet wound carelessly around her waist, her bare skin glowing from the lights coming through the portholes. Her cheeks were flushed with excitement, her eyes like jewels.

Beautiful girl.

Yours. All yours.

A satisfaction I hadn't felt for years stretched out inside me.

'But it wouldn't take you long to get up to speed. I think it would be perfect for you. Lots of different things to think about, lots of balls to keep in the air. And I'd be around to help and keep you focused.'

A crease appeared between her brows. 'Ajax, you can't put me in charge. I don't know the first thing about housing, or building, or project management. I have no experience of anything. I wouldn't even know where to start.'

'Like I said, I'd help.' I smiled at her. 'Little one, that brain of yours is a gift. It needs to be put to good use and I think you'd be perfect for this. The way you see things, all the details, plus those outside the square ideas. Shit, your energy alone is what this project has always needed, because I sure as hell don't have it. I had the idea, now I just need someone with vision to carry it out.' I brushed my fingers over her soft cheek. 'You have the vision. You have the energy. You have the interest. All you need is the confidence.'

'You really think so?'

'I wouldn't have said it if I didn't. Besides, choosing the right person for a job is part of what I do and I'm very good at it.' I let my hand trail down to her chin. 'I haven't been wrong about a person yet.'

'You might be wrong about me.'

'No.' I slid my fingers along her jaw and into her

hair, curling around the back of her neck, drawing her towards me. 'I don't think I am.'

She didn't argue with me, not after that.

Later, we came back out and watched the lights of Sydney drift by from the deck.

She nestled into me as we stood at the rail and I held her, her curvy body fitting perfectly against me.

And for the first time in my life I let myself think about a future that had all the things I wanted in it. A family with children, a wife.

The things my brothers had, that I'd never thought would be mine.

Do you really think that, after everything you've done, you deserve it?

An intense possessiveness gripped me tight, anger gathering along with it. No, I didn't deserve it and I sure as hell knew that. But I didn't care. I'd worked hard to ensure Sydney stayed clear of bastards like my father, to give my brothers a future after all they'd been through, and now it was my turn.

Next you'll start believing you're the hero she thinks you are.

So? Would that be such a bad thing?

A memory came back to me, of being in that warehouse with Dad, standing beside the broken and bleeding man in the chair, his hand resting on the guy's shoulder. Dad had smiled as he'd told me what was expected of me, how he couldn't allow disloyalty, most especially not from his own sons.

His gaze hadn't flickered as he'd held Xander and Leon's lives over my head, using them to keep me in line. And I'd let him.

You're no hero. Heroes don't let those they love get hurt.

I'd been thirteen years old. What the fuck else was I supposed to do? Becoming Dad's puppet was the only way I could save them.

Imogen was standing in front of me and now she leaned back, resting her head on my chest, her blonde hair bright against the black cotton of my T-shirt.

She didn't smell of roses any more. She smelled of my soap, plus something indefinable and sweetly feminine. Like she'd taken my scent and made it her own.

I leaned down and nuzzled against her hair, folding myself more protectively around her, trying to ignore the thoughts in my head.

I needed to get her home and safe, but there was plenty of time for that. Once I'd let her father know she'd be staying with me I'd have to review my security and deal with the threat he presented, but until then I could take this moment the way she did. I could live in the here and now, and not think about what was going to happen in the future.

Let her enjoy this taste of freedom while she could because, once her father knew she was staying with me, that freedom would end.

She deserves that freedom. She deserves better than you.

I shoved the thought away hard, slipping my arms around her waist and pulling her in tight to me.

She'd chosen me and I was keeping her.

'Being with me isn't going to be easy,' I murmured into the night. 'You understand that, don't you?'

'Yes.' Her voice was quiet. 'I'll be a target, won't I?'

'You will.' I didn't want to sugar-coat it so I didn't. 'And I have many enemies.'

'I can handle it.'

'It'll mean security. More guards.'

'I get that. I don't care as long as I'm with you.'

She will care. Eventually.

I gritted my teeth. 'I'll try and allow you as much freedom as I can. And maybe after I've dealt with your father—'

She turned in my arms, her head tipping back to look up at me. 'Don't hurt him, Ajax.'

The vehemence in her tone caught me off guard, as did the way she'd apparently read my mind.

That slippery slope? You're heading down it already.

'I'm not going to hurt him.' It sounded hollow to my own ears. Mainly because hurting him for what he'd done to her was exactly what I wanted to do.

Imogen just looked at me. 'Please promise me you won't put yourself at risk. He's not worth it.'

'If it keeps you safe, anything's worth it.'

'No,' she said quietly. 'It's not. Sometimes the end does not justify the means, especially if that end involves you being dead or in prison.'

She was wrong. The end was the most important part.

I stared down into her eyes. 'But what if it means your freedom?'

Her gaze didn't even flicker. 'I'm not worth that kind of sacrifice, Ajax, and I don't want to be. You've already had to give up too much. I don't want you giving up anything more.'

'Your mother thought you were worth that sacrifice.'

Her eyes darkened. 'My mother didn't have a choice.'

'Imogen,' I began.

But she reached up and laid her finger across my mouth, silencing me. 'No. This is one thing I'm not arguing with you about.'

So I didn't argue.

I bit the tip of her finger gently instead and then we found something else to distract ourselves with.

But I couldn't get rid of the feeling that somehow I'd just made a mistake.

For both of us.

CHAPTER TWENTY

Imogen

THE NEXT FEW days with Ajax were the happiest I'd ever had.

I spent a lot of time researching his social housing project and discussing how we'd approach it.

I still thought he was mad to put me in charge, but I couldn't resist how confident he was that I could do it. It made me want to show him that he was right to be confident, that I could.

With his help I put together a plan and it was exciting to see it take shape. There were so many details to get right. It suited the way my mind worked, especially when I thought of how to apply what I'd learned to other projects.

I really loved knowing that we were helping people too.

It made me feel like I was doing something valuable rather than mastering a lot of skills that ended up being useless.

But work wasn't all we did.

We talked, about everything from our favourite

pizza toppings to the price of property and whether the kids of today would ever be able to afford a house.

Once I asked him what he did in his spare time and he told me he never had any spare time. I told him that was bullshit, he must have some hobbies, and eventually he took me down to the beach below his house and the tiny boathouse at the foot of the cliff where he kept a small yacht.

He'd got it when he was young and had taught himself to sail, though he hadn't been able to take it out much since his father had kept him so busy.

I asked him to take me out in it so he did, and I sat in the prow, watching him work the sails and do things with the ropes, his strong hands sure on the rudder as we tacked across the blue water.

The sun turned his hair glossy black, his eyes the colour of the sky above us as he watched the sails fill.

His expression was concentrated but the lines of tension around his eyes and mouth, lines I'd never fully noticed before, had gone. And I realised that this, out here on the water with the sea and the wind and the sails, was freedom for him.

He had no one to worry about. No one to protect. All he had to do was keep an eye on the weather and concentrate on the boat.

Yet now he has another person to protect. You.

I didn't like what he'd told me that night on the harbour, how he'd do whatever it took to keep me safe. And I had an idea what that meant to Ajax, and it made me afraid for him. Afraid of what he'd sacrifice to protect me.

I didn't want him to have to sacrifice *anything*.

He'd already risked his soul to take his father down,

putting aside his own hopes and dreams along the way, ignoring the cost to himself.

It wasn't fair. He looked out for everyone else yet no one looked out for him. Sure, he had Xander and Leon, but they had their own lives. Did they know how much Ajax had done for them? Did they even realise what he was *still* doing for them?

The thought made me ache and the closer we came to the day where he'd tell my father I was his, the deeper the ache became.

Dad would never let me go and if I stayed with Ajax he'd make Ajax's life even more difficult than it already was. He'd probably force Ajax's hand, encouraging him to do something that would end up...

Well, I didn't like to think where that might end up because, wherever it was, it wouldn't be good for Ajax.

And, no matter what Ajax told me about me being worth the sacrifice, there was still a part of me buried deep that knew I wasn't. He was more important than my freedom and always would be.

Over the next couple of days, I made it my mission to figure out how he was planning on dealing with Dad, but he always changed the subject, or distracted me. Or simply told me not to worry about it.

He seemed to think that it was my safety that I cared about.

He was wrong. It was his.

The day before the planned meeting with Dad was a beautiful day and I made Ajax take me out on his yacht again.

I hoped he might be more forthcoming about what he was planning if he was in his happy place. Except, as the sails caught the wind and the boat skipped over the waves, Ajax grinning at how fast we were moving, I couldn't bring myself to broach the topic.

Then he pointed at something in the water. 'Look, Imogen.'

Distracted, I looked and saw a sleek grey shape cutting through the waves, keeping pace with the boat.

A surge of wonder went through me. 'Is it a dolphin?'

'I think so.' His voice was full of the same wonder, making me stare, because I'd never heard him sound that way before.

The expression on his face was the most purely happy I'd ever seen him. Then the dolphin leapt and he laughed, the sound full of delight. A boy's laugh. And in that second that's what I saw—a boy, caught up in the excitement and wonder of the moment.

My heart twisted like a wet towel being wrung out.

Out on the waves he was free and I could see that freedom written all over his face. In his smile and in his laugh. In the relaxed way he sat in the boat, the tension in his shoulders gone.

This was what he should be. This was how he should live.

This was what he should have—the freedom to be who he was, and that wasn't the dangerous man with the violent reputation that everyone was afraid of.

It was a boy who loved the wind in his hair and the sun on his face and the sight of a dolphin leaping in the waves.

I couldn't let him sacrifice that freedom for me.

'Did you see it?' Ajax grinned. 'Did you see him leap?'

My eyes prickled with tears. 'No, I missed it.' I

turned to focus on the shape of the dolphin in the water, blinking the moisture away.

If he wouldn't save himself then I would do it for him.

Because there was no one else who could.

He didn't seem to notice my overly emotional moment and when we got back to the house I made some excuses about having to work on my project plan and disappeared upstairs into his office.

But I didn't look at the project plan.

I emailed my father instead and told him I was coming home.

It was surprisingly easy to set up.

I'd tell Ajax I needed a car to go into the city for some spurious shopping trip and then Dad would meet me.

The thought of going back to Dad's prison made me feel cold and sick, but the thought of Ajax losing everything purely to protect me was even worse.

I could bear being Dad's trophy a few more years. It wouldn't be for ever. Eventually I'd find a way to get free. Tonight, though, I'd have to keep my plan secret because obviously if Ajax found out he'd try to stop me.

Arranging for a car wasn't a drama; in fact I was almost annoyed by how easy it was to convince Ajax that I needed a shopping trip. And then, when the car arrived, he barely looked up from his laptop as I came to say goodbye.

This would be the last time I'd ever see him and it hurt that he only gave me a quick glance as I bent to kiss him.

But that was good. If he'd seen the tears in my eyes

he'd have asked what was wrong and I didn't think I had the strength not to tell him.

So I only brushed my lips against his cheek, inhaling the scent of him one last time, imprinting him in my head for ever.

'See you soon,' he said, his gaze on his screen.

I didn't trust myself to speak, turning and walking through the door, letting the tears fall only once I'd got into the car.

I didn't want to leave him, but there was no other option.

I loved him and if there was one thing Ajax King had taught me it was that, unlike my father, who'd used my love to get me to do what he wanted, Ajax's love wasn't selfish. He loved his brothers and his city and he put them first. Before everything.

I couldn't do any less.

As the car pulled away I didn't look back, gritting my teeth and wiping away the tears.

We pulled up outside one of the department stores and I searched the footpath surreptitiously, looking for Dad's guards. He'd told me that they'd be waiting for me.

A man signalled from the crowd and fear caught me by the throat.

Ignoring it, I pushed open the door. 'I'll be five minutes,' I told my driver.

Hopefully he wouldn't come after me.

The streets were full of people and I had to bite down on the urge to scream for help as Dad's guard caught my elbow, beginning to usher me to another car, long and black and drawn up down the street a little way.

But I put my shoulders back as the guard pulled open the door for me and I lifted my chin, steeled my spine.

Then I got in and sat down, turning to look at my father.

Except the man sitting beside me wasn't my father.

'Hello, Imogen,' Ajax said.

CHAPTER TWENTY-ONE

Ajax

THERE WAS SHOCK in her wide green eyes, which I'd expected. They were also red from crying, which I hadn't.

My little one had been crying for me.

Pain sat between my ribs, like someone had sunk a knife into me, and I wanted to pull her into my arms and wrap her up tight, hold her and never let her go.

But that wasn't why I was here.

I was here to set her free.

'Ajax?' She sounded bewildered. 'What are you doing here?'

I glanced in the rear-view mirror and caught the driver's eye. Then I gave him a nod and the car pulled back into the traffic.

'I know what you were trying to do, Imogen,' I said quietly. 'I know you were coming to meet your father.'

She blinked and her mouth opened. Then she shut it again as if she couldn't trust herself to speak.

So I went on, 'I saw your email this afternoon.'

'No,' she said faintly. 'I deleted—'

'It wasn't deleted. One of the emails failed to send and it was sitting in my outbox.'

She'd gone very pale. 'I wasn't going to hurt you. That's not why I was going back to him.'

'No, I realise that.' I knew why Imogen had decided to leave. Given the type of person she was, only one explanation made sense. 'You're trying to save me, aren't you?'

Her eyes filled with tears. 'You can't keep me, Ajax. Dad would force you into doing something terrible to protect me and I can't let that happen. It's better for me to go back to him. Then we'll both leave Sydney for good and you won't have to worry about me any more.'

I wanted to laugh—if only it were that simple.

Letting her go back to White and make her grand gesture for me would have been the easiest way out of the situation. Certainly it would have been better for me.

Except there was no way in hell I could do that.

The past few days with her had only cemented her worth to me, made me more aware of how vital she was. And not just to me, but to the people whose lives she would one day change. Because she would change lives. She'd changed mine.

The moment I'd seen her email to her father I'd known that I couldn't keep her any more than her father could.

What Imogen needed was freedom.

She needed the chance to stretch her wings, find out who she was on her own terms, figure out for herself what she was worth, without her father holding her mother's death over her head.

Without me stifling her.

Because that would happen if I kept her.

I'd accepted the truth as I'd read her email to White,

telling him she wanted to come home. That she'd agree to return only on the condition that he'd leave me alone.

I'd wanted to save her in that moment. And I knew that saving her didn't involve keeping her here with me. It was only condemning her to more fucking captivity.

She deserved better than that. She always had.

'You're not going back to your father, little one,' I said gently.

She blinked, her eyes glittering. 'Then where am I going?'

'I'm taking you to the airport.' I tried to keep my voice steady, but the rough edge crept in all the same. 'There's a King Enterprises jet ready to go, with all the documentation you need. I have a friend in New York who's going to make sure you're set up once you get there.'

She was silent. A streak of red tinged her cheekbones, the glitter in her eyes not fear or sadness like I thought, but anger. 'No,' she said flatly. 'I'm not going anywhere. I *need* to see Dad. I won't let him put you in a position where you have to do something you'll regret.'

My jaw tightened. She was right to call me on that. It was the slippery slope staring me in the face—the one that would make me no better than Dad.

You are *no better*.

'Give me some credit, for fuck's sake,' I growled, ignoring the thought. 'You think I'd really put everything on the line just to get him out of the way?'

'Wouldn't you?' Her chin lifted. 'What if he hurt me? What would you do then?'

I gritted my teeth. 'I would—'

'Hurt him back. And you wouldn't care what happened to you after that. All you care about is that the people you love are safe.'

She's wrong. All you care about is yourself.

Fucking lies. If that was all that mattered, I wouldn't be sitting here ready to put her on a plane to goddamn New York.

'I'm not accepting that any more,' Imogen went on, not letting me speak. 'You protect everyone all the time and yet who protects you?'

'I don't need protection.'

'Oh, don't give me that alpha male bullshit,' she said fiercely. 'Of course you need protection. And I'm going to protect you whether you like it or not.'

I felt the knife in my chest twist. She was so strong and I kept forgetting that. Far from the delicate little thing she seemed, she was electric. She felt things passionately and deeply, and she didn't give up.

But this was one fight she wasn't going to win, not if I had anything to do with it.

'No,' I said. 'It's not happening and that's final.'

Her green eyes burned. 'Look, it'll be okay. I'm not the same person I was when you kidnapped me from that ball. I won't let Dad hurt me the way he did before. I'll figure out how to get away from him eventually and—'

'No.' I kept my voice hard and cold. 'You're not going to give up your freedom for me.'

'You can't stop me.'

'I can. I will.'

Her pale throat moved as she swallowed. 'Don't… do this to me, Ajax. Don't let it mean nothing.'

'It won't mean nothing. Because you won't be doing it at all.'

Anger had flushed her cheeks, made her eyes glow.

Her hair was in a loose ponytail at the nape of her neck and little wisps of hair were curling around her forehead.

She was so beautiful. Giving her up was going to hurt like fuck.

But I'd made my decision.

'Ajax,' she said hoarsely, 'I care about you. That's what I told you on the boat. You're worth ten thousand of my father and I'm not going to sit around and watch you—'

'And you're worth ten thousand of me,' I interrupted. 'That's why you're going to get on my jet and leave the country.'

Her eyes were liquid in the light coming from the freeway, but there was fire in them. 'You're wrong. You're worth the sacrifice, Ajax King. Don't you know that?'

No. You're not.

And that was the truth that had always been there, sitting inside me. I wasn't worth it and I knew it.

'Go and have a fucking life,' I said, ignoring her. 'Go and have the life you should have had.'

She stared at me a second then looked away. 'And what about Dad? What are you going to do about him? Because if you end up in prison, Ajax King, so help me I'll come back and…and… I don't know. Murder you or something.'

Tenderness caught at me, unexpected and sweet. Bittersweet.

I reached out, touched her cheek, her skin so soft against my fingertips. 'You won't murder me.'

She shivered at the contact, turning back to me. 'Tell me you won't hurt my father. Promise me, Ajax.

Promise me you'll do nothing that will end up with you in prison.'

I trailed my fingertips along her jaw.

You can't make that promise.

And if I didn't? Shit, I'd be no better than Dad.

Why fight it? Maybe it's time you embraced it.

'Imogen...'

'I won't go without a fight. I'll come home on the next flight and you won't be able to stop me.' Determination glowed in her eyes. 'If you want me to have my freedom then you have to keep yours. I won't go if you don't make me this promise.'

'Stubborn little one.'

'You're better than that. Promise me. Your word as a King.'

What could I say? That I wasn't better? That deep down there was a part of me who was just like my dad? Just as violent, just as ruthless...

You should claim your legacy. Once she's gone, there'll be no one to stop you.

I could. Except there was one thing stopping me and she was looking at me right now, demanding a promise that would hold me back from that slippery slope into the past.

She thought I was better. That was the rope that kept me from falling and I couldn't refuse to hold onto it, not without hurting her. And I would never, ever hurt her.

'I promise,' I said, staring deep into her pretty eyes. 'My word as a King.'

I'd broken that word with her father, but I wouldn't with her. It was an oath, a vow.

She seemed to understand, giving me a slight nod.

Then she pulled away from my hand, putting distance between us, turning to look out the window. 'Good. You can take me to the airport now.'

Her withdrawal was like the sun clouding over, leaving me in shadow. I felt cold. I wanted to reach out again and draw her back, let her warmth and brightness cover me.

But if I did, if I touched her again, I'd never let her go. So I stayed where I was.

The rest of the drive was spent in silence and neither of us broke it. There was nothing to say.

The jet was waiting on the tarmac, Imogen waiting with it while I spoke with the captain and the customs official who was handling the departure.

Once that was done I went to take her hand, only to check myself at the last minute. No, I couldn't touch her. That would be a mistake I wouldn't come back from.

If she noticed my hesitation she didn't show it, following along behind me as I led her to the jet and showed her up the stairs and inside.

The stewardess was there, making the cabin ready.

'Can you give us a few minutes?' Imogen said unexpectedly.

The stewardess looked at me and I nodded, so she went out, leaving us alone in the cabin.

Imogen turned to face me, a familiar glow in her green eyes.

It made everything inside me tighten.

'No,' I said before she could speak. 'Not now. Not here.'

She ignored me, closing the distance she'd put between us in the car, her hand reaching out, her palm flattening against my chest.

It stole my breath, froze me in place.

'I want one more thing,' she said softly, looking up at me. 'One last time with you.'

'Imogen—'

'Just one more time. If you're going to make me leave, you have to give me something to take with me.' Her eyes were liquid. 'Please.'

'I touch you and I might never let you go,' I said roughly. 'That's not what I want.'

'I know.' She swallowed. 'But you will let me go. And this would be for both of us.'

I didn't know where she got her certainty from, because God knew I didn't have it. But I couldn't refuse her.

My goddamn cock wouldn't let me.

I let her take my face in her hands and bring my head down, let her mouth brush over mine.

She tasted of salt and sweetness, and I had her in my arms before I could stop myself, crushing that soft mouth beneath my own. Taking and taking. Gorging on her because this wasn't going to happen again. I would never kiss her again. Never hold her again.

This was all I'd ever have and it was going to have to last me and so I fucking took it.

Two steps took us to the closed door of the cockpit and I pinned her against it, my hands shaking as I slid them beneath her ass and lifted her. She wound her legs around my waist, raining kisses all over my face, hot and hungry and desperate just like me.

I was instantly hard and I ached, but there was also a knife in my chest and she was twisting it with every kiss. Every touch. But I didn't let her go. I shoved up her little dress and slid my hand between her legs, finding the slick heat of her pussy. She was wet for me, shuddering in my arms as I stroked her.

I wanted to go slowly, to make this last so we had something more than desperation to take with us, but there was no time. Her hands were at the fly of my jeans, pulling down my zip and sliding inside my boxers, cool fingers on my cock.

I turned my face into her neck, biting and licking her skin, her taste more delicious to me than anything I'd ever eaten, finding her clit and stroking at the same time.

She gave a sob. 'Ajax…'

The knife worked its way deeper, a dull agony seeping through me. But it wasn't enough to stop.

I found my wallet and managed to get it open without loosening my hold on her, dropping it on the ground as I took out the condom.

She tried to snatch the packet but I didn't let her, ripping it open with my teeth and then rolling the latex down.

My hands were fucking shaking like she was my first time.

She is *your first time. Your first time with a woman you care about.*

I hadn't thought that would make it different. But it did.

I continued to stare into her eyes as I drew my hips back then pushed in deep. Again. And again. Harder. Faster.

We didn't speak, our breathing loud in the quiet of the cabin, and the world shrank down, getting narrower and narrower as the pleasure curled around us and wrapped us up tight.

There was nothing but this. Nothing but us. Me inside her, her around me.

Except she was going to let go of me and I had to make her.

How are you going to live without her?

The thought was as clear as the deep green of her eyes, and as vivid. But pleasure was dragging at me, choking me, and I shoved the thought away.

I would live the way I'd always lived. Cold and hard and certain. Wanting nothing. Needing nothing. Living for the big picture.

Except it wasn't the big picture I saw as she sobbed in my arms, the orgasm flaring in her eyes. I only saw her. And when mine hit, a deep, annihilating pulse of pleasure, for a second there was no past and no future. Only a perfect, shining moment of us.

Her and me. Together.

It took a supreme act of will to let her go, but I did. I was proud of myself for that, if nothing else. I moved like a fucking robot, lowering her to the floor, dealing with the condom and my clothes. She'd already smoothed down her dress, but she let me lead her over to her seat and buckle her in. I didn't rush, taking my time, savouring every last second of touching her.

But then it was done and I couldn't put it off any longer.

I kissed her one last time then I turned to go, moving towards the door of the aircraft.

'Ajax,' she said softly.

I paused, everything in me wanting to turn around

and grab her, take her back to my house and keep her there for ever.

'I love you.'

The knife in my chest found my heart and slid straight into it.

I walked away from the jet a dead man.

CHAPTER TWENTY-TWO

Imogen

NEW YORK WAS FINE. I had an apartment and a great job, one I'd found for myself—basic data entry at an office. The apartment was one Ajax had organised for me, and perhaps I should have found my own, but apartments were expensive and the one he'd found was too nice to give up.

I made friends and I went out to clubs and bars. Central Park for picnics and the Met for a dose of culture. I went shopping and to the theatre, discovered I loved musicals and the cheesiness of Coney Island. I even liked riding on the subway.

I enjoyed my life.

But there was an ache inside me. A space that wasn't ever going to be filled. An Ajax-shaped space.

After I'd first arrived, I'd thrown myself into my new life because that was what he'd wanted for me and I hadn't felt I could throw that away on feeling sorry for myself.

Besides, he'd promised he wouldn't do anything that would involve him going to prison so I could hardly do anything less than honour my promise to him.

Every so often I'd run a quick search to check on him, not to make sure of the promise he'd made—I knew he wouldn't break it—but to see if he was okay. Sure enough, he was. There were a lot of news stories about the King brothers and the waves they were making with their new luxury property development in Sydney.

I couldn't look at pictures of him, though, so I didn't. I pretended that my heart was fine and didn't have an Ajax-shaped hole right through the middle of it.

Once, I even tried to date someone, but it was an abject failure. He was a nice enough guy but he wasn't Ajax and after ten minutes of awkward conversation I told him I was in love with someone else and I was sorry I'd wasted his time.

Then I went home and consoled myself with my newly purchased vibrator and memories of Ajax beside the pool. In the bedroom. In the shower… Everywhere but the plane before I'd left Sydney.

The look in Ajax's eyes as he'd held me. The way his hands had shaken. The agony on his face as he'd kissed me goodbye.

The way he'd paused when I'd told him I loved him.

The way he'd walked out without a backward glance.

It was all too painful to remember so I didn't.

Six months after I'd arrived in New York, I got a phone call from an Australian number.

It was late in the day and I was at home, settling in for a night of crappy TV, and my heart nearly stopped when I saw the numbers on the screen. And then it started beating again, hard and fast, making my hands shake.

Was it Ajax? Or was it someone else? My father? Who else knew I was here? Who else knew this number?

I hit the answer button and a man's deep voice said, 'Is this Imogen White?'

It wasn't Ajax.

The combination of relief and disappointment was so bitter it nearly choked me. 'Yes,' I said, forcing it away. 'Who's this?'

'This is Leon King. I want to know what the hell you've done to my brother.'

Shock coursed through me. 'What? What do you mean?'

'Ajax has been a fucking bastard to deal with for the past six months, which, to be fair, is nothing unusual. But now he's shut himself up in his house and won't see either Xander or me.' There was a pause. 'We're worried about him.'

I closed my eyes, longing pulling at me, making the hole in my heart hurt worse than anything I could imagine. 'What makes you think I can help him?'

'Well, he got like this pretty much as soon as you left so I'm assuming it's got something to do with you.'

'It might not.'

There was a silence.

'I tried asking him about you,' Leon said, 'but he refused to answer any questions and at the mention of your name... Well, let's just say he wasn't happy.'

My voice didn't work, but I tried to speak anyway. 'I promised him I'd stay here. That I wouldn't come back.'

'Why not?'

'Because he wanted me to be free.'

'Christ,' Leon muttered, sounding exasperated.

'Look, I don't know what you two are to each other, but can't you come back to Australia and be free with him?'

'I promised,' I repeated, clutching the phone. 'I told him I'd stay.'

Leon sighed. 'Do you want to stay?'

I thought of the life I'd made for myself here. The job and friends and apartment. It was a nice life. It was everything I'd dreamed about. And yet...

There was something missing. Him.

My throat felt thick. 'Not really.'

'Then come back.' Leon's voice was flat. 'Come back and help him.'

The ache in my chest got worse. 'Can't you do anything for him?'

'You don't think I've tried? He won't listen to me and he won't listen to Xander. Which leaves you.' For the first time I heard a note of actual worry in his tone. 'Someone needs to help him, Imogen, because, God knows, if there's one man who deserves a fucking break it's my brother.'

A shiver went through me. When I'd left Sydney, I hadn't fought to stay. I'd gone to New York with only the most cursory of arguments. I'd told myself that getting that promise out of him was a victory, that leaving was the best thing for both of us.

Besides, he'd wanted me to go and I hadn't wanted to make myself into even more of a problem for him than I was already.

Lies. You know why you didn't fight.

It was fear. Fear that he didn't feel for me what I felt for him. Fear that I didn't deserve him. Fear that because my mother had died for me I didn't deserve to be happy.

Then again, if I wasn't, wouldn't her sacrifice have been in vain?

Ajax had told me she would have been glad that I existed and I was pretty sure she wouldn't have wanted me to exist unhappily. That wouldn't have honoured her memory.

You know what will.

Yes. There was only one way to honour that memory, only one way to repay the debt I owed her. And that wasn't with yet another sacrifice.

It was with happiness. With love.

With showing a man who'd given up too much that he didn't have to give up anything more. That if I deserved happiness then he did too.

Tears filled my eyes.

'Well?' Leon demanded, after I hadn't spoken. 'Will you come back?'

I didn't hesitate this time.

'Yes,' I said fiercely. 'Yes, I'll come back.'

That night I booked a ticket home and the next day I handed in my resignation at my job. And I packed up my life in New York.

But before I left I made one last phone call.

The phone rang for a while before it picked up, but my father's voice hadn't changed, hard and cold and suspicious. 'Who is this?'

'Hi, Dad,' I said. 'It's Imogen.'

There was a shocked silence. 'Where are you? Where the *hell* are—'

'I haven't got time for explanations,' I interrupted

firmly. 'I wanted you to know that I'm coming home. And when I get back I will be marrying Ajax King.'

'You ungrateful little—'

'And if you so much as touch me or harm Ajax or his family and friends in any way—and I mean *any* way, Dad—I'll take what I know about you and your business to the media.' I paused, letting that sink in, then I added, 'And I'll make sure *everyone* knows just what kind of man you really are.'

There was another long, shocked silence.

'Imogen,' Dad said and there was a hoarse tone to it that I'd never heard before.

'You'll leave Sydney,' I went on, 'and you won't come back. And in return I'll stay quiet. But the moment you hurt anyone I care about, I'll tell the world. And you'll never work in Australia again.'

I could feel his anger radiating clear across the Pacific. But all he said was, 'Okay. You have a deal.'

A day later I flew back to Sydney to reclaim the life I'd always wanted.

And the man I loved.

CHAPTER TWENTY-THREE

Ajax

Someone was knocking on the front door.

I ignored it the way I'd been ignoring all visitors to my house for the past few months. Instead I shoved the empty takeout boxes that were sitting on the coffee table to one side, put my laptop down, poured myself another liberal amount of Scotch, then stared at the screen.

I'd been putting off my housing project for too long and I couldn't put it off any more. I had to do something, because at the moment it felt like I was in limbo.

All I'd done since Imogen had left was take the boat out every day, trying to get rid of the dead feeling inside me, trying to shock it back to life with the things that usually calmed me. The wind, the salt, the sun. Ropes under my hands and the crack of the sails above me.

But even being out on the ocean didn't get rid of it.

Everything was muted and flat, what little joy I'd taken from life utterly gone.

I accepted it. It was all part of the sacrifice. And

knowing she was in New York and having the time of her life made it better.

I got updates from my New York contact about how she was doing, but after a while I told him not to send me any more.

It was easier not to know.

I'd flung myself into work, chasing down the last of my father's loyal lieutenants, mopping up the rest of his mess. It was hard work and I took a certain relish in it. But I made good on my promise to Imogen and left her father alone.

He'd tried to exact his revenge on me for placing his daughter beyond his reach, but I avoided it. I didn't retaliate, didn't engage.

She held me back from the precipice and I couldn't let her down.

Eventually White lost interest.

With Imogen gone, what was the point? For either of us?

My brothers tried to talk to me, but I didn't want to talk to them. There was nothing they could say that would make any difference.

They had the women they loved and if I was grateful for nothing else, it was that.

I was never meant to have the things I wanted for myself anyway and I didn't know why I hadn't remembered that.

I stared at the document that had come up on the computer—Imogen's management plan. She'd put so much work into it and had been so excited about it...

Pain shifted in my chest, so intense I couldn't breathe. It would fade in a minute and then I'd go back to being deadened and numb but, for the moment it lasted, all I could see was her face, luminous with excitement, her green eyes glowing.

For a second I tried to pretend that I didn't know why it hurt so much, but it was too hard and so I gave up.

I knew why it hurt so much.

I was in love with her. I'd probably fallen in love with her the moment her gaze had met mine in the mirror of the bathroom the night I'd kidnapped her.

No wonder I felt like a dead man walking half the time; she'd taken my heart to New York with her.

Not that love would have made a difference anyway.

Love was just another sacrifice I'd had to make.

The hammering on the door didn't stop.

Fuck. I was going to have to either keep ignoring it or answer the bloody thing.

Ignoring it took work though and for once I was glad of the distraction. Otherwise I'd have to think about who could take Imogen's place on the housing project and thinking about that filled me with rage.

Cursing, I shoved myself to my feet, stalking out of the room and down the hallway to the front door.

Who the fuck was it? And how had they even got to the front door? They'd have had to get past the guards at the gate so it had to be someone I knew.

I could have checked via the front door camera, but I couldn't be fucked looking.

God help me, if it was Xander or Leon disturbing me again I'd have their fucking balls on a plate.

I jerked open the door and the heart I thought was dead shocked suddenly back into life.

It wasn't Xander or Leon.

It was Imogen.

She stood on my doorstep, her gilt hair loose and gleaming down her back, wearing a simple turquoise cotton dress that gave her green eyes a tinge of blue and her skin a creamy glow.

I hadn't seen her for a whole six months and I felt like a man who'd been in the desert for years surrounded by nothing but sand, suddenly seeing green grass for the first time.

Fresh. Beautiful. Evidence of life…

'Hi,' she said, her familiar voice with its husky edge sounding shaken.

I couldn't think of a bloody word to say.

'Uh, are you going to invite me in?' She gave me a small hopeful smile. 'Or do you want to have this conversation on the front doorstep?'

'What the fuck are you doing here?' I demanded, graceless and rough, like I hadn't spoken for days.

She swallowed. 'I came back. Obviously.'

'But… I freed you.' My heart was thundering in my head, beating so loudly I could hardly hear a fucking thing. 'You were supposed to have a life.'

'And I did,' she said. 'It sucked.'

I stared at her, not understanding. 'What do you mean, "it sucked"?'

Imogen took a step forward and put her palm in the centre of my chest. 'Seriously, I'm not having this conversation outside.'

Her touch was pure electricity, delivering another shock to my heart and, before I knew what I was doing, I'd backed away from the door so she could come in, closing it behind her.

She made as if to remove her hand but automatically

I put mine over hers, keeping it exactly where it was, desperate for her touch.

Her skin was warm and I could smell her. Ah, fuck...roses.

I ached.

'You idiot.' Her eyes glowed with a familiar determination. 'Did you seriously think you could send me away and that I'd stay? I told you I loved you before I left. That hasn't changed.'

My jaw was so tight I could barely speak. 'You were supposed to stay in New York. Get a job and friends and an apartment and—'

'Yeah, yeah.' She waved a hand as if that was nothing. 'I did all those things. But I didn't leave Sydney because I wanted to, Ajax. I left to make you happy.'

Again, I could not think of one fucking thing to say.

'But you're not happy,' she went on, gazing up at me. 'I can see that you're not. And you know something? I'm not happy either.' Her hand pressed a little harder on my chest. 'Mum gave her life for me and I've spent a long time thinking that I didn't deserve to have anything because of that. But... I was wrong. You taught me that. She wouldn't have wanted me to be unhappy. That would mean she died for nothing.' Imogen's thumb moved caressingly over my skin. 'Her death needs to mean something, Ajax. And the best way I can think of to honour it is with happiness. With love.'

The ache inside me intensified. It was plain she believed every word she said. I only wished I could believe it too.

'If anyone deserves to have that, it's you,' I said roughly. 'But you can't have it with me.'

She didn't look away. 'Why not?'

My breathing was ragged from the effort it took not to grab her and hold her. Keep her with me. Never let her go.

'Because you know what will happen when you're with me,' I said. 'There'll be guards and security and threats and—'

'No, that's not what will happen.' Her finger was on my mouth before I could move. 'What will happen with you is sex and sailing and swimming. And food and more sex. And then some interesting projects that I can really sink my teeth into, and more sex, and then a dolphin or two, and then—'

I shook her finger away before the touch would overcome my control. 'Imogen, you're not listening.'

She pulled her hands from me and took my face between them. 'I am. *You're* not listening to *me*.' Her eyes were very green. 'I love you and telling me you can't be with me because you want me to be free is a bullshit excuse. You're scared. I can see it.'

Of course she did. She'd always been able to see right through me.

I said nothing. There was no point in denying it.

She searched my face. 'What are you so afraid of?'

'That promise I made you—remember it?' I met her gaze head-on. 'That was the only thing that kept me from hurting your father. The only fucking thing that stopped me from being just like him. From being like my dad. And yes, that makes me afraid.'

'It wasn't the only thing,' she said as if she knew it for truth. 'You wouldn't have done it anyway.'

'I wanted to. I wanted to hurt him so fucking badly for what he did to you.'

'But you didn't. You're not that type of man, Ajax.'

'I could have become him,' I went on, laying out just what type of man I was for her. 'I still could. I can feel it inside me, his violence. Christ, so much. I *hurt* people, Imogen. Including my brothers. Fuck, I just stood back and watched them suffer. How can I be allowed to have you—have anything at all—after that?'

'That wasn't your fault.' Her tone was quiet and absolutely sure. 'Your father threatened them, you didn't. And you did what you could to protect them.'

'But what if I didn't?' I couldn't stop the words from coming out, the secret truth I'd been trying to hide. 'What if I didn't do *everything*? What if there's a part of me that enjoyed it? What if there's a part of me that's just like him? That *wants* to be like him?'

She shook her head. 'You're not him, Ajax King. Not in any way. You don't hurt people—you protect them. I was the daughter of your enemy. You could have used my life to get Dad to leave Sydney, but you didn't. And those houses you're building, they're to improve people's lives.' Her thumbs stroked my cheekbones so gently. 'Everything you do is about keeping people safe, the way you kept your brothers safe all those years ago.'

'They weren't safe,' I almost spat. 'You don't know what they went through.'

'I think they would have thought it was worth it to see Augustus in jail.' Her mouth curved in a smile of such tenderness it hurt to look at it. 'Do you know that Leon called me in New York? He told me that I'd better come home, because something was wrong with his brother. They want you to be happy, Ajax. Don't you think you should honour them by, you know, actually being happy?'

My brothers. They were the reason for everything. Because I was the oldest and I had to protect them. And I'd told myself that I'd had to stand aside and let them get hurt in order to ultimately protect them.

The end justified the means, always.

But…what if that was a lie? What if there had been something in me that had let it happen? The same thing that had been in my father, who caused people nothing but pain.

'They don't know,' I said raggedly. 'They don't know that Dad threatened them. They don't know that I couldn't lift a finger to save them.'

'So tell them. Talk to them.' Her fingers were cool on my skin. 'But you'll have to let me stay first, because I'm not leaving you.'

That steely determination was in her eyes, her will as strong as mine.

She'd got under my skin the second she'd appeared, with her wide-eyed innocence, incessant questions and electric presence, and I had a feeling she would never leave.

But it wasn't her I was fighting. It was myself.

'I'll never be an easy man to live with.' My voice was cracked and broken, all the fight running out of me. 'I can't change my past and I'm possessive as fuck. And you're wrong. I'm a man like my father was through and through.'

That blindingly tender smile was a weapon, cutting me to pieces. 'Don't use him as an excuse, love. Don't let fear win. He destroyed things. You build them.

That's what you do. That's what you *and* your brothers are doing.'

Fear. Was I really letting it stop me?

I looked into Imogen's eyes, saw her love for me staring back.

It didn't seem possible that a man like me, broken and dark, violent and possessive, could catch a beam of sunlight in his hand and hold it for ever. And, because it didn't seem possible, I'd locked myself down, denied myself. Told myself I couldn't have it.

But then she'd come along and broken me wide open with her honesty and her trust. With her love. A love that terrified me because I wanted it so much.

She was right; I *was* afraid. And if I gave into fear he would win.

I couldn't let that happen. Because I had one thing he didn't: love.

Love made me keep my promise to her. Love kept me from the brink.

Loving her had saved me and it was still saving me, even now.

Love was the key. It wasn't a word my father would have said to anyone. He wouldn't have even known what it meant.

But Imogen did. And she'd taught me.

Love was the difference between me and my father.

Imogen was watching me and maybe she'd read my mind because she asked very softly, 'Do you love me, Ajax?'

All my fight was gone. She'd kidnapped my heart and she wasn't giving it back. And I couldn't lie, not to myself and not to her.

Not any more.

'Yes.' It came out low and guttural. 'I'll love you till I die.'

The warmth in her expression killed me. 'Then have me.'

'I'll never be good enough for you. I'll never deserve you.'

'You don't need to. What you deserve is happiness.'

I couldn't hold back then, couldn't keep the hunger at bay.

She'd brought me back to life and there was no way I could have that life without her.

I caught her in my arms, pulling her close, fitting her against me, and the constant ache inside me began to ease, like a part of me that had been missing had come back.

'Little one,' I murmured, nuzzling my face in her hair. 'I can't let you go again.'

'Good.' She pressed harder against me. 'Because I wouldn't leave. I'd camp out on your doorstep and play loud music and sing and generally make a nuisance of myself, and then I'd—'

I didn't let her finish. I kissed her instead.

Because I suddenly saw it, my big picture.

My big picture was her.

EPILOGUE

Ajax

'You're a fucking idiot,' Leon muttered, adjusting the rose in my buttonhole, because there had to be roses the day I married Imogen.

'Seconded,' Xander said, frowning at me. 'I can't believe you haven't told us this bullshit before.'

It had taken me a while, but I'd finally told them everything about my time as Dad's second-in-command—about his threat to their lives and how I'd had to stand back and watch them get hurt in order to protect them.

The timing wasn't great—I was getting ready for my wedding after all—but they seemed to take it well.

'Of course he hasn't,' Leon said before I could get a word in. 'Big brother thinks he knows what's best for us, right?'

Xander snorted. 'How long have you been torturing yourself with this then?'

'For fucking ever.' Leon adjusted the damn rose again. 'Jesus, Ajax. You should have said something.'

'If I could get a fucking word in?' I jerked my lapel

away from Leon before he ruined the rose. 'It isn't that simple.'

'Sure it is,' Xander disagreed. 'You just open your mouth and words come out of it.'

Prick. I was about to tell him exactly how not simple it was when something caught my eye out the window. We were in my bedroom at home and I could see the pool area by the cliff, all decorated for the ceremony that would take place in an hour's time.

A woman was hurrying after something white that was being blown across the tiles, another two women chasing after her.

She wore a simple white silk gown, a crown of roses wound into her gilt hair, and she was laughing. One of the other women running after her had long auburn hair, while the other had a riot of black curls.

Imogen made a grab for the white thing—her veil—and caught it, Vita and Poppy, my sisters-in-law, cheering as she held it up triumphantly.

'It's bad luck to see the bride before the wedding,' Xander said from beside me.

'Surely not today,' Leon murmured from the other side.

There was silence as we watched the women we loved fix Imogen's veil, their faces alight with laughter.

'Be happy, Ajax,' Leon said at last. 'If anyone deserves it, it's you.'

Xander didn't say a word, merely put his hand on my shoulder.

Down by the pool, Imogen looked up and caught me watching. She smiled and I felt my heart catch fire.

Turned out that my brothers knew what they were talking about.

Happiness *was* something I could choose and they were showing me the way.
So I chose it.
It really was that simple after all.

* * * * *

MARRIED FOR HIS ONE-NIGHT HEIR

JENNIFER HAYWARD

Who knew an unmitigated hair disaster would turn into an almost twenty-year friendship?

Grazie mille for your amazing input on this story, Silvano Belmonte.

Our brainstorming sessions were so much fun!

CHAPTER ONE

"So, what did they think?" Giovanna De Luca leaned back against the windowsill of her boss's office, a cup of coffee cradled between her fingers as she absorbed the brilliant sunshine that flooded through the space that served as the epicenter of power for Delilah Rothchild's luxury Caribbean hotel chain.

To look at her, one would have bought the deliberately casual picture hook, line and sinker. That she hadn't just completed the most important assignment of her life, with the decor she'd done for a series of private residences on Delilah's flagship Bahamian resort that would sell for upward of 20 million dollars each. That she was as cool as a cucumber as she waited for the feedback from the initial round of prospective buyers Delilah had met with this morning. But inside, her heart was racing.

Delilah, however, knew better. Knew she was a master at hiding her emotions. "I have verbal expressions of intent for all but two of the villas," she announced, a Cheshire-cat smile curving her lips. "Which will be snapped up in the second round, leaving them desperate for more. Due in large part," she allowed, tipping her head at Gia, "to you. The interiors knocked their socks off, Gia. They were mad about them."

Gia released a breath she hadn't known she was holding on a quiet, even exhale. A warmth flooded through her, spreading from her fingertips to her toes, then sinking deep to wrap itself around the thrumming beat of her heart. She had worked day and night to make sure those villas were perfect. To position them as the irresistible showpiece that would launch the opening of this phase of Delilah's development to critical acclaim. But it went much deeper than that.

The Private Residences at the Rothchild Bahamas had been her opportunity to give back to Delilah everything she'd given to her. To prove the bet the hotelier had made on her had been the right one. To prove to *herself* she could do this—that she could have the career she'd always dreamed of.

She closed her fingers tighter around the coffee cup she held, fighting back the rush of emotion that chased through her. "I'm so happy to hear that," she said huskily. "I know how much this project means to you."

Delilah fixed a laser-sharp, bright blue gaze on her. The woman was legendary for her ability to read a person in under a second flat. Her gaze was warm, however, as it rested on Gia, the bond they'd formed over the past two years undeniable. "You deserve every bit of the kudos. This wasn't personal, Gia, it was business. You earned it with your talent.

"Which is also," Delilah added, rolling to her feet and crossing to the bar, "a cause for celebration." She poured herself a cup of coffee, then turned and leaned against the counter. "I'm having a barbecue tonight to celebrate Junkanoo. Not a big thing—just some friends and a few business acquaintances. A chance to kick back and have a glass of champagne. Put on a pretty dress and come."

Gia shook her head in a refusal that had become customary. "I was looking forward to a night at home. A couple of hours with Leo, a good book and a glass of wine."

Delilah pointed her cup at her. "You need a life, Gia. It's been two years since Franco was killed. You are twenty-six years old. Working yourself to the bone, then spending all of your time with Leo, isn't any kind of a life."

She thought it was the perfect life. Her three-year-old son, Leo, meant everything to her. She had walked away from her family—one of the most powerful organized-crime syndicates in America—to protect him. He was happy and thriving and that was all that mattered.

"Besides," Delilah added, a crafty smile curving her mouth, "there is someone I want you to meet. A friend of mine who does international financing. He is single for the first time in forever, he is nice and he is loaded. *And*," she added on a low purr, "he is divine-looking. As in drop-dead gorgeous."

As in the last thing she was looking for. Getting involved with another rich, powerful man after her life had been ruled by such men held no interest for her. Getting involved with *any* man wasn't in her plans after her disastrous marriage to Franco. But she would never say that to Delilah, the woman who had given her sanctuary in the months following her husband's targeted assassination. Who had been her lifeline ever since.

"I'm not interested in being set up," she said firmly. "But maybe you are right about me needing to get out. Will I know anyone there?"

Delilah named a couple of women she worked with at the hotel. Gia thought about the hours after Leo went to bed, when there was no escape from the loneliness that had consumed her life. When she missed her mother so much it felt like her insides were being torn out. When what-ifs infiltrated her head, taunting her with what might have been.

Her stomach curled. She didn't want to go there tonight. Her new life was wonderful—*amazing*—and everything she'd always dreamed of. She was moving forward, not backward. Delilah was right, it was time for her to start living again. Tonight would be the perfect opportunity to dip her toe back in.

She lifted an eyebrow. "What should I wear?"

Delilah's eyes flashed in triumph. "Wear something summer fun. Sexy."

Gia shook her head. "I am not letting you set me up, Delilah. This is about me getting out to have some fun. That's all."

"You should still wear something sexy."

Gia settled for a dress that was neither sexy, nor conservative. A bright coral, with a wrap-front ruffle, it showed off the golden tan she'd acquired while living in the tropics, as well as the smooth length of her legs with its short, flirty skirt.

Anticipation nipped at her skin as she kissed Leo goodnight, left him with his babysitter, then walked the short distance from the villa where she lived on Delilah's exclusive Lyford Cay estate, up to the main house. To not have her bodyguard, Dante, tracing her every step was still a novelty she couldn't quite fathom. To step out her front door and not wonder what was going to be on the other side was a peace she couldn't articulate.

But there was also trepidation as she climbed the hill toward the sprawling colonial-style mansion, ablaze with light. She didn't remember what it was like to go out for a carefree evening of fun. Had no idea how to even approach it. Maybe because her life had rarely, if ever, afforded her that luxury.

Tonight, however, she was Giovanna De Luca, not Giovanna Castiglione. She was free.

The barbecue, held on the beachside terrace of Delilah's home to celebrate the popular Bahamian Junkanoo summer festival—a celebration of the arts on the island—was already in full swing when she arrived. A spectacular sunset stained the sky, a fiery pink-and-gold canvas for the festivities as the torchlight climbed high into the night. In the midst of that exotic atmosphere, the guests enjoyed fresh fried fish straight off the grill, rum-based refreshments and a steel band—the classic island experience.

Gia hesitated on the fringe of the group, an age-old apprehension slivering through her. Once upon a time she had been judged for who she was, the family that she came from, rather than the girl she'd been. It had broken her heart—that sense of always being an outsider no matter how hard she had tried. But Delilah quickly spotted her, drew her into the crowd and slid a drink into her hand.

The welcome cocktail, which was heavy on the rum, eased her nerves. As did the handsome financier Delilah introduced her to. He was charming and a gentleman to boot. She might have no intention of getting involved with him, but the clear attraction in his eyes was a boost to her ego, which had taken such a hit with Franco, she wasn't sure the wounds were ever going to heal.

Relaxing into the vibe, the alcohol warming the blood in her veins, she cast an idle glance over the crowd, surveying the new arrivals. A tall, fair-haired male that Sophie, the hotel's glamorous publicity director, was chatting up claimed her attention. Muscular and well-built, he was undeniably commanding in his white shirt and dark pants that showed off every rippling, well-honed inch of him. But it was when her gaze rose to his elegant profile that her breath caught in her throat.

It could not be. Not here. Not now.

But it was.

Her heart stuttered an erratic rhythm in her chest, its jagged beat reverberating in her head. Frozen to the spot, her companion's words faded to the background as she absorbed Santo Di Fiore's formidable, charismatic presence. Six foot two inches of lean, hard male, he had the perfectly hewn face and golden hair of an angel. A woman could drown herself in those velvety dark eyes.

And for a night, she had done just that. One kiss—one perfect passionate kiss on a stormy evening in Manhattan four years ago—had changed everything. An attempt to escape her fate had dissolved into a fire neither of them could extinguish—a hunger that had been almost a decade in the making.

She went hot and cold all at the same time, desperately wishing he was an illusion, because Santo Di Fiore had been her biggest mistake. Her most unforgettable, costly mistake—the repercussions of which had set into motion a chain of events she could never have foreseen. But he had also given her the most precious thing she possessed.

Santo looked up and cast a lazy glance over the crowd. Every muscle in her body seized tight as his gaze came to rest on her, a hint of male interest flickering through his dark eyes, followed by a frown that marred his brow.

Shock descended into fear—a bitter layer of it that coated her mouth. She turned away before he could focus on her, her purse clutched to her chest. *She looked different.* There was a chance he hadn't recognized her, but she doubted that luck would hold. She needed to get out of here *now*.

Spinning on her heel, she headed through the crowd. But before she could make an exit, Delilah descended upon her with one of the investors who'd purchased two of the private residences that morning and her escape route was blocked.

She pasted a smile on her face and tried desperately to pretend that her world wasn't crashing in on her.

He should be on a plane back to New York, stickhandling the most important launch in Supersonic's history, dispensing with the hundreds of emails that had piled up in his inbox while he'd spent the weekend playing in a charitable golf tournament alongside his brother, Lazzero. Instead, Santo Di Fiore was on a tropical island being schmoozed by the current queen of the luxury-hotel market.

Really, he'd had no time. But given he and Lazzero had bet the bank on Elevate—the new running shoe they'd promised investors would set the world on fire—gaining access to Delilah's exclusive clientele list wasn't an opportunity he'd been able to pass up. So after a tour of her impressive flagship property that afternoon, where the hotel maven had expressed her desire to house a half a dozen of his Supersonic boutiques in her hotels, he and Lazzero had been invited to soak up the local atmosphere before flying out in the morning.

He brought his glass to his lips and tipped back a mouthful of Scotch. Under normal circumstances, the delectable redhead, who'd been all over him in far more than a business sense ever since the tour, would have been adequate compensation for the expenditure of time. Instead, he was consumed by ghosts—ghosts he'd thought long ago put to bed. Because surely the sophisticated blonde across the crowd couldn't have been Giovanna. She had beautiful raven-dark hair she'd always worn long and wavy, swearing she'd never cut it short.

He brushed his wayward thoughts aside with an irritated twist of his lips. Giovanna Castiglione had married another man. *They* were over. End of story. That her husband had been taken out in a targeted hit, that she hadn't been present at any of the functions where their social circles might have overlapped since, that she was a widow, *available* now, was inconsequential to him. The Giovanna he'd fallen in love with had been an illusion. She'd never existed.

So why the hell couldn't he get her out of his head?

Lazzero, who'd finished his conversation with a slick-suited real-estate developer, joined him at the bar. "So what do you think of Delilah's offer?" he prompted.

"If we could get the pop-up retail in place in time for Elevate, it could offer us an entrée into a whole different clientele."

"Not a problem." Lazzero dismissed the *if*. "Our retail teams have done it in a month. So we scale—we make it happen. My only question," he allowed, tipping his glass at Santo, "is whose hotel chain do we like more for this? Stefano Castiglione's or Delilah's? They are two entirely different propositions."

A bitter taste filled Santo's mouth. Once he hadn't been good enough for Giovanna—Stefano Castiglione, her father, had made that very clear. Now, Stefano wanted to partner with him because he ran the most buzzed-about athletic-wear brand on the planet, because the famous personalities representing his clothing would make a huge splash at his casinos? Hell would freeze over before he did business with the man who had put those emotional bruises in Gia's eyes.

"Castiglione has a bigger reach," Lazzero pointed out. "Don't let your personal feelings about this cloud your professional judgment."

"What personal feelings?" Santo responded curtly. "The man is a criminal. Just because he's bought half of Washington and Hollywood with his money and influence doesn't mean I want to do business with him."

Lazzero had grown up around the corner from the powerful Castiglione family, just as he had. Knew that along with being one of the most powerful real estate and gambling czars in the United States, his empire reaching from New York to Las Vegas, Stefano Castiglione was reputed to carry darker connections beneath that smooth, charismatic facade of his as the head of an international crime syndicate.

"We aren't doing business with him, Laz." He dismissed the notion with a shake of his head. "End of story."

His brother hiked a lazy shoulder. "I wasn't actually suggesting we do business with him," he drawled. "I was merely yanking your chain to see how you would react. Which was predictable." His brother narrowed his gaze on him. "You're still hung up on her."

"Who?"

"Gia." Lazzero waved a hand at him. "You've gone on a tear through half the women on the planet since her, but you're not even remotely interested in any of them. Take tonight, for instance. You could have had that redhead—the publicity girl. What's her name… Sylvie? Sophie? Instead, you are completely distracted."

"Because I should be back at the office working."

"Says the man who likes to socialize more than he likes to breathe." His brother rolled the Scotch around his tumbler, the amber liquid flickering in the torch light. "So if I were to tell you that Gia is standing behind you it would be of no interest to you?"

He turned to stone. Fingers locking around his glass, he swiveled, his scan of the crowd pinpointing the woman he'd spotted earlier talking with Delilah and another guest. His heart stalled in his chest as he took her in. Confirmed what he'd instinctively known. *It was Gia.*

Clad in a vibrant coral dress that hugged every inch of her curvaceous figure, she was thinner than he remembered, her gorgeous long, dark hair cut into a sophisticated blond bob that gave her a completely different look. Her cheeks were gaunt under her perfect, dramatic bone structure, her eyes deep, dark pools of green that seemed to vibrate emotion.

Exactly as they had that night four years ago when she'd given him her innocence, then walked away, as if what they'd shared had meant nothing. When she'd married another man.

Turn around, he told himself. *Pretend she isn't here. Do exactly what you said you would do if you ever saw her.* But he stayed where he was. Gia looked up. She froze as their gazes collided, her eyes widening beneath long, dusky lashes. Like a curtain coming down over her face, the blood fled, rendering her whiter than a sheet.

A midnight storm darkened those beautiful eyes. Twisted something in his insides tight. *Maledizione*. Why tonight? Why here, when she hadn't been seen in public for an eternity?

"Santo," Lazzero said on low note. "She is bad for you. Nothing good ever came of the two of you. Leave it alone."

He was wrong, Santo corrected silently. They had been good that night. *Perfect*. Before she'd torn out his heart. And even though he knew he should stay away, he couldn't seem to do it.

He set down his glass on the bar, ignoring his brother's muttered imprecation as he threaded his way through the crowd toward where Gia stood. But when he got there, she was gone, Delilah and the other guest immersed in conversation. Instinct took him to where Gia stood at the edge of the terrace, looking out at the water, a silent, delicate figure silhouetted against a sparkling, dark blanket of blue.

The image struck him as particularly appropriate, because hadn't it always been Gia against the world? Gia, who'd hovered on the outside, sitting by herself in the high-school cafeteria the first time he'd ever seen her, shunned by her fellow students because of who she was. Because she'd been escorted to and from school by her bodyguards, her friendships vetted and discarded by her powerful father before they'd ever had a chance to take flight.

He would never forget the shy smile that had lit up her face when he'd plunked his tray down beside hers and asked if the seat beside her was taken.

She turned as he approached, as if she'd sensed his presence, that same invisible thread tethering them together that had always defied reason. Her spine rigid, her face set in a mask he couldn't possibly decipher, she looked haunted. Guarded. *Vulnerable*. It awakened a primitive need to protect inside of him that was as instinctive as it was irrational.

"Santo," she said huskily, unleashing that insanely sexy voice that had haunted his dreams. "I had no idea you would be here tonight."

He came to a halt in front of her. Dug his hands into his pockets. "Delilah is hot on the idea of putting our boutiques in her hotels. Lazzero and I were on the way home from a golf tournament in Albany. She suggested we drop in."

Her long lashes brushed the delicate line of her cheeks. "That's exciting. Delilah has some of the biggest key influencers on the planet on her client list. It would be the perfect partnership."

"We think so." He held her gaze. "I was sorry to hear about your husband."

She inclined her head. "Thank you. It was a shock. It's taken me some time to process it."

He would have bought her cool, collected act if it wasn't for the white-knuckled grip she had on her clutch. The tremor in her voice that dismantled his insides. "Gia," he said softly, stepping forward to sweep a thumb across her jaw. "Are you okay?"

She flinched away from his touch, a quick, reflexive movement that sent a hot rush of emotion through him.

"I'm fine. You know I didn't love him, Santo. What my marriage was and what it wasn't."

"I'm not sure what I know and what I don't," he growled, "because you walked away without a word."

"Santo—"

He waved a hand at her. "You dropped off the edge of the earth for two years, only to show up here tonight. Forgive me if I had to ask the question. Old habits die hard."

She anchored her teeth in her lush bottom lip. "I work for Delilah. I have for the past couple of years."

He frowned. "You *live* here?"

She nodded. "You know I never wanted that kind of a life for myself. When Franco died, it was my opportunity to reach out and take everything I had been denied. Delilah," she explained, "is an old friend of the family on my mother's side. She offered to help me create a new life for myself. Gave me a job as a designer for her hotels and a place to stay. No one," she stated evenly, "knows me as Giovanna Castiglione here, they know me as Giovanna De Luca."

And she wanted to keep it that way. He struggled to wrap his head around that revelation. "And what does your father think of all of this?"

Her chin hiked, a tiny, but imperceptible movement. "He doesn't know."

He frowned. "What do you mean, he doesn't know?"

"I mean he doesn't know where I am. No one does, Santo. I left the life. I walked away."

She'd left the life? Walked away? A surge of astonishment coursed through him. "You *ran* away?"

A fire darkened her emerald eyes. "I am a *Castiglione*, Santo. You know who my father is. What was I going to do? Tell him I wanted out? Tell him I was done? You don't simply walk away from a life like mine. You run and you don't look back."

He ran a bemused palm over his jaw. "So let me get this straight," he began. "You married a man you didn't love because your father decreed it. Because your family means everything to you. And then, when your husband is gunned down in broad daylight outside of his casino, you walk away from that family and all the protection it affords to hide in the Bahamas, where you are open and vulnerable prey?"

"It's been two years. There is no longer that kind of a threat."

There was always a threat. He dealt with it as one of the world's richest men. She faced it because of who she was. But apparently, he conceded dazedly, no one *knew* where she was.

He arched an eyebrow. "And what do you intend to do? Run for the rest of your life?"

"No." Defiance was painted in every centimeter of her ramrod-straight spine. "I intend to live the life I've always dreamed of. I have everything I've ever wanted here, Santo. I'm never going back."

He studied the visible tension etching the sides of her eyes and mouth. Two and two weren't adding up to four here. Something was way off. But he didn't have the opportunity to push it further because Delilah descended upon them with an effusive "Darlings" to talk about the pop-up retail she envisioned for the Elevate launch.

Gia had designed one of the retail spaces he'd admired earlier on his tour of the hotel, done in partnership with a French high-fashion brand. Delilah thought Gia and his own designers would be the perfect working combination, a suggestion Santo couldn't refute because he'd loved the poolside boutique space Gia had created, an oasis that drew the hotel's clientele in the highest heat of the day. She clearly knew how to meld two distinct brands into a show-stopping, utterly unforgettable space.

Unfortunately, his brain wasn't functioning on all cylinders at the moment as he attempted to follow the conversation, because none of what Gia had told him made sense. Why did she look so terrified if she had the perfect new life? Why would she leave her family to live on her own in the Bahamas when the blood ties that had always bound her had been sacrosanct?

Why had she not come to him?

Four years of not knowing, of wondering why she'd left that morning, piled up in his head until he couldn't think of anything else.

He needed closure—once and for all.

But first, he needed answers.

CHAPTER TWO

Gia pleaded a headache and escaped the party shortly after her conversation with Santo and Delilah ended. She'd barely managed to keep it together during that encounter with Santo, terrified she'd say something she shouldn't, reveal something she couldn't. But the need to ensure he didn't blow her cover had been paramount.

She'd thought she was safe. That she was finally free after all of this time spent creating a new identity for herself, avoiding any kind of a social life where she might have been recognized. Delilah would have comprehensively vetted the guest list. But Delilah couldn't have known about Santo. No one knew. Apart from her mother and Franco.

She said good-night to Desaray, her babysitter, then went to check on Leo. Her son was fast asleep, his thick, long lashes shading his cheeks, his thumb stuck in his mouth, his sturdy little body curled in the fetal position in his cozy, white-framed bed. She smoothed a hand over his glossy blond hair and pressed a kiss to his soft, scented cheek.

He was so peaceful, her love for him so all-encompassing, he calmed her nerves. But she still couldn't settle enough to sleep, so she changed and got ready for bed, then headed to the kitchen for some warm milk.

She had the feeling Santo hadn't bought her story for a minute. That he'd thought it was as full of holes as she'd known it was. But she was also sure he would never betray her trust—that he would keep her secret. The bigger problem was the business he was conducting with Delilah. If he was considering putting his Supersonic boutiques in her hotels, he would have ongoing interests in the Bahamas. Which would never work.

Dismay clogged her throat. Surely, he would send one of his minions to oversee the project? Chances were, he'd never be here.

But what if he was?

A rap at the door brought her back to reality. Thinking Desaray must have forgotten something, as she was apt to do, she turned off the burner under the milk, padded to the front door and swung it open. "What did you—" She stopped dead in her tracks at the sight of Santo, lounging against the door frame.

Her heart slammed against her ribs. Acutely aware of the expanse of bare skin her silk nightie revealed, she wrapped her arms around herself as the humid, floral-scented air pressed in on her lungs. "Santo," she croaked, "what are you doing here?"

"Getting some answers." He brushed past her into the house before she'd even registered he'd moved. Scared her heart might jump right through her chest, she turned to face him.

"How did you know where I live?"

"Your joke to Delilah about sliding down the hill to get home."

Dammit. She bit the inside of her mouth. Really, she hadn't been in her right head. She'd simply been desperate to get out of there.

She had to get rid of him. But how?

She looked up at him, then wished she hadn't, the connection between them crackling like an electrical storm. It reverberated all the way through her, right down to the tips of her toes. Sucking in a deep breath, she corralled her racing thoughts, reaching desperately for the aura of outward calm she had perfected as a Castiglione. "About what?" she enquired evenly, pressing a palm against the frame of the door.

"About why you are really here. What's really going on with you."

"We've been through that already. It is also," she said pointedly, "far too late for this type of a discussion."

"I wholeheartedly agree. I would have preferred to have had it four years ago, but better late than never."

Her stomach dropped. *He wasn't going to give up.* She knew Santo. He was like a dog with a bone when he wanted something. "My head is pounding," she prevaricated. "If you insist on doing this, can we do it in the morning?"

"I'm flying out tomorrow, so no." He gestured toward the living room. "Should we talk in there?"

Panic surged through her veins. "No," she said as calmly as she could manage. "We can do it on the porch. It's cooler out there."

He waved a hand at her. "Lead the way."

She closed the door. Directed him out onto the veranda that ran the length of the villa and overlooked the sparkling midnight waters of the bay. A gentle breeze lifted the leaves of the palm trees, the sweet smell of bougainvillea and frangipani filling the air. But she was too frozen to take in any of it as Santo lounged back against the railing and regarded her with a silent look.

Feeling far too exposed, she wrapped her arms around herself and lifted her chin. "What would you like to know?"

"Why the hell you are hiding in the Bahamas when your mother must be worried sick about you. What were you thinking, Gia?"

She hadn't been thinking. She'd been doing what she'd needed to do to protect Leo. And she'd do it a million times over.

"I left them a note. They know I'm safe."

A flicker of dark emotion moved through his gaze. "Why didn't you come to me?" he growled, the undertone of frustration raking a path across her skin. "You know I would have helped you."

Her lashes lowered. "We were over, Santo. We had both moved on. What was the point?"

"That's a lie," he countered softly. "Why did you leave that morning without saying goodbye, Gia? Why run?"

"Santo," she breathed. "Don't."

His mouth twisted. "Don't ask why you walked into my arms that night and gave me your innocence? How we could have shared what we shared only for you to walk away and marry another man? Why I woke up the next morning alone, without an explanation? Not a note. *Nothing.*" A lift of his eyebrow. "Which of those things do you imagine confounds me the most?"

She closed her eyes, a hot, searing pain moving through her until it hurt to breathe. "You knew I was promised to him, Santo. You knew I was going to marry him. There was never any doubt about that."

"I thought you'd changed your mind." He threw the words at her in a charged voice that skittered through her insides. "You were emotional that night, Gia. Intensely vulnerable. You didn't want that kind of a life for yourself. You wanted better."

"And then I realized what I was doing. I was getting engaged in front of half of Las Vegas the next night. How was I going to walk away? It would have destroyed my father's honor. His reputation. The Lombardi family's reputation… It was not *undoable*, no matter how much I wanted it to be."

She was Sicilian. A Castiglione. That she would marry Franco Lombardi, the heir to a Las Vegas gambling dynasty, was a fact that had been cast in stone since the day she'd turned fourteen, when her father had approved the match between his only daughter and the eldest Lombardi son. A match that would cement his empire.

Pursuing the career she'd always wanted, marrying a man she loved and walking away from her destiny had never been options for her, something she'd foolishly forgotten during that impulsive, explosive night with Santo.

There had been no more time left to wonder *what if*. To look for solutions that didn't exist. To want what she could never have.

She drew in a deep breath. Then exhaled as she met Santo's dark, tumultuous gaze. "I convinced myself it would be easier if I simply left," she said huskily. "There was no future for us, Santo. You know that."

He stepped closer, his expensive aftershave infiltrating her senses with devastating effect. "You know what I think?" he murmured, his warm breath skating across her cheek. "I think we will never know because you walked away, Gia. Because it was easier for you to surrender to the inevitable than to face what was between us."

The brush of her bare leg against the muscled length of his thigh unearthed a shiver that reverberated through her. Heat pooled beneath her skin at the memory of what all that hard muscle could do. How it could take her to heaven and back. How it might have been worth every disastrous moment that had followed.

She watched, hypnotized, as his gaze darkened to midnight. As the power of what they created together took hold. One step and she would be in his arms. One tilt of her head and her mouth would be on his.

It would be magical. *Unforgettable*. Which had always been the problem between her and Santo. Because if he knew what she really was, who she was at her core, what she'd *done*, he wouldn't want her anymore.

Her pulse was a frantic, flurried beat she couldn't seem

to control, and she took an unsteady step backward. "You're right," she agreed breathlessly, staring up into all that black heat. "It's history under the bridge. You have moved on and so have I. So maybe we should agree on that and call it a night."

A myriad of emotions flickered across his hard-boned face. As if he was debating whether or not to agree with her. She drew in a breath and waited, only to have his attention captured by something behind her, a bemused expression moving across his face.

An ominous thud started somewhere in the region of her heart. Warning bells rang in her head as she turned around slowly to find Leo padding out onto the porch, his thumb stuck in his mouth, his blue blanket trailing behind him. Clearly woken by their raised voices, he directed a big dark-eyed stare at Santo.

Gia stepped toward him, desperate to head off disaster. But there was no way to prevent it. Her son, cheeks flushed from sleep, golden hair ruffled, took his thumb out of his mouth, walked the last couple of steps toward her and held his chubby arms out to her. "Up."

She picked him up and cuddled him close to her chest, her pulse pounding so loud in her ears it was like a freight train running through her head. Santo took in the scene, a frown creasing his brow. The curiosity in his gaze deepened as he stared at Leo. Then his eyes widened, shock flaring in those midnight depths.

It was like looking at two mirror images of each other.

She saw the moment realization dawned in Santo's eyes. Watched the blood drain from his face.

Santo took an unsteady breath as he stared at velvety dark eyes that could have been his own. At the noticeable cowlick that had infuriated all three of the Di Fiore brothers as they'd grown into adulthood. He ruffled the hair of the child in front of him.

It could not be. The child could be Lombardi's... Except there was no sign of the angular-faced Italian in the little boy clinging to Gia—there was only the identical image staring back at him. A bone-deep recognition echoed through him—a deep, primal pull in his gut unlike anything he'd ever felt in his life.

And then there was the panic arrowing through Gia's eyes. The stark fear painted across her face as she held the little boy close. The events of the night started piling up in quick succession, bombarding him with the impossible. Why Gia had been so terrified to see him. Why she'd been so anxious to get rid of him.

Because she'd been guarding a secret she'd spent four years preserving.

Somehow, he found the presence of mind to pull himself together. "I didn't know you had a little boy." He set his gaze on Gia's stricken face. "How old is he?"

She didn't answer. For so long, so damn long, his heart climbed into his throat. "*Dannazione*, Gia. Answer the question."

"He is three years old."

The earth gave way beneath his feet, any reality he'd thought he'd ever known replaced by a grey haze that threatened to envelop him whole. But the little boy had settled now and was staring at him with big, dark, curious eyes that held the slightest bit of apprehension, and the silence on the porch was deafening.

"Friend?" the little boy whispered, looking up at Santo.

Friend? Santo almost choked on the word.

A strangled look crossed Gia's face. "Yes," she murmured. "A friend. And *you* should be in bed." She glanced at Santo. "I need to—"

"Go," he instructed curtly, as if she wasn't about to carry *his son* away from him. As if the world wasn't disintegrating beneath his feet. "We'll talk when you get him settled."

It was the longest ten minutes of his life as he paced the length of the porch, a chorus of cicadas keeping him company as a red haze built in his head. He had used a condom that night—he was sure of it. Except the night had been long, condoms had been known to fail and, quite honestly, the last thing he could remember was Gia stripping down to a skimpy piece of lace and then there had been nothing after that except the hot, sensual explosion that had followed.

Uncertainty dogging his every step, he forced himself to keep a lid on the violent emotion coursing through him until he confirmed what he already knew.

Gia's face was deathly pale when she returned, slipping quietly onto the porch. Dressed now in cropped yoga pants and a T-shirt, she smoothed her palms over her thighs as she came to a halt in front of him.

"He is mine."

The muscles in her throat convulsed. "Yes."

A fury, unlike any he'd ever known, rose up inside of him. He clenched his hands into fists at his sides, attempted to control it, but it escaped his bounds, rising up into his throat until all that emerged was a primal sound of disbelief.

"Santo," Gia said haltingly, "you need to let me explain."

"Explain what?" he exploded. "That I have a three-year-old son you haven't told me about? There isn't one possible reason on this earth you could give me which would explain why you would keep something like this from me."

"Franco," she choked out. "He was going to kill you."

His jaw dropped. "What are you talking about?"

She sank back against a pillar. Pressed a hand against

her temple. "I found out I was pregnant a couple of weeks before I married Franco. I was scared, *terrified*. It was a disaster, given the circumstances. I had no idea what to do. I couldn't go to my father—that was inconceivable. So I went to my mother. She told me I had to tell Franco."

"You should have come to *me*," Santo grated out. "It was the obvious choice, Gia."

"And done what?" Fire flared in her eyes. "I was about to marry one of the most powerful men in the country. A pivotal match that would cement my father's business interests in Las Vegas, which were, at the time, in jeopardy. There was *no way out*."

He gave her a thunderous look. "And so you simply chose to marry Lombardi instead, when you were pregnant with *my child*?"

"There was nothing *simple* about it." She threw the words at him with a ragged heat. "Franco was beside himself with fury. My impulse, my *walk on the wild side* had put the entire partnership in jeopardy." She dragged a hand through her hair. Sucked in a deep breath. "Once Franco had finally calmed down, he told me we would have to make it work. That he would take my son as his own and give him his name. As long as no one ever found out the truth. As long as I never saw you again."

Her eyes glittered a deep green as they lifted to his. "He said if I did, he would find out, he would hunt you down and he would kill you."

Maledizione. He couldn't believe what he was hearing. "I can protect myself," he rasped. "You should have come to me, Gia."

She shook her head, eyes bleak. "Nothing would have protected you against him. He had the power to eliminate anyone he liked. He could and would do it. There was no doubt in my mind he would."

His brain buzzed with incomprehension. He understood Gia was intimidated by her powerful, charismatic father. Always had been. It was why she'd married Lombardi in the first place. To humiliate her father by walking away from her marriage would have been unthinkable. But to have passed his son off as Lombardi's? To *lie* to the world about his parentage? It was unfathomable to him.

He fixed his gaze on hers, his fury a hot pulse against his skin. "So you allowed my son to be raised by Franco Lombardi? In the same culture of violence you were brought up in? That same culture of violence you hated so much?"

She shook her head. "I protected Leo. He was never exposed to any of it, Santo. I wouldn't tolerate it. Franco knew that."

Leo. His son's name was Leo. He absorbed that mind-boggling fact. "Why leave then? After Franco died? Why walk away from your family?"

An emotion he couldn't read flickered over her face. "Franco was murdered in broad daylight. I didn't feel safe. I didn't trust Leo's safety with anyone but myself. So I ran."

He bit back the surge of anger that coursed through him at the thought that his son could have been in danger. "To Delilah?"

"Yes." Her lashes lowered. "I had known Delilah from some work I'd done on Franco's hotels. We'd become friends even. I think she always knew there was something wrong with my marriage, but she never said anything. She just said if I ever needed anything, I could come to her. So I did. I explained my situation with Leo, that I didn't want him to live that kind of a life, and she offered to get us out."

"So your mother knows where you are?"

"Yes," she acknowledged. "She's the only one who does. We keep in contact via Delilah."

He rubbed a hand against the stubble on his jaw, brain reeling. Addressed the one point he couldn't wrap his head around. The obvious, simple choice she should have made. "If Franco was out of the picture, what stopped you from coming to me then?"

Color rode high on her delicate cheekbones. "You were with a different woman every week. In a different city on a different continent building Supersonic, Santo. You were not, in any way, prepared to settle down, that was clear. And you had obviously moved on."

"Gia," he growled, feeling himself slipping over the edge of reason. "Tell me the *truth*."

Her beautiful eyes shone a luminous green. "I was afraid," she admitted quietly, "that you would never forgive me for what I'd done. That you might take Leo away from me."

She might have been right. Because right now, all he could feel was the fury burning through his veins. The anger that rose in a wild flood, stripping him of the ability to think.

He was a father. He had a three-year-old son. He had missed so many moments, so many milestones, things he would never get back. *Priceless memories.*

It was so far from the vision of the perfect family he'd had for himself, he couldn't even begin to contemplate it. Because that was what he'd always wanted—the family he'd never had. A family like his best friend Pietro's growing up—a warm Italian brood he'd been enveloped in when his own family had been shattered apart. Instead, he had a son he hadn't known about, a woman who'd chosen another man over him, a woman he couldn't trust. A woman with whom the complications ran a mile deep.

He wanted to scream.

Nothing should have prevented Gia from telling him

the truth about his son no matter what the circumstances had been. *Nothing*. But he was also smart enough to know that he wasn't in any condition to be attempting rational thought at the moment.

He turned and braced his hands on the railing while he stared out at the sparkling bay. He was supposed to be leaving in the morning. He could safely say that wasn't happening. In fact, he didn't want to let his son out of his sight. But Gia and Leo—who he assumed had been named after her grandfather—were safe for the night, since Delilah's security was second to none. And he needed a chance to breathe.

Gia set a nervous gaze on him as he turned around, clearly attempting to anticipate his next move. "What are you thinking?"

"That I need time to think."

She gave him a beseeching look. "We have a good life here, Santo—Leo and I. He is happy. Well adjusted. He plays on the beach every afternoon and he loves his friends. He won't ever have to suffer the stigma of being a Castiglione."

"He should be a *Di Fiore*." The thick surge of emotion in his voice reverberated through the stillness of the night. "Goddammit, Gia. Have you any idea of what you've taken from me? *Stolen* from me?"

She blanched. Lifted her chin. "Yes, I do," she said quietly. "But I did what I thought was best for Leo."

A harsh sound choked its way out of him. "I know you think you did. That's what astounds me. You think so much like a Castiglione, you don't know the difference between what's right and what's wrong."

A shattered look spread across her face. He ignored it, his brain too full to think. "Here's how this is going to go," he said tersely. "I will contact you tomorrow. At which time you will *be there*, Gia, or I will use every legal resource I have to find you, and when I do, you can kiss your son goodbye, because there isn't a court on this earth that wouldn't award me custody of Leo with your criminal past. The time for running is over."

CHAPTER THREE

GIA COULDN'T SLEEP. She sat in a chair on the veranda, staring out at the ocean as the deep dark of a Caribbean night set in with all its requisite sparkling stars, attempting to absorb the fact that her secret was out after three long, painful years of keeping it. She wondered what the ramifications would be, because surely there would be consequences. Santo's parting speech had made that clear.

Her stomach curled into a tight ball. She pressed her palms against it, as if willing it would smooth out the knots that made it hard to breathe. Had she really been foolish enough to think she could keep her secret forever? That her love for Leo would be enough to sustain the two of them in this sanctuary she'd created? That somehow, somewhere along the way, the truth wouldn't eventually come out?

She'd pushed aside that fear every time it had surfaced, because Leo's safety had always been paramount. But her betrayal sat in the back of her mind, festering and dark. Because she'd known what she was doing was wrong. She'd been clear on that, despite Santo's scathing appraisal to the contrary. There had simply been no other way out.

But now, as the guilt pushed its way out into the open, filling her chest with its heavy weight, it threatened to consume her. Her decision had seemed so clear-cut in the moment. Protect her son. Do what was necessary. But after witnessing the naked emotion on Santo's face tonight, allowing herself to acknowledge what she'd stripped him of, it didn't seem so straightforward anymore. It felt selfish. *Unforgivable.*

And couldn't all of this, she acknowledged, hugging her

arms tight around herself, have been avoided if only she hadn't had that one weak moment?

She had resigned herself to her marriage to Franco on the eve of her engagement party. Had always known her purpose in life was to cement the Castiglione bloodline through a powerful political marriage, rather than to pursue the dreams she'd had. But running into Santo in the airport lounge they'd both been scheduled to fly out of that night had thrown her into disarray.

A stormy winter night had cast havoc across the eastern seaboard, grounding all of the flights for the evening. Flustered, because she'd known Franco would be furious with her, she'd accepted Santo's offer to find her a hotel room alongside his. They'd ended up having dinner together in the bar of the hotel because the weather had been that bad.

It had been time to catch up properly, both of their lives since high school frantically busy, with Santo building a company and her finishing off a design degree and an internship at a high-end Manhattan firm. They'd kept in touch—a party here, a coffee there—but both of them had accepted the fact that to put some distance between them was the wise thing to do. But she'd never been able to break that bond completely. Santo had been the haven she'd run to when life became too much.

Her thoughts had been a circular storm of emotion that had mirrored the gale-force winds raging outside, the knowledge of what she was about to do, the *fear* of what she'd been about to commit herself to, had clawed at her throat. Her decisiveness had stumbled, replaced by a desperate desire to control her own destiny, if only for one night. For the chance to know what it would be like to be with a man like Santo, who had grown from the eighteen-year-old boy she'd first met into a formidably beautiful man who made her heart race like one of the jet engines that had ceased flying overhead.

They'd polished off an expensive bottle of Amarone over a dinner she hadn't been able to eat, an ever-present, pulsing attraction throbbing across the table between them, a living force she'd never been able to quell. She'd watched Santo extinguish it with that superior self-control of his, her heart sinking as he'd suggested they should both get some sleep.

Which might possibly have worked, had they not ended up alone in a silent elevator as they'd been whisked high into the sky. Had her desperation not reached a fever pitch about halfway there, her fear and frustration closing the distance between them. And then there had only been Santo's arms. A hotel room she wasn't sure belonged to him or to her. A night she would never forget a second of no matter how long she lived, every single piece of clothing they'd removed a revelation of what it had felt like to be alive.

One night for herself before she'd married a man she didn't love.

And then had come the harsh reality of morning. Of what she'd done. Of what was ahead—a glittering, star-studded party at the Lombardis' Las Vegas home to announce her engagement to Franco. The day she would officially become his.

Maybe it *had* been easier to run than to face what she'd done. How she'd felt about Santo. Maybe she'd convinced herself he would move on as he always did and she would end up brokenhearted. And maybe, it had been the coward's way out, exactly as he'd suggested.

She finally stumbled to bed in the early hours. She woke bleary-eyed, sure her safe little world was about to be blown to smithereens, and there was nothing she could do about it.

She dropped off Leo at the hotel day care, her heart in her throat as she watched him toddle off to join the others, a smile on his face. *She couldn't lose him.* He was all that she had. It had been them against the world for the past three years. She felt helpless in a way she hadn't in forever and it threw her back to a version of herself she never wanted to be again. Never *would* be again. Powerless. At the mercy of the forces surrounding her.

Delilah, always a lethally accurate barometer of her moods, appeared in her office shortly thereafter. Clad in a brilliant scarlet suit, her perfectly manicured nails colored to match, she looked as impeccable as always.

"Clearly, I have failed in my efforts," she observed, her ever-present coffee cup in hand. "Poor Justin left brokenhearted. Although I think I might have been sabotaged by outside forces. Is there something I should know about you and Santo Di Fiore?"

Gia's stomach curled. "You picked up on that?"

"It was hard not to," Delilah said drily. "The tension between you two was palpable. He was barely paying attention to anything I said."

She swallowed past the giant knot in her throat. "Santo is Leo's father. His *real* father."

Delilah's jaw dropped. Coffee sloshed out of her cup and over the side. She set it down on the cabinet, shaking the liquid from her hand. "I'm sorry. Could you say that again?"

Gia found a napkin in her desk and handed it to Delilah. "Santo and I had a night together before Franco and I married. We conceived Leo."

Delilah stared at her, gobsmacked. "But how? *Why?* You knew you were going to marry him."

"I was frightened. Scared. Santo was there." She sat back in her chair and drew in a deep breath. "We had known each other since high school. He was a senior in my freshman year. The most popular boy in school—the star athlete everyone loved. *I* was persona non grata. A Castiglione. No one wanted to hang out with me, and even on the rare occasion they did, Dante made quick work of them."

"But Santo," she reminisced, her heart pulsing, "walked right up to my table in the cafeteria. Sat down and started chatting away as if it was the most natural thing in the world that the most popular guy in school would want to talk to me." She sank her teeth into her lip, remembering how tongue-tied she'd been. "I was completely dazzled by him."

"You fell in love with him," Delilah concluded.

"It wasn't so simple. I was promised to Franco. We—" she hesitated, searching for the right words "—became friends. We use to run together in the mornings. Talk afterward in the stands. And there was more," she conceded. "An attraction that grew between us. Dante caught on to what was going on and my father sent a message through him. That I was not a possibility for Santo. That I never would be."

She told Delilah how her friendship with Santo had grown into something special. How he'd been the one she'd always run to. The night her sixteenth birthday party had fallen apart at the seams when her new friend, the one she'd thought might actually become a best friend, hadn't shown up because she'd been forbidden to. The afternoon she'd found out she'd been accepted for a glamorous exchange program to France, only to be told it posed too much of a security risk. The day she'd secured a spot on the track team only to find out her father had ensured it instead with his strong-arm techniques. Santo had always been there.

And then, there had been that night with him that had turned her life upside down. She told Delilah about Franco's fury, and the promise she had made to him to never see Santo again.

Delilah's sapphire gaze deepened with understanding.

"Which was why your marriage to Franco was so rocky. Because of Leo."

"Yes."

Delilah frowned. "How did Santo take the news about him?"

"Not well." *The understatement of the year.*

Delilah sighed and took a sip of her coffee. "This is a mess," she said finally. "You know that. Santo is one of the most powerful men on the planet. Does he want his son?"

She nodded. That much was clear.

"Then I would suggest," Delilah advised, "that you attempt to reason with him. It's your only option. And," she added quietly, eyes on Gia's, "you might want to figure out how you feel about him while you're at it. There are clearly some unresolved feelings there between you two."

She intended to ignore the latter piece of advice completely, because Santo clearly hated her for what she'd done. She wasn't sure about the first part, either. The Santo who had walked away from her last night had been a cold, hard stranger she couldn't hope to know. She didn't think reasoning with him was going to work.

But she had to try, because everything banked on her succeeding. Convincing Santo she had done the right thing.

Santo stood leaning against the railing of the terrace of his suite as a stunning pink sunset blazed its way across the sky. He'd spent the night before attempting to absorb the mind-numbing news that he had a three-year-old son. Walking for hours on the beach in an effort to work past the emotion consuming him. To figure out his next step. Which had produced a single, yet irrefutable solution to the situation he now found himself in.

He'd gone through it with his lawyer in New York this morning, his proposed solution the one his chief legal counsel deemed "the cleanest one possible." The complex process of having Leo's paternity corrected was another story. It was a land mine of red tape to negotiate that left him with a dark cloud in his head. Which hadn't necessarily been lessened by his brother's parting words that morning.

You know what I'm thinking.

Yes. And it would never be him. His father had married his mother, a Broadway dancer, when she'd become pregnant with his child. Had been so blindingly in love with her, with the *thought* of her, he hadn't considered the consequences of tying himself to a woman who would never be happy. Who had never wanted to be a wife or a mother. Who had married him for his money and then proceeded to make his life miserable from that day forward.

Which was not how his relationship with Gia was going to proceed. His father might have allowed his emotion to rule him, *he* might have allowed emotion to rule him the first time around with Gia, but *this* iteration of their relationship would be based on rationality. On putting their child first.

She showed up at six-thirty sharp, exactly as he'd known she would, because he held all the cards in this unspeakably difficult situation she'd created, and he intended to use them. His plan, however, was momentarily derailed when he opened the door and found her on the threshold.

Clad in a knee-length, olive-green dress with a halter-style top, the soft drape of the material accented her perfect curves, doing particular justice to her amazing backside, which had used to make every boy in school stop and stare. Then walk the other way when they remembered who she was.

Hauling his gaze upward, he refused to allow himself to fall into that trap. He focused, instead, on Gia's pinched face. Bare of makeup, except for a light-coloured gloss on her lips, there were shadows painted beneath her brilliant green eyes. She looked vulnerable. Apprehensive. *Scared.* Which normally would have tugged at his heartstrings, but not this time.

He waved her into a seat. "Would you like a drink?"

She shook her head. Perched herself on the arm of a chair instead. He moved to the bar, poured himself two fingers of Scotch, because he sorely needed it, added some ice, then turned to face her, leaning a hip against the marble.

Gia dug her teeth into her lip, eyes on his. "Santo," she began haltingly, "I don't think we were entirely rational, either of us, last night. It was an emotional discussion. Perhaps we can start over—discuss this situation with a fresh perspective?"

He cradled the glass between his fingers. "Actually," he murmured, with a contemplative look, "I woke up with excellent perspective. You stole my son from me, Gia. You kept his existence a secret for three years, one you would no doubt have continued to keep had it not been for last night. So, from now on, I will be the one calling the shots and you will be the one listening."

She swallowed hard, the delicate muscles of her throat pulling tight. "You need to be reasonable."

"Believe me, this is reasonable after the thoughts that have been going through my head." He inclined his head. "Who is taking care of Leo while you're here?"

"His babysitter. I thought it better we spoke in private."

"And during the day when you work?"

"He goes to the hotel day care."

"Day care?" He said the words as if they were dirty, which they were to him, because the idea of his son being cared for by strangers was just that unpalatable to him.

"I work," she pointed out. "I have a successful career,

which allows me to support my son. The day care is amazing. Leo loves it. Everyone there is wonderful."

"So he is growing up without a father *and* a mother?"

Her head snapped back, her green eyes firing. "On the contrary. I start and finish work early every day. I spend the better part of the afternoons with Leo, as well as the evenings. He never wants for love or affection, Santo, and the socialization with the other children is good for him. He needs to learn to bond with other kids."

Which she never had. *He*, however, knew the flipside. What it was like to come home to a nanny who had never lasted, and then later, when he'd been a teenager, to come home to nothing at all when his mother had walked out on them.

He'd been thirteen when she'd left after his father's business had gone bankrupt and his family had lost everything—the house, the car, every piece of solid footing he'd ever known. His father busy drowning his sorrows at a local bar, Nico working to support the family, Lazzero off in his basketball-obsessed world, it had been unspeakably lonely to come home to the empty, dingy apartment they'd lived in. So he'd gone to his friend Pietro's instead. Enveloped himself in the freely given warmth that had been bestowed upon him there.

Something Leo was never going to have to do.

"I have no problem with my son socializing with other children," he bit out tersely. "In fact, I'm all for it, Gia. My issue here is that you have not only deprived Leo of his father, you have deprived him of his extended family as well, because you have walked away from yours and stripped him of mine." He pointed his glass at her. "Nico and Chloe have a two-year-old boy named Jack. A cousin he doesn't even know. How is that *fair*?"

Any color that had been in her cheeks fled. She hugged

her arms tight around herself, her eyes glittering with emotion. "I am so sorry," she said huskily. "I am, Santo. I do understand what I did was wrong, despite your opinion to the contrary. But I did what I thought was best for Leo at the time and I would do it a million times over, because I never want him to grow up like I did. As a Castiglione. That was the *only* thing in my head when I left."

He absorbed the defiant tilt of her chin. The fire in her eyes. *That* was what had kept him up all night. The fact that she believed, in her own misguided way, that she'd done the right thing. Because Gia had only ever known one world—a world in which the blood ties that bound her—family, *loyalty*—meant everything. A world in which power and intimidation reigned supreme—except that she'd held no power in that world. In her mind, there had been *no way out*.

He regarded her with a hooded gaze. "What were you going to tell Leo when the time came? The truth? Or were you going to tell him that his father was a high-priced thug?"

She flinched. Lifted a fluttering hand to her throat. "I hadn't thought that far ahead," she admitted. "We've been too busy trying to survive. Making a life for ourselves. Leo's welfare has been my top priority."

Which he believed. It was the only reason he wasn't going to take his child and walk. Do to her exactly what she'd done to him. Because as angry as he was, as unforgivable as what she had done had been, he had to take the situation she'd been in into account. It had taken guts for her to walk away from her life. Courage. She'd put Leo first, something his own mother hadn't done. And she had been young and scared. All things he couldn't ignore.

Gia set her gaze on his, apprehension flaring in her eyes. "I can't change the past, Santo, the decisions I made. But I can make this right. Clearly," she acknowledged, "you are going to want to be a part of Leo's life. I was thinking about solutions last night. I thought you could visit us here... Get Leo used to the idea of having you around, and then, when he is older, more able to understand the situation, we can tell him the truth."

A slow curl of heat unraveled inside of him, firing the blood in his veins to dangerously combustible levels. "And what do you propose we tell him when I visit? That I am that *friend* you referred to the other night? How many *friends* do you have, Gia?"

Her face froze. "I have been building a *life* here. Establishing a career. There has been no time for dating. All I do is work and spend time with Leo, who is a handful as you can imagine, as all three-year-olds tend to be."

The defensively issued words lodged themselves in his throat. "I can't actually imagine," he said softly, "because you've deprived me of the right to know that, Gia. You have deprived me of *everything*."

She blanched. He set down his glass on the bar. "I am his *father*. I have missed three years of his life. You think a *weekend pass* is going to suffice? A few dips in the sea as he learns to swim?" He shook his head. "I want *every day* with him. I want to wake up with him bouncing on the bed. I want to take him to the park and throw a ball around. I want to hear about his day when I tuck him into bed. I want it *all*."

"What else can we do?" she queried helplessly. "You live in New York and I live here. Leo is settled and happy. A limited custody arrangement is the only realistic solution for us."

"It is *not* a viable proposition." His low growl made her jump. "That's not how this is going to work, Gia."

She eyed him warily. "Which part?"

"All of it. I have a proposal for you. It's the only one on the table. Nonnegotiable on all points. Take it or leave it."

The wariness written across her face intensified. "Which is?"

"We do what's in the best interests of our child. You marry me, we create a life together in New York and give Leo the family he deserves."

Gia's stomach dropped, like a book falling off a high shelf. She stared at Santo, horrified, not sure which of his proposals she was most taken aback by. The idea of being forced into another marriage she had no interest in, that it would be with a man who now clearly hated her for what she'd done. Or the thought that he expected her to give up the life she'd made here to return to New York.

She shook her head. "I can't do that. My life is here now, Santo. Everything I *have* is here. Leo loves it. You can't just ask me to give all of that up."

His face was unyielding. "I run a *Fortune 500* company. My business is headquartered in Manhattan. I can't base myself in the Bahamas, however enticing that prospect may be. It is not logical."

She rubbed a palm against the back of her neck. Thought about how completely she'd severed herself from her life. How impossible, how undoable, it would be to simply pick it back up again. Her father had moved the family to Las Vegas a decade ago, when he had concentrated the business on the gambling end of things, but he still had business interests in New York. A collision would be guaranteed.

Her skin went cold. "I can't go back to New York," she said adamantly. "You know what that would mean, Santo. Leo would be exposed to my family. He would become a Castiglione."

A cold fire lit his ebony eyes. "Leo will become a *Di*

Fiore. He will be protected as such—as will you. Which leads me to the final part of my offer. Leo will have no contact with your family. *Ever*. Those ties will remain severed. Unless it's your mother on a supervised visit approved by me. If you break that condition, our agreement will become null and void."

And she would lose Leo. There was no need to even ask the question. She could tell from the look on his face. Ice formed on Gia's insides. "My father will never tolerate such an arrangement, you know that. My brother, Tommaso, has never had a boy. Leo is his grandson—his future heir."

"Your father has bigger things to worry about." Santo picked up a newspaper that was folded on the breakfast bar and handed it to her. She scanned the page. Found the story he was referring to near the bottom.

Castiglione Thumbs His Nose at Congressional Hearings. Her heart jumped into her mouth. She skimmed the story, which talked about the new attorney general's determination to crack down on the resurgence of organized crime in the United States with a series of congressional hearings set for next month in Washington. Her father, unsurprisingly, had been invited to testify on the subject. He had, also unsurprisingly, refused to attend, electing to take a lengthy sojourn to Calabria instead.

She inhaled a deep breath. This would kill her mother. Her father was everything to her. Her whole life was built around him.

"They will go after his business interests," she said huskily. "My brother, next."

"Perhaps," Santo agreed. "But that would take time. Meanwhile Tommaso will run things in Vegas while your father lawyers up. Which, I'm assuming, he will do."

Undoubtedly. Her father, meticulous with the details in which he protected his empire, would take his time to ensure he was fully shielded against the proceedings before he resurfaced. The battle he'd been fighting against law enforcement had been the bane of his existence, providing an undesirable spotlight when the *famiglia* would prefer to operate in the shadows.

"He will come back," she said flatly. "He will never trust my brother with the leadership. He will make himself impenetrable and then he will plead the Fifth. At which time, he will find out that Leo and I are back. I can't risk that."

"You aren't going to deal with him, Gia. I am."

Oh, no. Her heart dropped. That would never work. That would be a disaster. "You know how he feels about you, Santo."

A smile that wasn't really a smile twisted his lips. "That he thinks I'm not good enough for you? Oh, that message came across loud and clear a decade ago. Funnily enough though," he drawled, "we are on an equal playing field now. It will be interesting to see how that plays out."

Her stomach curled at the thought of it. But that fear was quickly replaced by the panic that surged up her throat. "You're going to tell him you are Leo's father."

His black eyes glittered. "You're damn right I am, because that man is never going to set eyes on Leo again. He needs to know that."

Gia felt the world dissolve beneath her feet. This was a nightmare. This could not happen. She needed to do something to stop it before it did.

She covered the distance between them with shaky steps, coming to a halt just centimeters from him. Her heart jammed in her chest at how gorgeous he was in a white shirt rolled up to the elbows and dark jeans that molded to his thighs to perfection. She had always been able to appeal to his softer side. He had never been able to resist her, and right now, she wasn't above using whatever means necessary to prevent him from shattering her world apart.

"Don't do this," she said softly, "You're angry—I understand that. What I did was wrong. But I can't go back there. I'm *never* going back."

His gaze slid to the fingers she had wrapped around his arm, tensile muscle that vibrated beneath her touch. It was, she recorded silently, her second mistake of the past five minutes, because everything went up in smoke then, the slow rise of heat between them palpable as he lifted his gaze to hers, dark as ebony. And, suddenly, she was so tangled up in him she couldn't get out.

"Santo," she murmured. *"No."*

He leaned forward until his mouth was mere centimeters from hers. Her pulse sped into overdrive, threatening to steal her breath. His warm breath fanning her cheek, his blatant masculinity surrounding her from every angle, his heat bleeding into her skin, her knees went weak.

"Nice try," he murmured, "but that isn't going to work this time, Gia. The only possible course of action here is us together, in New York, making this right the way we should have from the beginning. Your damsel-in-distress act no longer wields any power over me."

She took a step back, heat stinging her cheeks. "I was appealing to your sense of reason."

"And so I will give some to you. You are the one who created this impossible situation by not coming to me, Gia. You are the one who passed my son off as another man's child—a complex legal issue that's going to take months to unravel. You are the one who chose to run rather than to face your problems. So *you* need to wrap your head around the fact that *this* is the only option that exists for us."

She lifted her chin. "I'm not *running*. I am *free*, a concept that neither you nor my father would understand."

"Which you will be in New York," he countered. "You'll have every resource you could ever want. The ability to do whatever you please."

"Except live the life I want." She hurled daggers at him with her eyes. "I am not one of your side dishes, Santo, out to plunder your pockets. You know the dreams I had for myself."

He cocked a shoulder. "Stay, then. Take everything you want. But Leo comes with me."

It was a surgical strike. Precise. Deadly. A bolt of fury vibrated through her, her hands clenching into fists at her sides. "And if the courts side with me?" she challenged. "I walked away from my life to protect my son, Santo. I think that's a very powerful testament to the lengths I am willing to go to, to keep him safe."

"Your father is the head of one of the most powerful organized-crime syndicates in the world." Skepticism razed his face. "What kind of a leg do you think you have to stand on? And then," he added deliberately, "there's the part where this would become public if it were to go to court and your life here would be exposed."

She sucked in a breath. *So he was really going to go there?* She hadn't thought he actually would, but *this* Santo, she was realizing, was one she didn't know. Not anymore.

She tried another tact, because apparently, the gloves had come off. "Your father married your mother because she was pregnant with Nico, and look what a disaster that turned out to be. *My* parents' marriage was an arranged match in which my father was never faithful to my mother. *My* marriage to Franco was equally ill-advised. How can you think this is going to work any better for us?"

His jaw hardened. "My parents' marriage was a disaster because my mother was only in it for the money and when that ran out and reality set in, she didn't care enough to stick. *Your* father is an incurable megalomaniac who feeds his ego with power and women. Who never prioritized his family. *Our* marriage will resemble nothing of the sort because we will put Leo first. And," he added, "we have a history to build on together."

"We don't," she rebutted desperately. "We don't even know each other anymore." She jammed a hand on her hip, eyes fixed on his. "Do you really expect me to believe you're simply going to abandon your woman-a-week lifestyle to marry me and we are going to live happily ever after?"

"Yes," he responded, without missing a beat. "Because it's in Leo's best interests that we do. Although you," he said deliberately, "will play an equal role in making this potential marriage successful. It takes two, Gia, another lesson I've learned from the past. So if you agree to my proposal, it will be a real marriage in every sense of the word, because I only intend to do it once."

Her stomach bottomed out. All of this was inconceivable—everything he'd just proposed—but the prospect of becoming Santo's wife in the real sense of the word was the most terrifying thought of all. Because she remembered that night. She remembered how he'd stripped away all of her defenses. How he'd insisted she give him everything. How not one piece of her had remained intact.

Fear rose up inside of her—swift and all-encompassing. And suddenly, it was all too much. Much too much. "I need time to think," she breathed. "You are asking for the impossible, Santo."

"I'm asking for my son. Whom you should have given me in the first place." He downed the rest of the Scotch and set the glass on the bar. "You have twenty-four hours to decide, Gia. Make the right choice."

CHAPTER FOUR

Gia spent the next morning in a fog. She should have been jumping into a new project—the decor Delilah had asked her to do for her new resort on Paradise Island. It was an exciting, demanding project that would be exceptionally creative, with its fantastical edge. But she found it impossible to concentrate with Santo's ultimatum consuming her thoughts.

She understood he was furious with her. She didn't blame him. But his proposal they marry to give Leo the family he deserved was far from the simple proposition he had positioned it as. Yes, Leo was her priority—had been from day one. But Santo was asking her to walk away from her life for the second time in the space of two years, a life she'd chosen to protect Leo from her past. A life she loved.

Moving back to New York, exposing Leo to the influence of her family, seemed inconceivable. Almost as inconceivable as being locked into another marriage with a powerful man who only wanted to marry her for convenience. For his son. A man she still had unresolved feelings for, the only man she'd ever had those kinds of feelings for, a man who made her feel the dangerous, scary things she'd spent her whole life avoiding because she knew the rejection that came with it.

It seemed like insanity. Because eventually, Santo would resent her for forcing him into a marriage he didn't want and that resentment would eventually splinter them apart, exactly as it had done to her and Franco. Which wasn't an option when she had just managed to put herself back together.

Not to mention the fact that it wouldn't be good for Leo. He would sense the tension between them and it would be damaging to him. She knew it, because she'd lived it every day of her childhood, watching her mother's broken heart.

But what choice did she really have? She could fight Santo in court, tie up a custody battle in international red tape, but that would only prolong the inevitable, because she was quite sure that Santo would win. Which meant her only alternative was to get him to see that marriage wasn't an option for them. That Leo was better off here and that somehow, they could make this work for both of them.

She gave up any attempts at pretending to work by midafternoon, collected Leo from the day care and packed a cooler with some snacks for them for an afternoon on the beach. A half hour later, they were there, a picture-perfect Caribbean scene unfolding around them. The sky a cloudless blue, the sea a vibrant turquoise, the waves a soothing rhythmic roll against the sand—it calmed her fractured senses.

Knees drawn up to her chest, arms wrapped around them, she watched Leo play in the sand from the blanket she sat on as a cool, salty breeze slid across her skin.

"Mommy. *Dig*." Leo waved a shovel at her, his golden hair falling over his forehead as he crouched in the sand. Her heart contracted at the blindingly bright smile he bestowed on her. How could she give *this* up?

She forced a smile in return, too distracted to contemplate that particular pastime with the chaos going on inside her head. "Give me a minute."

Leo looked past her to the house, his eyes widening slightly. "Friend here."

Her stomach plummeted. She swiveled around on the blanket and saw Santo striding down the beach. Dressed in a white T-shirt and navy blue shorts emblazoned with a red Supersonic logo, every hard-earned muscle from the sports he played nonstop was on display. Aviator sunglasses shielding his eyes, his blond hair spiky and ruffled, he was outrageously good-looking in the jaw-dropping way that had made women lust after him his entire life.

She'd seen them do it time and again at school, some of them discreet, some of them not so much. A phenomenon that had only gotten worse by the time Santo had put Supersonic on the Nasdaq in his midtwenties. Every woman had wanted a piece of the business world's resident golden boy. But even when they'd had success, it had never lasted long with Santo, because although he loved women of all iterations, loved to charm and flirt with them, none of them had ever lived up to his exacting standards of the perfect woman.

I want a woman who is as interesting inside as she is on the outside, he'd told her once. *A soul mate*, he'd elaborated on another occasion at a party when yet another candidate had bitten the dust. Which had immediately discounted her. She didn't have the goodness inside of her that Santo was looking for. She was a Castiglione—something that would never change no matter how far she ran.

She was not Miss Arkansas, Santo's last girlfriend, who was a champion of underprivileged kids across the globe. The most stunningly beautiful woman she'd ever seen, *inside and out*. *She* was a massive work-in-progress.

Her stomach, having picked itself back up again, fluttered against her ribs as Santo dropped down beside her on the blanket. "Friend," said Leo happily, flicking up wet sand with his shovel as he shot Santo another of those curious, big-eyed looks. Gia cringed, but Santo appeared ready for it this time.

"Yes," he said evenly. "Are you having fun?"

Leo nodded and started to dig, keeping one eye on the

shovel and one eye on Santo. Gia slid Santo a sideways look, which wasn't necessarily the smartest move because she found herself all caught up in the hard muscle on display. The way his sunglass-clad gaze slid over her in an unapologetically slow perusal from her bare shoulders in the casual sundress she wore, to the tanned length of her legs and her cherry-tipped toes.

"We said five," she blurted out, her bones melting. "My babysitter isn't here yet."

A shrug of a muscular shoulder. "I finished my conference call early. You said you're always on the beach in the afternoon. I thought I'd join you."

Because he'd wanted to see his son. A hot lump formed in her throat as another wave of potent guilt swept through her. She'd compartmentalized her feelings these last couple of years, because it had always been a method of survival for her. Which was exactly what bringing Leo here had been. But now it wasn't so easy.

"Dig," Leo said again, his voice insistent.

Santo took off his sunglasses. Looked at Leo. "Can I?"

Her heart turned over at the thick edge to his voice. Leo gave Santo an appraising look. "Yes," he said finally, and handed Santo a yellow shovel.

Santo took the shovel and joined Leo in the sand. Leo began giving him imperious, one-word instructions, commanding and sure of his domain. They were building, according to Leo, a *supahero's house*. Santo, who had been born with an ingenious brain, as evidenced by the high-tech fabric he'd developed for the sports jerseys that had set Supersonic on the path to stardom, took to the concept like a duck to water.

"He should live in the middle of the mountains," he proposed. "A secret hideaway with a *supapad* to land on."

The idea was met with Leo's wholehearted approval.

They began work on the multitiered, elaborate structure. Santo went a bit overboard with the details, heaping sand high around the structure to simulate the surrounding mountains, adding a landing pad for the various aircraft, and a driveway for the high-tech vehicles their superhero would command. Leo ate it up, his eyes sparkling with excitement as he made the requisite sound effects, a chorus of *kapows* and *pishaws* filling the air.

Off went Santo's shirt as the still strong afternoon sun beat down. Leo gave his playmate's powerful, chiseled core an astonished look and asked him if *he* was a superhero. Which made Gia bite down hard on the inside of her cheek, half to prevent laughter and half to prevent other deeper, darker emotions from engulfing her.

Santo was a complete stranger to Leo, but her son was completely entranced by him. Part of it, to be sure, was Santo's charm, because he could beguile any living creature in the universe. But the connection between the two of them was also seemingly innate. It was simply *there*.

A throb built inside of her, curling her insides. Santo was Leo's father. How could she have ever convinced herself that her son would never need *this*? That the love they shared would be enough to replace the bond he and his father could have together?

She'd spent her whole life trying to earn her powerful, important father's love, something she'd never quite seemed to do. Maybe she'd convinced herself that because she'd never had it, Leo didn't need it, either. Maybe it had been a lie she'd been content to tell herself because to stay had been too high a price to pay. And yet, here was Santo ready and willing to offer that love freely to his son. *Passionate* about it.

Her heart expanded until it seemed too big for her chest.

She had done such a bad thing. An unforgivable thing. And she could never take it back.

Leo declared the *supafort* done. Trotting back up to her, he deposited the shovels and buckets in the sand. Gia handed them bottles of water from the cooler. Santo dropped down on the blanket beside her and downed half of his. Leo had a sip, then peered inside the cooler. "Hungry," he pronounced.

"That's my cue." Desaray materialized on the sand behind them, holding her arms wide for Leo, who ran into them. "I'm sorry I'm late. How is my little munchkin?"

Leo giggled and twirled a lock of Desaray's dark hair around his finger. "Good. Bana bread?" he asked hopefully.

"Banana," Desaray corrected. "And yes, Mamma sent some." She slid a curious look at Santo, her dark gaze admiring, before she redirected it to Gia. "School ran late. Sorry. I'll take him inside and get him changed? Give him a snack?"

"That would be perfect." Gia made the introductions to Santo. "I'll go change," she suggested, as Desaray and Leo took off toward the villa, "and we can talk?"

"Why don't we talk here?"

Which probably made sense, Gia conceded. It would be more private. But the romantic setting on the beach combined with the emotion clogging her throat didn't necessarily make for a wise combination. She was about to refuse again when Santo shot her a deliberate look. "Sit down, Gia."

She sat down on the blanket, keeping a safe distance between them as she resumed her pose with her knees curled up to her chest, arms slung around them.

"What's wrong?" Santo asked quietly.

Aside from the fact that he was half-naked and her heart was beating a mile a minute? That he was still the most gorgeous, compelling male she'd ever encountered and no amount of time she'd put between herself and that night seemed to enable her to blank it from her head?

She pushed aside the thought with a determined act of will, because *that* had been what had gotten her into this situation in the first place.

"It was seeing the two of you together," she admitted. "I thought that I was right in the decisions I made. That I could be enough for Leo—that if I just created a love big enough, *strong* enough, we could be enough for each other. But watching you two just now, I realize how wrong I was in keeping him from you."

An emotion she couldn't read moved through his dark eyes. "You were young and you were frightened."

"Yes," she agreed. "But I still believe Leo is better off here with me, Santo. Away from my family's influence. There are other ways to approach this than marriage. We can find a way to share custody of Leo that works for both of us."

An implacable look moved across his face. "I've already told you, you living here and me living in New York is a nonstarter. I'm not interested in some sort of a modern arrangement, Gia. A *pseudo family*. I want the real thing. I will not compromise on that."

Gia trained her eyes on the sea, her stomach a tight knot. Santo's gaze was hot on her profile. "What?"

"I'm just figuring out who I am. I *like* who I am here, Santo. I am *good* here."

"And you can't be that as my wife?"

No, she couldn't. She would spend all her time trying to live up to the vision of the ideal woman he had in his head, forever knowing she hadn't been his *choice*, she had been his *necessity*. Because whatever they'd once shared, she'd always known that who she was would eventually destroy everything they had. It always did.

She angled her body to face him. "You're ordering me to marry you, Santo. Exactly as my father did with Franco. You are giving me no choice. How can that be the basis for a healthy relationship? How can that be good for *Leo*—two people who are marrying for convenience?"

A dark challenge glittered in his eyes. "Because we are going to *make* this into something good, Gia. We had a friendship once. We can rebuild it."

She absorbed the iron set of his jaw. His utter immovability. Indecision flooded through her. She had been so sure that marrying Santo was a mistake. But after seeing him and Leo together this afternoon, after witnessing what she had denied her son, she wasn't sure of anything anymore.

Santo tipped her chin up with his fingers. "You know it's the right thing to do, Gia," he said softly. "Make the call."

Her stomach twisted. Once again, she was expected to make the *right decision*. Which was the right decision for everyone *but* her. It left a bitter taste in her mouth, because her dreams were precious to her, she'd fought so hard to attain them. But Santo was leaving her no other option. How could she fight him on every front?

Her head went back to the image of her son playing in the sand with Santo. The relationship they could have if he had a father who was in his life for every one of those moments versus the fragmented time he would have with him in a joint-custody arrangement. Leo could have everything she had never had. It was the thing that tipped the scale for her.

She might have made an unforgivable mistake in keeping Santo from his son, but she could rectify it now by doing the right thing. Even if it killed her to do it.

She swallowed past the lump in her throat that refused to produce the words that didn't seem to want to emerge. "All right," she finally breathed, "I will marry you."

Everything happened in a blur in the days after she'd agreed to marry Santo. Gia tried to take it one step at a time, to keep her world from spinning out from beneath her feet, but it was almost impossible with everything happening so fast it made her head whirl.

With the biggest launch in Supersonic's history on his hands and clearly not intending to let Leo out of his sight for even a moment, Santo took control of everything, including the logistics for their move back to New York, as well as for their wedding, which would be a private, civil ceremony held on the beach on Delilah's estate.

He was determined to see her named a Di Fiore before they returned to New York to protect her and Leo and, she suspected, to send a clear signal to her father that she and Leo belonged to him. And while the whole concept of *belonging* to Santo, belonging to any man ever again, stoked the anger that burned beneath the surface, she couldn't deny the necessity behind it.

She also couldn't deny the attraction a simple, private ceremony held after her big, glitzy wedding to Franco—an over-the-top occasion she had dreaded. Her mother, busy holding the family together in Las Vegas in her father's absence, the situation tense over whether he would testify in the hearings, thought it better they keep the ties severed between them until the political furor had died down. She was also, Gia could tell, concerned about the political ramifications of her return.

It hurt, because she missed her mother desperately. But she'd been doing this for two years now. She'd learned to separate herself from her emotions. What was a few more weeks?

Before she knew it, she was marrying Santo in a short, textbook ceremony on the beach with only Delilah, Desaray and Leo in attendance. The ceremony, conducted by a civil officiant, was over before it even seemed to begin. The brief, perfunctory kiss Santo brushed against her lips barely penetrated the ice-cold shell she had constructed around herself. It was the only way she knew how to cope, because the thought of what was ahead was terrifying.

Santo might have promised to protect her from her former life, but a collision with her father was assured. Her mother might have understood her struggles, have supported her decisions, but her father would not. He would be angry, *furious*. To him family, loyalty, was everything. And she had thrown that in his face.

Her head a circular storm of emotion, she refused to look back as they left for the airport and the private Di Fiore jet that was waiting. Leaving Delilah had been bad enough. Saying goodbye to the slice of paradise where she'd healed, where she'd become a different person, might break her.

The three-hour flight back to New York flew by as rapidly as everything else. Leo, who'd only been six months old when they'd left for the Bahamas, was beside himself with excitement in the luxurious confines of the jet, imagining himself a *supahero* on his way to a *mission*. Which was a welcome distraction for Gia, because with each mile the plane ate up toward the past she'd vowed to leave behind, the faster her icy calm faded.

New York was home, where she'd spent her entire life before she'd married Franco and moved to Las Vegas. But she had become a different person—strong and resilient—and she was fiercely protective of this new version of herself. She worried that by walking back into her old life, exposing herself to those influences, she'd become *that* Gia again. And that could never happen.

Soon, they were landing at a tiny, private airport in New Jersey on a spectacular mid-May evening. Benecio, Santo's driver, who'd had the foresight to install a car seat in the Bentley, was waiting for them. Leo, agog at Benecio's shaved head and ex-military presence, which oozed from every inch of his dark, perfectly tailored suit, soon found the skyscrapers of New York his next big distraction. He absorbed them with big eyes until he passed out halfway to Santo's Fifth Avenue penthouse, which left Gia to take in the pulsing energy of the city. The honking horns and endless cacophony of sound, which was complete sensory overload after her life in paradise.

Santo's five-thousand-square-foot duplex penthouse that fronted Central Park was unspeakably gorgeous, with its private wraparound terrace and infinity pool that offered breath-taking, panoramic views of the skyline. The double-height ceilings in the modern glass-and-gunmetal-inspired living room were spectacular, as was the art wall wine display and the sweeping metal circular staircase.

Santo, a fast-asleep Leo sprawled over his shoulder, intercepted the wary look Gia gave her surroundings as they climbed the stairs to the upper floor. "This clearly isn't going to work for us," he acknowledged. "I'll have my real-estate agent look for something else. Nico and Chloe bought in Westchester. Maybe that's something we'd want to consider. Or the Hamptons. I'd love to get out of the city."

Her stomach dropped at the speed at which it was all moving. But staying here would not be an option, Santo was right about that. She wouldn't be able to take her eyes off Leo for a second, or he'd be swooping down that sweeping banister. The pool, however, might be the perfect antidote for not having the sea at his doorstep, which Leo would surely miss.

Santo showed her to the beautiful blue bedroom his housekeeper, Felicia, had prepared for Leo. It held none of the adventurous boyish charm his bedroom in Nassau had. It was all smooth, perfectly designed angles, but the collection of stuffed animals they'd sent along ahead, arranged in a decorative pile in the middle of the queen-sized bed, would hopefully be enough to keep him from feeling too homesick for now.

She roused her son briefly to slip on his pajamas, then tucked him into the center of the big bed. She left the lamp on in case he woke, frightened in a strange place, then followed Santo on a tour of the upper level, which included the beautiful master suite. Done in more of those browns, creams and greys, and featuring another jaw-dropping panoramic view, it was overtly masculine. A sultan's den of pleasure with its massive mahogany four-poster bed, working fireplace and skylight that showcased the stars.

She could only imagine how many women Santo had entertained here. She pushed that thought out of her head and considered the rest of the room. The palatial walk-in closet, with its full dressing room, already contained her clothes, which Felicia had unpacked. The bathroom, almost like a spa, was glorious, as was the chandelier that sparkled in the ceiling—a decadent touch she had a feeling Santo hadn't chosen. It was all so beautiful, even her critical eye couldn't find fault with it.

"Why don't you relax?" he suggested. "Get settled in. I have a few emails to address before I join you."

For what? Her stomach swooped at the question, but she forced herself to nod. He'd been business-like ever since she'd agreed to marry him. Throughout the ceremony today, when he'd barely touched her. When he'd followed her wedding band with a magnificent, oval-shaped diamond that had stolen her breath.

Which had hurt, because whenever her life had gone sideways, Santo had been the one she'd run to. The person who'd made it all better. This time, however, she'd been the one to break them. Who'd crossed the line they'd so clearly delineated in their relationship that night and smashed a decade-long friendship she'd regarded as sacrosanct, only to replace it with something far scarier and far more powerful.

And maybe, she conceded, kicking off her shoes, that was another reason why she'd walked away from him that morning. Because she hadn't known how to handle what she'd unleashed.

Which left her with the question of what he expected of her tonight. The sparkle of the chandelier drew her eye to the gorgeous diamond glittering on her finger. She was his *wife*. Would he expect her to share his bed tonight? It made her brain blank to even think about repeating the devastating intimacy they'd once shared. But Santo had made it clear he expected this marriage to be real in *every sense of the word*.

Rather than face that daunting prospect, she ran a bath instead. Enveloped herself in lavender-scented bubbles in the luxurious tub, with its spectacular view of Manhattan. Which only gave her more time to *think*.

She leaned her head back. Found herself spiraling into a place she rarely let herself go. Her marriage to Franco had been the most painful years of her life. She had blocked out much of it, because by the end, it had been a disaster, but now the memories came flooding back.

If she'd found it difficult to be a Castiglione, she'd found it even harder to be a Lombardi. Franco had been aloof and hard to know, exactly as her father had been. Angry at her for what she'd done, he'd been cold until after Leo had been born. He had allowed her to do a couple of decorating jobs on his hotels to keep herself busy.

She'd had good taste and he'd appreciated it. It had led her to believe that their marriage could work. That once they'd had their own children, when they had a family together, they could forge a connection between them. But that had never happened.

She'd been so intimidated by him, had never been comfortable with him. It seemed the harder she'd tried to conceive a child, the more difficult it had become, until her husband's jealousy of Santo had become a living, breathing entity that had driven an impenetrable wedge between them.

She hadn't blamed Franco. Had known the whole situation was her fault. But her husband's cruel, careless comments about her inability to conceive, about her failures as a woman and wife, had cut deep. He'd taken a mistress, which had almost been a relief for the reprieve it had been. But he had also insisted she stop working so that she could focus on a family. Provide him with an heir. Which had only made her feel more trapped and isolated than ever.

She'd hosted his dinner parties, stayed out of his business, did everything she was supposed to do. But each day the gulf had been driven wider between them, until her husband's death had mercifully ended a marriage that had been barely limping along.

She stared out at the skyline, the lights of the city blinking like teardrops suspended from the tall, imposing skyscrapers. Perhaps it was true that her feelings for Santo had destroyed her marriage. But now that she'd broken *them* with her actions, she had no idea what they were. What they could ever be.

She felt utterly and completely lost.

* * *

Santo nursed a brandy in his study as a hushed blanket of black slipped over Manhattan. He'd called his brothers to let them know he was back. Dispensed with the dozens of emails that had filled his inbox during the flight home.

He should join Gia. Get some sleep before the insane day he had ahead. But he hung on a moment longer to finish the drink. To process everything in his head. And maybe, there was a little avoidance thrown in there, too.

He'd come back to New York a married man with a three-year-old son he hadn't known about. His life as he'd known it had been annihilated. He should be having some sort of an extreme reaction to it. Withdrawal from his bachelor life. Instead, he was numb, Lazzero's assessment of he and Gia from that night in Nassau running through his head.

You've gone on a tear through half the women on the planet since her, but you're not even remotely interested in any of them... You are completely distracted.

He wasn't actually sure that was true. He'd had a list of the attributes in the woman he'd been looking for. Abigail, the last serious candidate for a permanent role in his life, had lacked the fire and passion he was looking for, despite the heavy dose of altruism she'd possessed. Katy, the massage therapist who'd been so amazing with her hands in bed, had bored him out of it. Suzanne, the one before Abigail, had been both smart and sexy, but her promotion to assistant district attorney for the State of New York had called an abrupt ending to their relationship.

It was the one thing he wouldn't compromise on—a wife who wanted the same things out of life as he did. Who wanted to build the strong, impenetrable bonds of family that he did. Who was content to be at home, taking care of their child, putting her family first. Everything he'd never had.

He took a swig of the brandy, the aged malt burning a fiery path down his throat. In his defense, none of those women had been right. But to Lazzero's point, maybe the problem had always been Gia. That once, he'd thought she'd been *the one*. His soul mate. Only to have her shatter those illusions when she'd left.

At eighteen, he'd been no match for Stefano Castiglione. Gia had belonged to someone else. She was not *his*. It was a refrain he'd repeated to himself a dozen times over in the ensuing years. It was better, *easier* that way. Which had been the way he'd been content to play it until she'd crossed the elevator on that stormy night four years ago, blown his brains out with her innocence and passion, and he'd made the conscious decision to claim her as his.

He'd woken up the next morning, intent on speaking to her father. On taking her away from that life. On building a future with her. Instead, she had walked away from him and married Franco Lombardi without a backward look. Slammed the door on everything they had shared.

It had taken him months to blank the image of her with Franco from his head. To convince himself that she was just as emotionally damaged as his mother had been, just as unsure of what she wanted, and he was better off without her. And once he'd finally managed to put the memory to rest, he'd vowed she was a piece of his history never to be repeated.

His fingers tightened around the glass. So what the hell had he just done?

The necessary, a voice in his head responded. His marriage to Gia had been *necessary*. To secure his wife and son. To protect them as he'd promised.

So now, he acknowledged, downing the last sip of brandy, he was going to do just that. With his expectations firmly in place when it came to his wife, and fully aware of what she was and what she was not, he was going to put his relationship with Gia back on the rational, pragmatic plane he had promised himself. Piece together this family he'd been given and somehow make it work.

Dispensing with the tumbler in the kitchen, he made his way upstairs. His wife had taken a bath and changed into some filmy cream concoction that wasn't overtly sexy, with its silky, delicate material that flowed to her knees. It was the body beneath it that claimed his attention. He knew how perfect it was. The curve of her hips that filled the palms of his hands. How those curves nipped in to a tiny waist, then up to the voluptuous fullness of her breasts, with their feminine, dusky rose tips.

It was an image that would be imprinted in his head forever. Which didn't help him now as he lifted his gaze to her beautiful face, the lush fullness of her mouth, those emotive green eyes that made his body harden with predictable effect.

So he was hot for his wife. Wasn't that a good thing when this was *forever*?

The bath had dissipated some of Gia's tension, but she found her nerves ramping up all over again with Santo's reappearance in the bedroom.

His shirt sleeves rolled up in that sexy look he did so effortlessly, his shirt open at the collar to reveal hard, bronzed flesh, he was familiar, yet foreign, a new thickness and maturity to all that muscle she'd once known intimately.

The storm of mixed emotions coursing through her reached new heights, an inescapable awareness of him climbing up her throat. Which was not necessarily helped by the slow slide of his dark gaze as it worked its way from the tip of her head down to her toes, lingering on the fullness of her mouth, the swell of her breasts and the curve of her hip.

The aloofness he'd been wearing all day vaporized, replaced by a flare of heat that stole her breath. "How was your bath?" he murmured, keeping that whiskey-dark gaze on hers.

"Relaxing." She curled her fingers tight by her sides. "Did you get your work done?"

"Yes." He threw his phone on the table. "I have an early meeting in the morning. It's a quiet week on the social front, which is good because it will give you some time to get settled in. Benecio will be at your disposal. You will take him with you whenever you leave the apartment," he said emphatically.

A surge of frustration swept through her. "So it's back to me being a prisoner in my own life?"

"I wouldn't look at it that way," he countered smoothly. "Whether it's because you are a Castiglione or because you are my wife, Gia, you are a target. As is Leo. It is a reality you need to face."

Which she wouldn't have needed if she was still in the Bahamas. A wet heat stung the back of her eyes. Blinking it back, she snatched a short, silk robe from the wardrobe and shrugged it on. Santo covered the distance between them, his slow, purposeful stride accelerating her pulse. Stopping in front of her, he stuck a hand against the frame of the dressing room door and blocked her exit when she would have stalked out.

His deliciously enticing aftershave worked its way into her head as she sank back against the wall, a heady combination of bergamot and lime infiltrating her senses. His tall muscular body blanketing her with a wicked heat, she focused her gaze on a place somewhere in the middle of his chest.

Long fingers crawled up her nape, slid into her hair to tilt up her chin. He studied her face with such a thorough appraisal, she felt utterly transparent. As if he could see how desperately she was melting inside. "What's wrong, Gia?"

Frustration and fear and something else she was afraid to identify, something far more dangerous, bubbled up inside of her. "I am off balance, Santo. *Lost*. You've torn me away from a life I loved. Put me right back in the middle of this," she said, waving a hand toward the window and its unparalleled view of Manhattan. "Am I simply supposed to walk back into everything that I was as if nothing has changed?"

"No," he said evenly, "you need time to acclimatize. To establish a new life for yourself, which will be built around the family we create together."

Her heart gave a bittersweet twinge. And what was that going to look like? She couldn't see her mother right now, the one person who would have grounded her other than Delilah. The Di Fiores were hardly likely to be any more welcoming. She'd taken Santo's son and run. Had deprived him of three years of his life. She couldn't imagine they would understand.

And then there was her father, and the looming question of Leo. The political time bomb she carried.

She expelled a breath. Leaned back against the wall. "What happens when my father resurfaces? He's going to hit the roof when he finds out what I've done."

His expression hardened into one of pure determination. "I told you I will handle your father. Leave him to me."

"*How?* How are you going to handle him? He isn't simply going to play nicely because you ask him to, Santo. You know what he is."

"You don't need to know." His delivery was flat. Icy

cool. "I know exactly who and what your father is, Gia. I will deal with him. What *you* need to focus on is settling you and Leo into a new life. Getting your bearings back."

She shot him a deadly look. "I am not a china doll."

"Clearly not," he said softly. "You took your child and walked away from one of the most powerful organized-crime families in the world. That took guts. But now it's time to relinquish control and let me handle this."

She inhaled a shaky breath. She wanted to do just that. Wanted to let him fix this as he'd fixed everything else in the past. But she felt so vulnerable, as if her soft underbelly had been exposed to the world again. And her father was a wild card no one could predict.

Santo ran a finger down the heated surface of her cheek, the slow caress rippling a reactionary path through her. "What else is going on in that head of yours?"

"I may have agreed to do this," she said huskily, "but that doesn't mean I am happy about it. You have turned my life upside down. Taken away everything I've built. I am angry with you. *Furious.*"

"Good," he murmured. "That makes two of us. We can work through that. But I need all your feelings out in the open where I can see them, Gia. I can work with that—the icy shell not so much. And as far as you being angry with me?" He tipped his head to the side. "Honor it, wallow in it if you need to, but you are going to have to get over it, because we *are* going to make this marriage work."

She swallowed hard, past the inevitability clogging her throat. His powerful length imparting a seductive heat, a faint darkness on his jaw where his stubble was beginning to show, the thick fringe of lashes over those beautiful mahogany eyes decadently tempting, he was far too close for comfort. Too close for her to think straight.

Her hands curled tighter at her sides. "I thought I would

sleep with Leo tonight," she blurted out. "It's a strange place. He might get frightened."

His gaze drifted over the heightened color in her cheeks. The accelerated beat of her pulse at the base of her throat. "I think that's a good idea," he said quietly, lifting his gaze back up to hers. "Sleep with him for a few nights—he might need the comfort. But just to be clear, I am not okay with the concept of separate beds because I think it creates a distance between us before we've even started. And since I intend for us to start this relationship off on the right foot, that means we share a bed together, sex or no sex. We build an intimacy between us, which includes *you* opening up and sharing those thoughts and fears of yours."

The very concept of it made her brain freeze. She slicked her tongue over her lips in a nervous movement, Franco's appraisal of her as "ice-cold" and "not worth the effort" filling her head. "I'm not sure I can do that."

"You can," he rejected flatly. "You merely choose not to. You'd prefer to live in that safe, self-protective world of yours that has shielded you from real life as long as I've known you. It's how you've survived. But that isn't going to work for us."

She absorbed his utter implacability with a sinking heart. "Even if I can learn to open up, it's not going to happen overnight."

"I'm not asking for you to do it overnight. I'm merely telling you there is no more running and there is no more hiding. There is only going to be the truth between us, Gia, so get that through your head."

CHAPTER FIVE

GIA DID HER best to acclimatize to her new life over the next few days. A stunningly warm early summer heat blanketed the city as temperatures soared into the high eighties. She and Leo put on shorts and played in the park under Benecio's watchful eye while Santo worked, the two of them indulging in an afternoon ritual of ice cream and a dip in the spectacular terrace pool at the penthouse.

It was New York at its most glorious, the city transformed into a glittering, vibrant green jewel. It had an energy about it, an aura of excitement that Leo loved, regarding it all as a big adventure. But Gia missed the peace and tranquility of the islands. The simplicity of her life there. The job she'd loved so much. Her *freedom*. It was like a punch to the gut every time she thought about it.

Not to mention the fact that she was still so angry at Santo for taking it away from her, it was hard to find the peace she was looking for. She knew he was right—that she had to get over it if they were going to make this marriage work. But she *wanted* to wallow in it, to mourn what she'd lost, because it had meant everything to her to have that independence she'd fought so hard for.

And overshadowing it all was the news coverage of her father's flight from justice. The papers were positioning it as a glamorous international intrigue—a tangle between two foreign governments. Her father, through his lawyer, insisted it was all a tactic on the US government's part to expose holdings they imagined he had, but in reality, he did not. High drama played out for all to see.

It made her worry about her mother. How she was handling all of this. She was tough, she knew, because she'd had to be. She would have her family around her. But that didn't mean she wouldn't be reeling from it, her foundation rocked.

Meanwhile, in the shadow of it all, she was having dinner with the Di Fiore clan that evening, an event that didn't ease her nerves. She had grown up with Nico and Lazzero. Had known them since they were teenagers. But this was different. She was afraid they wouldn't understand the decisions she'd made when it came to Leo, exactly as Santo hadn't.

She had tried on and discarded five outfits before Santo came home from work. Standing in front of the mirror in the dressing room scrutinizing her latest choice—a turquoise, off-the-shoulder dress with a ruffle at the hem—she heard him blow through the front door of the penthouse.

Leo's excited greeting as he went running to meet him did something strange to her heart. If anything had felt right in all of this, it was the decision she'd made when it came to her son.

Every night, bar none, Santo had come home from work in time to have dinner as a family, then put Leo to bed, after which he would work until midnight with his grueling schedule. He was clearly committed to being the father his own hadn't, as Leone Di Fiore had been so caught up in his high-powered Wall Street career in the early years, then later in the bottom of a bottle, Santo had only a few distant memories of the bond they'd once shared. It made her heart hurt to think of it. To watch him changing history.

Her husband breezed into the dressing room, having left Leo to his collection of NYC first-responder toy vehicles he'd come home with last night, much to her son's delight. Dressed in a sharp navy suit with a pale yellow tie, with tawny blond stubble darkening his jaw, he looked so gorgeous he made her heart stutter in her chest.

She imagined the women of New York had spent the day watching him walk down the street drooling in his wake. And that was without the look he lavished on her, his dark, appreciative gaze taking in the flirty line of her short, feminine dress.

"You look amazing," he murmured, bending to brush a kiss against her cheek. "I only need five minutes to get out of this monkey suit. It's far too hot for this."

Which was such a shame, she opined silently, more than a bit off balance at the sight of him. Santo stepped back and stuck his fingers into the knot of his tie. "How was your day?"

She gave as casual a shrug as she could manage. "The same. The park. Ice cream. The pool. I'm exhausted. So is Benecio."

His mouth quirked. "Maybe we should switch. *I* sat through four hours of meetings this morning, spent my lunch debating our social-media strategy after one of our athletes decided to blow up Twitter by sending nude pictures to his girlfriend that were somehow leaked. Then," he continued, stripping off the tie and dropping it on a chair, "the icing on the cake was my afternoon spent ironing out a manufacturing flaw with the Elevate design team. *Not* what I needed at this stage of the game."

"Did you get it figured out?"

He lifted a brow. "The nude tornado or the potentially crippling flaw?"

"Both."

"Yes." He threw her one of those sexy smiles that could melt a woman's knees as he made quick work of the buttons on his shirt. The smooth expanse of rippling, bronzed flesh he exposed made her stomach contract.

"I will want my career back," she murmured, as a distraction more than anything else. "When Leo gets settled.

I can only wander aimlessly around Central Park and eat ice cream for so long."

"Of course," he agreed smoothly. "But there's no hurry. Meanwhile, you can focus on *us*."

On the fact that he was now stripping off his dark trousers, revealing snug-fitting black boxers that left little to the imagination. Which brought every second, every minute of that explosive night they'd spent together, roaring back with crystal clarity. Because she remembered how amazing he looked. How *virile*. How incomparable. It was not what her strung-out nerves needed at the moment.

Dear God. She fumbled around for earrings to wear. Found some simple diamond teardrops that would enhance the feminine lines of the dress.

True to his word, Santo had given her the space she'd asked for. She'd been sleeping with Leo ever since that first night they'd come back, avoiding these kinds of intimacies. But sooner or later she was going to have to address what was between her and Santo.

Clad now in a pair of dark jeans and a black T-shirt that looked just as deadly on him as the suit had, clinging to his lean, hard body in all the right places, he propped himself against the dressing table, eyes on her. "You're nervous."

"A bit." She refused to show just *how* nervous she was.

"Don't be. You know Nico and Lazzero and you've met Chloe a few times. Chiara," he added, "is amazing. You'll love her."

She sank her teeth into her lip. "What do they know about us? About Leo?"

"The truth. That I have a three-year-old son with you and that we are married. All they need to know. Nico and Chloe are thrilled that Jack will have a playmate."

Which she had denied him for the past couple of years. A whirlwind of conflicting emotions sweeping through her, she presented her back to Santo so that he could do up the top clasp of her dress. They weren't helped by his close proximity, which only got worse when his fingers, having deftly dispensed with the tiny hook and eye closure, trailed a path down her spine to her waist, sensitizing every centimeter of flesh he touched.

Her bare thighs brushed against the rough denim that encased his length and his palms heated her skin, making her awareness of him sky-high—it was sensory overload. "Stop thinking about the past," he said softly. "Think about the *now*, Gia. The *right* decisions we are making. About this fresh start we have."

Her skin fizzled beneath his touch, a golden heat invading her blood. Her eyes fixed on his in the mirror, a luminous green snagging a slumberous black. She couldn't deny how tempting the thought was to believe that they could make this work. That somewhere in the midst of all of this insanity, of the mistakes she had made, of the gulf that now stretched between them, something good could emerge.

But there was also fear. Fear that clawed at her insides at making herself that vulnerable ever again.

He bent his head and pressed a kiss to the delicate skin of her neck. An involuntary shiver raked through her. She moved closer in an instinctive reaction. His hands dropped lower on her hips to hold her more firmly against him. More of those fleeting, butterfly-light kisses pressed down the length of her throat until it felt as if her skin was on fire.

He tightened his hands around her hips and turned her around. Gia sank back against the dressing table. Her pulse a frantic, staccato beat at her throat she couldn't seem to control, she read the dark intent in his gaze before he lowered his head to hers. A mad anticipation fizzled through her, sizzling her blood, just before a tiny, dark-haired dynamo launched himself between them.

"Wee-oh, wee-oh," cried Leo, waving his fire truck in the air.

The heat in Santo's eyes cooled, replaced by a reluctant amusement. "The very epitome of an inopportune moment," he drawled. "One we will pick up later."

He bent to scoop his son off the floor. Her cheeks scarlet, her head a muddled mess, Gia went and looked for her shoes rather than let her mind go down that path.

Nico and Chloe's Westchester estate sat on the banks of the Hudson, the magnificent Georgian home sparkling in the late afternoon sun. Situated on three acres of lush, picturesque landscape, it offered unparalleled privacy and endless vistas across the water. Private gates opened to the main residence, which was surrounded by multiple stone terraces and an in-ground pool.

It took Leo about five minutes to warm up to his new cousin, Jack, a gorgeous little dark-haired boy with a big personality, before her son was off and running, Jack's nanny in tow. Which was a bit unnerving, because deprived of her son's lively presence, Gia felt completely under the microscope.

Chloe and Chiara were amazing—warm and wonderful. Nico and Lazzero, on the other hand, were guarded with her. Polite, but distinctly cool. Particularly the aloof, hard-to-know Lazzero. Which wasn't entirely unexpected. The three brothers had always been close, given the way their family had shattered apart. It would take time to earn back their trust.

A hand fisted her chest. But hadn't that always been the way? Guilty until proven innocent? Never had anyone given her the benefit of the doubt—she'd had to earn it every single time. *Prove herself.* This would be no different.

She pushed back her shoulders and absorbed their scrutiny with an unflinching look. Chloe, quiet and lovely, soon took her under her wing, suggesting she and Chiara join her for a glass of wine on the deck while the men threw a football around with the boys.

A brilliant scientist who'd developed some of the world's most popular perfumes at Evolution, the cosmetics company she ran with Nico, Chloe told them about the new fragrance she was debuting at the Met Young Patrons party, one of the biggest nights of the year. It would go into all the gift bags for the influencers in attendance, but she'd send Gia home with a bottle of it tonight to try.

Chiara, a talented, up-and-coming clothing designer, was the polar opposite of Chloe. Stunning with her dark Latina looks and fiery personality, Gia could understand why the impossible-to-catch Lazzero had fallen for her.

Alight with the news that her hip line of street clothing, which had been garnering so much attention among the city's fashionistas, had just been picked up by one of the largest department stores in the city, Chiara was brimming with excitement.

"I am dressing a few people for the Met party," she buzzed. "Speaking of which," she said, tipping her glass at Gia, "Abigail Wright is going to flip her lid when she hears Santo is married. Just last week she was telling me she is *not* over him. That she's only dating Carl O'Brien, the quarterback of the Stars, to make him jealous."

Abigail Wright. Gia's brain sifted through a mental list of who was who. *Miss Arkansas*. Abigail Wright. The paragon of virtue she was sure she could never live up to. Who was apparently dating New York's most famous quarterback.

"Half of New York's female population is undoubtedly in mourning," Chloe interjected drily. "No surprises there."

"Not that I'm going to dress her anymore," Chiara

amended hastily. "He never looked at her the way he looks at you, by the way. You have nothing to worry about."

Gia's lashes swept down. "What do you mean?"

"Like someone would have to walk through him to get to you. I've never seen him like that."

A flush warmed her cheeks. That had always been Santo's way. But in this case, it didn't mean anything other than he'd married her for his son and he was protecting his investment. Because he was determined to carve out that perfect family he'd promised himself.

"I think it's obvious why Santo and I married," she said quietly, aware these women were too smart and perceptive not to sense the truth. "We did it for Leo."

Chloe studied her for a long moment with that quiet scrutiny of hers. "Is it? I don't pretend to know what happened between you and Santo. Frankly, it's none of my business. But you know him as well as I do. The last thing he would do is commit himself to a marriage he doesn't want. He could have his pick of any woman on the planet. So clearly," she observed, "there is something there for him. Something he thinks can work."

Or, Gia countered silently, he was simply going to *make* it work because he had to.

Chloe's words, however, stuck with her as the lazy evening stretched on, a delicious dinner served on the terrace amidst a stunning, rose-red Westchester sunset. Maybe she was right. Santo seemed committed to making this relationship work. Maybe it was *her* that was the stumbling block. Maybe she had to let go of this anger. Believe everything he was saying. That she and Santo had a foundation to build this marriage of theirs on that could make it a success. That once, they'd shared something rare and special and maybe they could have it again.

When her husband suggested they should leave as the

sky darkened to black, the sound of an army of cicadas filling the air, a current of anticipation fizzled her blood at the promise of what was to come. She made a quick trip upstairs with Chloe to get the bottle of perfume she'd promised, and was about to join the others at the front of the house when she remembered she'd left her wrap on a chair on the terrace. Winding her way through the house to the patio, she had set one foot through the open sliding glass doors, before the low pitch of Santo's voice froze her in her tracks.

"What the hell is wrong with you?"

"I am attempting to hold my tongue, that's what I'm doing." Lazzero's voice held a dark frown. "Your shotgun wedding has us all a bit shell-shocked, Santo. I'm simply attempting to process it all."

"Some kind of a friendly welcome might be nice."

"She is a *Castiglione*," his brother said, biting out the words. "Her father is the topic du jour of the newspapers. She is a political liability. Immersing yourself in this, taking Stefano Castiglione on, is madness with the biggest launch in our history right around the corner."

"She is the mother of my child," her husband growled back. "There was no question as to what I'd do. You would have done the same."

"No," his brother said deliberately, "I wouldn't have. I think it's a mistake. I think *she* is a mistake. I can hold my tongue on your private affairs, Santo, but do not ask me to tell you lies about how I feel."

"You don't know her." Santo's voice was low, resonant. "You are judging her based on the family she comes from, not for who she is."

"I am *judging* her based on what I saw every day for a decade. Her running to you every time she had a problem. You playing knight in shining armor. You're going to spend the rest of your life trying to keep a woman like that happy. Dealing with her *backstory*. And you never will."

Gia's heart splintered into pieces. Unable to bear hearing any more, she turned on her heel and retreated the way she'd come, tears stinging the back of her eyes.

It wasn't anything she hadn't heard before. It shouldn't cut so deeply. It was the last comment that did it, because she knew it was true. Santo had always been her shelter. Her rock. She'd always run to him when she'd needed someone. It was exactly what she'd been trying to rectify when she'd started her new life in the Bahamas. To learn how to stand on her own two feet. And now, she'd lost that, too.

CHAPTER SIX

Santo followed Gia into the penthouse. He stripped off his watch and tossed it on the dresser in the bedroom, while she put Leo to bed, frustration seething through his bones. He'd been so sure they'd been making progress in this détente of theirs only to have her freeze up on him on the way home as if the temperature had been subzero instead of damn near balmy.

He absorbed the icy look on her face as she slipped into the bedroom, slid the clip from her hair and threw it on the dressing room table, her silky blond hair swinging against the delicate line of her jaw.

"What the hell is wrong with you?" He leaned a palm against the dresser. "Everyone was making an effort to make you feel comfortable tonight. We were good and then we were not."

"It's nothing," she said frostily. "I'm tired. I'm going to bed."

"Oh, no." He eliminated the prospect of that happening, covering the distance between them with swift steps. "We are not doing this again. I've made it clear that isn't how our marriage is going to work."

She stared him down with belligerent heat. "It's nothing. You are barking up the wrong tree, Santo. I'm tired. I want to go to bed. That's all."

"Gia," he growled, "you can tell me what's wrong or we can stay here all night." He spread his hands wide. "Your choice. I'm *easy*."

She hiked up her chin. "I overheard you and Lazzero

talking before we left. About what a mistake he thinks I am. A political liability."

Maledizione. He raked a hand through his hair. "You heard that?"

"I was coming back to get my sweater. I'd left it on the terrace."

He absorbed the cloud of hurt suffusing her eyes, his insides contracting. "It doesn't matter what Lazzero thinks," he said quietly. "This is our relationship, not his."

"Which he completely disapproves of. Both of your brothers do."

"So what?" He shrugged "I'm sorry you had to hear that. Lazzero is being… *Lazzero*. You know what my brothers are like. But that doesn't mean he is right. Which is exactly what I told him." He shook his head. "You have to stop worrying so much about what other people think and focus on *us*."

"How can I?" she bit out. "You haven't lived with the constant judgment like I have, Santo. You *saw* it growing up. It doesn't matter how hard I work to prove myself as something other than a Castiglione, I will always *be* a Castiglione."

"So you rise above it. Choose how you define yourself rather than let others do it for you. We've had this conversation dozens of times, Gia."

Yes, they had. And yet, every time it kept on happening.

He waved a hand at her. "You think I don't understand what it's like to live with a legacy? My father imploded in spectacular fashion, Gia. Thousands of people lost their jobs when his company failed. The analysts couldn't wait to savage the great Leone Di Fiore in the press. The golden boy of Wall Street's meteoric fall from grace. Lazzero and I have had to battle that legacy every step of the way. If we make a wrong move, they point to my father. When we succeed, they tell us we've risen too far, too fast. It is *always there*."

"You can't compare the two," she shot back. "Your father was an honorable man. My father is…" She stumbled to a halt, her cheeks blazing. "You know what he is."

"What?" he prompted quietly. "Why don't you just say it?"

"You *know* why."

"You aren't bound by those rules anymore. You walked away, remember?"

The storm in her eyes brewed darker. *"Fine,"* she said. "You want to get the elephant in the room out in the open? My father is a *criminal*, Santo. A monster in a slick suit. He rose to the top of the food chain by the exercise of extreme power and brutality. He has *blood* on his hands. Who knows how much?"

He stared at her, shocked into silence.

Her lashes lowered, brushing her cheeks. "People *assume* that I am guilty by association. How can I not be when I lived that life? When I *condoned* what he was?"

"You don't choose who your father is," he said evenly. "You were too young and too defenseless to make any sense of it, Gia. When you got older, when you could make those decisions for yourself, you left. You made your choice."

But she had been indelibly shaped by who she was, as he himself had pointed out in the Bahamas. Gia curled her arms tight around herself and paced to the window, everything she'd kept hidden inside of her for what seemed like forever bubbling to the surface. Pushing at the edges of her tightly held composure. The secrets, the memories, the *shame* of it all.

And suddenly, she needed to get it out before it ate her alive. Before it destroyed her even more than it already had.

"I didn't know what he was in the beginning," she said

huskily, turning to lean a hip against the sill. "I was dazzled by him. I *loved* him. I thought he was larger than life. I would see him for a few minutes before bed every night. I would make sure I had a witty thing to tell him, something to make it worth his while. A funny joke I'd heard, a cool fact I'd collected from my *National Geographic Kids* magazine." Her mouth softened at the memory. "He would laugh and tell me how smart or funny I was. It seemed, in that moment, like it was the best thing I'd accomplished all day."

Her innocence about her father, she acknowledged, stomach twisting, had still been alive and well then.

"But soon," she continued, "the rumors started. My father was climbing the ranks—gaining power in the family. He was always working. Even more distant than he was before. I would hear the whispers at school about what he was, something a kid's parents had seen in the newspaper or on TV. I would go home and ask my mother if it was true. She would tell me that successful people like my father were a target for those types of stories and that I shouldn't believe any of it. Nor was I to talk about it."

"You never did," Santo observed. "Not even when I asked."

"I was bound by the *omerta*—the vow of silence we take. Talking about the business could land my father in jail. We could be forced to testify. Or worse," she added matter-of-factly, "it could be used against us."

She wrapped her arms tighter around herself as the memories enveloped her. "I didn't know *what* he was until the night before my thirteenth birthday. We'd finished dinner. Mamma had gone to her sister's. I was bored and lonely, angry I wasn't out socializing like every other kid I knew. My father always held these secret meetings in his library at night. I was desperately curious about them. So, I slipped into the secret compartment behind the library wall."

The memory was burned into her head, an indelible image she'd never forget. Her heart had been beating so loud in her ears she'd thought it might thunder right out of her chest. Her fingertips clutched the gnarled old oak shelves in a death grip as she listened through the gap in the wood. She'd been old enough to suspect that what everyone had said was true, but hoped it wasn't. Had been desperate to prove all the catty whispers wrong. Because, of course, it *couldn't* be true. Her father couldn't be *that*.

"My father was meeting with my Uncle Louis. Who wasn't my real uncle at all," she acknowledged, her mouth twisting. "He was my father's top lieutenant. His right-hand man.

"My father and Louis were talking about Giuliano Calendri, the famous jazz singer my father hung out with. Giuliano was refusing to play an engagement at one of my father's casinos." The knots in her stomach pulled tight. "My father told Louis that if Giuliano *couldn't find the time* to play his gig, he would ensure he never did another date on the east coast. Then, he would break his knees."

"So then you knew," Santo said softly.

"Yes." But it had felt as if she hadn't known *anything*, really. Because if her Uncle Louis wasn't her real uncle, what *was* true? Were the stories in the newspapers true? How much else had her father lied to her about? Was *anything* real in her world?

"I almost got away with it," she reminisced. "Until one of my father's security men found me slipping back into the house." A chill went up her spine as she recalled her father's violent rage. The sting of his fingers as he'd slapped her face so hard, her head snapped back. She'd been in shock. Her father was hard. Undeniably ruthless. But he had never hit her before.

"He lost it with me," she said, lifting her gaze to Santo's. "He hit me. Told me I was never to do it again. That I should *know my place*. I never," she said quietly, "gave him reason to do it again."

Santo watched her with an unblinking look. "So you turned yourself into a straight A student. Won every track competition you entered. Did everything you could do to earn his approval, including marrying Franco. Walking away from what we had."

She lifted her chin, Lazzero's soul-destroying words slicing open jagged wounds inside of her. "It was never going to work, Santo. *That's* why I walked away. We both knew it. It's why we avoided the attraction between us."

"I ignored the attraction between us because you were promised to someone else," he qualified. "In case you have forgotten that pertinent fact. I was trying to be sensible for the both of us, Gia."

"And the fact that it was complicated, that *I* was complicated, never figured into it?"

The evasive look on his face cut a swath right through her. "It is inconsequential," he murmured. "Because we crossed that line and now we are here. *Together*. Stop trying to throw roadblocks between us."

A hot ball of hurt lodged itself beneath her ribs. At him for refusing to acknowledge the truth. Anger at herself for ever agreeing to a marriage she shouldn't have. For allowing herself to believe, even for a moment, that it could work, because she had never been, nor would she ever be, what he needed. Nor what he'd wanted.

She hiked her chin higher, refusing to show the pain and humiliation shredding her insides. "I am telling you the *truth* you refuse to admit. It wasn't going to work then, and it isn't going to work now."

* * *

Santo absorbed the hurt darkening his wife's big green eyes. Watched her shut herself down. It *had* been complicated. He had held himself back because of it. But he'd picked her up and carried her into that hotel room, anyway, because he'd thought it had been worth it. That *she* had been worth it. And it infuriated him that yet again, she was denying everything it had been.

He stalked across the room and came to a halt in front of her. "First of all," he murmured, tipping her chin up with his fingers, "*you* are the one who walked away, not me, Gia. It may have been complicated, but *I* thought it was worth it. Secondly," he qualified, "if you had stayed around long enough to hear the end of my conversation with Lazzero, you would have heard me say that he needs to open his eyes, because you are the strongest, most courageous woman I know to have walked away from everything you knew to protect Leo like you did. I respect that, even if I haven't understood all of the decisions you've made."

Her eyes grew large, glittering pools of emerald green in the lamplight. "And finally," he concluded, "*for the record*, I don't give a damn what anyone else thinks about us. I only care what *we* think about us. What we make of this marriage. So how about we focus on that?"

Gia sucked in a breath.

He swept the pad of his thumb over the trembling line of her bottom lip. "What are you so scared of when it comes to us?" he murmured. "Because I think it has to do with more than this."

"Nothing," she muttered.

"Gia." His tone commanded an answer.

"We went from zero to a hundred in one night," she whispered, eyes on his. "I don't know how to handle it. How to put the pieces back together."

"So we slow it down. Learn each other all over again."

She stared at him as if she wasn't quite sure how to do that. He braced both of his palms on the window on either side of her. Shallow, fractured with anticipation, her breath sat frozen, trapped in her lungs as he lowered his head. Waited, his mouth just millimeters from hers until she made the first infinitesimal move—a tiny lift of her chin. Then he closed the almost imperceptible gap between them and claimed her mouth in a slow, gentle kiss.

Lazy, sensual, *magical*—it was so unlike Franco's impatient, rough caresses, it rocked her world. Wiped the memories clean from her head. She slid her fingers into his hair and kissed him back, a leisurely, mutual relearning of each other that affirmed everything they had once been. Real. *Right*.

Gauging her responses, reading the softening in her body, he took the kiss deeper. She tipped her head back, slid her fingers to his jaw and accepted his questing foray. The slow slide of his tongue against hers was stomach-clenchingly erotic. The remembrance of a taste once savored and never forgotten.

It filled the jagged, empty holes inside of her. Banished the loneliness she'd felt for so long.

Heat swept through her—surged to every inch of her skin. Slowly, seductively, he made love to her mouth until she melted beneath him, her limbs lax as she plastered herself against the glass.

Santo lifted his mouth from hers and took her in. Cheeks aflame with color, her breathing erratic, she watched as he dropped his gaze to the erect peaks of her breasts, which jutted through the silk of her dress. Her pulse beat an erratic edge as he splayed a warm palm against her rib cage. Slid his hand up over the smooth expanse of skin covered by the silk until he found the pebbled peak that throbbed for him. Eyes on hers, he rubbed his thumb over the distended surface. Stroked the need higher.

"Santo," she whispered, arching into his touch.

"You like that?"

"Yes."

He transferred his attention to the other hard peak. Stroked it to erectness. The hot stillness that floated in the air between them and the electric tension that seized her throat were almost unbearable.

"You are so beautiful," he rasped, his mouth trailing a path of fire down her throat. "You make me lose my head."

He hit the ultrasensitive spot at the base of her throat. She gasped and arched her neck to give him better access. He took full advantage, nuzzling and exploring until she flattened her palms against the windows and surrendered completely.

He slid a finger underneath the strap of her dress and slipped it off her shoulder, revealing a full, rose-tipped breast. Cool air slid over her heated skin as he weighted her in his palm. Her stomach clenched at the look of lust on his face. Right before he took her inside the heat of his mouth.

The sweet, all-encompassing rush of pleasure almost took her to her knees. He slid a muscled leg between her thighs and brought her closer. He was hot, hard and male, and it excited her beyond belief.

She moved against him. Whimpered. "Santo..."

He slid the other strap off her shoulder and flicked his tongue over her nipple. Gave her what her husky plea hadn't been able to verbalize. Desperate, aching for him, she pushed into his touch. Absorbed his heady torture. Almost cried out when he stepped away. But it was only to move behind her to undo the clasp of her dress.

It hit the floor in a whisper of silk. She tensed then,

exposed to his gaze, because not even the heat pulsing between them was enough to wipe away the cruel taunts Franco had tossed at her when the tension between them had risen to a fever pitch. When she had failed to live up to his expectations on every level.

Ice-cold and not worth the effort.

Santo's fingers tightened around her waist. "Forget about him," he growled, pressing a hot, open-mouthed kiss to the delicate skin of her neck. She melted at the hedonistic touch. At the sensual kisses he pressed against her back as he worked his way down her spine. As desperate and urgent as the last time between them had been, this time was slow and achingly sensual. He lit her up with those skillful hands of his. Made her achingly aware of every centimeter of flesh she possessed as he trailed a path of fire over the rounded curve of her bottom.

She lifted a foot for him as he divested her of a sexy, high shoe. Pressed a kiss to the delicate arch of her foot that made her toes curl. Then he reached for the other shoe and stripped her of that, too.

Heat shimmered through her insides as he turned her around with firm hands on her hips. On his knees, every magnificent, muscled inch of him at her disposal, she thought her heart might crash through her chest. Naked, except for the flimsy panties she had on, she should have felt self-conscious, as lacking as Franco had painted her as. Instead, all she could see was the desire in Santo's eyes. The electric connection they shared.

He cupped the back of her knee. Slid a palm up the soft skin of her thigh to the rounded curve of her buttock. Eyes on hers, he traced the smooth edge of her panties. Absorbed the shiver of reaction that chased through her. "I want to take these off," he murmured. "Can I?"

She nodded, a barely perceptible movement of her head

because she couldn't breathe. He hooked his fingers into either side of the flimsy piece of silk, and stripped it off. Hands on his shoulders, her fingertips curling into hard, bunched-up muscle, she stepped out of them. He tossed the filmy material aside, then brought her closer.

"Santo," she murmured unsteadily as he pressed a kiss to the soft flesh of her upper thigh, "what are you doing?"

"Slowing things down," he said huskily. "All you have to do is relax and enjoy it."

She was not *relaxed*. She was ready to jump out of her skin because he hadn't done *this* that night. But she was also insanely turned on, her body hot and liquid as she reached for the window frame behind her and clutched it with both hands. Widening her stance with an insistent push of his palm against her thigh, she watched as Santo set his gaze on her most intimate flesh, as he parted her with gentle fingers and set his mouth to her.

Her body clenched hard at the first slide of his tongue against her silken warmth. Reverential, decadent, it washed over her in the most exquisite wave of pleasure she'd ever felt. Her legs shuddered beneath her, threatened to give way. Cupping her knee in his palm, Santo urged her leg over his shoulder and her fingers into his hair. And then, there was only the way he devoured her, *savored* her, in the most erotic, intimate way possible.

Oh, my God. She almost moaned with relief when he picked her up and carried her to the bed. But the torture didn't end there. He followed her down, spread her thighs wide and sought out her slick warmth with his fingers.

Talented, skillful, his deliberate strokes made her crazy. She arched her hips and moaned his name. He added a second finger, the sensation of fullness so exquisitely good it made her gasp out loud.

"Santo. Please—"

He bent to kiss her, his mouth against hers as his thumb massaged the tight bundle of nerves at the center of her. "Let go," he murmured. "Come for me, Gia."

She arched her hips to take him deep as his devastating caresses unleashed a hot, shimmering pleasure that radiated out from her core. Stroking her with those amazing hands, he drew it out, wringing every last ounce of pleasure from her until she collapsed on the bed, her orgasm all-consuming and never-ending.

When she finally emerged from the haze of pleasure, she found Santo sitting back on his knees, watching her with hot, dark eyes. A wave of heat suffused her cheeks at how completely she'd let go. How utterly abandoned she'd been.

She slicked her tongue over desperately dry lips. Averted her gaze. Only to find her attention captured by the erection pushing against the zipper of his jeans.

"You going to do something about that?" he murmured.

Had they not just shared what they'd just shared, had they not bared everything to each other on that stormy night four years ago, she might have been frozen right there. Instead, her head filled with images of what he looked like— hot, hard and silky smooth. *Heavenly.* And the temptation was irresistible.

She pushed herself into a sitting position. Went up on her knees in front of him. Lip caught between her teeth, she ran her fingers over the hard bulge under the denim that covered him. Explored the rigid length of him from top to bottom.

He hissed in a breath. "Maybe this was a bad idea," he murmured. But he let her play. Slide his zipper down, draw him out and find him with her hands. Velvety soft, he was sleek power over steel. Stomach curlingly masculine.

His breath grew deeper as she caressed him, the taut muscles of his abs convulsing as she ran her fingers over him with a firmer touch. A rough sound leaving his throat, he pulled her hands from him, rolled off the bed and shucked the rest of his clothing, until he stood, in the flesh, exactly as she remembered him—a perfect canvas of lean muscle that was breathtaking in its perfection.

But it was the possessive look in his eyes that scorched through her. The *way* he looked at her. As if she was something special to him.

It warmed her from the inside out as he joined her on the bed, scooped her up with one arm and brought her down on top of him, cradling her against his chest. The long, languid kiss he stole melted her insides. Annihilated the last of her defenses. "I want to be inside of you," he murmured.

His arousal, thick and ridged, jutted against her abdomen. The scent of their lust was heavy and humid in the air, a seductive, hedonistic mix that drove everything from her head but the need to have him. She raised herself up, her palms on his rock-hard chest, captured him in her hands and, slowly, carefully, lowered herself onto him.

Thick and powerful, he filled her like nothing else had. She drew in a deep breath as she absorbed the shock of his all-consuming possession. The first time between them there had been a fleeting moment of pain, before there had been pleasure. This time, it was all pleasure. Buried deep inside of her, she could feel the pulse of his heartbeat, a carnal kiss that echoed deep in her soul.

His velvet dark eyes anchored her in the moment. "You destroy me," he murmured. "Every single damn time, Gia."

Her heart pulsed at the admission. At the look of raw, uncensored emotion on his face. It did something to her to know that he wanted her this much. That he *felt* as much as she did. Healed a broken part of her she hadn't been sure would ever mend after Franco.

"Gia," he rasped, his voice a rough caress. "I need you to move, *cara. Now.*"

Emboldened by what they shared, by the want written across his face, she leaned forward, pushed his hands over his head and locked her fingers with his. Then she started to move, each stroke of his body inside of her raking across her nerve endings.

He let her take control. She lifted herself off him, then took him back inside of her, wriggling her hips as she adjusted to his potent possession. A dark flush of color stained his cheekbones as she drew out the moment. Took him harder and deeper with every stroke until they were both gasping at the pure sensation of it.

He freed his hands. She let him, because she wanted him to take control. To give her that pleasure she knew was waiting for her. He cupped her bottom in his palms and angled her so that the tip of his erection rubbed against a tender, aching spot inside of her. She threw her head back and moaned, each skillful, deliberate thrust he administered stealing her breath. Nudging her closer to the edge.

"Santo—"

His hands bit into her flesh as he throbbed and thickened inside of her. Brought her down to meet his punishing lunges. Told her in a guttural voice how good she felt. How perfectly she took him. How much he wanted her.

Her heart thundered at the magnificence of him. His chest heaving with the force of his breath, perspiration dotting the hard planes of his face, his body radiating a blanket of heat, he was as far gone as she was.

Her release began deep in her core, sweeping through her, tightening her muscles around him. Santo captured her by the nape, his fingers biting into her flesh as he watched her shatter around him. It was the most erotic, intimate experience of her life. Terrifying in its intensity.

She lowered her head to his, fused their mouths together and rode him to his climax.

Santo lay awake, Gia curled against his chest, her silky blond hair spilling across his shoulder as a sliver of moonlight filtered through the room. His head too full to sleep, too many emotions chasing through his chest to settle, he stroked a palm down the satiny soft skin of her back. Over the delectable curve of her bottom.

She had taken him apart tonight. Dismantled him with her truths. It illuminated so much about her, made sense of so many of the puzzle pieces he'd held, but couldn't seem to reconstruct. Why she hid behind those impenetrable walls of hers. Why she had walked away from them four years ago. Because she'd been taught that trust was an illusion. That the only person she could trust was herself. So she'd taken her son and ran.

Which hadn't been helped by her marriage to Lombardi if her reactions tonight were anything to go by, he concluded grimly. A place he wasn't about to let himself go, because it made him want to hit something.

He captured a lock of her hair in his fingers, rather than address the knot in his chest. Watched the moonlight play across its golden strands. The intensity of what they'd shared together replayed itself in his head. The *singularity* of it. Her particular combination of vulnerability and strength had always touched something deep inside of him. The loneliness that had always emanated from her. The sense that it was Gia against the world. Maybe because it mirrored a piece of himself.

That was why it had been so intense. It had been his protective edge talking—the one he'd never been able to dismantle when it came to her. That was the only place he was ever going to allow his emotions to go, because letting himself feel the things he once had for Gia wasn't going to happen. Not when she'd already shattered him once. Not when Stefano Castiglione would no doubt waltz back into town when he was ready to take on Washington—a land mine he couldn't ignore. Not when Lazzero had been absolutely right.

His future was on the line with Elevate. His attention needed to be fully on the business, ensuring this launch went off without a hitch, because one misstep could bring it all tumbling down around them.

Which meant preserving this bond he and Gia had built—smoothing out the rough waters of his marriage was paramount. Which he now thought might actually be possible. He had finally gotten inside her head. He was starting to understand what made his wife tick. Which was half the battle.

He could work with that.

CHAPTER SEVEN

GIA WOKE TO the bright light of another gorgeous, sunny New York day streaming through the floor-to-ceiling windows of the penthouse. It was not, she recognized with a start, the guest bedroom she had been sleeping in with Leo. It was the master bedroom. *She was in Santo's bed.* And *they* had just spent a steamy, passionate night together.

Eyes widening at the height of the sun, she threw off the sheets, ready to dash out of bed and confront disaster with a Leo gone wild, then remembered it was Saturday, and he was already up. Somewhere in the early hours, Santo had murmured to her to sleep and had taken her son down for breakfast.

The apartment, however, was silent, bathed in a hushed, luxurious glow as the city bustled to life below. She collapsed back against the pillows, her pulse settling with the knowledge her son wasn't sailing down the circular banister like a real *supahero*.

She felt vulnerable, turned inside out after what she and Santo had shared. Full of emotions she didn't know how to process. The last time she'd felt like this, she'd run. She'd thrown away everything she and Santo had shared. Which had been a total disaster.

This time, however, she couldn't run. She had committed to this new life she was building with him. To making this marriage work. Which left her to wonder what it was, exactly, that she'd walked away from.

It might have been complicated, but I thought it was worth it.

She dug her teeth into her lip. Had she walked away

from something amazing between her and Santo? Had she let her fears and insecurities destroy something that could have been everything she'd ever envisioned?

Her chest clenched into a fist. Secretly, desperately, in a part of her she'd refused to reveal, she'd wanted to be that girl on his arm. The one in the center of all that golden light. It had hurt to watch him move from one woman to the next, knowing she would never be the one. The one he chose, because she was who she was.

Had all of her assumptions been wrong?

She had thrown her worst at him last night. All of her secrets. Santo, however, had not flinched. Hadn't blinked. Had acted as if none of it had mattered. But what would happen when the news of his marriage to her became public knowledge? When she became that liability Lazzero had predicted? Because that part of what he'd said had been undeniably true.

Would Santo regret his decision then? It was hard to have faith he wouldn't, when every good thing she'd ever had in her life, every friendship, every fledgling bond she'd forged, had eventually been destroyed because of who and what she was. Could her relationship with Santo be any different?

Her thoughts were interrupted by the sound of voices, followed by an explosion of tiny limbs as her son launched himself into the bedroom and onto the bed. "Mamma," he cried, throwing his chubby arms around her. "We bought *bugels*."

"Bagels," Santo corrected, strolling in behind her son, a coffee from her favorite bakery and a brown bag in his hands. "Of which your son had two, by the way. He clearly likes to eat as much as I do."

Which did not show on his lean, sculpted body, *at all*. Gia's pulse did a ridiculous jump at the sight of her husband in a baseball T-shirt and another pair of those dark denim jeans that hugged every delectable inch of him.

"Sleepyhead," Leo chastised, ruffling her hair. "Mamma tired?"

Santo's gaze met hers over her son's head, a dark glitter of amusement lighting its midnight depths. "Mamma had a busy night. She needed the sleep."

"Santo," she breathed, giving him a you-need-to-filter look.

"What?" Her husband deposited the items in his hands on the bedside table, braced a hand on the headboard and bent his head to hers to press a long, lingering kiss against her lips. "You were...*busy*."

Leo watched the whole thing with a huge smile on his face. "And if he repeats that to someone else?" she challenged.

"He will forget about it in about sixty seconds," her husband drawled. "His attention span is that of a gnat. He was a menace in New York traffic."

Her heart skipped a beat. "Relax," Santo murmured. "I had him glued to my side the entire time."

Leo tugged on his T-shirt. "Look," he said proudly. "They're the same."

She took in the T-shirt her son was wearing. It was an exact replica of the one her husband had on, albeit a third of the size. It did something strange to her heart to see the two of them dressed alike, the same, unmistakable blond cowlick rendering them equally handsome.

"You went shopping?" she asked.

Santo lifted a shoulder. "He saw the T-shirt in a window. It was a Supersonic design. Also," he added with satisfaction, "establishing the right loyalties is something that needs to start young. We had a conversation about Joe DiMaggio on the way back. Although," he conceded,

"I was doing the most of the conversing. Leo was chasing a butterfly."

The lump in her throat grew to the size of Manhattan. Santo's gaze darkened as he read the emotion on her face. "You do, however," he murmured, tracing a thumb along the edge of her jaw, "have to get up. We have things to do."

She frowned. Snagged the coffee from the dresser. "It's Saturday," she said, taking a sip. "What do we have to do?"

"We're going house shopping. My agent gave me a call this morning. There's a property in Southampton that just came on the market. Ocean front. Amazing views. It won't last the day."

Southampton. It was one of her favorite places on earth, with its ethereal views and windswept beaches. *Heaven*. To buy a house there was her dream.

"Ocean," Leo echoed happily. "We need shovels."

Southampton, situated on the south-eastern end of Long Island's South Fork, had been home to famous family dynasties for over a decade. Its rugged beauty had attracted some of the great industry titans, New York's most influential financiers, as well as a who's who of the Manhattan social circuit. Alight with glamour in the height of the summer, the village was buzzing with flashy cars and designer outfits.

The house the agent showed them lived up to its billing. Located just a short walk from the village's trendy Main Street, with its high-end galleries, restaurants and shops, it sat at the end of a wide, tree-lined street, directly on the beach. A magnificent, traditional colonial-style Hamptons home, it had five bedrooms and a wraparound porch that offered up the most spectacular sunset views.

Gia adored its rugged ocean ambience, high-vaulted ceilings and massive fireplaces. It felt like a home even though it was clearly a showpiece, and it gave her a taste of the serenity she'd had in the Bahamas. Santo loved the beautifully manicured tennis courts, the expansive bluestone patios and the waterside gunite pool. Leo, as predicted, tripped over himself gushing excitedly about the ocean and the boats.

"You love it," Santo observed, as they stood side by side on the terrace drinking in the view while the real estate agent showed Leo the beach.

"*You* love it," she countered. "You are drooling over those tennis courts."

"And the running trail along the water. It would be incredible in the morning. You would enjoy the view while I annihilate you."

The thought of running here in the morning with him, like they'd used to, exchanging the confidences they'd had, squeezed something tight in her chest. "You mean while *I* annihilate *you*."

"As I recall," he murmured, "you only did that once. And it was because I had a leg cramp."

Which was true. She hated that. But she did love the house.

They bought it, on the spot. Leo, thoroughly overexcited by the whole adventure, was drooping by the time they walked through the door that evening, having missed his afternoon nap. Santo carried him upstairs to his bedroom and set him down on the bed to change him into his pajamas, while Gia went on a search of his blue blanket.

"Want my bed," Leo pronounced as he lifted his arms for Santo to slide off his T-shirt.

"You are almost there," said Santo, slipping off the T-shirt. "*Supaheroes* need their suit, you know."

Leo's bottom lip quavered. "Want *my* bed."

Gia paused in her search for the blanket. She'd known

this was coming—the moment when her son's new reality began to sink in. When he began to realize the big adventure was a permanent thing. When he started to miss everything that was familiar to him. But the desolate look on his face made her heart plummet to the floor.

"We live here now," Santo said gently. "Remember that blue room you saw today? It's going to be yours. We'll make it into a *supahero* hideout."

Leo shook his head. "Want *my* room. *Friends*. Want to go *home*."

Santo tried to comfort his son, but Leo was too overtired and too overwhelmed to see straight. A tear slid down his cheek, and he kicked his hands and feet, refusing to let Santo slide on his pajama bottoms. Gia scooped the blanket off the floor and moved swiftly to intercept, but it was too late. In the blink of an eye, her son descended into a full-scale meltdown, pummeling his fists against Santo's chest and demanding to go home.

She took Leo from her shell-shocked husband. Leo clutched his blanket, his sobs of "Mamma" dampening the fabric of her T-shirt. She sat down and pressed him to her chest, holding him tight.

"Leave him with me," she murmured to Santo. "It's been a big day."

Santo made himself an espresso in the kitchen, intent on returning a couple of urgent emails. The deadlines were piling up with the massive launch he had in front of him, so Saturday was no obstacle to the work that had to get done. But he was so thoroughly shaken by his son's temper tantrum, by the transformation of his earlier, sunny demeanor into the frightened, miserable boy upstairs, by his inability to comfort him, he was utterly distracted.

It sent him back to the day his own world had been

pulled from beneath his feet. He'd been thirteen. His father barely *compos mentis* in the wake of the collapse of his life, his mother gone in its dissolute aftermath. He'd spent the next week wondering which bike to take with him to the tiny apartment they'd rented above the hardware store where Nico had gotten a job, while attempting to process the fact that his mother was gone for good this time.

Walking into that dingy apartment for the first time had shocked him. Unnerved him. Everything had felt foreign to him—the neighborhood, with its gritty, boarded-up feel, the cramped, two-bedroom space he and his family had crammed themselves into. There'd be no defense against his father's first bender in their new, so-called home that night. The buffer of his mother's protection, her only nod to a maternal instinct, was gone for good. His new reality a shock to the system.

He'd had a massive temper tantrum that first night, unable to cope with all the changes. At having to share a bedroom with Lazzero. At becoming a part-time caregiver to his father, an experience he'd found terrifying with the shell of a man his father had become. At the train he would now have to take to school. Before Nico had put a halt to it with a grim command to "suck it up" because they were going to make this work.

And maybe, he recalled, his insides shifting, that was what had frightened him the most. How his eldest brother, strong, stoic Nico, had looked as lost and displaced as he had.

His brothers had been consumed by their own internal battles. The bonds between them back then had been all about survival. The difference for Leo, he determined, drawing in a deep breath, was that his son would never grow up in an emotional vacuum. He would have all of the love and support Santo had never had. The rock-solid stability of his world going forward.

He leaned back in his chair, coffee cup in hand, eyes on the skyline spread out in front of his office window. He'd been so focused on doing what he thought was right, what he thought was best for his son, he hadn't fully considered the impact it would have on him. But clearly, he conceded, the knot inside of him twisting tighter, he should have considered it. Because hadn't he done to Leo exactly what had been done to him? Pulled his world out from beneath his feet? Stripped him of everything that was familiar to him?

Except Gia. His head went back to how trustingly his son had curled into her. She was his world. The constant in his life. She made all the difference.

What he needed to do, he concluded, was stay the course. Keep the promises he'd made.

Gia padded into his office a short while later and perched herself on the corner of his desk. He looked up from the report he'd been studying. "How is he?"

"He's asleep." Her mouth softened. "The last couple of weeks have been a lot for his little brain to absorb. He has one of those meltdowns every once in a blue moon."

Santo's stomach coiled. He never wanted to see his son like that again. *Ever.*

"He's fine," she murmured, lifting a hand to brush against his cheek. "What," she queried, a wry note in her voice, "is going on in that head of yours? You're in another world."

He pushed aside the complex ball of emotion winding his insides tight. Moved his gaze over her in an effort to distract, finding himself more than occupied by the white cotton T-shirt she had on with cherry-red shorts that barely skimmed her thighs.

She flushed under the heat of his gaze. "I wasn't talking about that."

"I am." He pulled her onto his lap with a tug of his fingers around the slim curve of her wrist. He acknowledged why no other woman had ever been enough for him as he absorbed the flare of fire in her beautiful eyes, the voluptuous perfection of her body that fit so easily in his arms. Because none of them had ever been *her*.

Rather than consider that discomforting thought, he slid his fingers up to her nape and brought her mouth down to his for a kiss that soothed the ache inside of him.

Gia spent the next couple of weeks taking care of the details on the Southampton house, working on a design for the breezy, contemporary great room she'd envisioned. It kept her busy while Santo worked like a mad man getting ready for his big launch, gone by six every morning, home just in time to have dinner with them and put Leo to bed.

Which meant the only real time she had with him were the nights. Stomach-clenchingly hot affairs in which they couldn't seem to get enough of each other. As if once unleashed, their hunger was unquenchable. Which wasn't helping with her vow to keep her feelings for him on an even keel.

He might have said he'd thought they'd been worth it, but that had been then and this was now. Even if he did learn to forgive her for what she'd done, she would be a fool to think he'd ever let himself feel the way he once had about her.

Distraction seemed preferable. Particularly when the Met Young Patrons party lay ahead. It was one of the city's most prestigious events, thrown every summer to fund its annual initiatives, and would mark her debut as Santo's wife. Her reintroduction to Manhattan society. It was like being thrown to the wolves all over again. But since Chloe, one of the museum's largest donors in her role as chairwoman of Evolution, was patroness of the event, skipping it was not a possibility.

It wasn't until the afternoon of the party that she discovered her dress for the event had somehow acquired a stain on the front of it. Clearly, her efforts at distraction had been a little *too* successful.

She hadn't done any socializing in Nassau. Her wardrobe was limited. And since she couldn't just pull something out of her closet in the hopes that it would work, Chiara, thank goodness, came to the rescue. Not only did she have impeccable, trendy fashion sense, but she also had a curvy figure just like Gia's.

With Leo safely installed with Chloe's nanny, Anna, for a sleepover with his cousin Jack, she and Chiara went to a tiny boutique owned by a friend of Chiara's on West Broadway. Her sister-in-law made it clear she didn't need to pick one of her own designs, but Gia immediately fell in love with a sultry, bohemian number from her collection. A rich shade of cream, its twisted neckline was done in a halter style, her favorite, with the front plunging to a wrap waist.

Dress in hand, she set off for the quirky, luxe fitting rooms to try it on. She presented herself for Chiara's inspection, taking in her reflection in the large horizontal mirrors in the lounge. "Is it too much?"

Chiara inspected her from top to bottom, a slow smile curving her lips. "It's just enough. The color is amazing with your skin."

"But this," Gia said, gesturing to the expanse of skin the keyhole effect bared, including the tiniest hint of the swell of her breasts. "I can't wear anything underneath it."

"That would be the point." Chiara's dark eyes sparkled. "It's sexy without being overt. Perfect. Santo will be picking his jaw up off the ground. *Trust me.*"

She did trust Chiara. Although she wasn't at all sure what she wanted Santo's reaction to be anymore. Her head was too muddled. So she bought the dress instead.

Now, if she could only get rid of her raging nerves about the night ahead.

The Met Young Patrons party was hosted at The Cloisters, one of New York's hidden gems. The replica medieval monastery in Upper Manhattan, which housed the museum's superb collection of medieval art and architecture, was spectacular, harkening back to a different age.

Built in the 1930s by the American oil magnate John D. Rockefeller, to showcase the large collection of medieval art he'd recently acquired, then gifted to the Met, the Cloisters sat in a picturesque setting overlooking the Hudson River. All of the guests agreed it was worth the forty-minute trip from the center of the city as they made their way up the red carpet to the top of the steps, greeted by waiters carrying trays of champagne.

The main hall, where the cocktail hour was being held, was bathed in purple and pink light projections that cast the ancient artwork and stained glass windows in a luminous glow. For Gia, the dark atmosphere fit the tone of the night. Everyone who was anyone in Manhattan was in attendance tonight.

Some of the faces were familiar, some had changed. What hadn't evolved was Manhattan's predilection for gossip—the eternal, inexorable fuel it operated on. Santo was too high-profile a personality for there not to be talk about his sudden change in marital status. Which, of course, unearthed the subject of who she was and all the salacious gossip that surrounded her father.

It was the evening's tasty tidbit. She could see it in the sideways looks thrown her way. Hear it in the sly questions disguised as social niceties. She would have had to have been deaf, dumb and blind not to notice it. The difference from every other occasion in which she'd endured such speculation was that tonight, she had Santo by her side.

Lethally attractive in a silver-grey suit and a dark blue shirt, he curled his fingers around hers, his hawklike gaze never leaving her as they made the rounds of the affluent crowd. Which was helpful as they came face-to-face with a particularly notorious clique of women she'd known from school.

The three organizers of the evening had frozen her out in the past and they did so again tonight. A knot formed in her stomach as they fawned all over Chloe and Chiara, inviting them to join the committee they were chairing for the Central Park Conservatory, while ignoring her completely.

Her smile faltered, her carefully constructed exterior giving way beneath one too many knocks. Santo closed his fingers tighter around hers and murmured in her ear, "Tougher and stronger, remember?"

The low prompt took her back to another place and time. To the afternoon she'd found out that her father had strong-armed her coach into giving her a position on the track team at school. But she hadn't known that part.

It had been the best day of her life as she'd walked off the field confident in her win, cheeks flushed with victory, only to overhear two of the other girls talking about her father in the tunnel on the way to the locker rooms. How *unfair* it was.

She'd turned and walked in the opposite direction, tears burning her eyes. She'd thought she'd earned it. That, for once in her life, she hadn't been defined by who she was—she'd been judged by her performance on the field instead. Which had once again turned out to be an illusion, like everything else.

Santo, on the field for his football practice, had taken one look at her face and walked away from his scrimmage, which had nearly gotten him booted off the team. But instead of giving her the sympathy she'd expected, he'd shaken his head instead and told her that quitting wasn't an option. That she needed to be "tougher, stronger than all the rest. Prove herself better," because that was the only thing that would put the naysayers to rest.

So she had. She'd turned the other cheek. Trained harder, longer than all the rest. And recorded the fastest time for a female runner that year in the city championships.

She pushed her shoulders back as they moved on through the crowd. Lifted her chin. He was right. She was better than this. Stronger than this. She would not let them get to her.

Chiara, resplendent in a midnight blue beaded dress of her own creation and Chloe, elegant in white, ankle-length Roberto Cavalli, soon stole her away for a gossip as they enjoyed the atmospheric artwork. Gradually, enveloped by the warmth of the other two women, her stomach began to unfurl. She'd never had allies. *Friends*. Women who would look out for her, other than Delilah. A *family* who would protect her. And now she clearly did.

Santo leaned a hip against the bar, keeping one eye on Gia while he caught up with Lazzero after his brother's trip to Europe. The most beautiful women in New York were in the room tonight, but none of them made his pulse accelerate like his wife did in the knee-length cream dress that plunged nearly to the waist. She had the most jaw-dropping legs he'd ever seen. Followed by every other part of her anatomy that had held him spellbound for weeks, with no sign of that particular affliction waning.

She had handled all the gossip tonight with a quiet dignity he was coming to expect from her. With that iron spine she'd acquired. She might be thrown, but she was holding her own. Glittering like the brightest jewel in the night. It was a sexy, empowering transformation he couldn't take his eyes off.

"Everything okay in paradise?"

He transferred his gaze to his brother. Ignored his mocking gibe just as he'd avoided every other conversation about his wife over the last couple of weeks, because then it would devolve into a debate about Stefano Castiglione and how he continued to dominate the headlines. Which was already enough of a distraction, quite frankly.

"Actually," he drawled, "it's perfect. Thanks for asking."

His personal life was exactly where he wanted it to be. He had a beautiful wife, an amazing sex life and a confident, happy son who made him smile at the end of every day. As close to perfection as it came.

"Good to hear." Lazzero tipped back a mouthful of Scotch. Pointed his glass at him. "I bumped into Gervasio Delgado in the airport in Madrid. We're having dinner with him on Saturday night."

Santo blinked. Gervasio Delgado, the Spanish retail czar, had reinvented the way fashion was delivered to the masses with his on-demand manufacturing model. He also commanded the world's most popular clothing store chain, Divertido.

He arched an eyebrow at his brother. "Delgado is a notorious introvert. How did you manage that?"

His brother shrugged. "He asked me what we were up to. I told him about Elevate. His curiosity was piqued."

Santo's blood fizzled at the possibilities. "You think there's potential there?"

"He needs a shoe for the first wave of his spring campaign. It could be a massive win for us."

He got why Lazzero was tempering his enthusiasm. Gervasio Delgado was a passionate, creative personality whose whims changed with the wind. It could turn out to be nothing. Or everything.

"Delgado is bringing his wife," Lazzero continued. "Chiara almost fell off her chair when I told her who we're having dinner with. Which could be a problem," he observed, a wry note in his voice. "I might have to muzzle her. Gia, on the other hand, could be an asset. Delgado mentioned Alicia, his wife, is remodeling their house in Marbella. They can talk shop."

Which was perfect. His wife was a brilliant designer, the sketches she was putting together for the house in the Hamptons fantastic. She would be the perfect complement to Alicia Delgado. But right now, he allowed, all he wanted to do was take her home, strip that dress off her and avail himself of every inch of her beautiful body.

Dinner was served alfresco in the Cuxa Cloister Garden. It was a spectacular setting, mirrored banquets set alongside rose-pink marble columns, the candlelight flickering in the night as black-coated servers flitted here and there in an effort to get everything just right. By the time the elegant, sumptuous dinner had been served and Gia had consumed a couple of glasses of the delicious sparkling wine that accompanied it, she was feeling a bit light-headed.

Maybe it was the way Santo kept finding excuses to touch her. The hand he kept on her thigh throughout dinner, his warm palm burning a seductive brand into her skin. The looks he kept throwing her in between conversations. It was impossible to ignore the electricity that ran between them.

They moved back inside to enjoy the musical entertainment in the moody, spectacular Fuentidueña Chapel.

Reconstructed from pieces of a Romanesque-era Spanish church, the lights of the chapel had been lowered to a mysterious blue to focus attention on the magnificent dome and its beautiful Byzantine frescoes.

"I think," Santo murmured, catching her hand in his, "we should dance."

She couldn't actually find any reason to object, except the thought of it made her palms go damp and her knees weak. In the dark blue shirt that stretched across the rippling muscle of his shoulders, his jacket somehow having been lost along the way, *he* was the thing stretching her nerves over tenterhooks. Which wasn't a reason she could actually verbalize, so she followed him to the packed dance floor instead.

They had almost made it there when they were intercepted by the stunningly beautiful Abigail Wright and her big, wide-shouldered, square-jawed quarterback, Carl O'Brien. A tawny-haired Southern belle with a heart-shaped face and sparkling blue eyes, Abigail was, quite literally, perfection. Her sexy drawl when she greeted Santo only added to her devastating charm.

"Good news travels fast," Abigail murmured, with a wounded look in her eyes she almost, but not quite, smothered. "Your PR team reached out to me last week to emcee the event in Munich," she informed Santo. "I almost couldn't believe my ears when they told me the news. Congratulations."

Santo kissed her on both cheeks. "Thank you. And thank you for agreeing to do the event on such short notice. A conflict in schedules. I know they appreciate it. And you will be amazing. Carl," he said, turning to greet the quarterback, "good to see you. When are you going to come over from the dark side and join us?"

The quarterback, who was extremely handsome in a

rough, rugged kind of way, gave a lazy shrug of his shoulder. "My contract is up next month. We were just about to renegotiate. I might be persuaded to switch if the offer is right."

Santo's eyes glittered with opportunity. "Good to know. We will talk."

They chatted about the youth leadership conference Supersonic was sponsoring in Munich in several weeks, the event Santo's PR team had asked Abigail to emcee, at which Santo was also apparently speaking. Which unearthed a curl of jealousy in Gia. He and Abigail would be in Germany together. Sharing a luxury hotel, no doubt. Perhaps an intimate dinner together?

The claws of jealousy sank deep. Abigail asked all the right questions about the event. It was the platform she'd built her winning state title on, after all—the future of today's youth as the driving force of global change. It was impressive. *She* was impressive.

Gia wanted to hate her, but found that she couldn't. Abigail was clearly a serious and passionate supporter of the cause she'd chosen to embrace. She would have been the perfect wife for Santo. They would have been the ultimate power couple. Taken Manhattan by storm. *Abigail* would not have been causing waves by her mere presence at Santo's side.

Her stomach sank to the floor. She tried to push aside her thoughts as the conversation ended and Santo led her onto the dance floor.

Santo, ever perceptive, tipped up her chin with his fingers. "What's wrong?"

"Nothing."

His mouth curved at the lone word, imbued with far more emotion than she'd intended. "You're jealous."

"She would have been the perfect wife for you, Santo."

"Perhaps on paper," he conceded. "She is beautiful, talented and smart. She ticks all the boxes. But there was something missing."

"Which was?" It felt dangerous to ask the question. To expose more of herself to him. To find out what the breach in perfection had been, but she couldn't resist the need to know.

"Fire," he murmured, eyes on hers, "spark. Although," he added huskily, "I *like* that you are jealous, *cara*. That you *care*. It shows that you are invested in this relationship. That I am not the only one intent on making this work."

There was no hint of amusement in his gaze now, only a quiet message that the next step was hers as he tightened his fingers around hers and drew her close. She was terrified to let him in. Scared she was halfway to falling in love with him again. That maybe, she'd never stopped.

His palm spread against the small of her back to keep her from bumping into the other dancers in the packed space. They were close, his hard-packed body brushing against hers so she could feel every muscle and tendon of his powerful thighs pressed against hers. The faint abrasion of his stubble against her cheek.

Her pulse quickened as he slid a hand into her hair and tilted her face up to his. She felt the warm caress of his breath right before he claimed her mouth in a slow, deep kiss that was perfection. Everything faded to the background—the music, the other dancers, the spectacular setting—and each languorous slide of his mouth over hers pulled her deeper into the abyss.

She melted into him. Felt the thick, hard length of his arousal pressing against her thigh.

Her eyes flew open. Santo lifted his head to look at her, the potent sensual awareness that had been building between them all night exploding into flames that licked at his velvet, dark eyes.

"We are leaving."

They sought out the other Di Fiores to say good-night. Gia made a quick trip to the powder room while Santo filled in Lazzero on the opportunity with Carl O'Brien. She had repaired her lipstick and powdered her nose and was on her way through the main hall, walking toward the exit to meet Santo, when a voice hailed her from behind.

She turned to find Nina Ferrone, a hotelier who owned several boutique properties in the city, bearing down on her like the dynamic force of nature that she was. A sophisticated blonde in her early fifties, she was covered from head to toe in designer couture.

"I'm so glad I caught you." Nina brushed a brisk kiss to both of her cheeks. "I saw you earlier, but I couldn't get across the room. You know how these things are."

She introduced her daughter, who'd accompanied her to the event, then got straight to business. "Delilah mentioned you were back in New York. I need some help freshening up The Billiards Room on the Upper East Side. Delilah mentioned you'd done the work on the Rothchild Nassau I loved. Would you be interested in doing the work on The Billiards Room for me?"

Gia's heart jumped. The Billiards Room was one of Manhattan's funkiest, most exclusive hotels. It had a fantastic Regency vibe to it that transported you back to another time and place, complete with a gorgeous, hand-carved wood library Nina had brought over from England. She had always loved the place. But New York was New York and Nina would likely want the work done yesterday.

She swallowed back a pang of regret. "I don't think I can

do it. My son, Leo, is only three. He takes priority. I had a very flexible work schedule with Delilah."

"She mentioned that." Nina shrugged a shoulder. "It isn't a job I can give to just anyone. It has to be the right fit. Delilah says your work is flawless. I'm happy to be flexible with your schedule, my only stipulation being," she qualified, "that the work needs to be done by the spring. I can't miss the summer season."

Gia's pulse quickened. That would give her plenty of time to do it if she had the right team. Which Nina assured her she would.

Excitement began to build. Chloe had mentioned a friend who had an excellent nanny who would soon be looking for work. If she could arrange the same sort of schedule she'd had in Nassau this could work. She would feel less like the disenfranchised version of herself she'd been these last few weeks, she could have her career back and still be there for Leo.

Nina handed over her card. They agreed to meet for lunch when the hotelier returned to town the following week, said their goodbyes, then Gia tucked her purse under her arm and headed off to meet Santo, her steps as light as air.

Maybe everything was going to come together in this new life of hers. Maybe it was going to be everything she'd never thought it could be.

They ended up dropping off Lazzero and Chiara on the way home, the two Di Fiore men immersed in a heated discussion about a number for Carl O'Brien in the car. Her exciting news percolating in her head, Gia had to wait until they were back at the penthouse before she could tell Santo. Alone in the private confines of their plush, luxurious dressing-room space, the tension that had been building all night between them swirled against an impressive backdrop of Manhattan.

Santo's fingers paused on the knot of his tie. "Why don't you come over here?" he murmured. "You're much too far away."

His eyes an intense, unfathomable black, she felt the look all the way to her toes. "I haven't told you my good news yet," she murmured, dangling a shoe from her finger. "I bumped into Nina Ferrone on the way out tonight. She needs someone to freshen up the decor at The Billiards Room on the Upper East Side. She wants me to do it."

Santo froze in midmovement. "When?"

"Next month," she said happily. "She's willing to be flexible with my work hours, too. The only caveat is that the job needs to be done by the spring, which shouldn't be a problem at all given the team I'd have."

He stripped off his tie and tossed it on a chair. "Why mess with a good thing?" he said casually. "Leo is doing great. Everything is good between us."

Something about the careful tone of his voice made her pause. "Because I love what I do," she said evenly. "Because this is the perfect opportunity to get my name out there. To have an influential client like Nina to get things jumpstarted for me in New York. It's an amazing opportunity."

"You don't need to get your name out there." He crossed his arms over his chest and leaned back against the dresser. "My wife doesn't need to work, Gia. Leo is just getting settled. He doesn't need any more changes to his routine right now. He needs all of you."

Heat singed her veins. She wasn't sure which inflamed her more. That he was questioning her priorities after she'd spent the last three years putting Leo first, or that he was sweeping her career under the rug, as if it was the insignificant entity it clearly was to him. Exactly as Franco had done.

She came crashing down from her high with a resounding thump. Tossed the shoe on the floor. "I am aware of that," she said tersely. "Leo's welfare has always been my priority, Santo, and always will be. Working and caring for him, however, are not mutually exclusive. I don't *need* to work. I *want* to work."

"So find yourself some smaller projects," he suggested calmly. "Go nuts with the house in Southampton. My boathouse in Maine needs an update. So does my office. Both are sorely overdue."

"I see," she said, bringing her back teeth together. "And when I'm done with that, perhaps I can start on your new walk-in closet? Figure out a better arrangement for those flashy suits of yours? Devise a more economical space solution for your expensive shoes?"

He shot her a warning look. "Gia—"

She reached down and undid the strap of her other shoe, fingers shaking with anger. She slid it off, picked up both shoes, stalked past him to the elegantly appointed footwear closet and tossed the sandals onto a shelf, missing with her aim, the shoes tumbling to the floor.

Santo shot out an arm and barred her exit, a set look on his face. "What is your problem?" he murmured, in a voice too deadly to be soft. "I am giving everything here, Gia. The new house, this marriage, the *patience* I am exhibiting with you. Is it too much to expect that you could be agreeable on this point?"

"Yes," she stormed, heat flaring her cheeks. "I had a life in Nassau, Santo. A dream. A career. I was *happy*. And now I am back in New York, where I don't want to be, I am married to you, which was also not my decision, and now you are trying to take away the one thing that gives my life meaning."

"I am not asking you to give up your career. I am asking you to take a *breather*. To take a step back from ramping things up until Leo is in school, at least. Then, you can arrange your schedule so that you're home when he's finished at the end of the day."

"It's funny," she observed, the anger fizzling her veins threatening to spill over. "The only one who seems to be compromising here is me. You and your impressive career trajectory remain untouched."

He gave a shrug of his shoulder. "I am a CEO. I run a multibillion-dollar company. I spend every moment I can with Leo. I'm with him every morning and night. I think this arrangement works perfectly for us."

"I'll bet you do." Her hands clenched into fists at her sides. "This is all suiting you, perfectly, Santo. But not me."

"Then how about you try focusing your attention on *me*?" he murmured. "Maybe that will distract you. Leo is three. He's waited long enough for a sibling. Maybe we should get on that."

Her breath caught in her chest. The heat that had been smoldering between them all evening smoked to life. He was so gorgeous in his beautiful suit and sky-blue shirt that molded to every powerful inch of him, it was almost impossible to keep her head on straight. "You don't distract me," she said, biting out the words. "You *irritate* me with your antiquated, chauvinistic, close-minded opinions, Santo. With your *dishonest*, bull-in-a-china-shop approach."

"I didn't lie to you," he countered. "I was clear about how I felt about Leo being in any type of care. If anything," he drawled, "it was a sin of omission."

A haze of red enveloped her, her nails digging hard into the soft skin of her palms. "And that night we stood here and I reinforced the fact that I wanted to work? And you said, 'of course,' to me?"

Not a flicker of self-recrimination on his hard-boned face. "I do think it's okay. Just not *now*."

She caught her breath at the hard glint in his eyes. The *deliberation*. He had married her knowing he was never going to let her work. Had done it with calculated precision so that once she was married to him, she would have no choice in the matter. Because who else in the city was going to hire her? Who, other than Nina, had the guts to do it?

He took a step closer. Ran a thumb down her cheek. "Come on, baby. You knew my feelings on this. Don't mess this up when we finally have something good. When I am too damn busy to think."

It was the last comment that did it. That his work was so important it obliterated her need to be happy. The red surging in her head consumed her brain. She took a step back. Picked up the first thing that came to hand, a bright red stiletto, and threw it at him. He caught it with those high-octane reflexes of his before it could make contact with the rock-hard muscle of his chest. But it felt so good, so satisfying, she did it again.

It still wasn't enough. Frustration and fear, *fury* consuming her in a mad red haze, she scooped up another shoe and took aim. And then another, until she had emptied a whole row. One sole shoe remaining, she clutched it with shaking hands. Santo gave her a hard look, a glitter in his dark, beautiful eyes that promised retribution. "One more shoe, Gia," he murmured. "*One. More. Shoe.* And all bets are off. Do it at your own peril."

A combination of fear and excitement clenched her stomach tight. Eyes pinned on his, her chest heaving, she took aim, aware of exactly what line she was crossing if she did it, and doing it, anyway.

He moved fast like a cat, like the superior athlete that he was, catching the shoe midstride before he tossed it aside, strode toward her and scooped her off her feet. Stalking through the dressing room, he walked into the bedroom and deposited her on the huge, king-sized bed. He came down over her, his powerful body caging hers.

"We will find a compromise," he insisted. "But there will be no more drama, Gia. Enough of the Mafia Princess act."

That made her want to claw his eyes out. She tried to summon the rational part of her brain that should still be working, but the only word her brain could focus on was the word *compromise*. He was willing to *compromise*.

And then he was tracing an erotic path down the line of her throat with that talented tongue of his, his hot, hard erection nudging against her thigh, and she lost the plot completely.

"You should move now if you don't want this," he warned, giving her ample time to put a stop to the insanity that had been building between them all evening. But she couldn't find the words. She had been imagining this all night. Craving it. *Anticipating it.*

He slid her dress up her thighs with a warm palm. Pushed aside the lace panties she wore and traced the slick flesh of her cleft with the pad of his thumb.

"You want me here?" he murmured.

She didn't want to want him, but she did. *Badly.* She arched her hips against his devastating caress that delved deeper with every stroke. Against the thumb he rotated against the tight nub at the heart of her. *"Yes."*

His breath left him on a harsh exhale. Her fingers found the buckle of his belt, the button of his pants. Freed his thick, rigid length. Lifting her hips, she took him deep in a single, powerful stroke that stole her breath.

Buried deep inside of her, she could feel the hard pulse of him, his erection as silken smooth and powerful as the rest of him. He was so deep, so big inside of her—he filled every part of her.

She sucked in a lungful of air. Attempted to find a foothold in the moment. But then, he set those hot, dark eyes on her and they stared at each other for a long, suspended moment, absorbing the power of what they shared. It was almost unnerving, the intensity of it. And then he started to move. One arm at her back, the other in her hair, it was breathtakingly deliberate, every stroke a languid promise, building with every powerful thrust.

Her gaze was riveted to his face. His beautiful features imprinted with lust, his eyes so dilated and dark they were almost black, he was as lost to the moment as she was.

He lowered his mouth to hers in a deep, slow kiss. Gia closed her eyes and gave in to the storm. Spurred on by the intense fullness inside of her, his undulating, devastating strokes, his bitten-out command for her to come for him, her orgasm swept through her, all-consuming and uncontrollable.

She shook in his arms. Santo drank her cries of completion. Clamped a hand around her thigh, lifted it around his waist and positioned her for his unfettered penetration, so that she caressed his shaft with every stroke. She met his thrusts with a ragged breath, aftershocks of pleasure exploding through her dazed body and soul.

He made her scream before he was done. Made her fall apart all over again. And this time, he came with her, too.

Gia emerged slowly from the ecstasy of surrender. Spent, shattered, she curled up on the soft, silky comforter and watched as Santo rolled off the bed and stripped off the beautiful suit with swift efficiency.

"That was—"

"Insane," he murmured.

Yes. That was the word for it. She sank her teeth into her lip as he shrugged off his shirt. "So, regarding this compromise... I'll have lunch with Nina next week and I'll find out more details about the work. Chloe says she knows an amazing nanny who's about to lose a full-time position, which is *gold* in New York. We can meet her and you can dec—"

Santo held up a hand. "I said *compromise.* Meaning we will find a solution to this problem that fits both of us, Gia. Which is not you working for Nina. That job will be manic. You will be on call all hours of the day. There will be no controlling it. What *I* am envisioning is that you start a small business where you can work from home. Take on small jobs, with the nanny here for Leo while you're working. That way, you can have the best of both worlds."

The best of both worlds? Her rosy glow evaporated in the millisecond it took him to crush it dead. She sat up on the bed and yanked her dress down over her hips. "And who is going to take me on?" she rasped. "Who, other than Nina, is going to have any interest in working with Stefano Castiglione's daughter? In *associating* themselves with me?"

"If they judge you by your last name," he countered blithely, "they aren't worth your time. You have talent, Gia. If Nina is willing to break ranks, so will others."

"And you saw how well that worked tonight," she observed, a bitter taste in her mouth. "I was top of my class in design school, Santo. It took my fellow students in the top tier one, maybe two tries to get a work placement. Do you know how many tries it took me?" She arched an eyebrow. "*Ten.* They were all terrified of my father. And that was *before* he ended up on the front of every newspaper in the country."

A stubborn look claimed his face. "Then maybe you should focus on family for the time being. It is impossible for two people in a relationship to have high-powered careers, Gia. It simply doesn't work. The children are always the ones to suffer. I won't have that for Leo."

He wouldn't have that? "And what about Nico and Chloe?" she challenged. "How are they making this *untenable* situation work?"

The closed look on his face intensified. "They are not *us*. That isn't what I want out of my marriage."

"No," she agreed, flattened by his implacability, "you want everything. You want me to fall in line with this grand plan of yours. With your vision of what this perfect marriage of ours should look like. You want me to have faith in *us*. And just when I'm beginning to do so, you go and prove you are no more trustworthy than any other man I've ever met, because you knew, *you knew* how important this was to me and you went ahead and did it anyway."

His ebony gaze went wintry and cold. "I did what I needed to do to secure my son. If there is a lack of trust in this relationship, Gia, that would be all on you. You started this with your inability to do the right thing."

She jerked her head back at that cold, verbal slap in the face, any ideas that he might actually have forgiven her gone up in a wisp of smoke. But that didn't mean she was going to let him run roughshod over her. That she would let him strip her of everything she'd fought so hard to become. That she was going to spend her days in another corrosive, unhappy marriage trying to keep him happy while she died a little inside every day, exactly as she had with Franco.

She scrambled off the bed. Recovered her physical and emotional feet. "I'm not interested in your compromise," she told him, chin held high. "When you decide you are serious about making this marriage work, when you are willing to give as much as you are demanding, when you are willing to show that you *care*, you know where to find me."

Frustration painted itself across his face. "Gia—"

She ignored him. Stalked into the dressing room and snatched up a nightie to sleep in before she abandoned ship for the spare room, everything that had seemed so bright and shiny and full of promise demolished in an unequivocal, emotional wreck.

CHAPTER EIGHT

SANTO EXITED THE meeting he'd been attending with his design team at Supersonic's Central Park West offices, secure in the knowledge that the manufacturing flaw they had uncovered in Elevate had been successfully ironed out without detriment to the shoe's design, and production was back on a smooth schedule.

Which was key, because in just a few weeks, the sneaker would be winging its way across the globe and into stores for its worldwide launch, supported by the massive marketing campaign the company had planned. Elevate would soon become the most talked-about running shoe on the planet and all the critics would be silenced.

His marriage, however, was not on that same upward trajectory. It festered like an open wound that wouldn't heal as he picked up the messages his assistant, Enid, handed him before she left for the day, and continued on into his office. Gone were the intimate family dinners that had come to represent the highlight of his day, replaced by short, curt affairs in which Gia chose to communicate with him only when spoken to directly.

Gone, also, were the long, hot nights, replaced by an ice-cold version of her as chilly as the cherry-flavored Popsicles she served Leo after dinner. She wasn't happy, that was clear. Nor was he. In fact, it was so far from the vision of the marriage he'd wanted for himself, it would have been laughable if it hadn't been so damn disconcerting, because he and Gia were at a stalemate and he could not see a way forward.

Never, in his experience, had he seen a high-powered

couple make a family work. Nico and Chloe were managing it, but that was the operative word. *Managing.* Even Nico labeled it the supreme juggling act that it was. Chloe had confessed she wanted to spend more time with Jack and had plans to scale back her focus to make that happen. Which only proved his point. So he'd proposed the optimal solution to Gia, only to have her turn it down flat. Which left them exactly nowhere, because she'd gone ahead and had her lunch with Nina instead.

Lazzero strolled into his office. Surveyed him with a long look. If he made one more comment about *paradise*, he fumed inwardly, he was going to take off his head. His brother, however, seemed to recognize his perilous mood and leaned a hip against the front of his desk instead.

"Carlos just called. We're being asked to give input on the trade deal. He wants reinforcements."

Santo rubbed a hand over his brow. He was knee-deep in orchestrating a one-hundred-million-dollar marketing campaign for Elevate. He was having lunch with the best soccer player in the world on Wednesday, as the athlete was headlining their advertising campaign. And then there was Saturday's dinner with Gervasio Delgado. That the negotiations around the Mexican trade deal would heat up now, when they'd been lagging for months, was impeccably bad timing. But if Carlos Santino, the president of their Mexican subsidiary, had picked up the phone asking for reinforcements, he clearly needed it.

"When?"

"This week." His brother waved a hand at him. "I'll go. I'm better with the numbers and you have more on your plate than I do. Plus the daddy duties. But that means you have to handle Gervasio by yourself. I won't be back in time."

"Fine." He'd met Gervasio Delgado numerous times.

They had good chemistry together. Closing this deal would not be a problem.

"Chiara is going to crucify me," Lazzero said drily. "She will be devastated."

"She'll have plenty of time to meet him when we ink this deal." His wife, however, could be a problem. He needed her onside if she was going to charm Alicia Delgado at this dinner. *If* he could get her to talk to him. Which wasn't at all a guaranteed proposition at the moment.

"When will you leave?"

"Tomorrow morning. I need some time to acclimatize before I have to use my brain."

"Good idea." Santo stood and threw some papers in his briefcase, intent on a cold beer, a wrestle with his son and a resolution with his wife. Preferably in that order.

Gia shouldered her way through the penthouse door, a bag of groceries in one hand, a latte from her favorite bakery in the other. Expecting that Anna would have her son in the bath by now, she was instead greeted by Leo's peals of laughter and a rich deep baritone that accompanied it.

Her heart beat a jagged edge. *Santo was home?* She thought he'd be working late tonight, thus the reason she'd taken up Chloe's nanny on her offer of a few hours respite to get some errands done. But when she walked into the living room, her husband was indeed home, lying on the floor, bench-pressing her son as if he weighed nothing. Leo was waving his arms in the air as if he was a *supahero* coming in for a landing.

"Mamma," her son cried. "Look at me. I'm flying."

"Wow," she murmured. "You are."

Santo set down his son on his chest, all of that bulging muscle under his finely woven shirt doing something crazy to her insides. He was indecently gorgeous even when she hated him. "Maybe *Mamma*," he suggested, setting his gaze on her, "should come over and take a turn. She might like it, too."

Gia gave him a frosty look. She wasn't letting him charm his way out of this one.

Leo moved his gaze from one of them to the other, clearly attempting to decipher the mood. "I think," Santo confessed to his son, "that *Mamma* might be angry with me. What do you think I should do?"

"Flowers," Leo said confidently. "Pink ones."

She almost smiled at that, a memory of Leo emerging, shoulders deep, from Delilah's peony garden with a fistful of pink flowers in his hand and a wicked smile on his face, filling her head. She had been horrified, while Delilah had been thankfully amused.

But nope, that still wasn't touching the ice that encased her.

Santo rolled into a sitting position. "Good idea," he said to Leo. "I will keep that in mind. Did you know," he told him, "that even *supaheroes* need lots of sleep? *Especially supaheroes*, because that's where they get their power from."

Leo's eyes went round. He ran to Gia and gave her an enthusiastic hug, before Santo swooped him up and took him to bed. A discussion about kryptonite ensued, trailing off as they disappeared up the stairs.

Gia took the groceries into the kitchen, stowed them away, then opened a bottle of Chianti she had acquired from the art wall display. Intent on fine-tuning a couple of the drawings she'd done for the Hamptons house, she curled up in a chair in the living room with her sketch pad and a glass of wine.

Santo came downstairs shortly thereafter, dressed in jeans and a T-shirt. She nodded toward the kitchen, without looking up. "I bought home some antipasto from the deli if you're hungry."

"I had a late lunch. I'll join you for a glass of wine, instead."

"Don't bother." She kept her eyes on the sketch pad. "I'm sure you have work to do."

"We need to talk about this, Gia."

She looked up at him. "What's the point? You don't see me, Santo. You only see what you want to see."

Santo regarded his wife's frigid demeanor. Poured himself a glass of wine from the bottle on the table and sat down beside her, stretching his long legs out in front of him. "Tell me, then. Tell me why it has to be *this job*, *right now*. Why it can't be something more manageable. And yes, I know working with Nina is a great opportunity, but there will be other opportunities."

Her chin took on a stubborn tilt. "Because it's an amazing opportunity. Because I can *do it*. Nina has promised me a crack team. If I manage it correctly, it won't be a problem."

"And when the construction manager calls you at ten o'clock at night with an emergency?"

"I will handle it. Isn't that how *you* do it?" She arched an eyebrow at him. "Surround yourself with good people to get the job done?"

"Yes, but I also work sixteen-hour days. We can't both do that." He considered her over the rim of his glass. "If you don't want to do work for me, then come join Supersonic's design department part-time. We have a massive retail push on at the moment. They could use the help. You'd be a fantastic addition given the work you've done for Delilah."

The stubborn tilt of her chin intensified. "I can't work for you."

He threw up his hands. "I'm trying here, Gia. I'm offering you the money to front a business of your own. *Alternatives.* You have to give a bit, too."

Her long, dusky lashes swept her cheeks. "You need to understand my past. My history."

He swallowed past the bite of frustration that sank into his skin. "Which is?"

She pushed a lock of her hair behind her ear. "My mother never had what I have, Santo. She was *powerless*. She wanted more for me. She knew what I was walking into with Franco. So, she struck a deal with my father. That I would be able to go to college before I married him. So that I would have an education, something to fall back on if something happened."

"Like what?" Santo asked.

He watched her battle against those internal rules that would have kept her silent, until she finally broke the extended pause. "My father," she said, "has been to jail twice. Once for masterminding an auto-theft ring when he was in his early twenties. Another time for an illegal gambling operation when I was seven. In those days, he was still climbing the ranks. Paying his dues. The *famiglia* took care of us, but there was no money left for anything extra. No dance lessons for me, no cool sneakers for Tommaso. My mother was, essentially, devastated twice in those early years."

Cristo. He hadn't known that part. "That must have been difficult," he murmured. "Did you and Tommaso know what was going on?"

Her mouth twisted. "My mother told us he was running the business in Mexico. Another of the myths my childhood was constructed on. But I think," she recalled, eyes darkening, "that underneath it all, we knew something was wrong. My mother was always upset. *Stressed.* Though she hid it well. She is the strongest person I know."

"Like you are." Santo said quietly, eyeing the woman

he had come to learn had a core of steel. "You are a lot like her, Gia."

Her mouth softened, a glimmer of an emotion he couldn't read in those deep green eyes. "Which was why," she continued, "my career is so important to me. I told myself it would be my identity when I married Franco. My safety net. And at first," she allowed, "he was fine with it. He liked the work I did on his hotels. *I* loved it. But after I had Leo, when we tried to have our own child, everything went...*downhill.*"

A fist clamped around his chest. He didn't want to hear this part. Didn't want to think about her with another man. But he also needed to know the truth to truly lay those ghosts to rest.

"It wasn't happening for us," she said. "I was intimidated by him. He was cold. *Unyielding.* It seemed the harder I tried to conceive, the more difficult it got. Franco," she said, eyes on his, "was jealous of you. He punished me by refusing to allow me to work. Said I should focus on a family instead. Took a mistress. Which was almost a relief," she allowed. "He turned even colder, more distant, until our marriage fell apart."

A flash of red moved through his head. It was so far from the vision he'd had of her marriage to the powerful, arrogant Italian she'd married, he couldn't even reconcile the two. Franco Lombardi had been a consummate womanizer who'd had his fill of any woman he'd desired. In his head, Gia had been walking into his arms and out of his, no matter how much she'd dreaded it. But in reality, he conceded, consumed by a wealth of emotion he had no idea how to handle, it had been anything but what he'd envisioned.

"But you stayed," he murmured, "because you had to."

Gia nodded. "I thought about leaving. I almost did twice.

Delilah had made it clear she would help me. But every time I got as far as packing, I would think about my father and how angry he would be and I couldn't do it."

The misery, *helplessness* of those darkest days, washed over her like a dark cloud. The fear that this would always be her life. "So I stayed," she said. "Acted the part. I hosted Franco's dinner parties, kept myself out of his business—did everything that I was supposed to do."

"Until he was shot outside of his casino," said Santo. "Providing you with the opportunity to leave."

She nodded. "I called Delilah, she got passports for Leo and I under the name De Luca and she flew us out the night after Franco's funeral."

She remembered the wind whipping through her windbreaker, Leo bundled in her arms. How scared she'd been that Delilah's car wouldn't be where it was supposed to be. But it had been and they'd flown through the night to the private airport they'd flown out of.

"I was," she said huskily, "frozen when I arrived at Delilah's. I couldn't believe what I'd done. I was terrified I'd never get away with it. But Delilah made sure we didn't leave any tracks. And eventually, Leo and I settled in. When I was ready," she mused, heart pulsing at the memory, "Delilah gave me a job. I came into myself. I started to believe my life could be different. That *everything* could be different. I was Gia De Luca, not Gia Castiglione. I had a clean slate. I could be everything I ever wanted to be."

"Until I took it away from you," Santo said quietly. "That identity you'd created for yourself."

She nodded.

He dragged a hand over the back of his neck. "I was angry, Gia. You had taken my son. I had missed three years of his life. I did what I thought I needed to do. And yes," he conceded on a heavy exhale, "it's true. I have this vision of what I want my marriage and life to be, but there's a reason for it."

Gia eyed the stubborn lines of his face. "Because you never had it."

"Yes." He took a sip of his wine. "My mother was never mother-of-the-year material. I think on some level, I always accepted that. She was more interested in sitting on her high-profile charities. Expanding her influence. Spending our father's money. We had nannies when she managed to keep them. But she was there. She kept us clothed and fed. She enforced the rules, which we needed because my father was working all the time. She was a buffer between us and the drinking when that became a problem."

He rested his head against the back of the sofa, his eyes dark. "She walked out on New Year's Day. A week later, the bank arrived to repossess the house. I spent the next week in shock, telling myself that my mother would come back. She always did."

Except this time, she hadn't. Gia's heart lurched. "Thank god you had your brothers."

He nodded. "But they were immersed in their own internal battles. I would go home from school every day to that empty, depressing apartment and watch my father drink himself into the ground. Until word spread in the neighborhood of what had happened and Mamma Esposito, my best friend Pietro's mother, Carmela, insisted I come to their house after school.

"It was like culture shock for me," he reminisced, his mouth curving. "Kids and laughter everywhere. A basketball hoop in the front yard that attracted half the neighborhood. I didn't talk at all at first. Too heart-sore to do anything more than go through the motions. Mamma Esposito would put a plate of cookies in front of me and say nothing at all. She was just *there*. And gradually," he allowed, "I unfroze. I started to talk to her." His gaze dropped to the ruby-red wine in his glass. "I think she saved me, to be honest. I'm not sure what would have happened to me if it hadn't been for her."

The thought of him so lost, *helpless*, melted her heart. Melted all the ice around her, because all she could remember was Santo being the strong one. Santo and his dreams. His relentless refusal to accept anything less for himself. Everything that he had taught *her*.

She curled her fingers around his. "I'm so glad you had her," she murmured. "Carmela. She sounds wonderful."

"She was." He swirled the wine around his glass in a contemplative gesture. "I had a lot of guilt. That my brothers and I had been too much of a handful. That, maybe, we had driven my mother away. Carmela said something to me that really resonated with me. That maybe, it wasn't that my mother hadn't cared so much as she hadn't been *built for the job*. It was a concept I could understand."

Which was exactly what he wanted in a wife. Her stomach sank as she absorbed the insight into him. How it explained everything about him. About the vision he'd always had of the family he wanted. About the woman he'd wanted in his life. He wanted a *Carmela*.

"I can't be her, Santo," she said quietly. "Carmela. I saw how unhappy my mother was. I saw what her life did to her. I *know* how it affected me. I need my career. My independence. To stand on my own two feet."

"I get that," he murmured. "I do."

She watched the conflict in his eyes. How much it meant to him. And she knew, in that moment, it had the power to make or break them.

"You are a wonderful mother," he said huskily, curling his fingers tight around hers. "I watch Leo and I marvel at how confident he is. How utterly sure he is of his place in the world. You gave that to him, Gia. If you take this job with Nina, it will never contain itself to those hours. It *will* be madness. Leo will suffer. *We* will suffer."

She dug her teeth into her lip, lost in a sea of indecision. It was a big project, even with the team Nina would give her. There was no denying it. Nina was a perfectionist, just like Delilah. But in Nassau, it had been easy to pull out her laptop and work until midnight after Leo had gone to bed, because it had only been her to consider. Which would not be so easy now.

It seemed an impossible decision. She *knew* how unhappy she'd been with Franco. She knew she couldn't be in another marriage like that. But she didn't want to kill her relationship with Santo, either. Not when she had been the one to break them the first time.

"I can do it," she said huskily. "I promise you, Santo. I can make this work. And the reason that Leo is such a confident little boy is that I have learned to become that myself. What kind of a role model would I be for Leo if I didn't teach him to go after his dreams?"

A fleeting series of emotions shifted across his face. She watched him battle his need to control. To *make* this what he wanted it to be. To command this world he had created. Then he finally relented. "Fine," he murmured. "Take the job if you feel that's what you need to do. I can see how much this means to you." He set his wineglass on the table, then reached for hers. "Meanwhile," he said, sinking his hands into her waist and settling her into his lap so that she straddled his thighs, "I think you should kiss me. I am in severe withdrawal. Withering away from the effects of your icy facade."

"Sex will not change my mind," she told him, every cell in her body springing to life as he set his fingers to one side of her neck and his thumb to the other in a gesture of pure possession. "I need this, Santo."

"I know that. I just want you. *Badly.*"

It was the *badly* that did it, because she had been empty without him. Everything had been empty without him. And she wasn't sure how to fill the holes.

She buried her fingers in his hair and kissed him. Soft, achingly good kisses that unfurled a wounded part inside of her. Sighing her pleasure, she traced her mouth over the hard edge of his jaw.

His hands dealt with the buttons on her blouse, his mouth finding the soft skin beneath. Her skirt went the way of her blouse, hiked up to her waist by his sure hands. The fragile barrier of her panties ripped with a flick of his wrist. And then there was only his smooth, dominant possession that tore a gasp from her throat.

Her forehead resting against his, the last fragments of sunlight shifting across their bodies, she made it last as long as she could. Slow and undulating, they moved together, each lazy circle pushing her further toward the point of no return. Toward giving him her heart again. Until his overwhelming, unrelenting possession sent her over the edge, the tremors spreading outward from her center, rippling through her body like living fire, and they came together in a brilliant explosion of pleasure.

CHAPTER NINE

They dined with the legendary Spanish retailing giant Gervasio Delgado at Charles, the most celebrated French restaurant in New York, located on Park Avenue. Steeped in French culinary history, and run by famed chef Charles Fortier, it was renowned for its refined European cuisine, world-class wine cellar and gracious hospitality.

It was also, Gia conceded, one of the most beautiful restaurants in the city. From its soaring coffered ceiling to its elegant neoclassical architecture illuminated by custom Bernardaud chandeliers, its classic white color palette was a perfect blank canvas for the colorful artwork that adorned the walls. The vivid, vibrant works were those of a famous classical Spanish painter, a favorite of Charles, as well of Gervasio, as it turned out.

Santo, dressed in a navy suit and an ice-blue shirt, with a darker, contrasting navy tie, was as focused as she'd ever seen him. Which she completely understood. If Delgado elected to feature an Elevate shoe in the front window of his massively popular retail chain, Divertido, it would become an overnight fashion trend.

Gervasio, still intensely charismatic in his early sixties, had left school at fifteen, according to Santo, to work as a tailor's assistant, exactly as Nico had done to support his family. He clearly liked the Supersonic story…its Cinderella rise to stardom. But mostly, Gia thought, he loved the big-name athletes the company commanded and their potential to add glitter to his brand.

He was also intrigued by the concept of Elevate. Tonight was all about convincing him that Supersonic was the clear strategic choice to place in his front window.

Santo set about making the Supersonic case. It was jaw-dropping to watch him in action—something she'd never had the opportunity to do. His charisma and enthusiasm were infectious as he coaxed the notoriously introverted Gervasio out of his shell in that way he had that drew people to him like a moth to a flame.

Watching the man he had become—one who ruled the world around him so effortlessly—she felt helplessly aware that he had been the only one she'd ever had eyes for and always would be.

It was clear by the time they had polished off cocktails and the first bottle of crisp, delicious Pouilly-Fuissé, that it was going well, the conversation passionate and animated. While Santo focused his attention on Gervasio, Gia devoted hers to his elegant, beautiful wife, Alicia. With that flawless, classical, impeccable style that Gia found European women carried so effortlessly, Alicia had a passionate interest in interior design, because it influenced the fashion trends she created for Divertido. She was also remodeling her house in Marbella, which made for a wealth of conversation.

She and Alicia were talking color trends when a flutter at the front entrance caught Gervasio's attention. He blinked. Gave the front door a long look. "Is that Stefano Castiglione who just walked in?"

Gia froze in her chair. Her back was to the door, but everything slipped at the shocked look on Santo's face. *It could not be. Not here. Not tonight.*

She turned around. Followed Gervasio's gaze. Caught sight of her father's silvery dark hair and tall, elegant posture as he spoke with Charles, who'd materialized from the kitchen to greet him and the elegant blonde he had on his arm. His latest mistress, she assumed numbly.

Her fingers clutched tight to the sides of her chair. She

heard Santo murmur some sort of affirmation to Gervasio before her father trailed a glittering path through the crowd with his grey gaze, the customary combination of awe and respect he commanded rippling through the packed restaurant. And perhaps, she conceded, a fission of ice sliding up her spine, a tiny bit of apprehension.

She understood it. He was her father. She had loved him as much as she had hated him. *Feared* him. And therein lay the conflict that had ruled her existence. To adore someone—to revere them as larger than life—but to also know what they were capable of.

While the other girls in school had spoken about their fathers' affairs in the bathrooms, or the fast and loose lifestyle they'd acquired while working on Wall Street, she'd been wondering who her father had eliminated the night before.

Her father laughed at something the blonde had said, the rich, resonant sound making her breath catch in her chest. The hair stood up on the back of her neck as he flicked a glance her way, as if sensing her study. She saw his eyes widen, the proud set of his head as he cocked it to one side and took her in. And then there was only the buzzing in her ears as he acknowledged the table Charles had provided, then turned and made his way through the diners to where she sat, his beautiful companion at his side.

"Giovanna." His smooth, even tone betrayed not a hint of emotion as he came to a halt in front of them. It was all in his dark, deep-set eyes—fury mixed with a smattering of something she couldn't identify. "Forgive me," he murmured. "I had no idea you would be here tonight. Your mother only just mentioned you were back in New York."

Gia inhaled a deep, steadying breath as she stood to greet him, dimly aware that Santo had done the same. Her fingers reached back to clutch the edge of the chair tight.

"I've only been back in New York a little while," she murmured. "It's been a bit of a whirlwind."

"I see." Those two words held a wealth of meaning. Her stomach plunged another inch as her father turned to Santo and extended a hand. "Santo. I had been hoping I would run into you. We have some business on the table."

Santo shook her father's hand. *"Mi dispiace,"* he murmured. "I have been swamped. Unfortunately," he said, "we have signed an exclusive deal with Delilah Rothchild for our hotel-related retail efforts for the next couple of years. It will be our focus for the time being."

Her father's gaze glimmered. "So it is," he drawled, inclining his head. "The offer is there if you reconsider." He drew his beautiful blonde companion forward. She was thirty if she was a day, barely older than Gia herself. Her father's tastes clearly hadn't changed. "Julianne, this is my daughter, Giovanna Castiglione."

"Di Fiore," Santo corrected smoothly.

Her father's expression turned glacial. "Of course. *Scusi.* My mistake. An old habit. Julianne," he continued, "runs the Derringer Art Gallery on the Upper East Side. I am considering purchasing one of her pieces."

As if. Gia's chest burned as Santo made the introductions to the Delgados, who were watching it all with a bemused countenance. Gervasio, whom her father was clearly interested in meeting, looked distinctly standoffish through it all.

Tension climbed the back of her throat. She thought she might actually throw up, her stomach was churning so violently. Particularly when a long, painful silence then ensued. Her father finally broke the détente, setting his gaze on Gia. "Julianne was just mentioning she needed to visit the powder room. Perhaps we could speak privately outside for a few moments given we haven't seen each other in some time?"

Santo tensed beside her, ready to object. Gia put a hand on his arm. Sucked in a breath. She needed to defuse this situation. *Now*. She also needed to get this confrontation with her father over with before she jumped out of her skin. She'd imagined it in her head so many times, it was beginning to make her a little crazy.

If she was going to own this new version of herself, this strength she'd so painstakingly achieved, now was the time to do it. She could not let Santo fight this battle for her, no matter how much she wanted him to. She needed to do it by herself.

"I think that's a good idea," she murmured. She flicked a glance at the table. "My apologies. If you'll excuse me for a few moments."

Santo narrowed his gaze, as if considering trampling all over that idea. But after a long moment he nodded and bent his head to her ear. "Five minutes," he murmured.

Gia led the way outside into the lamp-lit courtyard at the back of the restaurant. It was deserted except for a patron smoking a cigar at the far end of the quadrangle. A sparkling fountain threw up a spray of gold into the lamplight, a series of beautifully cut marble figures running through it. It was a beautiful night, the air fragrant and warm as it wafted over her skin. But it was her father who claimed all of her attention as he leaned his tall, powerful frame against one of the stone columns supporting the restaurant's facade.

His anger had always manifested itself in one of two ways. Like a violent storm, which had often swept through their brick Georgian home like a thunderclap, flattening everything in its wake, only to die out just as quickly. Or the slow, silent type that was building in his eyes now as he took her in. "I'm not even sure where to begin," he murmured. "The fact that you walked away without a word, or that you showed up here married to Santo Di Fiore without even the courtesy of a warning."

Gia slicked her tongue along desperately dry lips. She had the feeling he was more caught up with Santo throwing his proposal in his face than he was with her return. Which was her father in a nutshell. She pushed her shoulders back and met the grey fury of his gaze. "I needed some time to find my feet. And you knew why I left, *Papà*. You *knew* I was frightened after what happened to Franco. I didn't feel safe. Leo was not safe. I explained all of it in my note."

"Your note?" Her father exploded. *"Your note*, Giovanna? You think it was acceptable to leave a note for your family before you walked out of our lives and disappeared? You thought that a *note* would prevent your mother's broken heart. *Cristo*." He waved a hand at her. "Were you thinking of nothing but yourself?"

Two years of fury and heartbreak caught fire. She drew herself up to her full height and met him head-on. "I was thinking of anything *but* myself when I married a man I didn't love. When I gave up the dreams I had for my life. My *future*. I *did* my duty. I have done it my whole life. And then, I watched as my husband was assassinated by some henchmen in front of his casino." She shook her head. "What if it had been Leo? What if a stray bullet had taken him instead?"

Her father waved a hand at her. "That would never have happened. You were protected."

"Like my husband was?" The fear she'd felt for herself, for her son, curled her stomach tight. "You were at war with the Bianchis. It was never going to end."

"It did end." Her father's mouth flattened. "Don't talk about things you can't hope to understand, Gia."

"At what cost?" She wrapped her arms around herself

and hugged them tight. "*At what cost, Papà?* I would do the same thing a hundred times over if I had to. Leo will never grow up in that world. He will never take Franco's place. I have seen what it has done to Tommaso. It will never happen."

Her father considered her for an extended beat, his grey gaze calculating. "Where were you? Before you came back?"

Her spine stiffened. "You don't need to know that." She would never, *ever* put Delilah or her mother in the crosshairs of her father's wrath.

"You could not have been with Santo," he concluded. "His inability to remain faithful to a woman has been well documented. Which means you were with someone else."

She glued her mouth shut. "And Leo?" he prompted. "Where is he? Clearly the Lombardis will be interested in his whereabouts given they are missing a grandson. It is a critical partnership for me, Gia, in case you have forgotten that particularly pertinent fact."

She cringed, the contents of her stomach roiling as if they might actually make an appearance. The truth had to come out. She knew it. But getting the words out of her mouth seemed impossible.

"Leo is not Franco's son," she finally blurted out. "He is Santo's."

Santo sat at the table as the minutes clicked by and attempted to concentrate on what Gervasio was saying, but failed miserably. His attention was focused instead on the path his wife had taken through the busy restaurant to the courtyard. On what was happening outside. Gia had looked frozen at her father's appearance. Stefano livid beneath that smooth veneer of his. He didn't want him anywhere near his ultravulnerable wife.

Nor had the buzz in the restaurant subsided. The most wanted organized-crime figure in the world was in the building. He'd apparently elected to testify in front of congress next week, and Charles Fortier's elegant establishment was a perfect foil for Stefano Castiglione's gilded image. His image restoration project. It was sending shock waves through the room.

Gervasio said something that flew right over his head. He set down his wineglass. "My apologies," he murmured. "I am distracted. Would you excuse me for a moment? I should go check on my wife."

"Por supuesto." The Spaniard nodded. "I would do the same."

He threw his napkin on the table and stood. "Please," he said, sweeping a hand toward the table as their main courses arrived, *"Adelante, por favor.* Enjoy."

He followed the path Gia and her father had taken through the restaurant to the courtyard. Emerged into the warm, sultry night to find them standing under the portico talking in low voices. Gia's voice, at least, was low. The bite in Stefano Castiglione's tone sliced through his skin like a knife as he listened to the exchange. Listened to his wife tell her father the truth about Leo.

Maledizione. Why couldn't she have waited for him to do it?

A slow burn slashed her father's aristocratic cheekbones in the lamplight. "Clearly none of the morals you were taught were in play that night when you chose to disrespect not only your husband, but me. When you acted like nothing but a common *slut.*"

A haze of red flared through his head. Gia, however, looked undaunted, squaring her shoulders. "And what about you, *Papà*? You disrespect *Mamma* every time you appear with your *mistress* in public. When you humiliate her and treat her as if she is a second-class citizen."

"You cannot compare the two," her father dismissed. "What you did was unforgivable, Giovanna."

"That's enough." Santo enunciated the words quietly as he moved to Gia's side and slid an arm around her. She was shaking like a leaf.

Stefano shot him a lethal look. "I was having a private conversation with my daughter."

"Which is over." Santo met the other man's wintry gaze. "Given you now know the truth, I will tell you how this is going to work."

Stefano arched an eyebrow. "How *what* is going to work?"

"Your relationship with your daughter. Gia has chosen to walk away from her family. She is no longer a Castiglione. You need to respect her wishes."

"Or what?"

"Or this becomes a public battle you want to avoid."

Gia blanched. It was the one thing her father couldn't abide. Negative publicity. It drew unwanted attention to his business practices. Shined a light on the family where it preferred to operate in the shadows. Drew attention to his leadership. Something he had more than enough of at the moment.

Stefano considered Santo with a calculating look. "You are stung because I declared her not good enough for you," he murmured. "Now you want revenge."

"Revenge has nothing to do with it," Santo said evenly. "You put those shadows in her eyes. It ends now."

A long moment passed, thick and pulsing with tension. It finally ended when Stefano lifted a broad, elegant shoulder. "Have her then," he said, flicking a cold look at Gia. "She is no longer my daughter after what she's done."

He turned and strode inside, leaving a stark silence behind him. Santo surveyed his wife's white, stricken face. She looked shaken, *disassembled*. And why wouldn't she? Her father had just disowned her. Struck her from his life as easily as he did one of his high-priced business deals. He didn't have to wonder how it felt. He knew how it felt, as his mother's parting words echoed in his head even now.

It's too much, Leone. Three boys and now this. I can't do it. I didn't sign up for this. As if they had been the dead weight, the *complication* she clearly didn't need.

He absorbed the shock reverberating in Gia's emerald eyes. Smoothed a thumb over her cheek. "Are you okay?"

"It isn't anything I didn't expect," she said huskily. "I knew he would react like that. His honor dictated it. I threw that in his face."

"That doesn't negate how it must make you feel," he said quietly. "Nothing gives him the right to do what he just did, Gia," he said quietly. *"Nothing."*

She blinked as if she was having trouble comprehending it all. Rubbed a palm against her temple. "You shouldn't have taken him on like that. It wasn't wise."

"He needed to know that you and Leo are no longer a part of the Castiglione family," he said grimly. "Now he does."

She inhaled a deep breath. "We should go back inside. The Delgados will be wondering where we are."

Could he ask her to sit through a meal with her father on the other side of the room after what had just happened? After he had taken his wife apart?

Gia read his hesitation. "I'm fine," she insisted, lifting a trembling hand to smooth her hair. "I will not let him ruin this, Santo."

She didn't look fine. But what choice did he have? He could not walk out on this dinner with the Delgados.

He tightened his arm around her waist. "Are you sure?"

"Yes."

Something inside of him shifted at the look of fierce determination in her eyes. He threaded his fingers through hers and led her back into the restaurant. Felt a dozen sets of eyes on them as they walked back to the table. Stefano and his companion were seated at a table near the window. Gia took them in, then resolutely shifted her gaze away.

Gervasio, quiet and circumspect, surveyed them both as they returned. *"Está todo bien?"* Everything all right?

Santo nodded. *"Mil disculpas."* *A thousand apologies.* "I hope you both enjoyed your meals."

The Delgados ensured him they had. Santo ordered another bottle of wine as he attempted to repair an evening gone awry. But the sight of his wife literally melting into her seat beside him, refusing to show how much she hurt, tore a hole in his insides.

And then, there was also the subtle temperature change at the table. Barely perceptible, but it was there. Gervasio was cooler and more distant than before. Back to his elusive self.

The gauntlet they had to maneuver on the way out was the final exclamation mark on an evening that had descended into a disaster. Spilling onto the sidewalk near the valet stand where the restaurant security held them at bay was a contingent of press, cameras at the ready to snap a shot of Stefano and his companion leaving the restaurant. Completing the debacle of a night.

It wasn't until they were home in the quiet, muted confines of the penthouse that Gia was able to breathe again. Numb, frozen with the protective coating she had formed around herself, she kicked off her shoes, walked to the bank of floor-to-ceiling windows and stood looking out at the lights of the city.

Santo appeared by her side, a glass of amber-colored liquid in his hand. She shook it off when he handed it to her, sure she did not need to feel any more numb than she already did. He pressed it into her hands. "Drink it. You need it. You're as white as a ghost."

She wrapped her fingers around the tumbler and took a reluctant sip. Felt the liquor penetrate her bloodstream, the color slowly returning to her cheeks. But as the shock receded, the nightmare the evening had been illuminated itself in crystal-clear clarity. Her father showing up with his mistress. The scene he had caused. How she had dismantled Santo's evening with Gervasio.

A burning sensation crawled from her stomach into her throat. She might have been out of it, but she could not have missed the way Gervasio had withdrawn after her father had shown up. The way the conversation at the table had never quite recovered. The taken-aback look on the Spanish retail scion's face at the media frenzy outside.

The fist clenching her chest tightened. The newspapers would be plastered with the coverage of her father's testimony. It was going to be a circus. Her mother would be completely unwound. And, she acknowledged, fingers of ice crawling up her spine, her father was going to have a target on his back, because the list of people he could incriminate, take down with him, was a virtual who's who of the criminal underworld. Of Washington. Hollywood.

No one would be safe.

He might elect to plead the Fifth. But would anyone wait to hear him say it? She was afraid they would attempt to eliminate him first.

She turned to Santo, the grim lines etched into the sides of his eyes and mouth making it clear he had already considered those possibilities. "I'm so sorry," she whispered, "about tonight. I've ruined everything. This was exactly what I was trying to avoid."

He shook his head. "It wasn't your fault. It was unfortunate timing. I will smooth things over with Gervasio in the morning."

She leaned against the window frame, jagged glass lining her throat. Blinked back the hot tears that stung her eyes. She would not cry over him. She had known from the day she'd walked away from her family that her father would never forgive her for what she'd done. It was an eventuality she had long accepted. So why did she feel as if she'd been gutted from end to end?

"I don't understand," she breathed, throwing a hand up into the air, "why I even care that he is disappointed in me. Why he still has this power over me when I know what he is. What he is *capable* of. When I came to terms with that a long time ago."

"Because he is your father," Santo said quietly. "Because you can't separate the two. Because you want him to love you."

Which was true. She'd always wanted her father's love. Always craved it. Even when she'd known better. Even when she'd known she was never going to have it. Even when she knew he wasn't *worthy* of it.

Santo brushed his knuckles across her cheek. "You are better off without him," he said huskily. "He is a sociopath, Gia. Sometimes, you need to let go of the expectations. Stop hoping he will love you and start believing that you are better than that."

The dark glitter of emotion in his eyes caught at her heart. She knew he was talking about his mother. That he learned that lesson the hard way. She also knew he was right. Knew that accepting the facts when it came to her father was a reality that was long past due. But coming to terms with that was another matter entirely.

A tear slid down her cheek. Pooled at the corner of her mouth. Santo closed the distance between them, removed the glass from her hands and gathered her into his arms. "He isn't worth your tears. He never was. You are worth so much more than that."

The tears fell harder, dampening her cheeks and soaking his shirt. He picked her up, sat down on the sofa and cradled her against his chest. Put his mouth to the hot, wet tears and kissed each one away. When she was done, he carried her to bed and held her until she slept, too emotionally depleted, too ragged and ripped apart inside to do anything more.

Unable to sleep, his head spinning from the events of the evening, Santo left a sleeping Gia, pulled on jeans and a T-shirt and went downstairs to his office to work.

He should call Lazzero, who was three hours behind him on west coast time, and give him an update on dinner. But what, exactly, would he say? That Stefano Castiglione had walked into Charles tonight and blown the whole evening to bits? That instead of tying up the deal with Gervasio, he had walked away with the distinct impression the Spaniard was backing off all over the place? That he'd been more concerned about his wife than he'd been about nailing down the most important retailer in the world?

A knot tied itself down low. He had promised himself he wouldn't get emotionally involved with his wife. But he was starting to realize that was an impossibility with Gia. That his instinct to protect her, to care for her, had always been his weak spot. His Achilles' heel. Which was going to be his downfall if he didn't watch it.

The phone call, he determined, could wait until the morning. He would call Gervasio first thing and smooth things over. Make sure he understood the ties between he and Stefano Castiglione were personal and not business.

But Gervasio was on a plane to Madrid the next morning when he tried to reach him, which meant that conversation would have to wait. Lazzero called at 8:00 a.m. while Santo stood with a cup of coffee in his hand, surveying the city as it came to life.

"Please tell me there is some way you were not sitting in Charles when Stefano Castiglione walked in last night."

Santo flicked his gaze over the morning papers, which were strewn across his desk. A photo of Stefano Castiglione and his mistress exiting the restaurant was emblazoned across the front of them. "You are fast off the mark."

"It's all over the internet, Santo. It's impossible to miss."

"We were there," Santo said carefully. "Stefano came over to introduce himself to Gervasio." *As well as to annihilate his wife.* Perhaps not in that order.

Lazzero exhaled a deep breath. "How was Gervasio?"

Tense. Standoffish. "I think," he began, "Gervasio is not a fan of Stefano's. But," he assured his brother, "the dinner was good. He loved the ideas we have for the launch. He is clearly hot on the athletes we have. There's a great deal of synergy between the two brands."

"So how did you leave it?" A suspicious note infiltrated his brother's voice. "You closed this thing, right?"

Santo winced. "Not yet."

"What do you mean, *not yet*?"

He gave up any attempts at delicacy. "The temperature was a bit off at the end of the night. Gervasio had his poker face on. I'm not sure what he was thinking."

Lazzero uttered a filthy word. "It doesn't take a rocket scientist to figure it out, Santo. He's the most conservative CEO on the face of the goddamn planet—reputation is everything to him. Your wife is the daughter of the most notorious organized-crime figure in America. What do you *think* he's thinking? He wants nothing to do with this."

"He didn't say that." Santo's gut coiled. "That is pure projection. He was cagey from the very beginning. I'm not sure I would have gotten a yes out of him last night either way. He needs time to think about it."

There was silence on the other end of the phone. Santo knew what was coming and he headed it off at the pass. *"Do not say it,"* he murmured. "I will fix this, Laz. I will make it happen. But do not go there."

His brother took a sip of his coffee, clearly restraining himself, before he moved on with a curt directive to keep him updated. After a brief status report on the Mexican negotiations, which had bled into the weekend, his brother went off to join the next round.

Tossing his phone on the desk, Santo paced to the window, watching as the sun climbed high into the sky. He would smooth things out with Gervasio. This was business, after all, and if the Spaniard was anything, he was a shrewd businessman. But the longer he stood there, the more he saw the potential for disaster.

He needed to retrieve this and fast. Strike before the damage became too catastrophic.

CHAPTER TEN

GIA WOKE BY herself in the big, four-poster bed, light pouring through the skylight and spilling onto the silk-covered sheets. The warm glow of another spectacular New York summer day evaporated almost immediately as the aftermath of the night before swept over her like a dark, ominous cloud. Her father walking into the restaurant and destroying everything in his wake. Him declaring her dead to him. Santo holding her until she'd cried herself to sleep.

Her father would cut her off completely. Which would mean he would forbid her mother to see her. A deep ache unfurled inside of her, one that had been a constant companion over the past two years. But it wasn't a prospect she had the capacity to even consider at the moment alongside her more imminent fear that her father might have done irreparable damage to the business relationship between her husband and Gervasio Delgado.

A sense of dread snaking through her, she threw on a T-shirt and shorts and went downstairs to the smell of freshly brewed coffee. Leo, who'd taken to getting up with his father on the weekends, was reenacting a *supahero* battle in the living room, while Santo paced the terrace, talking on his cell phone. He looked, she noticed from his rumpled appearance, as if he'd hardly slept.

She gave her son a big hug, then poured herself a cup of coffee and went in search of the morning papers. They were strewn across Santo's desk. The curl of dread inside her intensified as she flicked through them, scanning the headlines. Castiglione to Testify… But Will He Tell All? said one. Crime Boss Turns Himself in Amid Much Fanfare, said another. And from the most respected Washington daily: Castiglione to Take on the Capital in the Best Show in Town.

Oh, my god. Almost all of them included a photo of her father and his mistress, Julianne Montagne, leaving Charles in a hail of flashbulbs. Gia's stomach bottomed out at the glossy pictures. It would kill her mother.

She picked up the Washington paper. Scanned the story. Her father had indeed returned to the country to testify, confirmed his lawyers. But he had not given any indication as to whether he would comply with the attorney general's "witch hunt," or whether he would invoke his right to protect himself against self-incrimination, which she felt sure he would do.

Clearly, the attorney general had anticipated the same. According to the article, the brash new figure at the helm of the American justice system was considering prosecuting anyone who failed to participate in a "full and open manner." Which, the journalist opined, was undoubtedly directed toward Stefano Castiglione, the biggest and brightest star on his agenda. Which put her father in an impossible position. Betray his underworld contacts or risk being thrown in jail.

"You're up." Santo strode toward her, phone in hand, all loose, long-limbed elegance in jeans, a T-shirt and bare feet. Hair ruffled, dark eyes piercing, he looked so gorgeous, so warm, so solid, she wanted to throw herself in his arms and have him make it all better. But the distracted look on his face kept her where she was, the kiss he brushed across the top of her head disappointingly brief. "Don't read that," he murmured. "It is nothing but speculation."

She rested back against his desk. "He will have a target on his back."

"Which he is well aware of," Santo said evenly. "None

of this is yours to take on, Gia. You are a Di Fiore now. You are no longer a Castiglione. Let your father fight his own battles."

"I'm not worried about him," she said quietly. "I am worried about my mother."

"She is surrounded by family. She'll be fine."

She knew that was true, but she wanted to see it for herself.

He read the thoughts running through her head. "You aren't going anywhere near Las Vegas, Gia. We agreed on this. Your mother decided it was for the best. It is far too politically explosive."

Because of the Lombardis. She wrapped her arms around herself, knowing he was right. Hating how helpless she felt. "Did you get a hold of Gervasio?"

"No." A grim, one-word answer. "He's on a flight back to Madrid. I'll try him later."

She nodded. If she'd had any hopes she'd overblown the damage her father had done to Santo, they vaporized now with the look on his face. He was in problem-solving mode. He needed to fix this. And given the brewing media storm, it was only going to get worse.

"I'm sorry." She didn't know what else to say, except say it again.

"It's not your fault." He dismissed it with a wave of his hand. "Go take Leo for a walk. Get it out of your head. Concentrate on the life you have now. The family you have around you. All of the opportunities in front of you, rather than the circus show your father is putting on. That part of your life is over."

She inclined her head. Looked for some sign of softening in him, some tiny piece of the reassurance she craved, but he looked utterly preoccupied.

If the wounded, ragged edges inside of her found this

cooler, more distant version of him disconcerting after how tenderly he'd held her the night before, she pushed it aside. All she could hope was that Gervasio signed that deal.

She did her best to do exactly what Santo had said and put that piece of her life behind her over the next couple of weeks, rather than focus on the sensational media coverage of her father's pending testimony in Washington. Taking the job with Nina, putting her world firmly beneath her feet, was exactly how to do it.

If she thought Nina might back out of their agreement once the worst of the scandal hit, the worldly, hard-edged real estate tycoon surprised her, and merely lifted an eyebrow when Gia brought up the topic at lunch.

"Darling, if you've seen as many political storms as I have, you'll know this, too, shall pass," the woman insisted. "Put your head down and get the job done. And hold it high when you walk out of this room. If everyone in this city were defined by their pasts, we'd all be dead on arrival. It's what you do with it that counts."

Buoyed by Nina's firm backing and her sage advice, so like Delilah's, Gia buried herself in her work, excitement sizzling in her veins at the return of her creative outlet. Which was a welcome distraction, given how absent her husband had been in the lead-up to the Elevate launch.

He came home in time for dinner per the routine they'd established, but as soon as it ended, he went off to his office to work until the early hours, after which he came to bed and didn't wake her. She told herself he was swamped, buried under a mountain of work, but she couldn't shake the feeling that something was wrong. That he had withdrawn since that dinner with Gervasio. That it had torn something between them, that fragile bond they had been building. The situation wasn't helped by the complete lack of physical intimacy between them—the one part of their relationship that had always given her confidence in them.

It threw her. Unnerved her. Hurt her. Unearthed all her vulnerable points. Because this was exactly how it had started with Franco. He had wanted her, desired her in the beginning, but when it had become clear that she was less than the asset he'd signed on for, he'd grown cold.

Maybe, she acknowledged as she walked home from the hotel on another gorgeous, sunny day, she was overreacting. Maybe, she determined, pushing all of the negative thoughts out of her head, all they needed was a chance to reconnect. A nice dinner tonight before he left for Munich. Something to reassure herself that everything was fine.

An action plan in place, she picked up the groceries to make Santo's favorite dish, as well as an excellent bottle of wine to go with it, then went home to relieve Leo's new nanny for the day. Tia was Dutch, in her midtwenties and completely adorable. She reminded Gia of Desaray, with her energetic, enthusiastic manner, and Leo loved her. Which had been a huge relief, because Santo liked her, too.

She checked in with her husband, who said he'd be home a bit later tonight, after eight, he thought. Which fit perfectly with her plan. She'd put Leo to bed and have dinner waiting for him when he came home. They would have a romantic night together and she could put all these crazy doubts to rest.

She prepared the intricate beef dish she was making, put it all together and left it in the fridge before she went for a swim with Leo. They played together in the hot afternoon sun, enjoying the perfect weather, before she bathed him, fed him and put him to bed.

Dinner in the oven, she showered and put on the dress she knew Santo liked the best. The one he couldn't resist.

A body-skimming, knee-length, wrap design in a sky-blue, it made the most of her curves.

She set a candlelit table on the terrace and turned on some music, a sexy, Spanish guitar CD that fit her mood. Then she curled up in a chair in the living room with a glass of the wine and waited for Santo, her heart thudding with anticipation.

Eight o'clock came and went. Eight thirty. Nine. He finally walked in the door at nine fifteen, as night fell over the city. Dropping his briefcase on the floor of the marble entryway, he walked into the living room and threw his jacket over the back of a chair.

His gaze flicked to the candlelit table on the terrace. To the open bottle of wine. A frown knit his eyebrows together. "*Mi dispiace*. I didn't know you were cooking a special meal."

"It was a surprise." She uncurled her legs from beneath her and stood up. "I thought we could spend some time together before you left."

An apologetic look slid across his face. "I have a report I need to review for a meeting tomorrow and a contract to get back to my lawyer tonight."

Her heart slid to the floor. And so, he couldn't spend even half an hour with her? A man who ran a multibillion-dollar company, as he was so quick to point out to her? A man who likely had his whole legal team on a 24/7 retainer?

A slow burn lit her cheeks. "That's fine," she murmured. "It's probably burned anyway. It's been in there since eight."

He flicked a glance at his watch. "I could probably spare a few minutes."

"Don't bother," she said curtly. "Get your work done."

"Gia—"

She shook his arm off and stalked into the kitchen, where

she dumped the entire contents of the casserole dish into the garbage with no appetite to eat it herself.

Upstairs, she stripped off the beautiful blue dress and tossed it on a chair, her skin stinging. She hadn't been imagining the distance he'd put between them—it was a very real thing she'd been willfully avoiding.

A buzzing sound filled her ears. Spread through her body, sensitizing her skin until it hurt to touch. *It was happening all over again.* What always happened when she allowed herself to believe a relationship could work. That who she was wouldn't eventually destroy it. She always proved herself wrong.

She went through her bedtime routine in robotic fashion, consumed by her thoughts. She'd built up this hope inside of her that she and Santo could someday have what they'd once had. Something even more powerful and stronger with who they'd become. That someday, it might even grow into love. But he was never going to let himself feel the way about her that he once had. That he was always going to hold a part of himself back. Offer her the slim pickings of the emotional connection he'd put on the table. That he'd now, apparently, decided to rescind.

She curled up in bed, miserable and numb. She'd done exactly what Santo had asked of her. Put herself out there. Met him halfway. Sought that intimacy between them he'd demanded. And look where it had gotten her.

She woke for work after a terrible sleep, dark circles ringing her eyes. Santo had left in the early hours. He'd propped a handwritten note by the coffee machine that she was to take Deacon, his personal bodyguard, to work with her while he was in Germany and leave Benecio with Leo and Tia.

Nothing more. No added message.

Her stomach curled into another knot in a sea of them. She didn't think it was necessary, but she kept her mouth shut and took the big hulk of a man to work with her to keep her husband happy.

It was an exciting, busy day. But the more it stretched on, the more the confrontation played on her mind. Ate away at her insides. It made her feel even more lost in the storm than she already was. Her life had been blown wide open, and now the one person she had thought she could depend on wasn't there for her. The one person she needed desperately.

Her husband called only once, a short, stilted conversation when he'd been on the way out to a dinner. It made the apprehension inside her grow into a disconcerting force, because he couldn't have sounded more distant, more wrapped up in his busy trip.

By the time the week ended, she was exhausted. She put Leo to bed, poured herself a glass of wine and walked out onto the terrace as a resplendent pink sunset lit Manhattan in a golden glow. She could have accepted Chiara's offer to drop by with a bottle of wine, but she hadn't been able to face it. To try and pretend to the vibrant, happy, madly-in-love Chiara that everything was okay when nothing was. When Santo hadn't touched her in weeks. When she was in love with her husband and she was afraid he was never going to let himself love her back. When it felt as if her marriage was slipping away from her and there was nothing she could do about it.

She stood there for a long time, until finally, she picked up her cell phone and called her husband in Munich. It rang a dozen times before he picked it up. He was laughing, a husky sound of amusement in his voice, as he clipped out his customary greeting. "Di Fiore here."

Gia stilled, caught completely off guard by the sexy

laughter in his voice. By the sound of loud music pulsing in the background. He was at a party, she realized. *Relaxed.* Nothing like the version of him she'd encountered over the past couple of weeks.

She swallowed past the tightly constricted muscles of her throat. "It's Gia."

"Gia?" he answered, a frown in his voice. "Is everything okay?"

"Yes... I—" Her voice trailed off. What exactly was it that she'd wanted to say? She didn't even know.

"Gia." The frown in his voice deepened. "What's up? Why are you calling?"

Because she'd wanted to hear his voice. And wasn't that silly?

"Santo," a musical female voice sang out, close enough to the phone that she was undoubtedly hanging off his arm in that ritualistic exhibition she'd seen so many times. "I have someone you need to meet. We're opening a bottle of champagne at the bar."

Gia's stomach plunged. She knew that voice. That sultry, lazy drawl could only belong to one woman. She'd spent enough time that night at the Met gala obsessing over it. The fact that Santo was with Abigail Wright at an after-hours party that could hardly be all business caused her chest to tighten. The fact that she was introducing him to someone as if it was her rightful place to be at his side drove a stake right through her heart.

His inability to remain faithful to a woman has been well documented. Her father's cutting appraisal of her husband flashed through her head. The dozens upon dozens of women he had gone through in the past few years. Franco's extracurricular affairs that had cut a swath of humiliation through her.

"Gia?" Santo's voice deepened as he seemed to move farther away from the music. "Talk to me. What's going on?"

"Nothing." A bolt of fury moved through her. Here she'd been putting herself through the ringer over him. Agonizing over that confrontation they'd had. Desperate to right this thing between them before it capsized completely. But her husband clearly didn't feel the same. He was out partying with his friends. Cozying up with the woman who should have been his wife.

"I'm fine," she said evenly. "Leo wanted me to send you a kiss. There. Now it's done. You can go."

"Gia—"

She hung up the phone. Tossed it on the table. Stood looking out at the skyline, arms hugged around herself as her mobile vibrated with three more calls, then fell silent.

Let him stew. Let him feel one-tenth of what she was feeling. Her chest felt too sore to breathe. Too hurt to function. She braced her palms on the railing and drew in a deep breath. When had she started to believe this marriage was real? That it could work? That she could ever, even remotely be what Santo wanted or needed? When had she become that much of a fool?

A wet heat stormed the back of her eyes. She blinked it back, furious at herself. She'd thought she could do this. That she could live in another convenient marriage for Leo's sake. But she knew now that she couldn't. That it would break her heart to know that Santo had only married her for Leo. That she would always be his default choice.

That he would make it work, even as he resented her more every day for it. Because she knew he would. She'd been through this. Except this time, it would be worse, because she loved Santo. She always had.

She finally stumbled to bed in the early hours. Rose the

next morning to Leo's cheerful explosion of limbs in the big four-poster bed.

"Mamma," he cried, pressing a slobbery kiss to her cheek. It unraveled the tidal wave of emotion that had been inside of her all week, until the tears were a storm sliding down her cheeks.

Leo hugged her, bemused. *"Mamma* okay?"

She nodded. Pressed a kiss to the top of his head through the blinding tears. She cuddled him close until they finally slowed. She was about to get out of bed and get breakfast when her cell phone buzzed on the bedside table. She picked it up and stared at it through bleary eyes, wondering if it would be her husband. She was ridiculously disappointed when it was not. It was a Las Vegas number instead.

She sat up and took the call. The blood drained from her face at the sound of her Aunt Carlotta's voice on the other end of the phone. Short and to the point, her aunt told her that her mother had been admitted to the hospital with chest pains. A *cardiac episode.* How serious it was, they weren't sure.

Gia sank back against the pillows, her heart in her mouth. Her mother had never had any heart problems, but the stress of her father's pending testimony had been awful.

She pushed her disheveled hair out of her eyes. Santo had forbidden her to go to Las Vegas. She would be breaking their deal if she went. But she couldn't not go. It was her mother.

Grim resolve moved through her. To hell with Santo. To hell with her father. To hell with all the men in the world she'd let tell her what to do. She was going.

She took Leo down for breakfast. Benecio was in the kitchen making a coffee. "You okay?" he queried, eyeing her red eyes.

"Actually, I'm not feeling well," she lied. "I think Leo

and I will stay in and watch some movies today. If you have things to do, feel free."

He studied her for a moment, then nodded and melted off. Gia, aware that her window of opportunity was short, fed and dressed Leo in record time. Her son eyed her as she carried one of Santo's expensive, high-tech suitcases out of the storage closet and threw it on the bed. Started dumping their clothes into it.

His eyes lit up. "Going on a trip? Take a plane?"

"Yes," she confirmed.

"To see *Papà*?" he asked excitedly.

"No," she said. "To see *Nonna*. Go find Rudolfo," she instructed. "And your blanket."

Leo rounded up his teddy bear and blanket as fast as his little legs would carry him. Gia finished packing while she booked flights on her mobile. In less than an hour she and Leo were wheeling the suitcase out the door.

Her son looked up at her, confused. "Take Benecio?"

"No," she said evenly. "We're giving Benecio the day off."

Santo stepped into the penthouse at close to noon as a brilliant summer day cloaked New York in bright blue sunshine. His eyes were burning, his brain shot, every muscle in his body making itself known after his whirlwind four-day trip to Europe. But it had been imminently successful.

He'd engineered a meeting with Germany's largest retailer, followed that with a slew of smaller appointments, then closed out the conference with a keynote speech that had brought the audience of thousands of youth to its feet. If that hadn't been enough to make him a dead man walking, he'd tacked on a last-minute side trip to Madrid to talk Gervasio around.

Which he had. *Grazie Dio.*

In the end, it hadn't simply been his business arguments that had won the Spaniard over, but Supersonic's impeccable track record, too. It had overshadowed any doubts the Spanish CEO might have harbored about his personal connections to the Castiglione family. And so, with a request from Gervasio to pass his best along to Gia, they had shaken on the deal and Santo had headed home.

Which, he conceded as he set down his suitcase in the marble foyer, had been an issue he'd put on the back burner for the last couple of weeks. Allowing himself to engage with his beautiful, tempestuous wife, immersing himself in the passionate relationship they shared, sinking any deeper into that emotional realm with her than he already had was exactly what he couldn't do when everything depended on him getting through this next week, this last big push to the Elevate launch, with a clear head.

He had, however, brought with him an olive branch in the bouquet of red roses he held in his hand. He stepped into the living room, where he was greeted by silence. Maybe Gia and Leo had gone out for a walk. Impatient to see his wife and son, he fished in his pocket, found his cell phone and called Benecio.

"Ciao," he greeted him. "Where are you?"

"On my way back to the apartment," his security team member said. "Gia isn't feeling well. She's staying in today."

Santo frowned. "She isn't here."

There was a pause on the other end of the line. "I'll be right there."

Santo tried Gia's cell, but it went to voice mail. Maybe she'd gone to the drugstore for some medication. But why, then, hadn't she let Benecio know? And why wasn't she answering her phone?

He tried her cell again with the same result. Tamped down the frisson of unease that slid through him. She and

Leo were undoubtedly fine. But the fact that there were those who would use anything they could as leverage against Stefano Castiglione as he stood poised to testify, including his wife and child, was a reality he couldn't ignore.

He called Gia's cell a third time. This time, she answered. Relief settling through his bones, he frowned at the echo of public announcements in the background. "Where are you?"

"I'm in Las Vegas." Her short, cursory statement had him straightening like an arrow. "My mother has had a heart attack. She's in the hospital. Stable. They think it was a minor one. They're going to run some tests and see how much damage was done."

He raked a hand through his hair. "Thank goodness it was a minor one. Why the hell didn't you call me?"

There was a pregnant silence on the other end of the line. His eyes widened. "Your mother is in the hospital, Gia. What did you think I would do?"

"I thought you'd forbid me to come. I know I'm breaking our deal, Santo, but I need to do this. She is all I have."

"In your family," he corrected in a distracted voice. "You have Leo and I. My family." He buried a hand in his pocket and strode to the window, the skyline spread out before him. "*Cristo*. I have back-to-back meetings in the morning and the launch event on Wednesday. I can't get out there."

"It's fine," she murmured. "I don't need you here."

Something in the way she said it, the dead tone to her voice, raised the hairs on the back of his arms. As if all her walls were back up and she'd built them ten times stronger. "Gia," he said quietly, "I realize things were a little off between us before I left. But it's been crazy, you know that." He glanced at his watch. "I can fly out there for a couple of hours now."

"No." Her voice was flat. Decisive. "I need to do this on my own. I need some time to think."

"About what?" he asked carefully.

"About us. About everything."

Us? Everything? It was a big, blinking red caution sign that chilled his blood. "What are you talking about? You can't just throw this at me."

Someone calling his wife's name sounded in the background. "I have to go," she said. "Give me some time, Santo. It's what I need."

The line went dead. He stood staring at the phone, utterly unsure of what to do. He could not believe she had just thrown that at him. Now, when he was utterly unable to do anything about it.

Benecio chose that unfortunate moment to walk in. Santo gave him a savage look. "Which part of 'do not let them out of your sight' did you misinterpret?"

His bodyguard gave a helpless shrug. "She said she was sick. This building is beyond secure. I came back to check on her earlier and the bedroom door was closed. I assumed they were taking a nap."

Should he have gone in? his bodyguard's raised eyebrow queried.

Santo blew out a breath. Truthfully, it was not Benecio's fault. Gia was a professional at evading her bodyguards. One helpless look from those big green eyes and she would have had Benecio eating right out of the palm of her hand.

"She's in Vegas," he rasped.

Benecio's eyes widened. "Do you want me to go after her?"

He debated the thought. It would make him feel better to know Gia had his security team with her. But the Castiglione family would be under lockdown right now. It would be an armed fortress. They wouldn't be in any danger. And his wife had made it clear she wanted nothing to do with him.

He shook his head. Dismissed his bodyguard. Made himself an espresso and stood, nursing it in his hands as he considered the day unfolding around him.

He had known he had hurt Gia, blowing off dinner like he had. But it had been all he could do to keep his head straight. To get to the next thing in front of him. To get through the storm he'd been in. He had, however, intended to smooth things over when the madness was done. Which had clearly been a mistake.

His wife might have sounded confused, but he couldn't mistake the message that had come through. It had been loud and clear. She was having second thoughts about them. *Reconsidering them.*

His head flashed back to the words he'd heard from the hallway, his softball glove in his hand, before his mother had walked out.

I can't do this, Leone. I didn't sign up for this.

It paralyzed him for a moment, a bolt of pure fury moving through him. Because wasn't this always the way with Gia? She held things inside, bottled them up and refused to address them. Except, he allowed with a sinking realization, she *had* reached out to him. The night she'd cooked dinner for him. When she'd called him in Munich. When she'd sounded so lost on the phone.

He'd been preoccupied, focused on the networking he'd been doing. Had, in his defense, tried to call her back. But she hadn't wanted to hear what he'd had to say. Now his wife was in Las Vegas without his protection, he had no idea where her head was at, and he had a wicked week ahead of him in which he had no time to breathe.

Gia and her Aunt Carlotta took turns at her mother's bedside over the next couple of days as her condition continued to improve. The damage to her mother's heart, according to the doctors, had been limited in nature. Nothing that was irrecoverable with the right medication and the opportunity to heal.

A crush of family came and went, most of it from her mother's side, which was a relief, because the cool response she received from the Castiglones, including her brother, Tommaso, made it clear they would prefer she not be there at all. Her Aunt Carlotta, formidable by anyone's standards, silenced them all, installing she and Leo in her home and ensuring her nephew was surrounded by his cousins, whom Leo bemusedly seemed to accept as yet another facet of his new life.

Her father, she discovered, planned to take the Fifth when he testified later this week, rather than reveal his inner circle. He believed his expensive legal team would prevail. Which, her aunt declared with dismissive disdain, was what had driven her mother into the hospital in the first place, Stefano's *arroganza*. This circus show he was performing.

Finally, Gia got a chance to spend some time alone with her mother. It was disconcerting to see her like this, her mother's olive skin pale beneath its usual warmth, her familiar bergamot scent an elusive whisper against a sterile hospital backdrop, her dark, exotic features, so like her own, strained from the trauma of the past seventy-two hours. To watch her mother's almond-shaped eyes fill with tears at the sight of Leo, whom she hadn't seen since he was six months old.

"He is so much like Santo," her mother murmured. "The spitting image. I think if you had stayed, it would have been difficult to hide it."

Gia's throat tightened at the mention of her husband. At the distance between them it seemed impossible to bridge. Her mother's gaze sharpened. Issuing a request for Carlotta to take Leo off to get a treat, she motioned for the nurse to leave the room. Alone, she wrapped her cool, frail-boned hand around Gia's.

"Tell me what's wrong."

Gia lashes swept down. "Am I that transparent?"

"Only to me." Her mother's mouth softened. "You have been telling me about this beautiful new home you and Santo have bought on the beach. About your fabulous new job. How much Leo loves his new life in New York. Everything seems wonderful, no? So why do you look so sad?"

Tears stung her eyes, a reflexive reaction only her mother could provoke. As if she was five years old again with a scraped knee.

"It's Santo," she confessed. "He's been distant. *Off*. Ever since that dinner with Gervasio Delgado. I'm afraid it's broken something between us and I don't know how to make it right. That it's turning into my marriage with Franco all over again and I don't know what to do about it."

Her mother rested a dark-eyed stare on her. "Santo is not Franco, Gia. Nor is he your father. He is a good man who cares about you. Your marriage is never going to turn into the one that it was." She arched a dark eyebrow at her. "You said he has been busy with this big business thing of his. That he has a great deal of pressure on him right now. Maybe that's all it is."

Maybe it was. She'd told herself that a million times. But she also knew in her gut, that Santo had been different. That he had withdrawn. And the ghosts from her past were too strong to ignore.

Her mother's gaze softened. "Have you talked to Santo? Told him how you feel?"

"I'm afraid to." Her biggest fear uprooted itself and came tumbling out of her mouth. "I'm afraid he's never going to let himself trust me again. That I broke something between us when I walked away with Leo. That I will never be his first choice."

Her mother's brow furrowed. "Why would you think that? He was crazy about you, Gia, that was clear. It was enough that your father stepped in."

"Because of who I am," she said quietly. "Because I'm afraid it will break us over and over again until he won't want to be with me."

Her mother sat back against the pillows, a dark glint in her eyes. She was silent for a long moment before she spoke. "I think you are assuming a great deal of things, *mia cara*. That you will never know the answers to these questions unless you ask him." She shook her head. "You have an opportunity to have everything I never had. A marriage of your own choosing. One that is based on love and affection. And yes," she conceded, "I know Santo pushed you into it, but given that you are in love with him, that once, he was all that you wanted, is it not worth the effort to find out if you are right or if you are wrong?"

Gia swallowed hard, past the lump constricting her throat. It wasn't about the effort. She wasn't sure she could bear to hear the answer. That of all the rejection she'd suffered in her life, Santo was the one person she didn't think she could handle it from. The one who could break *her*.

Her mother squeezed her hand. "You've been running from your feelings for a long time, Giovanna. It's time you stopped and admitted what they are."

She knew her mother was right. In her heart, she knew Santo still had strong feelings for her. It was there in the things he said and did. In the way he'd held her after her father had taken her apart. It was the fact that he might never fully let himself go there that terrified her.

It might have been complicated, but I thought it was worth it.

Her heart took a perilous leap. Maybe, it was her turn to take the next step. To tell Santo how she felt. To make everything right she'd wronged four years ago when she'd walked away from him. To jump in with both feet and hope that her gamble that he could love her again wouldn't shatter her.

She had fought for everything else in her life. Maybe it was time she fought for Santo.

CHAPTER ELEVEN

Flashbulbs reflected off the step and repeat banner at Liberte, Manhattan's new hot spot in Chelsea, as celebrity after celebrity arrived on a sultry summer night that held the city in a steamy, breathless thrall. The club had its outdoor misters firing, showering the crowd with a cool, refreshing spray, but nothing could quell the guests' enthusiasm for Supersonic's big night.

The invitation-only Elevate party was, officially, the hottest ticket in town. Every fashion, sports and celebrity influencer from around the globe was making their way up onto the dais for their moment in the spotlight. And if the stacked guest list wasn't enough to prove it, the buzz from fashion's inner circles was. The celebrity-backed shoe was about to become the most coveted accessory on the planet, and no one wanted to miss its debut.

From the lit, buzzing entrance, guests descended a flight of stairs into an ethereal oasis. A world of sensory pleasure. The entire space was done in black and white to reflect the sleek, impactful ad campaign, accented by splashes of Supersonic red. Beautiful waitstaff dressed in black circulated with trays of a dark-fruit martini, while projected against the stark white walls were massive video images of the elite athletes who starred in the Elevate ad campaign, accompanied by inspirational messaging of how Elevate had helped raised their game. It was the only nod toward business on a night meant for celebration, other than the sneaker itself, subtly interwoven into the decor on raised, lit displays.

Santo stood at the center of it all, leaning a hip against

the gleaming gold bar. To his left stood the president of America's biggest retail chain. To his right, Carl O'Brien, the star quarterback he'd signed today, minus Abigail, who'd decided it wasn't a match made in heaven. In front of him, the highest-paid soccer player in the world partied with his entourage. And somewhere in the crowd was Gervasio Delgado, who had flown in from Madrid for the event.

It should have been the most important night of his life. The culmination of a decade's worth of work spent developing and bringing to market the most important product in his company's history. The night Elevate took the world by storm. Instead, he felt numb. Dead inside. Unable to work up the enthusiasm he should have possessed in what was undoubtedly a triumphant moment, because his wife wasn't there to share it with him. And nothing felt right without her.

Worse, he was beginning to think it was all his fault. That he had been so busy trying to keep it all together, with trying to make this night happen, with keeping his wife at a distance, so afraid strong, spirited Gia would shatter his heart again, he might have destroyed the amazing thing they'd been building.

He tugged at the collar of his silver-grey Armani as an A-list Hollywood actress droned on about her latest effort, his mistakes imprinting themselves in Technicolor detail. He'd made so many of them when it came to Gia, he didn't even know where to start.

He'd forced his wife into a marriage she hadn't wanted. Had excused his bullish behavior by convincing himself he was doing the right thing. By telling himself it was all about his son and his well-being when, in actual fact, what he'd wanted was Gia.

Then, he'd compounded the problem by refusing to

admit how he felt. By fooling himself into believing he'd never let himself love his wife again, when he clearly did. By distancing Gia in the moment she'd needed him the most.

Which, he acknowledged, knocking back a sip of bourbon on a bitter wave of self-recrimination, illuminated his true Achilles' heel. That he was so afraid of becoming his father—of repeating those same mistakes he'd made— he hadn't seen what was right in front of him. That in the imperfect family he'd been handed, he had everything he could ever want and more.

The actress wandered off, finally absorbing the fact that he'd heard nothing of what she'd said. Nico and Lazzero materialized by his side, a bottle of vintage champagne and three glasses in his eldest brother's hands.

"For a man about to take over the luxury sneaker market," Lazzero drawled, "you are looking a little less than over the moon."

He shrugged a shoulder. "The adrenaline rush. You have to come down sometime."

An enigmatic smile touched his brother's mouth. "Not for a while, *fratello*. I just got the first day's sales. They are through the roof."

That made a little dent in the numbness encasing him. But not much. He summoned a modicum of enthusiasm as Nico poured the champagne and proposed a toast. "To Elevate. May it wipe the competition from the face of the planet."

He took a sip of the excellent vintage. Attempted to follow the conversation as Nico made a very male comment about the beautiful dancers he was studiously ignoring on his wife's command, a topic Santo couldn't add to because he'd only glanced at them once to make sure they were doing their job.

Nico gave him a long look. "What the hell is wrong with you? This is your big night."

"Her name starts with a *G* and ends with an *A*," Lazzero supplied drily. "I feel like this is becoming a bad habit," his brother drawled, "but maybe you should just turn around."

Santo spun on his heel to find Gia standing at the entrance to the club, perched at the top of the stairs that led to the crowded space. Clad in a fire-engine-red dress, her hair tucked behind her ear in a sleek, sophisticated style that skimmed her cheeks, her legs endless in the figure-hugging outfit, her dark looks contrasted against the bloodred color, she looked ravishing.

Apparently, he wasn't the only one to notice, because a whole contingent of men had turned to stop and stare. It was her confidence, however, that held Santo riveted. Shoulders squared, head thrown back, she looked utterly sure of herself. *Defiant. Determined.* Not a trace of the hesitancy he was so used to seeing in her.

Something deep in his chest constricted. Filled him with a deep throb that bloomed and grew into something so big and powerful, it was hard to catch his breath. She had weathered the storm of the last couple of weeks with that backbone of steel she'd acquired. Had refused to succumb to it. She was, without a doubt, the strongest, most courageous woman he knew.

In that moment, everything was crystal clear. He'd told himself he'd wanted a cookie-cutter wife. A woman who would fit perfectly into the seamless, even-keeled world he'd constructed for himself. When instead, he'd wanted Gia. The fire and the flame. What he'd always wanted.

Her survey of the crowd came to a halt when it reached him, her gaze meshing with his. The vulnerability on her face, the layer of confidence that had slipped, kicked him hard in the ribs. He had put it there—that uncertainty in her eyes. It sent a rush of anger pulsing through his chest.

His feet were moving before he'd fully registered it, carrying him through the packed, vibrating space. He reached the bottom of the stairs as Gia took her last step, his hands spanning her waist as he lifted her down. Hungry to see her, to touch her, to make things right between them, he kept his hands on her waist and pulled her close.

"You came," he murmured. "You look incredible."

"It's your big night. I didn't want to miss it." She tucked a chunk of her hair behind her ear in a nervous movement. "I'm sorry I'm late. My flight was delayed, then I had to get Leo to Chloe's. Then I couldn't find a dress that was right and I was going through Chiara's closet and I—"

He saw it then, the tears glittering in her eyes. The emotion bubbling beneath the surface. His heart beat a jagged rhythm in his chest as he pressed his fingers to the trembling line of her mouth, cutting her off midstream. "It doesn't matter. You're here. How is your mother?"

"Almost herself. She goes home tomorrow." She flicked a distracted look around them. "Is there somewhere we can talk?"

He wrapped his fingers around hers and led her through the thick throngs of partygoers to the small private lounge at the back of the club they'd used for media interviews. Directed her through the door and locked it behind them.

Filled with a tiny bar, a couple of sofas and a coffee table, and lit with low-light lamps, it was a small, intimate space. The silence between them as they turned to face one another was deafening. Unsure of what to do with his hands, because they wanted to be on her but they clearly needed to talk, he jammed them in his pockets.

"Gia—"

She held up a hand. "No. I have things to say. I need to get them out."

He didn't like the wounded, painful look in her eyes. Wanted to extinguish it. But since he was also responsible for it, he closed his mouth and forced himself to listen.

"I'm sorry I threw all of that at you on the phone. I run, avoid my feelings, all of those things you say I do. But I was hurt. *Confused.*" She leaned back against the bar and raked a hand through her hair. "When you pushed me away after the dinner with Gervasio, I thought I'd broken something between us. It felt as if my marriage to Franco was happening all over again and I didn't know what to do about it. How to fix it. So I cooked you dinner that night. Which you blew off," she said, stating the painfully obvious detail he'd been kicking himself from here to Sunday for. "Then, when I called you in Munich, I heard Abigail in the background. Offering to introduce you to someone. As if the two of you were together."

He uttered an inward curse. He'd been so preoccupied with the party going on around him, about how lost she'd sounded, he hadn't even thought about it. For him, it had just been Abigail acting like the professional networker she was. "It was nothing," he said quietly. "You know that. You know *me*, Gia."

She shook her head. "I wasn't being rational. I was hurt. You had triggered all my insecurities the way you'd shut off on me." She dropped her gaze to the sparkling diamond on her hand. Twisted it to sit straight. "After I failed to conceive a child for Franco, he withdrew. He called me frigid, *ice-cold*. The affairs," she conceded, "were a relief, because he left me alone. But they also decimated my self-confidence. I started to believe the things he was saying. How worthless I was. It didn't help," she added on an achingly vulnerable admission, "that I didn't have a very strong base to start with."

He hated himself so much in that moment, it was palpable. "I was trying to keep things afloat," he murmured. "Every time I engaged with you, we ended up in some deeply emotional place where I couldn't think. Couldn't function. Which wasn't a place I could allow myself to be. Not with everything riding on this launch."

She fixed steady green eyes on him. "I needed you."

That gutted him like a knife. He closed his eyes. Absorbed the far too powerful insight of hindsight. "It was my own history talking. *My* baggage talking, because it reminded me of my father. Of the relationship he and my mother shared." He blew out a breath, struggled for the words to explain. "It was passionate. Fiery. Never calm waters. Which only got worse when my father started his own company. My mother didn't want him to do it. She wanted him to stay on Wall Street, where the money was assured. But my father was addicted to the chase. To the *win*. He wanted this one to be his own.

"Their fights," he recalled, "were house-shaking affairs. Instead of having his eye on the business where it should have been, my father spent all of his time trying to keep my mother happy. The pressure—it was too much. He lost a big contract, one he'd bet the bank on, the business failed and he imploded."

Hurt flared in her dark eyes. "So you were afraid the same would happen to us? That I would be that destructive force for you?"

"All I could see," he said quietly, "in that moment, was that I was going to mess this up if I didn't rein it in. *Us*. This passionate relationship we share. So I shut myself down. Withdrew. It was wrong," he admitted. "If I could take it back, if I could do it all over again, I would, because I would never want to hurt you. *Ever*, Gia."

An emotion he couldn't read darkened her gaze. "What?" he prompted.

She drew in a deep breath. Issued a shaky exhale. "I'm afraid you're never going to let yourself feel the same way about me again," she said in an unsteady voice. "That I broke something between us when I walked away with Leo and I'm not sure you will ever let yourself go there again. That you will make this marriage work because you have to, but I will never be your *ideal* choice. I will be your *necessity*."

He blinked as she threw that loaded statement at him. At how utterly and completely misguided it was. How it was equally his fault, because he'd let her go there.

She lifted her chin. "You had a list of the perfect woman, Santo. You rhymed it off to me countless times. She needs to be smart, with an impeccable social pedigree. Able to hold an interesting conversation over the dinner table with your business associates, but not too focused on business, because family takes priority. 'Martha Stewart by day, a sexual fantasy by night,' wasn't that how you put it? And then there was stipulation number four. She can't have too much *baggage*, because baggage is a *problem*."

He absorbed his own words. It *was* his list. He knew it backward and forward. But none of it had ever mattered with Gia, because how he felt about her had always superseded rationality. He opened his mouth to tell her that, but she gave him a look that said let her finish.

"I am afraid," she said quietly, "that I will always be that political liability for you. That weak link, just like your mother was for your father. That every time we get somewhere good, *who I am* will destroy us. That it will break us over and over again until you decide you don't want me anymore."

He absorbed the heart-wrenching vulnerability on her face. How stripped down and bare she looked. It made his heart ache from deep within. And now, he decided, he'd had enough.

He stalked the few paces across the room and came to a halt in front of her. Stuck a hand on the bar beside her. "First of all," he said, "nothing your father ever says or does is going to break us. *Ever*. I promise you that. I signed Gervasio in Madrid, Gia. He's here tonight. He asked about you. So that is done. And when things get complicated in the future, which they will," he conceded, "because life is complicated, we will deal with it together.

"Secondly," he murmured, pressing a palm to her chest, absorbing the wild beat of her heart, "*this* is the only thing I care about. What's in here. Who you are. It's all I've ever cared about. And yes, I had a list. But you have always meant more to me than any list. You *supersede* it. It's why we keep coming back to each other time and again. Because no one else will do."

Her eyes widened into shining emerald orbs, glittering in the lamplight. "And finally," he said huskily, "I fell for you the first time I ever saw you, sitting at that cafeteria table by yourself. So brave. *Strong*. Determined not to let the world defeat you. And then," he added, "I watched you grow into this amazing woman, more comfortable in your skin with every day that passed. I told myself I couldn't have you. That you were promised to someone else. And then you kissed me in the elevator, and all my good intentions went out the window."

He brushed a thumb across her cheek, unable to resist touching her. "I was in love with you, Gia. I was going to go to your father the next morning and tell him you were marrying me, not Franco. But I never got the chance, because you walked away without a word."

Gia's heart tumbled right out of her chest and crashed to the shining dark oak floor. He'd been going to go to her father? *He'd loved her?* It was almost too much to imagine, how much she'd ripped apart, *destroyed*, by walking away.

"I didn't know," she whispered, lifting a hand to trace the sexy golden stubble on his jaw. "We didn't say anything that night."

A wry smile curved his mouth. "We were too busy doing other things...like making our beautiful son, who means everything to me."

A wave of heat engulfed her at the memory of that hot, torrid night. How perfect it had been. How it had changed her in every way. But it also unearthed the uncertainty of the past few weeks. All the nights he hadn't touched her since.

Santo read her in one even look. "You think I don't love you?" he said huskily, his hands cupping her cheeks. "You think I'm not crazy about you, Gia? You don't think I want you every minute I'm with you? When I saw you at that party in Nassau, I knew it wasn't over. That it would never be over for me. Why else," he prompted softly, "do you think I showed up at your doorstep at midnight like the raging bull that I was? Because it's always been you, Gia. It will always be you."

She sank into the wall, her knees weak. To wonder about it for so long, to *dream* about it for so long, to be so afraid she was never going to hear him say those words to her, made it almost surreal to hear. Her heart was pounding so loudly in her chest, she thought it might thunder right out of it.

"I love you," she whispered. "So much it terrifies me. I always have."

He brought his mouth down on hers in a hot, hard kiss. She wound her arms around his neck and moved closer, her hands tangling in his hair as they exchanged soul-searing kisses, every hot breath, every stroke, every taste of each other a confirmation of what they were. What they could be. A consummation of the promises they'd made to each other.

"We should go back to the party," she murmured reluctantly against his mouth. "You are the host."

"Later."

Air became something she gasped in between indulging in the heated recklessness of his kiss. But soon even that wasn't enough. She wanted more—to obliterate the misery of the past few weeks. To drown herself in the connection they shared. To make *everything better.*

He took control, backing her up against the wall, his hands moving over her body in a sensual exploration that set her on fire. Caught up in the madness, desperate for him, she arched into his touch and sought closer contact. Begged him for more. The sparkly material of her dress a barrier to more intimate contact, he swept his hands up the back of her thighs and took the dress with him. Then it was only the hard, muscled length of him blanketing her with heat. He was hot and hard and she wanted him inside of her.

He palmed her thigh and curved it around his waist until she cradled the throbbing length of him at her core. Broke the kiss on a soft groan as she rocked against him in a rhythm that set him aflame.

"Santo," she whispered, eyes on his, "*love me.*"

"Always," he murmured, his gaze hot and smoky with passion.

And so he did, long and slow, every deep thrust, every

achingly good caress, imprinting on her how much he loved her. Needed her. Cementing the bond they had always shared.

"I have to give a speech," Santo groaned when they finally came back from the sensual abyss, straightening their clothing with shaking hands. "A few more hours," he promised, "and I'm taking you and Leo home. And then *we* are spending a week at the villa in Nassau *alone*. And if I mention the word *Elevate* once, you can punish me. In all the right ways of course," he purred, sliding her a heated look as he straightened his tie.

Gia peeled her gaze away from how utterly gorgeous he looked in the dark grey suit, because he would always make her heart race like that. "A week alone?" The idea melted her insides.

"A belated honeymoon, courtesy of Delilah. No newspapers, no interruptions, just us."

She frowned as an obstacle to that plan presented itself. "What about my work with Nina? I've already been away a few days."

"I cleared it with her," her husband responded with his usual indomitable confidence. "I was prepared to spend the week convincing you to forgive me using whatever methods necessary."

She went a little weak at the thought of it. Which wasn't necessary, she conceded, because she loved and adored him. But this time, it was an adult love that had grown into everything she'd ever imagined it could be.

"Sold," she murmured, rising on tiptoe to give him a kiss. He returned it with a hard one of his own, then slipped his hand through hers as they walked toward the door.

"Ready?"

She nodded. She wasn't afraid of what was behind the

door anymore, of what life would throw at her next, because she knew that whatever it was, she had Santo beside her and that was all that she needed.

Hand in hand, they walked into the buzzing, electric night. A tiny smile curved her lips as they joined her new family, congregated near the champagne fountain that threw up a luxurious, golden spray. Because this time, she was the girl at the center of the light.

* * * * *

LET'S TALK
Romance

For exclusive extracts, competitions and special offers, find us online:

- **f** MillsandBoon
- **X** @MillsandBoon
- **◎** @MillsandBoonUK
- **♪** @MillsandBoonUK

Get in touch on 01413 063 232

> For all the latest titles coming soon, visit
> millsandboon.co.uk/nextmonth